the
MOMENT
BETWEEN

Center Point
Large Print

the MOMENT BETWEEN

NICOLE BAART

CENTER POINT PUBLISHING
THORNDIKE, MAINE

Library of Congress Cataloging-in-Publication Data

Baart, Nicole.
 The moment between / Nicole Baart.
  p. cm.
 ISBN 978-1-60285-480-2 (library binding : alk. paper)
 1. Large type books. I. Title.

PS3602.A22M66 2009b
813'.6--dc22

2009007328

For Aaron

So we must keep apart,
You there, I here,
With just the door ajar
That oceans are,
And prayer,
And that pale
sustenance,
Despair!

†

EMILY DICKINSON
"I CANNOT LIVE WITH YOU"

I had been hungry
all the years;
My noon had come,
to dine;
I, trembling,
drew the table near,
And touched the
curious wine.

†

EMILY DICKINSON
"HUNGER"

the
MOMENT
BETWEEN

She left the world the same way that she had entered it: swathed in robes of scarlet so red and angry and portentous as to be mistaken for black.

The latter crimson swaddling was the result of a ruptured placenta, a condition which separated mother from daughter for hours while the doctors worked to stanch the flow and which nearly left the seven-pound infant motherless from the moment she took her very first wailing breath. The former was a dirty, ruby-colored wash that spread like a morbid inkblot a few inches up the concave line of her taut stomach and dragged the edges of her white T-shirt into the shallow pool of water where I found her. She was anchored in a bathtub so small she had to bend her long legs. Beneath the water, the bottom of her jeans and her perfect, manicured feet were indistinct and suffused with carnelian.

I tried not to look at her, not to notice the droop of her pale, waxy arm or her skin like rice paper dotted with fine, translucent hairs. She was so white against all that blood. So white and small and sad that the thought fled through my mind that she was floating in wine, an attempt at salvation instead of blood. Maybe someone—the thought made my heart seize agonizingly with hope—had touched her lips with Eucharist wine. Maybe she was too sick for the host, but someone had still taken pity on her and offered viaticum with a vintage so sacred it drowned her in forgiveness. I could almost imagine dipping a fine-stemmed glass beneath the surface and lifting the heady merlot to my lips. A toast to a grand entrance now bookended by an even grander exit.

Instead, I vomited into the toilet beside her upturned wrist.

Later, wiping my mouth with the back of my hand, I sat beside her and watched her face. I was waiting, maybe for a flicker, the smallest breath of movement across her carved features, but I knew she was long gone. She had tried to close her eyes at the end, and her lashes almost rested against smooth, unlined cheeks the exact color of gulf sand. There were no tracks of tears streaking her perfect skin, and her lips were even slightly parted in the semblance of a half smile, a secret crescent moon of understanding, as if she knew something I didn't.

I wanted to shake her. Why? What do you know? Or, more importantly, how could you?

But I didn't shake her; I couldn't. She was my waking nightmare, lying there with the razor positioned perfectly on the edge of the white porcelain tub and two bloody fingerprints beside it as if she had touched the pads of her fingers there on purpose. A signature of sorts. The dips and whorls an admission, her own posthumous confession to the crime she had committed.

There was something in me that hated her for what she had done. But beneath that and rising, swelling upward and outward in a dark, smoky thunderhead of impenetrable clouds was grief. Consuming, enveloping, absolute grief.

When I began to scream, it echoed through the glass-tiled bathroom like thunder.

I

ca ABIGAIL BENNETT WAS the definition of unexpected. She was one year on the wrong side of the knife blade that was thirty, but if she turned up at your restaurant and ordered a glass of wine, even high-heeled and clad in a black sheath, you'd card her every time. Petite and narrow-waisted, with a pixie flip of hair the exact color of coffee beans, Abigail could easily pass for sixteen in a pair of ripped jeans and an Abercrombie T-shirt.

Not that she liked looking younger than her age. In fact, most of the time Abigail hated the constant reminders that no matter what she did or where she went, she would not be taken seriously. This explained the harsh line of bobby pins that held her wayward hair out of her face as if the severity of it could add years. It also explained the almost-dowdy clothes, the earth-toned makeup, and the hard, thin line of a mouth that could have been very beautiful.

Once people got past the fact that she wasn't a teenager, Abigail looked very much like the ideal kindergarten teacher. Her stature and dress were the opposite of intimidating, yet there was a spark in her dark eyes as if from time to time a match was struck behind the velvety chocolate of her corneas. These eyes could freeze hell over with a well-timed look, a piercing arrow of unmistakable meaning. But there was also the hint of tenderness in Abigail that translated into quiet strength when paired with the sharp edges that were inevitably unveiled before anyone had a chance to form a false opinion of her. But then again, maybe it was all a facade. She didn't let people get close enough to find out.

In reality, Abigail was not a kindergarten teacher, nor could she remember a phase in her life when she ever wanted to be one. She was an accountant. Numbers were stable, unchanging, and best of all, incapable of being mysterious or of forcing people to act and think and feel in ways that they would not normally act and think and feel. Numbers were predictable; people were not. And because Abigail trusted the reliability of her chosen field, she was good at her job, meticulous and capable of holding the smallest detail in her mind for as long as it was useful.

During tax season Abigail worked more hours than anyone else at her firm, and that was saying a lot. It was why she was made a partner after only five years with the company and why she occupied one of two corner offices, the one with a view of the swampy man-made pond that graced the complex of professional stucco buildings on Key Point Drive. Johnson, McNally & Bennett was a Rosa Beach institution, and though Blake Johnson and Colton McNally could claim most of the honor behind their prestigious position in the community, Abigail knew she filled an important and indispensable role. Southern Florida had its share of widows and divorcées, and for some not-so-surprising reasons they preferred to have a woman handle their money. Abigail was happy to oblige. It kept her busy and the firm in business.

Keeping busy was what Abigail did best. When she wasn't working, which averaged sixty hours a week, she was either running or reheating days-old Chinese takeout in a dented wok. Both activities were little more than a personal experiment; they were representative of the only two things in Abigail's life that she really, deep down hoped to accomplish someday: run a marathon and learn to cook.

The marathon was a goal that she had already partly achieved. On the day of her twenty-ninth birthday, she ran a half marathon in Miami. Abigail could have easily completed it, and in fact, the finish line was in sight only two blocks ahead when she realized it was enough to know that she *could* do it. Crossing the finish line would have meant that she ran for someone else, that she ran for the glory, the recognition.

So Abigail had slowed down a little and then a bit more until someone thrust a cup of water in her hand and yelled, "You're almost there!" She smiled her thanks, sipped the water, and folded herself into the crowd while all eyes were watching the other runners throw their arms into the air for the last few triumphant yards.

The cooking, on the other hand, was little more than a pipe dream. Abigail's greatest accomplishment was adding a diced chicken breast and some soy sauce to leftover chicken chow mein. It was too salty. But propped on her counter in an antique, wrought-iron bookstand was a Williams-Sonoma cookbook with full-color photographs and extensive instructions on how to cook homemade delicacies like potato gnocchi with wild mushroom sauce and baked clams with pine nuts and basil. Every morning, while she waited for the last few drops of coffee to drip into her Gevalia carafe, Abigail would thumb through the glossy pages of the cookbook and imagine what it would be like to make a wine reduction sauce as the sound of laughter filled her apartment. *Someday,* she told herself.

And though there were many somedays in Abigail's life, she tried not to let the particulars of her existence get her down too much. It didn't matter that she didn't have a boyfriend. It didn't matter that every day plodded on with the same pitfalls and small successes. It didn't matter that her apartment was quiet but for the hum of her empty stainless steel refrigerator. It was the life that Abigail had chosen, and she was a grim optimist, resigned to the path she was on—she was getting exactly what she had always wanted. So what if it was tilted heavily toward work, personal discipline, solitude? So what if it left little room for the things other people craved? So what if her cupboards were as bare of exotic ingredients as her apartment was bare of cheerful company?

But sometimes, alone in her apartment with the shades drawn tight, Abigail would stand in front of the full-length mirror on the back of her bathroom door and relax enough to admire what she saw. Tousling her wet hair and practicing a self-conscious smile that showed her teeth—her impossibly white, perfectly straight teeth that were a genetic legacy instead of the result of extensive dental work—Abigail could almost pretend that she was ten years younger and that the world was unfurling itself before her.

For those moments in the steam and warmth, dark ringlets of hair curling around her temples as if she were some Grecian empress, Abigail wished much more for herself than what she had. She wished that she could rewind the clock and find Abby, the girl she used to be, perched on the cusp of her life instead of entrenched in the middle of it with no apparent way out.

Every once in a while, she could gather the courage to admit that it would be a very different life if she had it to do all over again.

When Abigail first came to Johnson & McNally, she had a chance at a different life.

It was no secret around the office that Colton McNally had a thing for the new accountant. He was twelve years older than Abigail and divorced, and that seemed somehow estimable according to Abigail's less-than-high expectations. It wasn't that she would settle for just anyone, but she also didn't enter into much of anything with a long list of prerequisites.

In truth, Abigail found Colton very attractive. She thought his salt-and-pepper hair was distinguished—even though she suspected it came from the hands of a very talented colorist as he wasn't quite forty—and she liked the way his tailored suits fell across the straight line of his shoulders. Best of all, he was nothing like the immature, self-absorbed boys Abigail had dated in college. They had nearly turned her off of men altogether. So when Colton turned his attention toward her, Abigail let him flirt. For a while, she even stopped wearing the stern bobby pins so that her dark curls framed her rather nicely arched forehead.

And yet Abigail wasn't naive. She knew that her employer loved her because of the photo. It would have been too much to ask for Colton to love her, or at least think he did, because of herself. But while she probably should have been reticent of attention resulting from such a faint and improbable notion, Abigail accepted—almost *expected*— the source of Colton's desire.

The photograph in question hung neatly

squared and centered on a fabric-covered board adorning the west wall in the reception room. It was a concession to the more traditional bulletin board, replete with employee photographs that were intended to look candid but often looked overposed.

Abigail knew of the board, she even shot glances at it whenever she could to detect updates and changes, but she was not aware upon settling into her position that tradition dictated a spot for her photo front and center ASAP.

It was her third day of work, and Abigail was immersed in balancing infinitesimal details, worlds away from the air-conditioned office she inhabited when Colton startled her with a quiet "Ahem."

Her head was bowed, and her forearms rested on endless pages that sprouted like an unruly crop of paper weeds across her generous desk. Abigail blinked and raised her eyes, just her eyes, in time to be blinded by the flash of Colton's expensive Canon. He laughed and snapped a few more pictures for which she cleared off her desk, sat up straight, and smiled, thin-lipped and toothy and even coy, trying them all in the hopes that one would be right.

But the next day, Abigail was surprised to see that the photo gracing the quasi bulletin board was the first of the batch. She knew she was looking at herself because seeing the small, hunched form over the crowded desk was a sort of déjà vu—she had been there before. If not for that, Abigail would have never believed that the woman staring back at her was her own reflection. The woman in the photograph had luminous—there was simply no other word for them—*luminous* black eyes of the starry-sky variety: endless and opalescent and dark like a time before the genesis. Like the event horizon of identical black holes—no way out, but no matter, for who would ever want to leave? Beneath the twin universes of those eyes, her lips were slightly parted, pink and full and evocative of bruised raspberries. Her skin glowed faintly (fluorescent light reflecting off all that white paper?), and her shadowy curls were framing and soft. The woman was lovely.

But what unnerved Abigail the most was that Colton had caught her at a moment between. A rare, uncovered moment between expressions: a moment of evaporation before the advent of her surprise became the dutiful smile that spread across her face in the split second after the shutter snapped. This woman was a living mystery.

Abigail wished she knew her.

One day, a few months after she started at the firm, Abigail went into Colton's office to ask him a question about the tax return of a dual citizen living out of country. It was a legitimate question, but Blake's office was closer than Colton's, and her admirer acknowledged that fact the second Abigail rapped her knuckles on the doorframe. She realized almost too late that her presence would be read as an invitation, and sure enough, a smile unfolded across Colton's face like a flag pulled taut in a billowing wind.

"Come in, Abigail! Why don't you close the door behind you? There's something I've been meaning to talk to you about."

Abigail did as she was told and crossed the plush, carpeted floor of Colton's office with her heart stuck fast in her throat.

"But first—" Colton set aside what he had been working on—"what can I do for you?"

Passing him the papers, Abigail lowered herself to balance on the arm of one of the leather chairs facing the wide, black walnut desk. But Colton raised an eyebrow at her, motioned that she should cross behind the desk to stand beside him.

They had flirted before, secret half smiles conveyed across crowded rooms and careful conversations littered with possibilities. And it seemed that the unmistakable chemistry between Colton and Abigail was a favorite topic around the water-cooler, boasting far more people in favor of a match than against it. It was impossible for Abigail not to get caught up in it a little. But she also couldn't help being cautious, and suddenly, with the door closed and Colton looking far more handsome than she remembered from only the day before, she knew that he was a man who wouldn't play games for long.

Colton waved her over again and Abigail moved slowly, explaining about the nonresident and his recent payout from a life insurance death benefit. She had just gotten to the part where he intended to give enough of it away to slip below the line of taxable income when Colton grabbed her wrist and, in one smooth movement, pulled her forward until her face was inches from his. He studied her, still smiling, then kissed her full on the mouth as if he had been intending to do so for a long time.

It wasn't that Abigail didn't want to kiss him back. Actually quite the opposite. It wasn't even that she was stunned by the inappropriateness of such a gesture. Instead, it was a Tic Tac that ruined everything, a burning little grain of peppermint that she inhaled when Colton's lips touched hers.

She drew back, pulling out of Colton's embrace and coughing violently until tears collected at the corners of her eyes. Abigail struggled for a moment, choking mutely as she watched Colton bolt out of his chair and grab her upper arms. When the breath mint was dislodged from her throat and she could feel it hot and peppery on her tongue, she knew it was a very small thing that would be significant in ways that might cause her years of lament.

"I'm sorry," Abigail murmured, utterly mortified for one of the first times she could remember. "I . . ." She couldn't continue.

Colton stared at her, concern and disbelief gathering foglike across his forehead. At first, Abigail thought he might fold her into his arms, that the almost-pitiable comedy of what had just happened would become the sort of story they laughed about months down the road when they told people the tale of how they came together. But then Colton laughed, rubbing his hands up and down her arms. The moment shattered and fell away, disappearing in a shimmer of doubt that made Abigail wonder if she had merely dreamed it.

"As long as you're okay," he boomed. And then he sat back down and pretended nothing had happened. He never mentioned it again and neither did she.

Eighteen months later, Colton married Marguerite, the receptionist who was hired at the same time as Abigail. Marguerite was a few years younger than Abigail, but she looked much older due to a succession of bad dye jobs and what appeared to be a lifetime of sun damage spotting her skin. Colton seemed happy; from what little Abigail could discern of her boss's marriage, he genuinely longed for companionship and Marguerite's horselike laugh didn't turn him off so much that he considered her a poor match.

Although it was against her nature, shortly after

the happy couple's beach wedding, Abigail went through a brief stage where she fixated on what might have been. The entire office had once been invited to Colton's sprawling house only a block off the ocean, and Abigail could almost picture herself the mistress of his columned colonial. What sort of a woman would she be if she were Mrs. McNally? What would she look like offering guests a second martini and lounging in some bright sari that she had bought on their honeymoon?

It was a nice scenario, but Abigail wasn't one to waste too much energy on regret, and she abandoned such nonsense the same way she set aside every other impossible dream: she placed it firmly out of her mind. A few years later when Blake and Colton approached her about being a partner, she was even able to congratulate herself that her business card would read *Johnson, McNally & Bennett* instead of *Johnson, McNally & McNally*. She convinced herself that it was much more satisfying this way.

For his part, after their less than romantic encounter in his office, Colton was nothing but a gentleman to Abigail. He treated her with the same respect, the same quiet yet somehow condescending pride of a father figure. Abigail was reduced from a possible lover to the discarded role of a dependable daughter. It was a character she was rather good at playing.

* * *

Lou Bennett was a father when he could have been a grandfather.

He met Melody Van Bemmel at Chevy's Café a week after he turned forty-five. It was nearly a blizzard outside, and she blew into the warm restaurant off-balance and trembling as if she were a leaf driven by the vicious wind. When the door slammed behind her, Melody gasped, stomped her booted feet, and flung the hood of her parka back. She smiled shyly, looking around as if her entrance had been staged, as if she were taking her place beneath the spotlight and now that she was front and center she had forgotten her lines.

Everyone in the café glanced up at her for the blink of an eye and then turned back to their coffees and specials of the day without a second thought. Everyone except Lou. He had fallen in love the moment Melody raised her hands to turn back her hood. They were little hands swimming in a pair of men's work gloves that were so big on her fingers they nearly slid off. Lou imagined they were his gloves. He wished they were.

And just as quickly as he longed for her, Lou hated himself for it. She was a child. Her eyes were too clear, her skin too bright for her to even look twice at a man whose own skin was as deeply lined as those etchings he had seen on display in the American National Bank. But when she caught his eye, when her lips pulled up slightly just for him,

Lou knew there was nothing that could be done about it. He was hers, even if she never acknowledged his existence. Even if he loved her in secret until the day he died.

As it turned out, he didn't have to. Melody came to Lou in the most natural, ordinary way: she brushed against the edge of his life and found herself inexorably pulled in. He didn't even know he was drowning until he felt himself reach for her and cling for dear life.

They were married less than a year later, and though Melody was not as young as Lou had imagined, when she walked down the aisle in a confection of white, a little shiver crept up Lou's spine because she did not look twenty-five. *Twenty years,* he thought in the second before the preacher asked him if he would have her and hold her until "death do you part."

Lou said, "I do" without hesitation, but somewhere in the back of his mind he faltered. There was a nagging suspicion, an accusatory guilt that made him wonder if he had made her the happiest woman alive like she claimed or if he had involuntarily ruined her life.

It took Melody almost six years to get pregnant, though they tried to make a baby on their wedding night. She saw doctors and gynecologists and fertility specialists, but no one could tell her why her womb would not swell with a child. For a while, Lou entertained the possibility of joining her at one of her appointments, but those sorts of things made him unbearably uncomfortable. He avoided the conversation he knew Melody wanted to have the same way that he avoided the drawer where she kept her neat pile of lace-trimmed underwear.

When Lou was fifty-one, Melody's cheeks took on a greenish hue in the early morning, and the waist that he so loved to encompass in his enormous hands began to expand. She wouldn't admit it at first—maybe she was scared to hope—but Lou knew almost immediately. Something about Melody had changed, the scent of her skin or the complexity of the air around her when she entered a room. Maybe both. Either way, Lou was relieved. It wasn't him, it had never been him, and now she would be happy. They would be a family.

Lou didn't think much about the baby until the doctor handed him a tiny, tightly wrapped bundle with a pink cap sliding down over her lashless eyes. They were two little commas, those eyes, a break amidst all the words that comprised his many years of life, though certainly not a beginning or even an end. Lou stared at her and realized that he had planned on having a son.

"Abigail Rose," Melody called weakly from the bed. She smiled at him with all the energy she could muster, and her eyes were dancing with tears. "Rose for my mother and Abigail because it's the most beautiful name I've ever heard. I think we'll call her Abby."

What was there to say? It was a fine name, and Lou hadn't wasted a single thought on another. "Pretty," he said finally and brushed his lips tentatively across the soft forehead because it seemed like the right thing to do.

CR I didn't know what to do with her.

She was cold, her skin was so cold, and she seemed dirty to me. I wanted to wash her hair and make her lips look pink again instead of the sickly gray that taunted me for not getting here sooner. For not paying attention. For not being everything she needed me to be.

When I got over the initial shock, when I had cried so hard I had emptied myself of every fighting, aching thing inside, I moved her arm half a degree and sat on the edge of the bathtub so I could be near her. There was nothing to be afraid of. This body beside me was only an empty shell; she was gone, and yet I wanted to be close enough to study every detail. I wanted to imprint her on each scribbled page of my memory so that when they took her away, I could remember how her collarbones rose in mirrored harmony and almost met in the shadow of her long neck.

My skin was tight from crying, and I could taste the salt from my tears when I licked my lips. There was blood, too, and it was insulting somehow that I could feel the metallic tang of life on my tongue when hers was spilled beneath me. Then I felt a jolt of shock at the blood in my mouth. How did it get there? Had I bled with her? Had I inadvertently touched where she lay broken and partaken in some unholy communion?

I raised my palms and studied their whiteness, then put them to my face and knew: the edges of my mouth were cracked from forming the scream that tried to clear a way for my heart to leave my body. It would have climbed up through my throat and escaped—it wanted to; I could feel it thrashing around, dying for an exit, a way to escape this pain—but it was held fast by each vein that anchored it to my fingers, my toes, the rest of my numb body. The blood in my mouth was my own.

It took me what felt like hours to reach for her. And when I did, her fingers were firm and limp like molded plastic as I wrapped my hands around them. I fought back my revulsion and reminded myself of who she was. Rubbing her lifeless hand between my own warm ones, I willed her to squeeze me back even as I knew she never would. A longing stabbed through me and was gone: I want to be where you are. *But that was impossible.*

I would have to live in this new reality.

I didn't know what to do without her.

 CR ABIGAIL LEFT EVERYTHING when she went to find Tyler.

At first she convinced herself that she could forget about him. She told herself that this consuming, breathing thing inside her would slowly fold and fade and crumble away so that she could live again. But instead of eventually cooling into ash and ember, the flame that had been lit for the elusive Tyler only fanned into something burning and fierce. In the end, Abigail didn't really even have a choice. She went because she had to.

It happened almost unexpectedly, the leaving, and when Abigail turned off the final light in her apartment and drank in one last, long look as the sunset laid an offering of orange flowers across her honeyed laminate floors, she felt like she was saying good-bye for good. And then the cat—the tabby stray she had adopted and forgotten to name—brushed against her legs, and she realized that she almost left it to die behind locked doors.

"Pretty girl," she murmured absently, picking it up and pressing her face into the ginger fuzz. "You can't come with me."

Abigail carried the cat outside under one arm and pulled her sleek suitcase on wheels with the other. One item would find its way into the trunk of her midnight blue Passat. The other she could hardly bring herself to think about. Maybe the nice men working for the Department of Homeland Security wouldn't notice a cat hiding in her calfskin attaché.

It was difficult to balance the cat as Abigail descended the two flights of stairs and slid a shiny silver key into her mailbox for the last time in weeks. Maybe months? She had put a hold on her mail, but Abigail knew there was a small accumulation of post that she had been ignoring for several days.

They had told her that she could expect the parcel in eight to ten weeks. For exactly two and a half months, every time she slipped her hand inside the tall, metal cavern that contained nothing more threatening than paper and envelopes, Abigail's heart wrenched and she had to force herself to stand still.

This time, as she was leaving, Abigail hardly gave the package a second thought. And there it was. Her fingers stalled for a moment on the manila envelope, then withdrew so quickly it seemed there was poison on the heavy-grain paper that stung her skin.

"Not now," Abigail whispered.

The cat mewed in reply.

"Shhh," she murmured. The deliberate hushing could have been meant for the cat. It could have been meant for Abigail.

She stood there staring at the mailbox for what seemed like hours. Finally Abigail thrust her hand back in the cool mail slot and grabbed everything without looking at it. Jiggling the attaché on her shoulder, she unzipped it with her arm bent corkscrew-like and jammed the papers inside. She stuffed the manila envelope down deep, sliding it between a slim folder and a bunch of maps she had printed off that resided in the niche usually reserved for her laptop. Slamming her mailbox closed, Abigail strode out of the building, trying with each purposeful step to fight the slick veneer of nausea that the envelope had spilled down her throat.

"Going away?" The unexpected voice seemed disembodied.

When Abigail turned, she saw the neighbor girl perched on one of the benches in the shade of the pergola crowning the entrance to Gulf Wind Estates. She was twelve or thirteen years old, and Abigail could never remember her name. Sierra or Sienna. Maybe Savannah. Something Southern and airy like a slow exhalation.

"Yes," Abigail said, trying to coax a smile onto her face. This was a welcome distraction. "I forgot to find a kennel for . . . ," she fumbled, shrugging to lift the plump cat a bit higher.

The girl's eyes widened. Her legs were crossed beneath her but she lowered them now, putting her hands on her knees as if she was waiting for Abigail to say something else.

"Do you know . . . ?" Abigail started and then

drifted off because she didn't know what else to say.

"How long are you going to be gone?" the girl asked.

"I don't know."

The girl had long, blonde hair like a cascade of sun-drenched water, and sitting as she was in the fading evening light, Abigail thought her very striking. Abigail's breath caught in her throat for a second and she swallowed with difficulty, suddenly eager to escape the strange conversation with her anonymous neighbor. But then the girl swept her hair over her shoulder and secured it in a ponytail with an elastic band she had looped around her wrist. Any resemblance to the ghost that haunted Abigail's dreams immediately disappeared.

"I'll take care of your cat," the girl said without preamble. She didn't put out her arms for the tabby, though it looked like she wanted to, like she was stopping herself from doing so.

Abigail didn't feel quite right about it, but what choice did she have? She knew she should ask the girl if it would be okay with her parents, or better yet she should ask the parents herself, but it seemed too complicated an endeavor. Instead of opening her mouth to form a single question, Abigail nodded slowly and took a step toward the girl.

The young lady stood and reached for the cat,

smiling as she accepted the ball of fluff and tucked it into her thin arms. "What's her name?"

"Whatever you want it to be," Abigail answered. Her reply echoed in her own ears like a tacky pickup line. She tried to soften it a bit. "I just called her Cat."

"We can do better than that, can't we?" the girl whispered, burying her nose in the scruff of furry neck.

Abigail wavered for a minute before walking away. It was easy—almost *too* easy—to leave. The cat was a charade of connection, an artificial reason to stay that resolved itself without any effort on her part. Abigail had already said her good-byes. There were no complicated loose ends to tie up. There was nothing to worry about. There was no one for her to miss when she was gone. Or anyone to miss her. Everything she was leaving behind was as unnamed as the girl and her cat. Meaningless. Vague.

Taking a deep breath, Abigail sliced through whatever slim bonds had tried to hold her back. She felt like she was emerging from the hazy aftermath of a storm.

As the sun set, it jettisoned thick shafts of brilliant light, bright and furious in their daily closing rite, across the earth below. It was so piercingly splendid in the moment before the horizon swallowed the scarlet sun whole that it was almost as if it was all—the cat, the sunset, the impending absence—an act of intention. All of it seemed purposed to break through the soft, gray mists that clung like cobwebs to Abigail.

It illuminated with startling intensity the only thing she sought: Tyler.

Leaving Florida to chase after Tyler was something Abigail never planned on doing. But obsession is rarely premeditated, and by the time she admitted that her life could not go on as long as Tyler only existed nebulous and uncertain in the shadowy corners of her mind, he was already gone.

Abigail had tracked him down to a modern apartment building that was only blocks away from the beach. In fact, it was so close to the ocean that as she walked the tree-lined street to Tyler's Tuscan-style apartment complex, she caught glimpses of white-capped waves frothing the surface of the blue herringbone gulf water. There was a slight breeze chasing itself around the corners of the rambling houses in the upscale neighborhood, and it would lift Abigail's cropped hair off her neck and cool her skin. She stifled a shiver, knowing that the soft wind on land was a mighty force to be reckoned with over the waters she could see in the distance.

The water frightened her a little, and though the ocean was one of the primary reasons Abigail had left Newcastle, Minnesota, her prairie blood had never quite warmed to the fathomless depths that surrounded her on three sides.

When she first moved to Rosa Beach, Abigail had a recurring nightmare that included a tsunami wiping Florida off the map. In her dream, she was standing in a parking lot with bags of groceries slung over her arms. Suddenly the sky went dark, and she looked up to see the wave—an impenetrable fortress of black water—swell and spread as if it would consume the heavens before crushing the earth.

All at once people screamed and ran for their lives, but Abigail was frozen by the immensity of the water and traumatized by the fact that it could stand there, upright, as if it lived and had risen out of the sea to stalk her. She dropped her groceries and strangely felt a surge of worry that the crusty baguette she had just purchased would get soggy. And then it began to sprinkle, the top curl of the churning wave dripping and crying in anticipation of crashing, and Abigail felt the full weight of the knowledge that she was about to drown.

The horror was so absolute, the fear so real and consuming that Abigail would inevitably wake up. She would be gasping and damp, sure that she was dying in the second before she realized that the paved parking lot beneath her was really her stiff-mattressed bed and that the drops on her skin were sweat and not seawater.

The nightmare eventually began to taper off, haunting Abigail less and less frequently until it was nothing more than the memory of a feeling, a sour aftertaste that lingered in her soul and could not quite be identified. But something about Florida forever felt changed to Abigail. It was as if the state was a floating, unstable peninsula. She stumbled at times, sure she felt the movement.

Approaching Tyler's apartment, desperate to see him yet afraid of that very thing, Abigail was actually forced to stop and steady herself against the trunk of a tree. She fitted her fingers against the bark and swayed once, an unwilling dance partner. But Abigail was a grown woman and this feebleness was nonsense. She forced it out of her mind and angled her steps away from the distant patch of sea.

As it turned out, Abigail need not have expended such agony—Tyler didn't live there anymore. His roommate, an attractive young man who was adjusting a neat, cranberry-colored, raw silk tie, informed Abigail that Tyler had moved out several weeks earlier.

"And I don't think he's coming back," the man offered, trying out a charming smile on Abigail to see how she would respond to his subtle flirtation.

Shock must have rippled visibly across her face because the man smoothed his pin-striped charcoal shirt with an irritated flick of his wrist and said, "Lover? What, he didn't leave you his number?"

In accordance with the sarcastic note in his voice, Abigail half expected him to add a caustic "boohoo" or some other less-than-sincere condolence. And though she didn't want to beg, though she didn't want to give this man the satisfaction of knowing that she sought Tyler with a steadily growing passion, she asked quietly, "Do you know where he is?"

The man sighed hard through his nose and put his hands on his hips. "You know, you're not the first girl to come looking for him."

"I don't care," Abigail said evenly.

"You can do a lot better than him, pretty thing like you."

"It's not . . ." But Abigail couldn't finish. She didn't know how to explain it all. "I just really need to talk to him."

"I don't have a phone number, sorry."

"An address?" she pressed.

He smiled wryly and gave in. "I'm supposed to send some of his stuff to him. What do you think? Tyler and I are a pretty close fit, wouldn't you say?" He held out his arms and admired his own outfit. "I guarantee you, I look way better in it than he ever did."

Abigail gave him a stiff nod.

Rolling his eyes, he moved to shut the door in her face. "Stay here. I'll see if I can find that stupid address. You can have it and I'll pretend I lost it."

Waiting for Tyler's ex-roommate to return was a taste of eternity for Abigail. If he didn't have what she was looking for, she didn't know what she'd do. She was hardly a detective, and the only things she had that even assured her that Tyler was real and not some creation of her overactive imagination were his name and a photograph with his striking face in profile.

Some of the panic that Abigail had left behind at the foot of the tree only steps from his front door began to creep up the sidewalk to claim her. If he didn't have the address, if it was lost or he was lying or he refused to give it to her, what next? All her days up until this point had led to this one place in her life, and Abigail could not see another future no matter how hard she tried.

But then the door swung open and the man thrust a rumpled receipt at her. "For what it's worth, I wouldn't waste another second on him if I were you."

"Thank you," Abigail muttered thinly.

"I'd say good luck, but I wouldn't mean it." He shut the door for a second time, and Abigail heard a dead bolt slide home.

Numb and suppressing a shudder that would quickly become a tremor throughout her entire body, Abigail looked down at the address scrawled in slightly smeared blue ink.

GIA'S BAKERY AND EUROPEAN DELI
5467 Crescent Drive
Surrey, British Columbia V4S 2H2
Canada

Canada? She hadn't expected that.

• • •

Nothing in Lou's life was quite how he expected it would be.

Sure that he was destined to be single forever, Melody had been an apparition that slowly took shape in his reality. She was all mist and magic in the beginning, but she solidified a little every day, reversing the normal pattern of life and becoming more real, more present and vivid and *possible* as the years progressed. What had once seemed impossible was now a beautiful, breathing actuality.

When they were newly married, Lou woke up every morning half-expecting his wife to have dissolved as his dreams slunk away in the fading night. But there she was, day after day and week after week, until one morning he woke up and knew that she would be there. Lou wasn't dreaming it. He was living it.

Then Abby came. She was quiet and contemplative for a child, but she was still a child, and suddenly the unexpected bliss of six unimaginable years was interrupted by nighttime feedings and the impulsive needs of a newborn. Lou didn't resent his daughter, not exactly, but she arrived at a time in his life when most of his friends were empty nesters or even grandparents who could coddle the children in their lives for small bits of time before returning them to their mothers. For Lou, it was as if God rewound the clock but forgot to rewind Lou. In the split second after the doctor announced, "It's a girl," Lou was transformed into an old husband playing the role of a young one. And a new father on top of it all.

So he quit the farm.

Just like that. He harvested the corn and soybeans for the last time while Melody nursed and cooed over her precious infant, and then he called the only Realtor he knew and listed the farm.

"What have you done?" Melody cried when she learned that the farm was for sale. And she *was* crying—huge, shining tears that Lou wiped away with his calloused thumbs.

"It's for the best," he said. Though what he meant was, *I have to do* something.

How could life go on as it always had when the truth was that it would forever be changed? The farm was an emblem to the way it had been and could never be again. It was a living photo album of sorts, for Lou couldn't look at the sagging fence around the pasture without seeing Melody standing on the bottom rung, hands on her hips as she balanced and her hair stroked wild by the wind. He couldn't see the freshly painted barn without watching his wife, remarkable and forever preserved in his mind's eye, color the splintering wood with her own carefully wielded brush. She was everywhere he looked, and he wanted it to remain that way. He didn't know if there was room for Abby in his dream of Melody.

So Lou tried to invent a new dream. It had to change—all of it—and he knew that one truth as certainly as he knew that the sun would continue to rise in the east.

"We're moving to town. I'm getting a steady job. We're going to church." He ticked off each imperative, calculating and measuring out the ingredients that, if left to simmer, would create the perfect life. Lou figured he could love Abby if he could only make room for her, if he set aside all that had been and focused hard on all that could be.

The farm sold quickly but only because Lou was willing to take less than what it was worth. By the time the final papers were signed and initialed, Melody had warmed up a bit to the idea of moving and had picked out an appealing little two-story only a block from the public library. The siding was lemon yellow, and the former owners had painted the shutters a blinding lime green. Melody chirped that it was "cheerful and fun," though when Lou looked at the house, it gave him such an impression of citrus that he actually had to fight a pucker.

Finding a job proved more difficult than finding a house, and when Lou and Melody moved in he still hadn't secured employment. He scoured the local paper for applicable want ads and circled them with a red pen purchased solely for this purpose. But either the job felt beneath him or he felt beneath the job, and Lou couldn't bring himself to drop off a résumé. Not that he had a résumé.

For the first time in his life, Lou felt the beginning twinges of something that threatened to suck him under: a depression with claws. Of course, he had been depressed before. But this felt like depression with a capital *D*. Just when it became alarming, when Lou could feel regret and bitterness glower menacingly on the horizon, Melody saved him for a second time.

"I got us a new phone number," she said one night over supper.

Abby was just learning to eat solid food, and pureed peas were lining her mouth like a foul, furry lipstick. Lou found it hard to focus on his wife, but he tore his eyes away from his daughter and tried. "We don't need a new number. We can transfer our old one to this house."

"This one is better." Melody smiled. "655-4357."

Lou shrugged.

"Do you know what 4357 spells?"

He shook his head.

"Help."

"Help?"

"655-HELP. It's the phone number for your new business. Temporary, of course, until you work something else out." Now that the confession was over with, Melody seemed afraid of Lou's reaction and explained what she had in mind. "I was thinking about you today, and all that you can do and all that you are, and I decided that you are a jack-of-all-trades."

"I'm not sure that's a compliment."

"But it is. You're a jack-of-all-trades and a *master* of them all, too. You can do everything from hang drywall to repair small engines—" Melody cast around, fumbling to encompass everything—"to fix the kitchen sink! Honey, you're the whole package, plus the kitchen sink." She reached across the table and took his hand, temporarily turning her back on the little girl who was taking up more and more of her attention—the little girl who was taking attention away from Lou.

Though Melody made him weak even sitting there without makeup to brighten her face and her hair in a sagging ponytail, Lou felt a stab of irritation at her self-satisfied smile. But she was trying and she loved him—he had to remind himself of that daily, sometimes hourly. He filled his mouth with another forkful of mashed potatoes before he could say something he regretted.

"Don't you see?" Melody asked. "You can run your own fix-it business. You can do everything, whatever people need you to do. Whenever they need help with something, they can just call you. We'll charge six dollars an hour."

"Six dollars?" Lou almost choked on his food. "That's almost double minimum wage."

"People will pay it." She shrugged. "I was

thinking of calling the business Mr. Honey Do or something like that, but now I kind of like the idea of incorporating the kitchen sink. . . ."

"I will not be Mr. Honey Do."

Melody laughed. "No, I suppose not. That sounds silly, doesn't it?"

"Ridiculous."

And though Lou initially hated the idea, though he was certain that people would continue to call their plumber instead of him when they had a leaky faucet, a year after they took their first ad out in the local paper, he had a truck with Handy Lou painted on the side. There was a custom-built storage unit in the bed of the truck with panels and compartments for his tools and equipment. It was fire engine red with bold yellow lettering. It was recognizable wherever he went. Lou both loathed it and loved it in equal measure.

The Bennetts took the truck to church on Sundays when Abby was old enough to find the color and size of her daddy's vehicle to be something akin to a clown car or an amusement park ride. When Abby was four and they took her to the county fair, she wouldn't go near the pastel-painted merry-go-round. Something about the prancing horses, the tinny music, or the blinking lights offended her. And yet at every opportunity she scrambled to sit high in the cab of her daddy's obnoxious truck. Lou didn't get it.

In fact, there were a lot of things Lou didn't get.

Five years after he made the decision to change everything, his life was exactly what he had intended it to be. The Bennetts had a well-kept little home smack-dab in the center of town. He had steady work. And they all attended St. Mary's Catholic Church. Melody, true to her name, sang soprano in the choir. Abby tottered off happily to Sunday school every week. Lou even knew the priest by name and considered him as close to a friend as he had ever had—they talked from time to time about things more consequential than sports or the weather.

All the ingredients were there. Lou should have been happy, ecstatic even, with a life that he had never dared to hope for himself, let alone expect. But he couldn't shake the feeling that something was missing. Some mysterious, gaping hole that he hadn't even realized existed sank deep and empty in his heart. It may have gone unnoticed forever but for the fullness of his present life. What manner of greed was this? The cavernous depth of his need was only felt when everything else in his life was exactly as it should be.

It wasn't until he stood in the delivery room a second time that Lou found himself hoping against all hope that Melody had given him a son. Maybe this was the ache that gnawed at his soul when he stared at the ceiling instead of sleeping every night. Maybe this child would complete whatever inside him was lacking and broken.

Lou didn't realize that Hailey was what he wanted until her baby hand curled around his own massive index finger for the very first time.

She was what he had been missing all along.

ᐒ I thought about pulling the plug on the drain.

It was an old-fashioned knobby plug with a slim, beaded chain. I knew this because I had noticed it before, not because I could see the plug now, slick with diluted blood and hidden beneath the murky water.

Remembering such a peculiar, insignificant detail stunned me, but for some reason, I could see everything with the same stark clarity. It was as if all my senses, even my memory, had been set to a higher frequency. Suddenly each detail—the hum of electricity in the lightbulb, the earthy-sick scent that hung weakly in the air, the occasional drip from the end of the corroded faucet—was backlit and brilliant, impossible to ignore. I was momentarily thankful, because in this new dynamic, knowing everything stopped me from having to feel everything.

I wanted to, but I couldn't bring myself to pull the plug in the bathtub. All that water—crimson and consecrated by her willful transgression—prevented me. And yet that didn't stop me from realizing that I was all she had; I was the only person who could prepare her for her dismal wake.

I knew that I should be calling someone. But who was I supposed to call? the police? the coroner? the ambulance? Dialing 911 seemed out of the question. This was not an emergency. Nothing could save her now.

But it didn't matter just yet. I wasn't ready to call anyone. There were things she would have wanted me to do.

I found a clean washcloth in the cabinet beneath the sink. It matched the narrow row of blue glass tiles surrounding her bathtub, but it bore neat, round scars from a few drops of spilled bleach. It seemed important to find a spotless cloth, but when I rifled through the half-dozen others neatly stacked beneath the curving s-pipe, I couldn't find one. They were all marked.

Choosing the least disfigured rag, I turned on the sink and held the blue cloth beneath the ice-cold stream. Because the world had sharp edges, I had to do more than just stand there. I counted the seconds it took for the water to warm up. "Thirty-nine," I whispered when I could turn off the tap and pinch out the hot, sopping rag. It had to be warm, even though I knew she wouldn't feel it.

Hesitation gripped me when I was back at the edge of the tub. Why? What could I possibly accomplish by doing this? But there was a smudge of mascara at the corner of her right eye, and I couldn't stop myself from tenderly wiping it away. The soft pile of cotton loops erased the powder of her makeup in an uneven little circle at the height of her cheekbone. I thought it was beautiful, that exposed skin, and I turned the cloth to rub the clean side over the rest of her cheek.

I returned to the sink three times, rinsing the cloth in steaming water until her makeup ran in dull rivulets of color against the porcelain bowl. When it was done, she looked faded somehow. But she also looked clean; her skin was unmarked, almost fresh, as if she were newly born instead of newly gone.

III

CR IT WAS ALMOST midnight when Abigail landed at Sea-Tac Airport.

The terminal was dim and quiet, nearly devoid of passengers. Most of the gate counters were closed, and there were only the occasional harried fliers leaning against overstuffed bags with eyes half-closed and a look of fatigue shadowing their faces. It was hollow feeling and desolate, as if the world had expired while they flew thirty thousand feet above the earth.

The passengers of flight 842 from Denver moved as one through the silent airport, and Abigail let herself be swept along. She had just spent three hours trying to sleep, and she hadn't achieved even a moment of rest. Now she was beyond weary and incapable of doing anything but following.

Clutching the soft, supple strap of her attaché, Abigail tried to conjure up some of the excitement that she knew she should be feeling. She was close! According to the map that she had printed from MapQuest, Tyler was 136 miles away. Or 218.8 kilometers if she felt like measuring it according to the standard of her destination. True, in Florida Tyler had lived less than a twenty-minute drive from Abigail. But this was different. Then she hadn't known who he was or what he meant to her. Now, with nothing but an international border and a relatively short drive between them, Abigail knew she should be frantic with anticipation.

Instead, she was exhausted. And afraid.

The thought hit Abigail so hard she actually let out a stifled gasp.

"You okay?" An elderly gentleman with a houndstooth cap mistook her muffled cry and put a steadying hand beneath her elbow.

"I tripped," Abigail heard herself say. "I'm fine." She tried to smile her thanks.

He smiled back uncertainly before turning to step on the underground train that would take them to the baggage claim.

Abigail followed the crowd to the silver carousel. She stood there for a couple minutes, watching the bags drop gracelessly off the edge of the conveyor belt and begin their slow rotation around the oval track, before she remembered that she hadn't checked any luggage and her bags were already in her hands. Nothing was stopping her from walking across the threshold of those sliding doors and facing everything she knew she had to face.

But she wasn't quite ready to face anything, and her subconscious noted this fact by refusing to recall which rental car agency she had booked her car with. Avis? Advantage? Dollar? They all looked the same, lined up in a neat row against the wall between the air-lock doors that opened onto

Seattle, Washington. Abigail studied them until she felt silly just standing there, and she hesitantly approached the nearest counter to ring the summons bell. She had to start somewhere.

A young clerk emerged disheveled and bleary-eyed from the back room.

"Abigail Bennett," she said in response to his tacit query. Abigail fully expected him to check his computer and roll his eyes, sending her away in aggravation because she interrupted his late night nap. Instead, the scruffy-haired attendant slipped her some paperwork to sign and initial, then offered her a ticket for the underground car claim.

When Abigail traveled for work, she rode in austere luxury sedans with uniformed drivers and muted, leather interiors filled with classical music. In contrast, the electric metallic orange Kia Spectra that the parking garage attendant led her to was a bit of a shock, but she had tried to be frugal when she booked the compact car; after all, she was traveling alone and had no need for a large vehicle. Frugality was the same excuse she had used when arranging her flight to Seattle instead of Vancouver. She just couldn't stomach the five hundred dollar price tag difference or the inflated cost of rental cars across the border. Abigail didn't have to worry about money, but her Midwestern upbringing refused to let her squander it.

However, the Kia was a bit more economical— not to mention garish—than she had intended to be, and Abigail thought about requesting another car before she was left alone in the dreary parking garage. But the overwhelming residue of exhaust fumes hung in the air, and it was simply too much work to do anything other than climb into the little car and drive away.

The West Coast air that nipped at Abigail in the underground garage crept through the cracks in the car doors and around the windshield the second she emerged into the dark night. It was drizzling slightly; the sky was thick with wet that seemed intentionally positioned to make sure there wasn't a single pinprick refuge of air that was not damp.

Abigail cranked the heater in her car and still managed to shiver uncontrollably. After Florida, the Pacific Northwest was almost oppressive in its soggy chill. Though it was probably near sixty degrees outside, the cool hung against the exposed skin at Abigail's neck like a mist of perfume that would not evaporate.

I-5 was slick and busier than Abigail would have anticipated for one o'clock in the morning. Trucks churned up the thin sheet of water on the asphalt and dispersed it in a burst of gray to hover like a fine cloud around all eighteen wheels. Abigail tried to avoid the trucks, but whenever she switched lanes, she was sure she could feel the wheels of the Kia hydroplane and skim across the surface of the road before settling safely between the dotted lines again.

Abigail had planned on driving straight into Canada. She figured the border crossing would be empty at this time of night and she'd sail through into her destination before finding a place to sleep. But the road and the rain were slowly eroding that haphazard plan. By the time the lights of downtown Seattle hovered in the distance, iridescent and wavering between the veil of drops, Abigail was looking for a roadside hotel.

If she couldn't see the hotel from the road, she refused to stop. Abigail was quite good with directions and perfectly capable of being on her own, but for some reason the interstate felt safe—she couldn't shake the feeling that if she lost it she would not find her way back, and she would vanish in this place of inexhaustible, sodden night. Even as she thought it, Abigail laughed at herself. How ridiculous was this? How childlike and simple were her nocturnal fears? She had never been afraid of the dark; she convinced herself that there was no reason to be afraid now.

And yet Abigail drove past a dozen signs for lodging. It wasn't until she had reached the far outskirts of Everett that she finally saw a Holiday Inn immediately accessible from the highway. She turned onto the off-ramp in relief.

By the time Abigail had secured a room, her head was throbbing and her body so chilled that her skin was clammy and her muscles were tight from shivering. Grabbing her room key from the desk clerk, she double-checked that the doors of the Kia were locked, even though she had left nothing inside it to steal. Then she mounted the wide steps to the second floor and found room 238.

A hot shower did much to disperse the cold, until Abigail stepped out into the humid bathroom and found that the cool air could reach her even here. She crawled into bed with wet hair still wrapped in a towel and bundled the blankets around her body, tangling herself into the sheets so that every inch of her skin was covered with the scratchy cloth.

Abigail lay in the semidarkness and found herself staring at the long lines of light foursquare around the window. She forced her eyes closed but realized that the numbers of the alarm clock were imprinting themselves in fluorescent green against the backs of her eyelids. Rolling over with a frustrated grunt, she squeezed her eyes shut yet again and willed herself to sleep. But it was useless. Abigail flung back the blankets, sat up straight, and opened the nightstand drawer.

It was there. A neat, brick-colored book with a two-handled jar emitting a small, careful flame. Abigail didn't open it, but she carried it to the desk, fumbling around in her attaché for the letter.

The edges of the letter were ragged and worn, torn and thin from being handled so much. She had read it maybe a hundred times. Maybe a thousand. Abigail had memorized it the moment she read it, but there was something powerful about holding it anyway. She bristled, touching the paper now. But she wanted to sleep, so instead of flicking on the light to scan the words one more time, Abigail slid the folded note into the cover of the Bible and put them both in her bag.

She hoped the Gideons would forgive her for her theft.

Abigail finally slept hard and deep, a solid and utterly dreamless sleep except for the vague and fleeting feeling that something was missing. It was less a dream than a sensation that evaporated as she faltered between sleep and wakefulness. Though the alarm clock assured her that she had over seven hours of rest behind her, Abigail woke to find herself still tired and crawling out from beneath the weight of something intangibly heavy. She didn't know what to do other than take another shower.

Checkout time was noon, and Abigail loitered in her room until five minutes before the lenient deadline. She wanted to leave, but she couldn't go back to the Kia and the road that held so much uncertainty and not a single definable promise. Now, at the moment when what she longed for was close enough to touch, Abigail was positively frozen. She hated herself for her immobility even as she longed to drive back to Sea-Tac and hop on the first flight home.

So Abigail procrastinated. She snuck to the little

kitchen near the reception desk and took a stale muffin that she dawdled over one crumb at a time. She agonized over the thin line of her charcoal eyeliner. She even finger-fluffed her curls to the point of frizz and had to soak her hair in the sink and start all over again.

At one point, Abigail went to her bag and retrieved the book that she had already claimed as her own. She held it in her hands, enjoying the weight of it, the familiar feel in her fingers. It felt right somehow, yet she had to acknowledge that she had left her own Bible behind in Florida. The abandonment had been intentional, and she couldn't quite understand why she wanted the book in her hands now. Abigail rubbed her thumbs across the cover and wondered how many people, if any, had picked it up as it lay inert and unassuming in the top drawer of the nightstand. A part of her wanted to open it, but she couldn't bring herself to do so.

When Abigail finally left the safe harbor of the Holiday Inn, she drove as hard and as fast as she had slept. She pointed her car north and put as many miles between herself and the road home as she could.

The clouds that blanketed the sky the night before had been blown inland by a stiff breeze off the ocean, and the midday light was warm and bright as it glared off the hood of Abigail's car. The sun was behind her as she drove, and the moist fog was a collection of gossamer shawls amidst the sweeping arcs of the jewel-toned mountains.

Abigail had never been to the Pacific Northwest, and she found it haunting and magical, illusory and almost fragile, as if she could reach out and dispel the fantasy with a touch of her finger like an interruption on the clear surface of a deep, cold lake. It was all merely a reflection.

But when she pulled over at a rest stop to stretch her legs, the cedars were decidedly solid and the air was infused with the earthy scents of moss and decay, wood and stone. Dressed in jeans and a designer T-shirt with a belted jacket, Abigail found that she wanted to tie up her coat when she stood in the shade and discard it in the sunshine. The air was so crisp, clean, and unfettered by the same sticky-hot humidity she had become accustomed to that it stung her lungs, and she drank it in greedy, gulping mouthfuls.

It did much to calm her soul, the weather, the unexpected fairy tale of landscape. In some ways it seemed to affirm Abigail's self-appointed mission, and she found herself believing in her own intentions much more than she had only hours before.

The map she had printed out afforded her two different ways to enter the country, and Abigail opted to stay on I-5 and access Canada via the Peace Arch crossing. It was the touristy border crossing, awash with color from fuchsia rhododendron bushes and clumps of splattered paint–colored pansies that had yet to overrun their border beds. To her right, perfectly manicured lawns and gardens rolled over soft hills. To her left, Birch Bay sparkled in the sunlight with an almost-cheerful abandon.

As she wound through the lush landscape and past the whitewashed arch between the two countries, Abigail couldn't help but feel the consequence of what she was doing. Crossing a border felt significant somehow. Here were the markers that divided peoples and nations, ideologies and accents. Here was the place where the vigilantly drawn lines that kept everything neat and orderly converged. And Abigail was blurring the separation.

But so were twenty cars ahead of her and another few dozen headed the opposite direction, going south on their way into the States. Abigail chided herself for being melodramatic, then focused on locating her passport.

What would she say to the border guard? *I'm traveling for business.* That was a blatant lie. Though Abigail was a rather accomplished liar when she needed to be, she couldn't stomach the thought of lying to a man in uniform, a man with a gun at his hip. Okay, then: *I'm visiting a friend.* He'd probably ask for a name and address. Abigail had those things but didn't want to disclose them. *I'm looking for someone.* It was the closest approximation to the truth. She could work with that.

Abigail practiced being vague as she watched the taillights in front of her slowly approach the covered vestibule where a handful of stern-faced roving officers studied each and every car through dark sunglasses. When they walked past her car, she debated: make eye contact and smile or pretend that she was engrossed in the pages of her nearly empty passport? She decided anonymity was key and so was the truth . . . or at least a watered-down version of it.

But when the young guard walked up to her open window and asked her, "Business or pleasure?" she couldn't think of a single intelligent thing to say.

So she ended up doing exactly what she had promised herself she wouldn't do. She lied. "I'm here for pleasure."

"Where are you headed?"

"Surrey."

"How long do you plan to stay?"

Abigail thought quickly. She had rented the Kia for three weeks. What was a reasonable time frame? "A couple weeks."

At this, the guard looked up from Abigail's passport and studied her. "Pretty open-ended trip. Where are you staying?"

The question seemed loaded. But the answer came easily to her; the falsified address was a few streets over from Gia's Bakery and European Deli on the map she had printed off. The names of her imaginary Canadian friends she stole from her parents, with her mother's maiden named tagged hastily and convincingly onto the end. "Louis and Melody Van Bemmel," Abigail said without blinking.

The border official downright warmed up at this point, obviously convinced that Abigail was not a national threat, and advised her to obtain a visitor record if she decided to stay in-country any longer. "You can't work and you can't vote," he said, actually smiling. "Other than that, welcome to Canada. Enjoy your stay."

Abigail thanked him and pulled away, completely unaware until the checkpoint was behind her of how her heart had filled her chest as if swollen against a rib cage far too small to contain it. She breathed deeply until everything began to fit as it should and she felt something akin to normal.

Then, pressing the pedal of the Kia all the way to the floor, she accelerated to merge with the traffic speeding up Highway 99. She knew from her map that it wound through the heart of Vancouver and beyond, finally merging with the Sea-to-Sky Highway and coiling deeper still until it nestled taciturn and snug among the mountains of Whistler and Blackcomb. Though her destination didn't take her nearly so far, Abigail was seized with the desire to keep driving. She could drive until she ran out of road. She wouldn't look back.

• • •

When Abby was born, Lou spent a whole lot of time looking back. Deep down, in a place where he only admitted even bits of the whole to himself, he secretly resented her for stealing Melody's love and attention and making it her own. He didn't understand the new feel of their marital unity—the way two had become one, then, inexplicably, three. What had been unbroken and full in its perfection was suddenly disjointed, divided and distant, as Melody became a rapturous mother and he a reluctant father to this infant intruder. Lou couldn't help feeling like he had lost everything he loved to Abby.

But when Hailey deigned to grace his life, Lou began to believe in a different sort of loss. He couldn't explain it, couldn't qualify it or even begin to unravel what it meant, but he would give himself freely, gladly, to this tiny baby with her feather white hair and eyes like the thinnest chip of blue blown glass. She only made his love for his wife more real. Hailey was the reincarnation of the whole that he and Melody had achieved the day they said their marriage vows.

Maybe it was because Hailey was so small, so fine. When Lou held her in the delivery room while they worked on Melody, she quivered in his hands and peered everywhere but at him. She cried a little, as if calling for someone just out of earshot, but she also sneaked peeks at Lou, and it seemed to him that she was wondering if he could provide what she needed.

"I will," he said. And he meant, *Yes, whatever you need, whatever you want, to the best of my ability and until the day I die.*

But maybe Lou loved Hailey because she reminded him in some elusive way of the woman he fell in love with in a diner. Or he adored her because she was beautiful and coy and nearly ethereal in her delicacy and grace. Maybe he was just finally ready for everything he had not been prepared for when Abby became his firstborn. Whatever the rationale, it was surely not rational, because every single principle Lou had ever held to be true became irrelevant to the point of absurdity. The whole world tipped on its axis and spun recklessly, delightfully out of control.

While Lou exulted in the dawn of his universe, Abby agonized over where she fit into hers. Though she tried to rewrite it a hundred different ways, it all came back to the same incident, the same few hours that left nothing unchanged. It seemed that everything hinged irrevocably on the night Hailey was born.

Years later, when Abby both loved and hated her sister, when she knew that Hailey was beloved and that she herself was neither unloved nor truly loved, when she hung in the balance between where everything was muted and lifeless and infuriating, Abby tried to console herself by imagining that Hailey was born of magic and moondust. Or more accurately comet dust. Who could do anything but love unconditionally such a consecrated child? How could she not do the same?

Hailey was born on March 14, 1986, while Halley's Comet passed overhead, glazing the night sky with a tepid stroke of glittering light.

It was the first clear night in nearly two weeks and the first decent chance that anyone who cared to observe the comet from the Bennetts' little corner of the world could do so with relative success. For the rest of her life, Abigail would remember the night as if it had been forever preserved, full-color and high resolution, in a carefully maintained and easily accessible part of her mind.

There was the almost-tangible excitement that hovered over the house all day—Melody was infatuated with the celestial sighting and, eight months pregnant or not, couldn't wait to attend a midnight viewing of the starry spectacle. There was the scent of melting snow, the early spring runoff that had lulled Abby into believing that it was much warmer outside than the thermometer indicated; her resulting sniffly nose caused Lou to shoot her glances that were less than adoring. And then there was the special supper—chicken kiev and brown sugar glazed carrots, Lou's favorite—

that was immediately forgotten the moment Melody groaned.

Abby was jarred from her plate by a quick and stabbing fear. Melody was white, as white as the dirty trail of the comet light that she longed to see, and trembling.

"Mel?" Lou dropped his fork and reached for her.

"I think it's time," Melody managed. Her lips were blanched and wilting on her startled face, but she managed to direct a shaky smile at Abby.

Lou didn't question his wife and he didn't waste a single second. He threw himself back from the table and raced for the hospital bag that Melody had leisurely begun to pack. She was just under four weeks from her due date, and the urgency with which Lou pulled things together was filled with the intensity of the omitted three weeks of waiting, wondering, and worrying.

From her vantage point at the kitchen table, Abby could see her father reflected in the bathroom mirror. Toothpaste and dental floss went into the duffel bag but no toothbrush. Lou grabbed the understated tube of petal pink lipstick that Melody only rarely wore but not the stout bottle of Oil of Olay that she smoothed on her cheeks every morning and night. Glasses but not Melody's contact case or soaking solution. Perfume but not deodorant.

Abby watched him unswervingly until little

black dots appeared at the edge of her vision, and she realized that she had forgotten to blink or breathe. Then she gasped and remembered why Lou was frantically filling a bag. When Abby looked at her mother, Melody was sitting very still and upright, and her eyes were closed. Abby slid away from the table to rush to her mom and tuck herself under one of those warm and comforting arms.

Skidding across the pockmarked, hardwood floor, Abby stopped when she saw the alarming glare of reflected light off the pool of dark water beneath Melody's chair.

The following minutes melted into a hot and simmering interlude in Abby's otherwise-perfect memory. She felt a swell of emotion, a panicky tightening in her throat that made her swallow hard even decades later whenever the moment was unearthed. Even when she learned that nearly every childbirth was filled with the same sudden uncertainty and potential darkness, Abby remembered the look on her mother's face and the water beneath the table and stifled a shiver.

Abby was shuffled around while Lou and Melody sped to the hospital. Lou had deposited his daughter on their neighbors' front porch and unceremoniously entrusted her well-being to their good graces; Melody was waiting, pale and vulnerable, in the backseat of the car—what else was he to do?

"We have to go," Lou spat out as if it was enough of an explanation.

Mrs. Manning wrapped a kind arm around Abby in an inexact facsimile of the gesture Abby had wanted from her mom. The older woman waved Lou away and promised they'd be fine, but the first thing she said to her husband when the front door was firmly closed behind them was, "We have card club tonight. We'll have to bring her somewhere else after supper." Turning to Abby, she said, "Can we drop you off at a friend's house, honey?"

Together, Mrs. Manning and Abby collected her pajamas, toothpaste *and* toothbrush, and a change of clothes for the morning. Then the Mannings drove Abby to Heather's house (no one was home), Cara's house (Cara had the flu and her parents didn't want to spread it around), and finally Tanya's house, where Abby was somewhat warmly welcomed into the chaos that invariably ensued when five children under the age of ten lived under the same roof.

"I'll call the hospital and have them let your parents know where you are," Mrs. Manning assured Abby as she handed her the plastic grocery bag that contained her overnight things. Then she even gave Abby a quick, awkward hug and a kiss on the forehead, as if Abby were a dear niece instead of the little girl she barely knew.

Tanya was ecstatic about the arrangement. She dragged Abby to the room she shared with her younger sister, skipping all the way and making Abby's arm bob as she clung to her friend's hand. Newborn siblings were no longer enchanting as far as Tanya was concerned, and she glazed over the reason for Abby's appearance on her doorstep as if it didn't exist. Abby was left feeling jumbled and tired, and though curling up on Tanya's bed was the most inviting scenario she could imagine, the night had already been planned without her consent.

"Since it's Saturday tomorrow, Daddy said we could stay up late and watch the comet!" Tanya informed Abby with a grin.

While Abby should have been thrilled that she would be able to see Halley's Comet and recount it in perfect detail for her mom, something in her balked. Seeing Halley felt wrong somehow. It felt like a betrayal of her mother. They were supposed to have enjoyed seeing the comet together—before the baby was born, before everything changed. Abby might have been young, but she felt the once-in-a-lifetime weight of what they had missed.

Much later, when Abby's stomach was sour from homesickness and Tanya's enthusiasm had worn thin with exhaustion, Tanya's father bundled his kids plus one into their new minivan and drove out of town. They turned off the highway onto a narrow gravel road and followed it until the light pollution of town was lost behind the gentle slope of a rolling hill. Here they got out, everyone except for the littlest, who had fallen asleep with her cheek pressed implausibly against the cold window.

Abby curled into herself as much as possible and felt the brisk night air sweep over her winter coat and razor through her cotton pajamas. They were a two-piece set, with plaid bottoms and a long-sleeved shirt that sported a matching plaid ruffle along the bottom and at the cuffs of the sleeves. Across the chest were the words *Daddy's Girl*. The gift tag had told Abby that the pajamas were a Christmas present from Lou, but she knew that Melody had done the shopping and wrapped the gift. It was Melody who tried hard to orchestrate a relationship that refused to resonate in tune.

Nobody was much impressed by the comet, even though it was heralded and pivotal, something they would most likely never have the chance to see again. But to Abby, who couldn't begin to articulate what she felt, Halley left her oddly unsettled. Her mother was in the hospital. Their family would never be the same. Abby was too young to understand what it meant, but the irony of what her pajamas boldly declared pinched uncomfortably around her slender five-year-old shoulders.

Worst of all, branding the sky above her was Halley. The comet was maybe lesser than Abby had expected, but it was significant all the same. It was bold and mysterious, special yet strange, and it moved leisurely through the darkness, shedding a dim but perpetual light.

☙ *The room was beginning to sway.*

It didn't spin, not exactly. It didn't roll and tilt like it sometimes did when I was sick and my body rebelled against the pull of gravity—falling upward, floating, trying to fly. But the walls shimmered and I found myself slightly off-balance.

I knocked my hip on the counter and was surprised by the jolt of pain that stabbed through the taut ridge of bone. I stumbled on my way to the sink and, reaching for something to steady myself, pulled the hand towel from the brushed bronze ring beside the counter. It fell almost gracefully.

I wanted to sit down for a minute, but I couldn't bring myself to reclaim the toilet seat, where I had collapsed when I first found her. Nor could I prop myself on the edge of the tub again. In fact, now that I had done what I could with her, now that I had held her, loved her, and washed her beautiful face, I discovered that I could not physically go back to her.

But neither could I leave.

"It's time," I told myself, steeling my nerves to dial the three numbers on my cell phone that would conclude the solitary, final moments that we had spent together. Final moments that were far from the hoped-for eloquence of farewell and more a fumbling attempt to simply endure. Survive. Go on.

Could life go on?

I couldn't go forward and I couldn't go back, so I knelt to do the one thing I was able to: I picked up the fallen towel. It was laced with multicolored lint and it smelled faintly of sour milk. It seemed wrong to hang up a dirty towel—jarring and indecent, as insulting as dirty underwear on an accident victim—so I found a clean one in the cabinet and folded it carefully to hang just so.

There were cleaning supplies beside the neat stack of towels, and because I had to, because there was no one else in the world who could do it, I hauled them out one by one and began to perfect the bathroom that had become her mausoleum. The cleaning was nonsensical, and somewhere in the back of my mind I was fully aware of this. But it was also compulsive. I couldn't stop myself. And as I played my part in the purification of her tiled tomb, the room felt momentarily solid again.

I buffed away the fingerprints, scoured the toilet, and polished the sink fixture that curved like the neck of an impossibly flawless silver swan. I replaced the toilet roll. I swept her hair from the corners of the room and threw the curling filaments into the garbage can. Then I filled a little bucket with water and Mr. Clean and went to my knees to mop the floor.

There were corners that hadn't been touched in weeks and a fine film of sticky hairspray over everything. The slender lid of a tube of eyeliner was collecting dust behind the toilet. And lying next to it, I found an empty container of musky-smelling men's deodorant. I was so thrown by the incongruity of the heady fragrance and the impossibility of it in her apartment that I shoved it to the bottom of the garbage can and attacked the floor with new vigor.

My thumb began to ache from working over the black smudges that I assumed were from the pair of heels I had seen uncharacteristically abandoned by the couch when I first came to her apartment. I had almost looped my first two fingers around the inside curve of the heels to set them neatly by the door. But I had known enough to understand that the apartment was thick with something invisible and threatening. I had turned and walked toward her instead.

How long ago had that been? Only minutes? Hours maybe?

I never imagined it would end like this, with me kneeling before her, prostrate in some futile act of servitude that she would never know. I never imagined I would back away from her, my eyes fixed on the floor as I tried to erase what she looked like the very last time I would ever see her.

When I reached the doorjamb, I found that I could back right over it. I was shocked by how much I wanted to. My knees sank into the carpet, and I finished the last foot of tile with my bare toes curling in the plush flooring. Then I dropped the rag in the gray water clouding the bucket and raised my arm to pull the bathroom door shut.

She was there, across from me. Perfectly silent and eternally still. I could feel her presence as if she were pressing herself against me, as if she were waiting for me to wrap my arms around her and I was being the obstinate one. As if I was the one resisting her.

I didn't look at her. I closed my eyes and I whispered, "Good-bye."

After the door clicked shut, I leaned my forehead against it and listened to the sound of my own breath wheeze and fail and gasp in the hushed catacomb of the airless apartment.

IV

ᏠᎡ GIA'S BAKERY AND EUROPEAN DELI was nothing like Abigail had pictured. Maybe it was because she had grown accustomed to the sparkling newness of nearly everything in Rosa Beach, but she had expected a glass-fronted shop in a modern strip mall. She imagined something neat and brightly lit and filled with the occasional North-Americanized nod to assumed European stereotypes: a handwritten sign announcing a sale on Black Forest ham and a basket display with a well-arranged collection of Kinder Eggs.

But Gia's was nothing of the sort.

As Abigail neared the address that she had so carefully researched and printed out in various routes and forms, the neighborhoods of Surrey, British Columbia, slowly began to deteriorate. Sprawling buildings with interesting architecture and trendy coffee shops on every corner gave way to low-lying stores and run-down houses covered in a fleece of soft, green mold. The mossy rooftops seemed almost primeval, as if BC merely suggested the facade of civilization. Beneath the surface, an elemental rainforest only just tolerated the presence of so many cars, structures, and people. Abigail couldn't shake the feeling that the earth could rise up at any time and reclaim its own.

The effect was only heightened when Abigail

started to descend into the heart of the old city. Streets began to sweep downward in sharp diagonals that rivaled the hills of San Francisco. Through the shrinking buildings and side-street vistas, Abigail could catch the occasional glimpse of muddy water in the distance. The Fraser River. And beyond, lining the North Shore and sprawling all the way up and up into Alaska, were the mountains. They hovered, indigo and jagged with snowy peaks that lingered still as a reminder of the brutality of winter at seven thousand feet.

It was against this backdrop that Abigail finally found Gia's nestled beneath the steel girders of a small bridge crossing a tributary. The building seemed to sag against the corroded beams, and ivy clung to the rotting exterior like barnacles on the hull of an old ship. It was two stories tall but narrow and angled, exactly how Abigail imagined a centuries-old store in some undiscovered German village might look.

The deli was so out of place amidst the industrial feel of the area that Abigail was sure for a minute that her eyes had been tricked. She blinked twice only to find that though Gia's Bakery and European Deli was drooping ever downward, it did indeed exist. A wooden post outside supported a dangling placard that confirmed it: Gia's, it simply said in a scrawling, ornamental font.

Abigail parallel parked behind a rusty van and stepped out into the shadow of the building. A cool breeze filtered off the water and she felt her skin prickle, though she couldn't tell if it was a result of the air or the beginning twinge of anxiety that was clawing its way up her throat.

He's here, Abigail told herself. *Tyler is here.*

The thought nearly leveled her, and she leaned against her car for support.

As she was collecting herself, the front door of Gia's opened and an elderly woman with close-cropped curls walked out. The woman caught sight of Abigail and smiled. "They have the best Gouda, *ja*?" Her thick accent betrayed her immigrant status as she raised her paper bag in salute.

Abigail nodded and hoped her smile looked sincere. Then she watched the woman fumble in a lumpy purse for her keys and finally get into the van. When the woman pulled away, Abigail's Kia was the only vehicle left on the street. She was alone. Maybe she was alone with Tyler. Abigail had to ball her hands into fists to stop them from trembling.

Now that she was on the threshold of actually seeing him, Abigail realized that she didn't have a plan. Not a well thought-out one, anyway. What was she going to do? What was she going to say? Would Tyler recognize her?

Abigail fought the urge to retrace her steps and instead put one foot in front of the other to approach the heavy, wooden door. If she didn't go *now*, she might never work up the courage to follow through. She had come this far; she had to at least see him. Besides, standing beneath the silhouette of Gia's felt like entering a fairy tale; maybe everything else would unfold with equal magic. Abigail crossed her fingers.

The interior of Gia's was everything that the exterior had promised and more. It was dimly lit and almost cavelike with a wide planked floor that was worn smooth from decades of traffic. Dutch-lace curtains shrouded the windows on the inside, and ivy leaves unfurled in layers of lush green on the outside. Best of all, the scents of fresh meat and pungent cheese lent an appealing acridity to the air. There was also the faint but lingering hint of baking bread, though the ovens that must have been busy throughout the morning were cool and empty now.

Abigail didn't see anyone right away, and aware that she should at least appear like she had business in the store, she walked absently to the meat counter. Trailing her fingers along the cold glass as if to ground herself, Abigail studied the fat wheels of foreign cheese and curled links of spicy sausages. At the end of the case was an aquarium, and Abigail approached it with some trepidation: the slithering forms amidst the murky water were not lobsters.

Eels? Abigail stifled a gasp and backed into a little round table filled with embroidered towels. The table tottered and she spun to steady it.

"Can I help you with something?"

The voice came from above her, and Abigail had to cast around for a moment before she found him. Along the far wall was a curving staircase leading to a small, open loft. At the top of the steps stood a portly man with a large, red nose and thinning hair. His hair was either very blond or completely white. Abigail couldn't tell which in the muted light. And she couldn't decide if she was happy or disappointed that the man was not Tyler.

Whoever he was, he was looking at her expectantly and obviously waiting for her to tell him about whatever friend of a friend had directed her to his unlikely store in the middle of suburban Vancouver. Abigail glanced at the meat counter to stall and wondered what exactly the woman outside had gushed about. Gouda? That was a cheese, right?

"We have a wonderful, not-too-salty prosciutto," the man offered.

Abigail could hear him start down the stairs.

"A nice Edam, too, and spiced if you prefer it that way."

He was standing next to her now, and when Abigail glanced at him, she caught a grin. His bottom teeth were all crooked and gnarled like shards of broken porcelain; his top teeth were pin straight.

"Maybe you like the eels?"

So he had seen her jump. Abigail smiled sheepishly at him in spite of herself, and in that very second of tenuous connection she decided to drop the subterfuge. "Actually I'm looking for someone."

The man's face fell a little, and he reached out to touch Abigail's arm. "You knew my Gia, too? It's funny how now that she is gone all these people come to see her. You are the third person since . . ." He trailed off and fixed her with a sad and meaningful look. "Gia passed away almost three weeks ago."

"Oh, I'm so sorry." The words came out automatically, but even as she said them, Abigail wondered how she would explain to this man that Gia was not the person she sought.

"She was so beautiful, my Gia. Remember how she smiled?" The man continued as if Abigail were a close relative or at least a dear friend. "She loved this store so much. But you don't look familiar to me. Maybe you knew her from the class downtown? Were you a teacher, too? You don't have an accent. I don't think you could be one of her students."

Abigail struggled for words. "I'm sorry. I don't . . . I didn't know Gia."

The glow of fond remembrance faded from the man's eyes. "You didn't know Gia?" he repeated, his voice ripe with disappointment.

Abigail shook her head.

There was a heavy silence before the old man

sighed and put his hands on his hips as if to steady himself.

"Maybe I have the wrong place," Abigail heard herself say. The unexpected words startled her, and she instantly wished to take them back. She had the right place! She couldn't back out now.

But though the man was disappointed, he quickly settled the appropriate mask over his momentarily naked features. "No, I shouldn't have assumed." He fit a smile on his face again. "Who exactly are you looking for? Because now that Gia is gone, there is only me."

Abigail swallowed. "I'm looking for Tyler. Tyler Kamp. Do you know him?"

The man's smile flashed genuinely. "Yes, I know Tyler. I should have known, pretty girl like you . . ."

"Did he work here?"

"No, Tyler is Gia's son. He's my stepson."

It made perfect sense, but something in Abigail balked at the word and refused to let it pass her lips. "Tyler came home for . . . for the . . ."

"Funeral." The man studied Abigail. "I'm sorry. I've completely forgotten my manners. I'm Murray Kamp."

"Abigail." She shook his hand firmly and was surprised at how warm and reassuring it was.

"It's nice to meet you." Murray moved behind the counter and slid open the glass door to peruse the selection before him. Choosing a small wedge, he knifed a crumbly section and offered it to

Abigail on the tip of his blade. "Queso Iberico. It's Spanish. A little hard, a little oily, but very smooth and mild. Once we got a wheel of Iberico with fresh strawberries stirred into it. Can you imagine? Strawberries in cheese."

Abigail took the cheese and bit off a corner. "Delicious," she affirmed after a moment.

"One of my favorites," Murray agreed. Then he laid the knife on the counter and looked directly at Abigail. "Now, because I like you, I'm going to be honest. Tyler has lots of girlfriends. If I were you, I'd buy a nice quarter wheel of something exotic and go home. Find another boyfriend."

Abigail couldn't stop the blush that spread across her cheeks. "He's not my boyfriend," she said. It sounded like a lie even to her ears.

Murray spread his lips in a thin, thoughtful line. "I love Tyler. He's been my son for almost twenty years. But I have to tell you, he's not a bad boy, but he is trouble."

"I know," Abigail said softly. And she thought, *If only you knew.*

Murray continued to study Abigail. "Gia would have liked you," he said eventually. "If I can't dissuade you, I will tell you that Tyler isn't here."

Abigail's heart plummeted. All this way. All this heartache, worrying, and wondering. All her planning.

Her distress must have been evident on her face because Murray looked at her with concern.

86

"Don't chase him. You're not the first, and I don't think you'll be the last."

I will, Abigail thought. *I will absolutely be the last.* But she didn't say that. Instead, she asked, "Where is Tyler?"

"He decided to work for his uncle this summer, take some time off before he decides what to do from here," Murray answered.

"And his uncle is . . ."

"The owner of a vineyard. It's called Thompson Hills Estate." Murray stalled, then obviously decided that Abigail would not be deterred. "It's in the Summerlands. In between Revell and Larson."

"Thank you," Abigail said.

Murray sighed. "You're welcome. But let me give you his cell phone number. Call him before you race off across British Columbia."

"No thanks," Abigail said. "I want to surprise him. Where exactly is the Summerlands?"

Realization blossomed across Murray's face. "You're not from BC, are you? Tell me you didn't come from Florida. Are you one of his friends from Florida?"

Abigail shrugged and offered him a little wave as she started for the door. "Thank you very much, Murray."

"Don't do something you'll regret," he called after her. "Tyler's a nice kid, but he's not worth it."

His words rang in the air like prophecy, but Abigail left them behind the moment the door fell shut.

• • •

Abigail pulled into a Tim Hortons for dinner.

The man behind her in line was more than helpful in giving her directions to Revell. All she had to do was take Highway 1 eastbound to Highway 3—the Crowsnest—head through Manning Park, and find herself on a straight shot to Revell.

The Crowsnest? It sounded almost menacing to Abigail, as if she would be precariously perched on top of the world. She pictured hairpin passes and thousand-foot cliffs with knee-high guardrails that served as little more than a warning. Caffeine was in order. But it sounded like an easy enough route, and Abigail figured that if she could make it to Revell, she could find her way to Thompson Hills without too much trouble.

"Beautiful country," the man in line assured her. "You'll love it. Wineries, orchards, warm weather . . . It's Canada's only desert, you know."

Abigail nodded, trying to discourage his cheerful conversation.

"Lots of Quebecois go there in the summer for work. The whole place has a sort of . . . Bohemian feel." He looked her up and down, taking in her tailored, dark jeans and Bindi leather flats.

She wanted to tell him that she got the Christian Lacroix shoes on clearance because it was obvious that he thought her a far cry from her sandaled, cutoff-wearing peers at BC's hottest vacation destination. But it was her turn to order, and she turned away from him gratefully rather than try to defend herself.

Abigail got a large black coffee, a chicken salad sandwich on a whole wheat kaiser roll, and a cup of broccoli cheddar soup to go, eager to be on her way.

Revell was about a five-hour drive according to her friendly fellow customer, and since it was already close to six o'clock, Abigail planned to get a hotel room when she arrived and locate Thompson Hills the next morning. When she was fresh. When she had a little more time to prepare. After a few hours of driving and the emotional upheaval of finding Gia's to be more and less than she had bargained for, Abigail was happy at the thought of having a bit more time to pull herself together before seeing Tyler. She felt like she got a reprieve. She got one more day.

Highway 1 wound through farm country before curving into the dark line of mountains that obscured the horizon. Abigail searched for a station on the radio, but nothing kept her interest, and she decided to drive in silence, chewing slowly on her sandwich and watching the sharp outlines of the glacier-carved peaks loom ever closer. She regretted buying the soup because once she was in the car, she realized that she couldn't eat it as she drove. The aroma filled the tiny interior and teased her, but Abigail let it sit in the cup holder and ignored it the same way she ignored any misgivings that tried to prevent her from driving deeper into British Columbia.

And though she had been told that she'd hit the junction for the Crowsnest before the little town of Hope, Abigail found that her informant had been wrong—it was just beyond Hope. Abigail almost laughed out loud at the irony. She didn't consider herself beyond hope, but something about the way the sun was setting behind her as the dark hills split to consume the road ahead seemed foreboding.

Abigail pushed such morbid thoughts out of her head and pressed forward into the growing twilight. For a few kilometers she could see the lights of Hope flickering in her rearview mirror. Then the road angled behind the rising hills that were bent in anticipation like an archer's bow, and she found herself almost immediately and unsettlingly disorientated in the jigsaw of the darkening mountains.

Abby was oriented to the irrepressible pull of Hailey's compass long before she could understand the implications of her sister's immediate and absolute control of everyone around her. The situation was unfortunate in many ways, but most disturbing of all was the fact that due north was a moving target when it came to Hailey. No matter how carefully Abby studied her sister, no matter how sincerely she tried to understand, Hailey refused to be predictable. She refused to make it easy.

The first few years weren't so bad. Abby had just turned five when Hailey was born, and though part of her mourned the division of her mother's attention, Abby was also pleased to have a living, breathing doll to play with. And she was too young to be jealous of the features that transformed Hailey into the flawless representation of a porcelain doll.

Hailey won a beautiful baby contest when she was six months old, and everyone who laid eyes on her gushed about her perfection, yet Abby was young enough to enjoy the attention directed at her sister almost as an extension of something that she herself had done well. Somehow Hailey was tied to her, and Abby didn't let her sister's distinction translate into feelings of inadequacy or competition. At least not in the beginning.

As Hailey got older, infant fussiness translated into toddler irritability that transformed into a preschool ferocity, assuring Hailey the lion's share of any attention that was to be doled out. Friends and family joked that she was a difficult child, but the enchanted beauty Hailey possessed ensured that people forgave and even forgot her eccentricities. She could be a bright and happy little fairy; the tips of her delicately fashioned ears were slightly pointed as if to prove it. But then she could also be a paradoxical nightmare—ethereally beautiful but dark and wild. Her tantrums became legendary, and she was uninhibited by the thought of unleashing herself anywhere on anyone.

Abby became the most likely target for Hailey's childish rages, but instead of turning against her, Abby defended her sister, rationalizing the episodes away because Hailey was indeed a child. And a spoiled one at that: Lou doted on her, Melody enabled her, and Abby vacillated between unreservedly adoring and barely tolerating her. It wasn't until Hailey was six and Abby was eleven that the balance began a slow and eventual decline, and Abby's tolerance finally wore thin enough to tear.

It was a gorgeous, early summer afternoon, and in celebration of the end of the school year, Abby had convinced her mother to let her have a sleep-over. The plan was to take advantage of the warm weather and bunk side by side in sleeping bags on the wide platform that comprised the top level of the two-tiered tree house Lou had built for Hailey. The little girl was both possessive and dismissive of the elaborate gift, and she vacillated between protecting the fort from even an innocent, way-ward glance, then offering it to the neighborhood kids for the rock-bottom price of a mere mini candy bar.

Although Abby had already secured her mother's permission, she sought out Hailey to ask her about using the tree house before she made any permanent plans. Her sister might be almost half her age, but Abby was well aware of Hailey's ability to use her influence to make life miserable for anyone who crossed her. It wasn't worth the heartache.

When Abby found her, Hailey was lounging in the grass with her legs propped on the ladder of her wooden swing set. Abby studied the matching white-blond plumes of her sister's long ponytails and admired the way all that corn silk shone golden against the new, pistachio green grass. Hailey's arms were already turning a soft, nut-brown shade; the summer was kind to her. Abby glanced at her own milky skin in faintly veiled disappointment before remembering why she had come in the first place.

"May I join you?" Abby asked.

"Indubitably," Hailey answered, without looking at her sister. She enunciated every syllable of the grown-up word, then repeated it in an equally careful whisper to herself: *In-du-bi-ta-bly*. Do you like my new word? Dad taught me. It means 'of course, without a doubt.' "

Abby let her head sink back in the grass and tried to follow the line of her sister's sight. There wasn't a breath of wind against her skin, but the sky was filled with a profusion of cotton ball clouds that raced across the expanse of blue.

"Aren't the clouds pretty?"

Abby mumbled a reply.

"Where are they going? Where did they come from? Who made them? How fast are they going?" Hailey asked in rapid succession.

"I don't know," Abby cut in before Hailey could rattle off more questions. She focused on the ones she could remember. "God made them, and they're going pretty fast, I guess." The truth was, they were absolutely flying. The wind, so high above them and so seemingly impossible on such a still and beautiful day, was whipping the outline of each individual cloud. It made subtle alterations to the throng of glaringly white puffs, tearing them all along as if they were incapable of keeping up on their own.

"Look." Hailey pointed.

Lying beside her, Abby could train her eyes on the tip of Hailey's long finger.

"Why doesn't it pop them?"

At first Abby had no idea what Hailey was talking about. But then as she followed her sister's unswerving aim, she focused in on the little flagpole at the top of Hailey's swing set. Last summer a rainbow flag had fluttered at the top, but it had been ripped off and lost in a winter storm. All that remained was the thin, wooden dowel affixed with an arrow-point finial that thrust almost violently heavenward. As she watched, a cloud floated toward it, and though she almost expected it to snag on the point of the flagpole, it swept along intact and unharmed.

"The clouds are too high," Abby reasoned for Hailey's sake.

"I wish they weren't. I want to see one hit the pole. Do you think they would bleed?"

"The clouds?" Abby turned to her sister. "A cloud can't bleed. Don't be silly."

Hailey rolled on her side and fixed her eyes on Abby. They were the same color as the sky, Abby noted, and flecked with the polka-dot reflections of the dozens of clouds above her. "I'm not silly," Hailey said very seriously. There was a familiar edge to her voice.

Abby realized her mistake and reached out to correct it, to erase it with her fingers. She laid her hand on Hailey's cheek and said just as seriously, "I know you're not."

They were quiet for a minute, looking at each other. Abby held her breath, waiting for the possible outburst to fade and pass. It did. When Hailey's face softened, Abby pretended that none of the earlier conversation had taken place and quietly posed her request. "Can me and some friends sleep in your tree house tonight?"

"Indubitably." Hailey turned her face into Abby's hand and kissed her solemnly on the palm. Then she hopped up and raced across the backyard, down the gravel alley, and out of sight.

But it became apparent when Abby's friends arrived and unrolled their sleeping bags in the beloved tree house that *indubitably* actually meant "no way, over my dead body."

Hailey stood in the backyard and watched them unfold three neat bags and toss backpacks on top of each. She didn't say a word. The older girls laughed and made plans, but Hailey never raised a complaint. They even leaned over the railing, surveying the neighborhood and enjoying the view, without fielding a single protest from the little girl beneath them. It wasn't until Abby and her friends walked past her to get snacks from the house that Hailey proved her volatility and collapsed in an explosion of fury on the ground at their feet.

Abby rolled her eyes in affected annoyance, a charade for the sake of her friends. "All little sisters throw tantrums," her expression insisted. "No big deal." But in reality, she knew it could be a very big deal. Her heart was pounding, and the hair on the back of her neck had risen in response to something that felt a lot like fear—fear of being embarrassed in front of her friends, fear of what Hailey could do if she wanted to.

"Go on," Abby mouthed over the screams that were intensifying beneath them. She motioned that her friends should head into the house without her, and mercifully, they complied.

"Stop it," Abby spat out when they were gone.

Hailey was writhing on the ground, jerking her limbs as if she were caught in the throes of a seizure. Abby knew better than that. Every motion, every sound was an act of Hailey's iron, unbending will. All at once, it infuriated her. All of it. She had *asked*. Hailey had *no right*. Hailey was ruining *everything*. Glancing around the yard to make sure they were alone, Abby dropped to her knees and tried to pin Hailey's arms to the ground.

The little girl froze for the span of a blink and fixed Abby with a look so hard and ugly that Abby's grip momentarily slackened. Then Hailey redoubled her efforts and Abby was thrown off-balance.

"My tree house! It's my tree house! Mine!" Hailey yelled, her voice cracking in a contortion of rage.

Abby's rage rose to match her sister's, and she threw herself back on top of Hailey, this time straddling her narrow waist and trapping those fragile, skinny arms beneath her own suddenly strong hands.

"Hailey. Anne. Bennett." Abby clipped every word as if the straight angles of sound could snap Hailey out of whatever wild world she was in. "Stop. It."

Nothing happened.

Abby growled, "Stop it!"

"Mine!" Hailey shouted back. "It's mine! Get out! Get out! Get out!"

"You said we could!"

"No! No! No! No! No! No! No! No! No! No!"

Abby interrupted the fusillade of verbal bullets

by clamping her hand down on the twisted, lovely mouth. "Stop!"

For a second, Abby felt the slight body slacken. And just as quickly as she comprehended what Hailey was going to do, she felt her sister's lips pull back in a reversal of the kiss that she had bestowed only hours before. Hailey exposed the hard rim of her flawless, pearly teeth against Abby's palm. Then those teeth sank *into* her palm, and Abby's screams were rivaling Hailey's.

The child didn't let go, her teeth ground into the flesh of Abby's hand and coaxed blood to form a masquerade of clown makeup around her mouth. Worst of all, she stopped her mindless flailing; she became perfectly still but for the slow and deliberate closure of her jaw. Instead, Abby moved. She squirmed and writhed, and before she could think to try to stop them, hot tears dripped off her chin to match the hot blood dripping off her palm.

Though it felt like an eternity, only moments later Abby saw her father throw open the back door and race across the lawn toward her. She nearly folded in relief. "Daddy!" she called, her voice breaking on a sob.

Hailey let go in an instant and cried out the very same thing: "Daddy!"

When Lou's hands found Abby, they didn't curl her into his arms. He heaved her off Hailey and went to his knees beside his baby girl. Hailey looked pitiful lying there in the grass. Threads of tangled hair had pulled loose from her ponytails and formed a haphazard halo around her head. There were tracks of tears cutting a path through the thin layer of dust and grime on her cheeks. Abby was nauseated by the sight of the blood at her mouth, glossy and sickening and dark in the spaces between her teeth.

"What were you doing?" Lou demanded. His indignation should have been directed at the pair of girls, but he glared at Abby alone. Even as he glowered at her, his fingers found Hailey and he lifted her tenderly into his lap. "What in the *world* were you doing?"

"Dad . . . ," Abby began, but she couldn't begin to explain what had happened. Rather than try, she lifted her hand as evidence and let the eight perfect points of broken skin speak for themselves.

Lou was unconvinced. "What did you expect her to do? I saw you sitting on her! She's half your size, Abby!"

Abby's mouth opened and closed. She pressed her lips together and shut them tight.

And Hailey, held snug against her father's chest and encircled by the protection of his arms, raised her eyes to Abby in wordless accusation.

The whole thing turned on its head, and Abby understood that it wasn't Hailey's fault.

It would never be Hailey's fault.

ᘓ *I don't remember making the call, but I must have done it because suddenly the phone was pressed against my cheek.*

A woman's voice was tinny and insistent, far-away sounding and followed by a small, hollow echo. "The authorities have been dispatched," she assured me. "They'll be there soon. Stay with me, okay? Stay on the line. Are you all right? Are you going to be okay?"

It was the stupidest question I had ever heard. I clicked the phone off and dropped it on the floor because it felt heavy in my hand. It was charcoal colored and sleek, and it shone in dark harmony against the muted carpet. I left it there.

Now that the door was shut between us, I didn't know where to go. Hadn't I already done every-thing I could? I consecrated. I cleaned. I called. I ticked off each imperative on my numb fingers and realized that I had become superfluous. This was her tragedy, and I was little more than a prop or at best the makeup artist who prepared her to look the part.

I couldn't just go and sit on the couch while I waited for the apartment to explode with people, so I stumbled down the hallway to her bedroom. It was hard to keep my body upright between the two narrow walls—they seemed to angle together as the bedroom door approached. My right shoulder slid against the taupe paint. My left knuckles rapped it on the other side. When I finally reached the doorjamb, I leaned heavily against the pressed particleboard. I breathed. And breathed.

Shock? *I wondered.* Can shock be delayed? Is it possible to limp along like a normal, sane person before crumbling to pieces? *But the idea was insubstantial and formless; it evaporated the moment my eyes found the photo on her bedside stand.*

Her bed was unmade, and I lowered myself to her mattress, aware for a second that her body had warmed the white cotton sheets only hours before she made the bathtub hot with her blood. My mind skittered away from the thought. I simply couldn't think, not anymore, and I wasn't surprised to see my hand tremble when I reached for the small, black frame. Everything was shaking—my mind, my body, my spirit—as if I could dislodge all I had seen and all that I felt if only I shuddered violently enough.

I grasped the photo in two hands and tried to stare beyond the quivering glass.

My eyes felt heavy and refused to focus, but I knew the picture well. It wasn't a recent photo by any means; she was entering young womanhood and I was just leaving it. She was behind me, her arms thrown over my shoulders in casual intimacy and her cheek pressed against my temple. Her rich skin was flawless and almost exotic next to my own pale complexion. Her eyes were a piercing and cloudless blue in contrast to my muddy brown ones. We smiled up at the photographer with mismatched grins; hers was radiant and white, mine a thin-lipped and slightly crooked smirk. We exhibited more than enough differences to prove that we were the perfect contradiction. Night and day. Light and dark. Yin and yang.

And against all odds, paired by blood. Sisters.

V

ଔ ABIGAIL FINALLY LEFT the protective fortress of the mountains when the moon was a thin crescent of pale yellow dangling from the apex of the sky. The heavens had slowly unwrapped themselves, an impromptu gift, as Abigail descended from first thousands and then hundreds of feet. As each corner revealed more of the sparkling, velvety black, Abigail was struck by the sheer beauty of this new world as it spread itself before her.

It had been years since she had experienced the deep dark of such a night. Buildings, cities, and the never-ending simulated day of south Florida life had masked the splendor of nighttime shadows. But here, the air was stark and clear, so achingly pure that she found herself convinced that she could have slipped a hand out of the window to pluck a dazzling sequin from the glorious fabric of the darkness. She could almost imagine the icy-hot burn of a tiny, glittering star in her hand. Such a thought made Abigail feel small and young, and something shifted inside her to expose a still and hidden place that she had forgotten about. The night was something mysterious and magical when Abigail was a child; it took growing up for her to realize that it was prudent to be afraid of the dark.

She purged the vulnerable feeling by turning her attention away from the sky and back to the road before her. It continued to change with the land-scape, undergoing such dramatic conversions that Abigail had the strange feeling of timelessness, of having been on the road for days or even weeks, not hours.

Just when Abigail was convinced that she could descend no farther, that she had taken a wrong turn and was nowhere near Revell, the road curved down one last switchback, and she was on the edge of a high cliff. The lights in the distance glowed golden and warm, as inviting as the white blue stars above were aloof. Beyond the softly curving clusters of streetlamps and neon, Abigail could see a fat and flowing ribbon of water. The surface shone like smoky glass, mirroring the evidence of the dim but luminous night. In smooth arcs and coils, the lake sidled up to the town and then wandered off above and below it, disappearing into the miles beyond more bluffs.

Revell was utterly foreign and strangely beautiful, cloaked in night and hidden from view. But it was also somewhat jarring, exploding out of the darkness as if the town took pleasure in surprising visitors. The effect muddied the waters for Abigail, rendering the tenuous calm of her bittersweet and solitary nighttime road as a mere illusion of a short-lived peace and nothing more.

The Sunny Grove Inn and RV Park was the first motel on the outskirts of town. The vacancy sign was burned out and the packed parking lot didn't look promising, but Abigail pulled in anyway. Inside the cramped office a television set was humming softly, and behind a large counter Abigail could just make out the top of a silver head, parted into disorganized rectangles and curlicued with foam curlers.

The gray head bobbed when the door shut, and Abigail felt a stab of guilt knowing that she had disturbed the woman's upright doze.

But her remorse subsided as the motel proprietor perked up almost instantly when she realized a customer had darkened her doorstep. An easy, albeit sleepy, smile spread across her face as it peeked over the tall laminate desk. "You must be Mrs. Conner! We thought you weren't going to show."

"N-no," Abigail stammered, confuscd. "I don't think you could possibly be expecting me."

The woman fluttered some papers on her desk before lifting her eyes to the oversize clock on the wall. "They should have been here hours ago," she murmured almost to herself. She looked disappointed for a second, and then her expression was replaced by a carefree grin. "Well, they forfeited the room at eleven, so I guess you're in luck. You do want a room, right?" She glanced behind Abigail, presumably through the dark windows that opened onto the parking lot. "Just one guest?"

"Yes," Abigail confirmed, stepping forward and

dropping her purse on the counter. "I'm exhausted."

"Me too, honey, me too. You are also extremely lucky. Rooms in Revell book up almost a year in advance. Without a reservation you should be sleeping in your car tonight."

Abigail hadn't considered the popularity of the Summerlands or the fact that it was newly summer when she took off down the highway on a whim. Her plan suddenly seemed sloppy and feeble. It made her tired just thinking about the possibility of being stranded in the middle of Canada with nowhere to stay. "But you do have a room for tonight?"

"Tonight." The woman wrinkled her nose and consulted a wide logbook with dozens of penciled notations and scribbled lines.

Abigail almost laughed wryly. Nothing was computerized.

As if she could feel Abigail's amusement, the proprietor looked up and pursed her lips. "But if the Conners show up tomorrow, you're out. We're booked solid. If they *don't*, well, I guess you may have their room. They're scheduled for the whole week."

Abigail didn't quite know what to say. Did she want the room for an entire week? Did she plan to stay that long? What if she decided she wanted to stay longer?

Obviously Abigail wasn't the only one wondering about timing. "How long are you—" the woman studied Abigail and seemed to come up at a loss—"vacationing in Revell?"

Abigail knew she didn't look anything like the typical laid-back tourist with a car full of excited kids and a gently snoring husband. But was there industry in Revell? Could she chalk her trip up to business? Probably not. Abigail decided to say nothing at all in explanation. "I'm not sure," she finally offered.

The woman shrugged. "Tonight then."

Within minutes the necessary papers were signed and Abigail clutched a rusty key on a plastic key chain inscribed with the Sunny Grove name.

"Room 117 across from the pool," the woman instructed. "Your parking spot is directly in front of the room and marked with the same number. Oh, and we'd appreciate it if you'd leave your dirty towels in the bathtub."

"Of course," Abigail said, tired and very thankful that she had a place to lay her head. She turned to leave and heard the woman click the television off and flip a few switches. Apparently she was allowed to retire for the night now that all the beds in her motel were filled. "Good night," Abigail called weakly.

Although the woman was already half-gone, she shouted a cheerful "good night" in reply.

Abigail woke at dawn, jolted from sleep by a rectangle of light that sprang through a gap in the cheap hotel curtains. It pounced upon her face the moment the sun burst the edge of the horizon, and though she squinted and mumbled halfhearted curses, the day refused to wind back even a second. Clinging to sleep was no use. The sun was up on the little desert town, and Abigail hadn't come all this way for a holiday. Sleeping in posed no other purpose than to postpone the inevitable.

The inevitable was what she had come for.

The roadside motel that Abigail had lucked into finding was out-of-date and shabby, but it boasted a large, sparkling pool surrounded by a lush, desert oasis. From what Abigail could see from her room window, the Sunny Grove Inn and RV Park was indicative of the rest of Revell. It was a quaint tourist town, maybe aging and kind of dusty, but much loved and homey all the same. Many of the buildings were old, but they were well kept and tidy, and from the profusion of flowers in whiskey barrels, pots, and hanging baskets, it was obvious that the residents had an eye for aesthetics. Or at least a love for flora. The overall effect was one of down-home comfort and hospitality, a feeling that was granted further credibility by the somewhat-warm welcome Abigail had received when she arrived in the middle of the night.

Abigail showered and got ready quickly, using the single-cup coffeepot on the bathroom counter to brew a mug of flat coffee. She pulled a pair of sandals out of her suitcase and slipped on her sunglasses, then let herself out of room 117, planning to finish her coffee poolside. Something about the four walls of another rented room felt stifling and oppressive to her.

The pool area was deserted at such an early hour, even though the day was already pleasantly warm and dry, bursting with the promise of a hot and sunny afternoon. It was so strikingly different from the climate of the coast that Abigail almost lowered herself to the side of the pool so she could dangle her feet in the inviting azure water. But unlacing the stranglehold of tension that had slowly tightened around her over the years would take more than the refreshing lure of a glassy pool. She thought of her pale skin and the blistering sun and sat on a lounge chair in the shade instead.

"Did you sleep well?"

Abigail glanced up from her mug to see the woman from last night unhook the gate latch and let herself into the pool area. She still had the curlers in her hair, and she was wearing a zippered housecoat. It was the sort of square-shaped, floral and lace pajama that Abigail remembered her mother wearing when Abigail was a child.

"Yes, thank you. I slept very well," Abigail said.

"You still look tired," the woman observed, her statement shrewd but not unkind.

All the same, Abigail was taken aback. "Still unwinding, I suppose."

"I'm Jane." The elderly woman walked over and

extended her hand to Abigail. "Sorry. I should keep my prying comments to myself. Or at least let you know who I am before I start to make such personal remarks."

Abigail took the wrinkled hand. "Nice to meet you, Jane. I'm Abigail. And don't worry about it. I like people who aren't afraid to speak their mind."

"Good." Jane moved away and took a long pole with a net affixed to the end from the pool house wall. She began to skim the surface of the water, trapping the little leaves that were floating there.

The women were silent while Jane cleaned the pool and Abigail worked up the courage to ask the question that plucked insistently at her mind. She opened and closed her mouth a few times before managing casually, "Do you know where Thompson Hills Winery is?"

Jane didn't turn from her task. "Sure I do. But it's not the best winery around. Getting better every year, but it's a pretty small operation compared to lots of the wineries around here."

"I guess my interest is personal," Abigail improvised.

"You know Elijah Dixon?"

"No."

Jane peeked at Abigail, seemingly relieved. "He's a miserable old bear." She turned back to her work. "Thompson is about five kilometers north of here. It's past Mack's Sweets and up on the bluff opposite the lake. The buildings are canary yellow, but you won't see them until you've turned off the main road."

"Thanks."

Jane looked up suddenly. "What day is it?"

"Saturday."

"Then you're in luck again. Thompson wine might be mediocre, but they offer an amazing brunch menu on Saturdays from nine to eleven. Look at you." Jane hummed with an amused smile. "Not only do you manage to get a room in Revell, but you have an incredible breakfast to look forward to on top of it. Lucky twice in the same day. Does everything else go your way, too?"

Abigail forced a reluctant smile to mirror the one on Jane's friendly face, but she didn't feel like smiling and she certainly didn't feel lucky. Instead of struggling through more small talk, she quickly finished her coffee and rested her head against the high back of the comfortable lounge chair. Though she didn't mean to close her eyes, she couldn't help it. The air was still and warm, and her body was heavy with the knowledge of what was to come. Abigail drew inside herself and lay quietly behind the barrier of her eyelids. She didn't think. She didn't move. She didn't plan.

Before she knew it, the sun had slanted across her face and Jane was long gone.

With Jane's straightforward directions, Thompson Hills Winery was easy to find. There was one main road heading north and south beside the lake, and once Abigail had traveled through one small corner of Revell, she found the land mostly agricultural. She drove on long, flat stretches, gently curving tracks that wound with the progress of the lake. The hills along the west side of the road were brown and sandy, the soil apparently as shallow and dry as any desert. And yet the ground must have harbored much more than Abigail could perceive because the landscape was lush with trees and grapevines and fields—verdant, thriving, and every shade of green imaginable.

Every kilometer or so there would be a ranch or a fruit stand or a sign indicating that a vineyard existed beyond some gravel path curving into the mellow hills. But the only real witnesses to Abigail's journey down the hot ribbon of pavement were dwarf trees and flourishing bushes arranged in rows like pleasant but unexpected sentinels.

Mack's Sweets was actually a vegetable stand with a huge poster of an ice-cream cone on the side. As Abigail drew closer to the clapboard building, she realized that what she had assumed was a swirl of strawberry ice cream topping the waffle cone was actually a glossy red pepper. *Have you had your sweets today?* the poster questioned. The concept didn't work for Abigail. Rather than whetting her appetite for vegetables, the poster made her long for an ice-cream cone.

Just as Jane promised, immediately past Mack's

was a narrow road sporting an unobtrusive sign for Thompson Hills. If she hadn't been looking for it, she probably would have sped right past. As it was, she still had to step on her brakes harder than usual and snap on her blinker at the last possible second. Then she was alone on the little road, curling into soft hills and past yet another orchard blossoming with newborn fruit.

By the time the tiled roofs of the winery buildings burst into view over the tops of the trees, Abigail had climbed substantially from the valley floor. To her right the hills cut away to form a high bluff, fortresslike and seemingly impenetrable—the perfect place for the cluster of handsome structures that were suddenly before her. To her left, the orchards gave way to the long rows of an old and well-established vineyard; the vines sliced picturesque paths across the sandy soil, curving off over the hills until they disappeared in the distance.

And directly in front of Abigail, behind a rather small parking lot, there was a long, chevron-shaped building with an enormous double door in the angle between the two oblique walls. The heavy, carved doors were propped open with two oak wine barrels that were topped by matching arrangements of fresh flowers in wide glass decanters.

It was like something out of a dream for Abigail. Thompson Hills reminded her of southern Italy. Or maybe France. It didn't really matter which; she had never been to Europe. But the hidden buildings, the sprawling vineyards, and the casual splendor of it all was as intensely foreign as it was inviting. Everything had the effortless air of uncompromised, natural beauty.

Abigail couldn't help but be intimidated. Here? She had to meet Tyler here? Nothing was familiar. Nothing felt solid. And beneath the breezy, romantic overtones of the place, Abigail felt naked, exposed. The feeling made a pit gape hollowly in her abdomen; no matter which way she twisted, she couldn't cover the sudden bare and unprotected place.

By the time she found a parking space among the thirty or so cars that crammed the lot, Abigail's damp hands were slipping on the steering wheel and her heart beat a wild, heavy rhythm in her chest. She lowered her window and then turned off the car, letting the fresh air roll over her in an effort to steady her uneven pulse. Even now, after all she had done to find him, after how far she had come, turning around and walking away felt like a very real possibility.

But no. To leave now would mean that this would never end. Ever.

Abigail couldn't live with that.

Abigail was seated at a tiny table that straddled the wide doorframe separating the main tasting room from an enormous outdoor patio. The tasting room was airy and light with a vaulted ceiling and two matching bars on opposite walls that were lined with shapely bottles of wine. The patio was merely an extension of the indoor space. It was a half hexagon arching out over a sheer, twenty-foot drop that opened dramatically on the tidy vineyards below.

Everything had been designed with maximum sun exposure in mind. The midmorning rays poured over the entire patio and spilled into the lofty room, bathing Abigail's table in light. She herself was shadowed, strategically positioned behind a supporting pillar so that she did not bake in the sun. But instead of feeling protected, Abigail felt shifty. Though she sat perfectly upright and perched on the end of her chair, she couldn't shake the impression that she was crouching in the shadows.

Upon her waitress's strong recommendation, Abigail ordered a mimosa and a platter of fresh fruit. The mimosa was sunrise colored and tart, served in a tall wineglass with a perfect sprig of mint. She gulped it down gratefully until a gentle warmth spread through her shoulders and she grasped that it was barely ten o'clock and she was drinking. The realization left her oddly uneasy, as if a few sips could alter everything, could render her incapable of doing what she had come to do, and she set the drink aside to finish her entire glass of ice water in one long drink.

When the fruit came, it was arranged on an attractive, deep plate overflowing with chilled berries. At the center there was half a grapefruit, disparately hot and bubbling with what looked like brown sugar so molten that it had nearly candied on top. Abigail couldn't help but be pleased. There was something about the extravagance of elegant food that resonated with her. She thought of the cookbook on her counter at home, then imagined herself serving up such austere delicacies as what lay before her to someone who would appreciate them. But the daydream was over almost before it began, and as she lifted a fork to spear a raspberry, she found she had no appetite for it at all.

Instead of eating, Abigail furtively skimmed every single face in the room. There were two waiters, two waitresses, and one good-looking hostess, who had seated Abigail when she arrived. None of them looked familiar, and none of them were the man that she was looking for. If Tyler had a brother, sister, or cousin working with him at his uncle's vineyard, Abigail doubted it was one of the people present and working today. Nor did she see anyone who could even pass for what she assumed was the middle-aged owner of Thompson Hills. All the employees were young and attractive. And the patrons were far too eclectic of a mix for Abigail to even consider. One thing she did know: Tyler was nowhere to be seen.

It would come down to asking. Abigail would

have to flag someone down—maybe her bright-eyed waitress—and make the object of her obsession public knowledge. She could almost imagine the kitchen chatter that would inevitably surround her request: "She's looking for Tyler! Can you imagine? . . . No, not her. The one at the corner table in the shadows. The one . . ." But what would they say about her? Though she tried, Abigail could scarcely imagine how she appeared to other people.

The whole process of being self-aware, or at least trying to be, often proved to be a downright daunting task for Abigail. She had always considered herself the definition of a wallflower: plain, unobtrusive, forgettable. But then sometimes people chipped away at that insular perception and treated her as *more*. It always left Abigail feeling mildly baffled, as if she needed to peek over her shoulder to discover who exactly was the object of this unfamiliar attention, this occasionally thinly veiled admiration. Colton made her feel this way, and Abigail wondered sometimes if her subconscious had derailed that potential relationship long before a wayward Tic Tac did.

But that was then and this was now. This was Abigail's present reality. It didn't matter what anyone thought of her; she had to ask—it was what she had come to do. Abigail decided that when the waitress came back with her bill she would casually mention Tyler. Until then, it was enough to simply watch the breeze play with the profusion of perfectly formed grape leaves and sip on her mimosa.

"Can I get you anything else?" The friendly voice that tore Abigail from her nervous reverie was not the voice she had expected to hear. It was not female.

As Abigail turned to face this newcomer, this glitch in her monumental morning, she knew that this was no casual coincidence. Jane had called her lucky twice, but Abigail knew that the world functioned along the rule of three. Everything had a beginning, a middle, an end. There was up, down, and that nebulous place in between. Life consisted of before and after, but who could ignore the interim? the time that joined the irrevocable commencement and cessation with a thin thread of existence, forever shaped and affected by the events that bookended it? And though she wasn't superstitious, Abigail had to admit that even religion followed this threefold pattern. She had grown up knowing the solemnity of the supreme trio: the Trinity. And creation, fall, redemption. Heaven and hell, with earth balanced forever between, tilting first one way, then the next. Ultimately, there was the triangle of eternity that Abigail could never quite take in: life, death, resurrection.

Now Abigail's third was complete. She had been lucky twice, but as she turned to face him, Abigail knew that this made three times. She was looking at Tyler.

"Sorry," he said, the corner of his mouth curled into an apologetic but amused smile. There was a dimple nestled beside the curve of his lip. "Natalie has been here since five without a break. I'm taking her tables." He paused, then startled Abigail with a brilliant grin. "Don't worry. I won't skim her tips."

Abigail shook her head almost imperceptibly. Blinked. Tried to absorb the sweep of sandy brown hair that he pushed nonchalantly from his forehead, the sparkle of his blue green eyes that seemed to tease her.

"Hey." Tyler's eyebrows narrowed. "Don't I know you from somewhere?"

I'm the girl in the photo, Abigail longed to say. *The one on the nightstand where you fell asleep beside her.* The words bubbled in her throat, choked her. What she wanted to say was imprisoned behind the cruel shock of his proximity. What she wanted to say was an ugly, living thing that threatened to eat her up inside. She wasn't ready for this, not ready at all.

Tyler stared at her, confused, wondering, and Abigail couldn't say a thing. But she thought it over and over and over: *You killed my sister.*

When Hailey was nine years old, she almost killed herself.

If Abby had known at the time that this was the first in a long line of other close calls, she probably would have paid more attention to the before and after. Maybe if she could have begun to pinpoint the "why?" and the "what next?" she would have been able to start anticipating the frantic downslide and the ensuing colossal fallout. But instead of recognizing the initial incident for what it was—the first in an emerging destructive pattern that highlighted Hailey's eccentric life—Abby merely reacted like anyone else would. She recoiled in concern and fear over what might have been, then pushed the occurrence out of her mind as if forgetting it entirely could undo it. *It never happened,* Abby told herself, and eventually she began to believe it. It never crossed her mind that it could happen again.

The trouble began because Hailey was too old for her age. She was too pretty, too wise. Too capable of manipulating any situation to her advantage, too triumphant when she won, and too moody when she didn't. Actually Hailey was too much of nearly everything. It seemed as though her spirit was simply too much for her little body to contain. *She should have been twins,* Abby once thought. Abby was in biology and could imagine the cellular split that was supposed to happen when Hailey was smaller than a pinprick but didn't—Hailey was left with soul enough for two. In some ways, Abby wished that the clock could be rewound and the problem fixed. But then there would be two of them, and she couldn't even deal with the implications of that.

It's not that Abby didn't love her sister intensely—she did—but when Abby started high school, Hailey became too much to handle. Abby was ready for freedom and friends, maybe even a boyfriend or two to collect and admire along the way. Hailey thought she could tag along for the ride.

After a tumultuous freshman year, a distraught Abby convinced her mother to draw a line in the sand between the sisters. Melody made it clear that Abby was the young woman; Hailey was still a child. The little girl was banned from her sister's room without explicit invitation, forbidden to touch the subdued collection of new pastel makeup, and warned about interfering when Abby had friends over, was on the telephone, or was involved in anything even remotely adult or personal.

Hailey was furious and made her feelings known by taking sharp fabric scissors from her mother's sewing kit and hiding herself in Abby's closet. Hailey pulled down one shirt at a time, making the fabric slide heavily from the hangers and sending the thin metal hooks flying off the closet rack. It was the sound of the hangers hitting the closed closet door that alerted Abby to the fact that something was going on. *Thump.* Then nothing. And again, a few minutes later: *thump.*

Abby found Hailey buried in a chaotic pile of shredded clothes. She had obliterated a dozen shirts, and the tangled pile of colorful strips spread across her lap like the beginning of a memory quilt. Abby wanted to strangle her and probably would have if Melody had not heard her daughter's low, anguished cry and come running.

Melody pulled them apart, panting, gasping, weeping, although it was impossible to know who was doing what as they grappled, all twisted limbs and tousled hair. "How could you?" Melody cried. And while the plea was directed at Hailey, Abby felt blame radiate—surely she had done something to cause this, surely she had had some hand in it, too.

After that, Melody brought up the topic of counseling for the first time. She had carefully approached the issue before, sidling up to the outskirts of suggestion but backing away immediately when Lou bristled. This time, she finally plunged in and said it. "Therapy," she muttered, barely above a whisper, as if it were a matter of massaging sore muscles back to health.

Lou glowered. "Who? Hailey?"

Melody nodded, a calculated little flick of her head that could have been interpreted as dissent if Lou completely flew off the handle. "She has some . . . behaviors that we should probably examine."

"She's a kid, Mel. A tailender who might as well be an only child. Abby doesn't give her the time of day except to provoke her. You can't blame Hailey for being jealous."

"Abby doesn't provoke her," Melody defended weakly. "And I don't think Hailey is simply jealous."

Lou only grunted.

"Abby's way older than Hailey. She—"

"Exactly my point," Lou interrupted. "Abby's older and Hailey's just acting her age."

Conversation over.

But Abby had heard it and so had Hailey as they perched together on the landing above the living room. They were cloaked in darkness, but when the grown-ups were quiet, the sisters peered at each other across the narrow hallway. There was nothing to say that could bridge the gap between them, and they crept back to their separate rooms wordlessly.

Things started to change then. Hailey plummeted over some invisible precipice and continued to freefall for weeks. The child that had been almost fanatical in her desire to be a part of it all withdrew. Where she had been loud and vibrant and electric she became subdued. Her colors flickered and dimmed. Her too much became too little. Way too little.

The cataclysmic switch upended the very structure of the Bennett home.

Abby vacillated between anxiety and anger, because although Hailey had always been a roller coaster of emotions, she had never dipped so low nor stayed there for so long. Abby worried about her and then despised her for throwing everything out of whack. Where was the inevitable upswing? Where was the eventual turnaround that would restore everything—their family, their relationships, their understanding of themselves and each other—to its natural state?

Lou and Melody were also far from blind to Hailey's sudden and absolute reversal. Melody teared up often and chewed her fingernails down to the quick. Nail biting was a habit that Lou detested, but he either didn't notice or didn't care when Melody picked up the addiction that she had kicked years ago. Besides fretting, Melody poured all of her nervous energy into cooking, cleaning, and creating things for Hailey. She seemed to think that peanut butter cookies or a new, fluffy purple scarf could coax Hailey out from under her dark cloud. With each offering, Melody tried to force cheer into the house. She laughed thinly to cover up the deep lines of concern that creased her face and carried on a limping form of life as normal.

While Melody fought the unhappy fog, Lou almost seemed to embrace it. He followed Hailey down her sad path and joined her in whatever strange and solitary place she had decided to hide. They curled on the couch together, father and daughter, arms entwined but eyes faraway and blank. Abby couldn't help wondering if each was aware of the other's presence. Sometimes she doubted it.

It was in this dismal and echoless facade of a home that Abby decided life could not possibly go on like this—Melody pretending, Lou singing funeral dirges with his sighs, and Hailey becoming a phantom of the girl she used to be. It was horrible. And somehow the responsibility to fix it seemed to rest on fourteen-year-old Abby's shoulders. Lou ignored, Melody tried to fix the wrong problems, and only Abby could stand outside and see the brokenness for what it was, even if she didn't understand what caused it or why. And she certainly didn't know how to begin to make things right.

So instead of trying, Abby started to drift away. She began the slow and difficult process of disentangling herself.

Disentanglement proved more difficult than Abby had imagined it would be. True, Lou and Hailey were impervious to her subtle change of attitude, but Abby could tell that her mother was present enough to realize that her eldest daughter's place in their family was slowly eroding. Abby prickled with a sort of mild shame around Melody, but what was she to do? She had been a virtual outsider in her own family since the day of her birth, the day her father grudgingly learned that love was designed to be shared. Of course, she could not put any of this into words, but she was definitely perceptive enough to be fully aware of the dynamics in her family and her father's simmer of something that smacked of resentment toward her.

But although Abby tried to convince herself that detachment was the way to go, family ties are never easily broken. When Abby's life started to sway in happy directions in spite of the confused muddle at home, the first thing she wanted to do was share her joy with her mother.

The truth was, Abby had an almost boyfriend. His name was Luke, and while he wasn't a starter on the fabled Newcastle Public School basketball team, he did a handsome job of warming the bench. Luke was a junior, and in addition to being a year older than Abby, he was an entire head taller. Best of all, he had a swath of strawberry-colored hair that was so softly waved it was almost pretty. But his features were angled and distinctive; Luke was the opposite of effeminate. And he was everything Abby could have ever hoped for.

"Devastating," Abby called him.

She whispered about her crush to her friends: his looks, his sense of humor, his inexplicable and utterly glorious interest in her. Abby lived and breathed Luke with the ardent passion of first love. And though she couldn't articulate what she felt or why, she longed to introduce him to her family. Maybe if they could see in her what Luke saw in her, everything would change.

Surely Luke, man-to-man, in some secret male rite of understanding, could impress upon Abby's interested father the depth of her inherent worth. Luke and his shy attentions had begun to convince Abby that she was a treasure. She was a small treasure, to be certain—a collection of shiny coins instead of an overflowing trove of diamonds, rubies, and riches—but a treasure all the same. If only Luke could somehow make them all see . . . He could be the impetus for change at the Bennetts'. Maybe Abby wouldn't have to disengage after all.

Abby's opportunity came in late January when Luke invited her to go to the winter dance with him. Of course, he had to play (sit on the bench) in the basketball game first, but after the double-header there was an all-school dance. Luke would escort Abby and then take her out with a large coed group for late-night appetizers at the local twenty-four-hour Perkins. Abby was ecstatic.

And she was ready to facilitate a meeting.

After the game, Abby made plans with a friend to be dropped off at home rather than wait around for Luke to shower and get ready for the dance. This would ensure not only that Abby had time to freshen up herself but also that Luke would be forced to pick her up from home. He was fine with the arrangement, and Abby excitedly began to count the days.

On the night in question, Abby floated through the front door of the Bennetts' still-citrus two-story and practically skipped into the living room.

"How was it?" Melody asked, turning from the television with a limp smile.

"Awesome," Abby shot back. "We won, of course."

"The big games are always stacked," Lou muttered. "The coaches schedule it so they play some loser team that will go down without a fight."

Abby shrugged. Nothing could dampen her exuberance on this night, not even Lou's cynicism. But instead of sticking around for more grumpy commentary, Abby headed to the main floor bathroom, where she brushed a fine coat of powder on her forehead and chin and reapplied a seashell pink lip gloss. She didn't realize that she had left the bathroom door open until Hailey poked her somber head in.

Actually, Hailey didn't poke her head in; she just materialized, all of her, out of nowhere. She hovered, a translucent fog of child that seemed to be more ghost than girl. "What are you doing?" she asked, her voice a monotone.

"Don't sneak up on me," Abby chided. But she wasn't angry, nor was she surprised by Hailey's abrupt appearance. "If you must know, I'm *primping*." Abby savored the last word, knowing that Hailey would immediately understand it within context and then file it away for later use.

"What for?"

Abby could have said a dozen things. *For the dance. Because I feel like it. Because I want to look pretty.* But Abby ached to say the truth and she spilled her secret. "I have a date."

Hailey's eyes were sunken and rimmed in a pale, unhealthy blue, but she was still striking and even more so when her eyes flashed silver beneath the icy blue. "A date?"

"Yes, a date." Abby pursed her lips and smacked them softly, watching the effect in the mirror and liking it. "His name is Luke. He's so hot."

Hailey took turns studying her sister's reflection in the glass and her profile in the flesh. For the first time in weeks, she seemed to be aware of the fact that Abby was moving forward while she moped around in some sorry state of self-inflicted distress. "You're dead, you know," Hailey finally said, breaking her silence when Abby spun from the mirror and reached to flick off the bathroom light. "Dad is going to be livid, irate, completely *incensed*. He's going to go ballistic."

Abby's heart pumped a single shot of ice-cold blood through her entire body. She shivered and then shook the feeling off. "Don't be ridiculous."

As Abby breezed down the hallway, she heard her sister call, "Did you ask Dad if you could go on a date?"

The thought had never crossed Abby's mind. Never. Last year she had attended the dance with a group of friends, so the issue of securing permission for a date was unnecessary. Boys and girls, the birds and the bees were not routinely or ever dis-

131

cussed in the Bennett home. There was no rule book for this sort of thing. No protocol. But Abby should have known better.

Suddenly panicked, Abby rushed through the kitchen and into the living room. She would wait by the window and slip out the door the second Luke pulled into the driveway. She'd abandon her plan to introduce her new boyfriend to her unstable family. She'd forget that she ever naively wished for some semblance of normalcy to result from the conventional unfolding of her own unimportant life.

But it was too late.

Luke was a gentleman and he had come to the door. He stood on the threshold, caught between the mild, uncomprehending gaze of Abby's mother and the startled, hard look of her father.

"I'm here for Abby . . . ?" Luke fumbled. He was awkward, young and beautiful and guileless, obviously waiting for a girl who he hoped would be more than a friend.

"Here," Abby said breathlessly. "I'm here." She hurried across the room, slid her feet in her shoes, and allowed Luke to hold her coat as she twisted into it in one smooth but trembling motion. Abby had intended to say, "This is my mother, and this is my father. And there—the little girl on the couch— that's my sister." But she didn't say any of that. Instead, she ushered Luke out the door.

Before the latch fell shut, Abby peeked at the still

life that was her family. Melody was frozen near the door, a confused frown furrowing her lips as she watched her stationary husband. Lou was seated, but his hand was on the arm of the couch as if he intended to rise, and his eyes were dark and cold. And just as the door swung closed, Abby caught a glimpse of Hailey. She was leaning against the entryway wall, her arms crossed and her face warm with something living and bright that Abby couldn't quite place.

Abby had hoped for change, but this wasn't what she had in mind.

Abby was grounded and Hailey came back to life.

The little girl resuscitated as quickly as she had suffocated; the reversal was absolute and mostly complete by the time the Bennett family gathered for breakfast the following morning. In a way it was a relief to have the old Hailey back, but the cause of her regeneration plagued Abby. Did Hailey turn around because Abby got into trouble? Did she take pleasure in her older sister's pain? Or was it simply the drama of the incident that breathed life back into the flagging Hailey? After all, the focus was finally off her. But then again, Hailey usually *liked* to be the center of attention.

The possibilities were endless, and they kept Abby busy during the homebound hours when she would have been continuing to develop her fledgling relationship with Luke. But one strange possibility niggled at the corners of her mind and made Luke a topic that she hardly even dared to think about at home lest his presence be made tangible by her thoughts. As Abby had pulled on her coat that unfortunate homecoming night, she had caught a startling look on Hailey's face. The girl was examining Luke, taking him in with wide-eyed, sweeping glances that seemed drenched in wonder and admiration. Hunger? Was there something hungry in her look? Abby flung the thought from her mind.

And Hailey, bizarrely, implausibly, flung herself from the roof.

It had snowed and frozen, snowed and frozen, and Lou had propped the extension ladder against the roof so he could pour boiling water down the frozen septic vent. It was just another winter chore, and it never occurred to him to promptly put the ladder back in the garage. Who could have possibly known what Hailey had in mind?

One morning, a few days after Luke stepped into their home and broke whatever spell had cast its wicked magic on Hailey, she bundled up in all her winter gear and climbed the icy ladder to the low, flat line of roof over the narrow porch. According to the neighbor who claimed to see it all from her bathroom window, Hailey stepped to the end, lifted her face to the sky, and swan dived off the edge with her arms spread wide in some imitation of a willing virgin sacrifice. She landed prostrate, her head buried in the snow and her arms still open as if she were making a snow angel instead of lying there unconscious. Only her legs were akimbo, leaning gawkily aslant as if somewhere in the back of her mind she was a reluctant offering after all.

At the hospital the doctors determined that Hailey had sprained her right ankle, bruised a number of ribs, and split her upper lip bad enough to require six small stitches. The damage was rather minimal, all things considered, but the whole world was enraged. "If it wasn't for the snow . . . ," a doctor warned them, trailing off to leave room for every horrible scenario they could think up.

But Lou didn't need help imagining the worst. "What were you trying to do?" he demanded as huge tears dripped through the five o'clock shadow that he could never quite make smooth. Lou pinched Hailey's shoulders in his massive hands. He shook her. He thundered. But then he pressed her to himself and rocked her as if she were the tiny baby that he had held all those years ago. "Were you trying to kill yourself?"

Maybe it would have been easier if she had been. As it turned out, Hailey wasn't trying to commit suicide at all; she was trying to fly.

When I heard them pounding on the apartment door, I panicked.

It didn't make sense. There was no reason for me to be afraid of their arrival. After all, I had called them; I had invited them to come. And yet, when the whine of those sirens whispered almost menacingly through the thick walls of her apartment, I surged off the bed as if I was caught in the act. Of doing what? thinking about her? remembering? Or was it the content, the sad slant of my memories that convicted me?

I stood there in her bedroom, just stood still in the middle of the floor while the seconds spun away. Then they were at the door: hard fists on wood, firm voices fixed just below a shout. I didn't go to let them in. They let themselves in.

Everything went gray around the edges. I gasped in shuddering, little breaths. I shook so hard I nearly collapsed again on the edge of the bed. They were calling for me. They found the bathroom instead. I could tell by the sudden sense of purpose in the unfamiliar voices. They would find me in a moment.

I hadn't believed the weight of my own remorse before, but now, with them sketching edges around what she had done, drawing conclusions about when and why and how, I realized that there was only one thing that mattered. Words gurgled up from the stronghold of my throat. "I did it. I did this to her." But I didn't say that. My voiceless confession rang only in my head.

Substituting denial for admission, I turned from the door because I couldn't bring myself to confront them when they did come through it. They would see the guilt written all over my face, and I was afraid of the disgust that I knew I would find in their eyes.

And that's when I spotted it. On the bedside stand, leaning against a dog-eared spy novel behind the place where the photo of the two of us had once stood, there was an envelope with my name on it. Abby, *it accused, as if she knew that I would try to defer the blame. Abby—an indictment as bold and undeniable as her pointed finger. I couldn't let them see it and know. I lunged for the paper, hastily folded it in two, and crammed it in the back pocket of my jeans.*

"Ma'am? Are you the young woman who called 911?"

I didn't even get to see his face before everything went black.

VI

ↁ ABIGAIL ESCAPED.

The need to feel her blood pound a hard and steady rhythm consumed her. Her heart was beating erratically and she longed to harness it, to bend it to her will instead of allowing it to be swept along by emotions that she was unable to control. If Abigail couldn't command her life, she'd discipline her body.

Thompson Hills was only a speck in her rearview mirror, and Abigail tried to convince herself that it was nothing more. It was unimportant, diminishing from view even as it faded from her life, and she would never see the stately yellow buildings again. But Abigail knew better. And the knowledge that this was only the beginning made her ache. Her foot quivered on the gas pedal.

Abigail turned left at Mack's Sweets and drove north, away from Revell. She didn't know where she was going, but she knew what she was looking for: a deserted road. Ten minutes stretched after leaving Thompson Hills before the perfect place presented itself. Abigail slammed on her brakes to make the sharp turn and pulled down a dirt drive amidst a cloud of dust and a spray of tiny rocks. She was in a small clearing surrounded by gnarled apple trees that were years past their prime. The grove was obviously untended, and there was a weathered real estate sign declaring that the property was sold. But Abigail wasn't concerned about trespassing. It looked as if no one had given the place a second thought in years.

Behind the trees, Abigail felt totally hidden. She parked in the shade and reached into the backseat of the Kia to riffle around in her suitcase for running shoes, shorts, and a tank top. Abigail changed in the car and discarded her carefully pressed capris and tailored, button-down blouse on the passenger seat. She removed the car key from its key chain and stuck it in her sock, then locked the car and took off.

Abigail hit the ground at a dead sprint. Even though she knew that she should warm up or at least slow down a bit, she could no more stop the pulse of her feet than she could prevent the sun from beating down on her back. Abigail gave in. She ran.

Fled, more like it.

Fled from Thompson Hills. From Tyler. Abigail tried to convince herself that he was just another predator in a long line of selfish, egocentric losers, but she recoiled at the very thought of him. She hated what she suspected he had done to Hailey.

Hailey, Hailey. Even in death she was always there. Sometimes it seemed to Abigail like there had never been a time in her life when Hailey didn't exist as close as her shadow, as constant as the breath of air on her skin. The few years that

Abigail had existed as an only daughter were far-away and forgettable—she had been a small child. Those years were as lost to her as the months spent in her mother's womb. They might as well have never been. In the beginning and even now at the apparent end, it always came down to Hailey.

Failure nipped at Abigail's ankles, threatening to trip the hammers that she hurled to the ground with increasing intensity. She fought it. *Let go. Let go. Let go.* Abigail's feet thundered in perfect rhythm. And then: *Good-bye. Good-bye. Good-bye.* A staccato of muted pain in every footprint she left in the sandy shoulder of the road. Although Abigail used her body to punish her mind, though she squeezed her heart with the exertion of her pumping arms and nearly frantic legs, she couldn't wring out the poison of her desperation.

In the weeks after Hailey killed herself, Abigail did everything she could to rearrange what had happened and why in her mind. *It was inevitable,* she rationalized. Hailey had always been, well, Hailey: one small step beyond reason. Even when the doctors got involved, little had changed. *There was nothing I could have done to stop her,* Abigail excused. But then, as much as she tried to convince herself, there was the truth, crouching in some corner and biding the time until she let down her guard. In those naked moments, the full force of it all would suffocate her and Abigail would know:

There was much I could have, should have done to stop her.

And as if her own self-flagellation wasn't enough, her father reminded her of her failure every single day.

Just the thought of Lou made Abigail run faster.

By the time the road finally curved close to the lake, Abigail radiated with exhaustion. Thinking only of the unbearable heat and the sweat that now poured from her body, Abigail slipped down a shallow ditch and wove through a few brushy shrubs as she made a beeline for the water. There were a couple of boats crisscrossing the enormous lake, but the beach here was narrow and rocky and there were no people around.

The shoreline curved away from the swath of stony sand and created a small cove. But there were no trees near the water's edge and therefore no privacy. Abigail didn't care. She kicked off her shoes and stood on the toe of each sock in turn to slip it off. Then she pulled her shirt over her head with one sharp tug. Her sports bra was black and so were her shorts; what did she care if a stranger on some distant motorboat suspected she was swimming in something other than her swimming suit?

Abigail was a bit shocked when she hit the water at a jog. It was colder than she had anticipated, and it stung the back of her legs with droplets as piercing as pinpricks. She plunged forward anyway, working hard to ward off the chill that tempted her to escape to the shore. When the edges of her shorts began to get wet, Abigail dived. She broke the surface of the water with her fingertips and angled the rest of her body to sweep along behind the line of her outstretched arms.

The cramps hit almost instantly. Abigail's right calf knotted like the spring fiddleheads of the potted fern she kept in her Florida apartment, and her side twisted angrily as if punishing her. But Abigail wasn't stupid. She knew the water would make her body seize, and she hadn't gone deeper than her waist. Settling her left foot on the uneven bottom of the lake, she burst out of the water and began to flex and point her right foot to work out the muscle spasm. The stitch in her side was a different story: no amount of stretching or twisting would rid her of that ache. Abigail didn't mind the pain. It was temporary.

Back on the beach, she sank to the ground and let her body unwind. A hot, dry breeze licked the water from her skin, and Abigail's nerves settled somewhere between the extremes.

"Go home," she told herself, her voice raspy and slight before the great expanse of water and sky.

It would be a simple enough thing to do. Abigail could get back in her car and retrace her steps: past Thompson Hills, over the mountains, through the blue cool of Vancouver, across that scenic border, and then back on a plane to reality. Johnson, McNally & Bennett awaited. In the arms of her cute neighbor girl, so did that nameless tabby. But then, Lou waited in Florida, too. And so did Hailey, in her haunting, unforgettable way.

Hailey. This was the thought that Abigail carried with her when she laced up her running shoes for a second time and made her way back to the rented Kia. This was the thought that galvanized her resolve. This was the thought that made Abigail realize, probably for the first time, that even if she wanted to she couldn't go back. Not until the scales stacked so pitifully against Hailey had somehow, someway, been balanced.

"I wondered if you'd be back," Jane said with a smile when Abigail returned to the cramped Sunny Grove office. The TV was on again, and this time it was turned up enough that Abigail could hear the insipid dialogue between some chisel-chinned leading man and his doe-eyed lover. Both were terrible actors. Jane followed Abigail's line of sight and turned the ancient television set so Abigail could see it better from where she stood.

"I just love soaps," Jane admitted. "Are you old enough to remember the original cast of *General Hospital*? Of course not," she sighed, answering her own question. "Nothing quite compares these days, but I still like a good dose of romantic tragedy on a daily basis."

No thanks, Abigail thought. *I already have more than my share of tragedy.* Out loud, she said, "I don't suppose you still have that room."

"Believe it or not, I do. The Conners called this morning to say that the baby's sick and they can't make it." Jane put up a warning finger and turned enthusiastically to the TV. "Shhh, I've been waiting for this. She's going to tell him she's pregnant."

Abigail was repulsed by the sight of all those fake tears and wrung hands. But rather than alienate her benefactor by being snide, she waited for the show to cut to commercial and Jane's attention to switch back to her. When an advertisement for laundry detergent took command of the orange-hued screen, Jane seemed to emerge from a trance.

"He's gonna leave her," she predicted with a glint in her eye. "It's a foregone conclusion."

"The room?" Abigail reminded.

"Oh, of course." Jane heaved her logbook across the counter and made a quick notation above the scratched-out line that indicated the Conners' stay. "How long?"

"How long can I have it?"

"They had it booked from Friday until Friday, so I guess you can have it the whole time if you'd like." Jane looked up. "But if you commit to the week, you pay for it—even if you change your mind and leave early."

Abigail nodded, even though she suspected that

the Conners were paying a hefty fee for canceling at the last minute themselves. "I can pay you up front if you'd like."

"Your word is enough," Jane said with a sudden jovial shake of her head. "I just had to let you know."

Abigail waited impatiently for Jane to get her key. She was eager to retreat from the older woman's cheerful company and even more eager to take another shower. Sweat, lake water, and a dusting of gritty sand mingled on Abigail's skin in a fine, itchy film.

"I'm sure the girls haven't gotten around to your room yet. Check-in is at four, and we're usually cleaning rooms up until the last second. You can wait by the pool if you'd like."

"Don't worry about it." Abigail took the proffered key from Jane's outstretched hand. "You can take my room off the list for today. I already made the bed, and everything else is pretty much as I found it."

"It's up to you. Would you like another coffee packet at least?" Jane held up a frayed basket with dozens of single serving packets in premade filters.

"No thanks." Abigail forced a smile and promised herself that she'd make work of finding the nearest Starbucks.

Abigail spent the rest of the afternoon tossing fitfully beneath the sheets of her hard-mattressed bed and trying to think of a way out, a reason to leave.

But no extraordinary solution presented itself, and Abigail knew that she had no choice but to do what she had come to do. She had already indulged her fears and tried to exorcise them in a run that left her well-trained muscles sore. Now, whether her weaknesses had been expunged or not, it was time to put all her misgivings and worries aside and focus on crafting a plan: Abigail had to get close to Tyler.

The truth was, Abigail had no desire to ever see Tyler again as long as she lived. But she also knew that she didn't have a choice. Her presence here, her every action was a small piece of the whole that would eventually help her atone for whatever role she had played in Hailey's death. This fundamental purification was as natural to Abigail as washing her hands when they were dirty. A quick wipe with a wrinkled napkin or a hurried rub against stiff jeans was not enough to clean the filth that Abigail was sure had accumulated on her hands and her heart. This penance demanded time, dedication. Some serious scouring. And a whole lot of water.

Just before dusk, Abigail locked up her musty motel room and set off on foot into Revell. The Sandy Grove overlooked the little town, and from her perch above it, Abigail could see the buildings angle gently toward the water. She knew from a number of brochures that there were restaurants and parks, docks and walking trails along the lake.

Even though her legs were a little wobbly from her run, Abigail looked forward to the two-kilometer walk and the chance to let the fresh air clean the foggy corners of her mind.

The road to the lake slanted ever downward, and Abigail let gravity pull her toward the water at its own leisurely pace. There were people everywhere: families still dressed in beachwear with swimming suit straps peeking out from rumpled T-shirts, young couples with fingers intertwined, clusters of teenagers trying to look tough and failing because of the telltale innocence of youth.

Under different circumstances, Abigail could have liked this place. She could almost envision coming here as a child for some uncommon family vacation. The Bennetts didn't usually take trips, but Abigail could imagine the roles that they would have played if things had been different and they were a normal family unit.

Melody stood center stage in her mind, decked out in a white linen shift, grinning as Lou mouthed the word he reserved for her: *stunning*. There was Hailey, drawn to the sun and sand, charmed by the old-fashioned ice-cream stands and carnival-like feel of the place. And as always, Abby would be peripheral but necessary, the ignorable skin that held the muscle, bone, and heart of her family together. How would she have seen this place at the age of twelve? fifteen? eighteen? Abigail was convinced that her childhood self would not have reacted much differently to Revell than her adult self did; she was a lone visitor and, frankly, prevented from being interested in the sunny tourist trap by obligation.

Whether or not she was particularly enamored of her surroundings, Abigail had to admit that she was starving and needed to find a place to eat. She hadn't had anything, and after her agonizing run and the subsequent sleepless nap, Abigail's stomach felt cavernous. She passed two pizza parlors, an ice-cream stand, and a burger joint that claimed to have the best onion rings in town. Instead of making her salivate, the options left her feeling disappointed. Abigail wasn't a vegetarian or even a picky eater by any standards, but she longed for a veggie wrap or a huge Greek salad with some of those bell peppers like she had seen advertised at Mack's.

The sun was slipping down the horizon, and a cool breeze wafted inland from the rippled surface of the water. But the sand was warm when Abigail stepped off the road, and since she could tell that it was obviously maintained and sifted, she took off her shoes to let the fine grains massage her tired feet.

Abigail headed north along the water because there was a restaurant that looked promising farther up the beach. She wove through groups of people carefully so as not to step on anyone's abandoned towel, shoes, or bag. Mostly she looked down to avoid making eye contact, and she tried to blend into her surroundings as much as possible. It was a bit of an exercise in futility. When Abigail did look up, she realized that not only was she practically the lone person on the beach wearing more than a swimming suit or cover-up, she was also as white as the little pools of foam that lapped gently at the sand. Everyone else had the beginnings of a summer tan; they were relaxed, laughing, enjoying themselves. Abigail caught someone staring at her and averted her eyes.

She didn't even notice that the dog was there until she nearly vaulted over him. He was a mangy thing with scruffy hair and long, clumsy limbs that indicated he was still little more than a puppy. The dog burst in front of her and grabbed a stick from the edge of the water, then turned in one fluid motion and tangled himself hopelessly in Abigail's legs. Though she had managed to stay upright the first time he passed by, when the dog crossed her path again, Abigail landed on the sand with a thud.

In less than a second he was all over her. The dog attacked her face with enthusiastic, sloppy kisses and thumped her leg with his madly wagging tail. His beloved stick was abandoned on her stomach, forgotten because Abigail had deigned to play with him.

"Fernando! Get off her! Down, boy! Bad dog!"

Abigail felt rather than saw someone haul the energetic puppy off her. Her chest felt momentarily light at the absence of his quaking weight, and she followed the buoyant feeling to a sitting position almost involuntarily. Sand slipped from her curls in dusty rivulets and trickled down her back. She shuddered and slapped her hands against her capris, trying to rid herself of some of the grime.

"Sorry 'bout that," a gruff voice said in a less than convincing tone. "Nan's just a puppy. He thought you were playing with him."

"It's okay," Abigail murmured, her own tone as unconvincing as his. She sighed and gave her legs one last hard pat, then shaded her eyes to survey her rescuer. He was tall and thin with hair that was more gray than brown and skin as wrinkled and dark as tree bark. He reminded Abigail of a hermit; she could picture him living off the earth with nothing but a backpack and his dog for company. But there was also something gentle in his eyes, and though his face was hard as he watched her, Abigail sensed a certain concern in his manner.

"I'm fine, really," Abigail said again, partly for herself and partly to wipe the shadow of care from the stranger's shielded eyes.

The man nodded in satisfaction and pushed a hard breath between his teeth. Then his gaze flicked away from her and he concentrated on his dog. Knotting his hands around the collarless scruff of golden fur, he gave Nan a deep and loving scratch. "You're just a puppy, aren't you, Nan? It's not your fault."

Maybe it was your *fault,* Abigail thought, staring at the man. After all, he was the one who had thrown the stick right in front of her. But Abigail was saving her accusations for Tyler, so instead of prolonging their encounter, she made a move to stand up.

"Here." The man offered her his hand.

Abigail didn't want to accept his help, but it seemed rude not to place her hand in his. She did so reluctantly.

The man gripped her hand in his own leathery fingers and hauled her to her feet with an unceremonious tug. He let go of her the second she was upright.

"Thank you," Abigail said stiffly.

"You have some sand on your back," he grunted.

Abigail twisted away from him quickly, afraid that he might offer to help brush her off. She didn't want to just stand there craning her arms around as she tried to reach unreachable places, but the man seemed intent on detaining her.

"You from around here?" he asked. "I haven't seen you on the beach before."

"No." Abigail looked over her shoulder and tried to dissuade his brusque conversation.

"Vacation, then?"

"No."

"Those are your two options, honey."

Honey? The way he said it implied that she was anything but.

He caught the angry cast of her features. "All I'm saying is unless you're a trucker—and I don't think you are—living and vacationing are the only two reasons you'd find yourself in Revell."

"I'm a trucker," Abigail spat out.

The man smirked. "Yeah, right."

Abigail glared at him for a moment and then spun on her heel to march off.

"Aw, come on. Don't be so sensitive."

Although it was against her better judgment, Abigail gave him the satisfaction of one last backward glance. This man was old enough to be her father, maybe even her grandfather, and the comparison didn't warm her heart any. But something about him made her think twice, and when he caught her eye, he grinned unreservedly.

"I'm a crusty old man," he said. There was a self-deprecating tilt to his features, and Abigail couldn't tell if he was serious or joking. "I shouldn't tease but I can't seem to help it."

Abigail paused, and when she did, the man took his hand off Nan. As if he had commanded the dog to do so, Nan trotted up to Abigail and pressed his muzzle against her open palm. She traced the warm head with her fingers and then gave in and scratched the puppy hard behind the ears. He was a handsome dog, though rather unkempt. Part golden retriever and part Lab, she guessed. If it was true what they said, dogs were usually pretty good judges of character. Too bad

153

this sweet young thing was obviously lacking in judgment.

"Look," the man entreated her, shoulders half-hunched in supplication, "I figure I owe you one."

"You don't owe me anything," Abigail cut in.

His raised eyebrow was enough to make her clamp her mouth shut.

"I lied," he continued. "If you're not vacationing in Revell and you don't live here, there is one more reason why a person might find herself here in the summertime."

Abigail kept her expression blank.

"Work," he finished with a crooked smile that said, *I've got you pegged.*

She opened her mouth to relieve him of that misplaced notion, but the truth was that the thought had crossed Abigail's mind and she couldn't stop it from crossing her face as well.

"I might be able to figure something out," the man offered.

Warning bells went off in Abigail's head, but before she could respond, he bent down to pick up her forgotten shoes. Tossing them at her one at a time, the man asked, "Where are you staying?"

Abigail answered almost obediently, her mind on the sandals as she snatched them out of the air. "The Sun—" She broke off, catching herself at the last second. "I'm not staying in Revell," she lied.

It was obvious he wasn't convinced. "I'll catch up with you tomorrow."

"No, I—," Abigail tried to protest, but the man's sharp whistle cut her off.

Nan's ears pricked instantly, and he let out a happy bark before taking off after his owner. The man was already making his way up the beach, and Abigail was left standing alone, holding her shoes and wondering what in the world she had just gotten herself into.

By the time Hailey was thirteen, she was adept at getting herself into situations so deep, so weighty and complicated and consequential, that she had more than her share of trouble getting out. As far as Hailey was concerned, there were only two people she deemed worthy enough to come to her rescue. Abby didn't appreciate being one of them.

Mercifully, counseling had been a part of Hailey's life since the incident on the roof. *The Incident*—that's the way it was referred to around the house, if it was referred to at all, which it was very rarely and usually by Abby. But the few times that conversation about The Incident was necessary required them to have an innocuous way to mention it, as if there were something hazardous about remembering too accurately what Hailey had done. The Bennetts worked hard to forget, and the only lasting consequences of Hailey's nosedive into a snowbank were a small, jagged scar on her lip and the introduction of Dr. Madsen into the knotted circle of their family. The scar was soon covered by lipstick. If not for those weekly, hour-long visits to Dr. Madsen, they could have almost believed that The Incident had never happened.

Hailey cycled in and out of Dr. Madsen's office for years. And for years his request to prescribe "a little something" was vehemently denied. He talked about ADD, ADHD, depression, and even personality "issues." But Lou didn't want to hear it, and truthfully neither did the women in his life. To them, labeling Hailey felt heavy-handed somehow, like the persuasive doctor was trying to finish a sentence that was yet to be written. *Wait,* became their mantra. *Just wait and see what happens.* Even Abby bristled when Dr. Madsen became too pushy. After all, Hailey might be eccentric, occasionally obnoxious, and even impossible to handle, but she certainly couldn't be *sick.*

Though the Bennetts rejected the idea of medication, they quietly accepted the counseling. At first, Hailey's pediatrician had recommended a few months' worth of visits, but as the months turned into a year and the years began to number two and three and four, the plush little office in the neighboring town of Kent was simply a part of their routine.

The fact that Hailey seemed to almost enjoy her hour-long meetings with the good doctor definitely helped the family accept them. Though the sessions were always private and no one had a clear idea of what went on behind the closed mahogany door, Hailey usually emerged with her shoulders relaxed and her mouth held in a thin little smile. Without fail, there would be a small period of calm after her time with Dr. Madsen. Sometimes the peace lasted days. Sometimes it had worn off by the time Hailey got in the car.

Once Dr. Madsen had tried to terminate his counseling with Hailey. They had been meeting for just over a year, and he insisted that she wasn't making any progress. If something didn't change, Dr. Madsen saw no point in continuing. He pushed medication hard then and gave Lou and Melody pamphlets about different mental disorders with nearly all of the symptoms circled in red.

"Hailey fits the demographic," he insisted.

"Of all of these?" Lou fanned the papers and threw them back on Dr. Madsen's desk.

"Well, definitely ADHD, though Hailey exhibits symptoms of some of these others, too."

"And ADHD is . . . ?" Melody refused to take her eyes off Dr. Madsen, refused to follow her husband's already-heated lead.

"Attention deficit/hyperactivity disorder," Dr. Madsen finished patiently. He rummaged through the discarded brochures in search of more evidence.

"Hailey's not hyper."

"Sometimes," Melody whispered.

"All kids are," Lou said darkly.

"It's not just hyperactivity," Dr. Madsen explained for the hundredth time. "If you'd just take the time to—"

But his entreaty was cut off by the sharp crack of Lou's hand coming down on the enormous oak desk between them. Then Lou grabbed his wife's arm and practically dragged her out of the office.

Hailey didn't see Dr. Madsen again for nearly six weeks. And for six weeks life unraveled at the Bennett house. Hailey's toxicity mounted and then crashed as she became needy, dependent, and unstable. She vacillated between fierce autonomy and an almost animal-like fear of separation. She went through brief phases of uncharacteristically productive multitasking and hard work, tempered by periods of laziness that required a huge effort to even coax her out of bed. It was all up and down, back and forth, until one night she threw an explosive fit in the kitchen and ended up slicing her arm with a paring knife.

The cut wasn't intentional, nor did it seem to be her intent to harm anyone else, but the ferocity of her mindless rage left the entire family speechless. Whatever set Hailey off was inconsequential—no one could even remember why after the fact—but her reaction was blind and senseless fury. And in the midst of the flailing and screaming, she somehow managed to carve a deep little wedge out of her forearm with the knife that she had been using to peel carrots only moments ago.

Hailey was such a whirlwind of motion, such a loud and commanding presence, that at first no one even noticed the cut. Not even Hailey. But then suddenly there were dots of crimson on the counter and more on the floor. Lou moved to stop her, but before he could get a grip on her wrists, she flung her hands up and away, past her face. It was the miniature tracks of warm blood across her cheek that finally stunned Hailey out of her frenzy.

It took three stitches to knit the skin back together. It took no coaxing whatsoever to convince Lou that Hailey needed to spend more time with Dr. Madsen.

Hailey's life had been chaotic up to the pivotal year that she officially became a teenager, but something about the momentous birthday seemed to herald a definitive change. It seemed as though Hailey had been holding her breath, and now that she had crossed a measurable milestone, it began to feel to the Bennetts that everything they had endured up to this point was merely a prelude to the cacophonous din that was Hailey's personal soundtrack.

As if to highlight her special evolution, the morning after her thirteenth birthday—her induction into the exalted world of everything adolescent—Hailey announced at the breakfast table: "I want to go on the pill."

There was no confusion over which pill she was

referring to. Melody gasped and covered her mouth with the back of her hand in a theatrical gesture of shock. Abby sighed. And Lou choked on the steaming mouthful of coffee that he had just gulped.

Lou sputtered into a balled-up paper towel, his cheeks turning a mottled shade of bruised pink while his eyes watered. Abby looked up just in time to catch the pure confusion in his wounded face. Lou's look whispered, "You did not say that. My baby could not have said that." Because he couldn't handle it, because he didn't want to know, Lou left. He slid back his chair and melted out of the room almost unnoticed.

Only Abby watched him go, and as his back disappeared around the corner, a cold fury raked across her heart. *Ignore it,* she thought viciously. *Ignore it if that's the only way you can keep pretending.*

Melody couldn't ignore it, though. And by default neither could Abby.

"Don't be ridiculous," Abby snarled, spearing her last bite of pancake and then abandoning it on her plate the very next second.

"I'm *thirteen.*"

"Exactly." Abby pushed away from the table, making her chair legs screech in protest while Hailey flipped her long hair over her shoulder with a condescending flick.

"We don't even believe in . . . that," Melody

whispered. She lifted her hand to the cross that didn't exist at her narrow throat and ended up curling her fingers around the collar of her shirt as a tangible alternative. Her breath shuddered shallowly.

"What, are you telling me you're not on it?" Hailey's eyes darted between her mother and her sister, finally fixing on Abby with a look of artificial surprise.

"Of course I'm not."

"Of course she's not," Melody echoed.

"I thought . . . I mean . . . you are eighteen, Abby."

The room was silent, and Abby willed her mother the strength, for once, to stand up to Hailey. But then Hailey shrugged as if to say, "to each her own," and Melody appeared to interpret her gesture as defeat. Melody watched her newly teenaged daughter finish her last few bites of yogurt, and seemingly satisfied that the subject had been dropped, she consulted Abby with a hopeful, pleading look that begged her to confirm that it was indeed over.

Abby knew it wasn't over, knew that Hailey would demand much more than a few awkward words and the assurance that "we don't even believe in that." But she was also going through another season in her life when Hailey irritated her far more than she cared to admit. On the brink of high school graduation and ready to start her own life apart from the stifling atmosphere in the Bennett house, Abby didn't have time to put out all of Hailey's little fires. She simply didn't feel like it.

Tradition dictated that Abby drop a kiss on her mother's cheek before leaving, and she did so perfunctorily, extricating herself from the situation before Hailey could make things worse. But as she turned to go, she cast one last look in Hailey's direction and noticed the incendiary purse of her sister's lips. That mouth betrayed that Hailey considered Abby to be naive, maybe even somewhat ridiculous, and she had no intention of letting her request go unfulfilled.

"I just want to be prepared," Hailey began.

Melody groaned. "Honey . . ."

"Keep your pants on," Abby advised coolly.

"Abby!" Melody cautioned.

Abby skewered her mother with a hard look, then slung her backpack over her shoulder and stormed out of the kitchen. She had intervened with Hailey a hundred times. She had been the mediator, the counselor, the arbiter who doled out discipline when Melody couldn't and Lou wouldn't. This was the last straw. It was up to someone else to handle Hailey this time.

And astonishingly, Melody chose this particular opportunity to rally her flagging reserves and rise to the occasion. She finally gathered the courage to do what should have been done years before.

• • •

"I'm on the pill," Hailey stated the moment Abby walked through the door that evening. She was sitting on a barstool at the counter in the kitchen, and indeed there was a bag in front of her bearing the distinctive graphic of the local pharmacy. A creased instruction sheet was spread out before her, but Hailey wasn't reading it. She was fixated on Abby and unveiling a slow, sardonic smile.

Abby was too shocked to be angry, and she whipped around to confront her mother as she stood stirring something in a pot for supper.

Melody sighed in defeat and glanced around the kitchen to make sure Lou was nowhere to be seen. "Not *the* pill, Abby. *A* pill."

Abby didn't flinch.

"A pill from Dr. Madsen," Melody explained.

"Ooh, but it's the good stuff. No expense spared. 'Possible side effects,'" Hailey read, clearing her throat. "'Reduced appetite, headache, jittery feeling, gastrointestinal upset, sleep difficulty—'"

"Stop, Hailey. That's enough," Melody warned.

"'—irritability, depression, anxiety, blood glucose changes, increased blood pressure, rebound . . .'" Hailey paused at that one. "What's *rebound*?"

"Bounce back," Abby said almost automatically.

"From what?"

"Feeling irritable, depressed, jittery, anxious . . . ?" Abby guessed.

"Makes sense. Where was I? . . . Oh yeah, the

good part. Check out these last side effects: 'tics and stereotyped movements, paranoia or psychosis, seizures, and—' last but not least—'sudden death.' " Hailey slapped the papers down, her mouth twisted almost cruelly. "At least sexual side effects weren't listed."

Abby snorted, unable to stop herself from appreciating Hailey's dark sense of humor.

Melody pursed her lips. *"Honey . . ."*

"I mean, seriously. Seizures? Sudden death?"

"Dr. Madsen said that the chances of you reacting like that are next to none. Zero. Zilch." Melody pushed a strand of hair from her forehead, but when it fell right back over her eye, she ignored it. "Hailey, those things aren't going to happen to you."

"They happened to somebody."

Although Abby had been livid only moments before, with Hailey across from her looking so furious and fragile, something inside Abby deflated. How could Hailey do that? How could she unveil her vulnerability at just the right moment and leave Abby feeling protective? She wanted to tell Hailey, "It's about time. You should have been on meds years ago." Then she would stomp off to her room, leave Hailey to think about all she had done. But Abby couldn't do it.

Sometimes Abby wanted to hate her sister. And sometimes she could admit that the tug of love she felt for Hailey was so acute, so taut that there were times it stung like loathing. Love for Abby was a slow revolution. There were two sides to her tenderness: a gentle, hopeful acknowledgment of Hailey as she was meant to be, and a sharp, painful knowledge of all she inflicted by falling so far short. Abby had felt herself orbit these two feelings with predictable accuracy for years. She was the hand and Hailey the flower: *I love her; I love her not; I love her; I love her not.* On and on, on and on, spinning the wheel ever tighter as each emotion cycled into the next. Abby was beginning to learn that the love she felt for Hailey was a circle without end.

"Those things won't happen to you," Abby parroted her mother with a sigh.

"You don't know that," Hailey accused. Her shoulders were rigid, her eyes afraid.

Abby shrugged off her backpack to cross the kitchen and stand behind her sister. A part of her wanted to hug Hailey, but the bitterness of their morning was a bad taste in her mouth. Abby reached around and took the medication sheets. "Sleep difficulty doesn't sound so bad," she said lightly, studying the effects. "Just think of all you'll get done while the rest of the world is sawing logs."

Hailey elbowed Abby in the stomach, but it was a gentle bump.

"And listen: 'this problem can often be eliminated by using one of the more intermediate-length stimulants. Clonidine or guanfacine—'" Abby intentionally butchered the pronunciation—" 'may help decrease agitation and may also help facilitate sleep.'"

"Clonidine," Hailey muttered, the word perfectly formed and fluid on her tongue. "Guanfacine. Whoop-de-do." She twirled her index finger in the air halfheartedly.

"What about irritability? It says here that they can prescribe an SSRI or an alpha agonist to combat that symptom." Abby thought her mild teasing would make Hailey laugh.

But all Abby got was a defeated little moan.

Giving in, she wrapped her arms around Hailey's narrow frame and rested her chin on her sister's shoulder. Within seconds, she could feel the warmth of a single tear mingling on their pressed cheeks. "Hey," she whispered.

It was all Hailey needed. The slight girl spun around on her stool and buried her face in Abby's chest. She tangled her arms around Abby's waist and sobbed.

Abby wasn't used to this sort of emotional frailty from her sister, and it was so sudden and so unexpected that tears sprang almost instantly to her eyes, too. She laid her cheek on the top of Hailey's head and stroked her back, making quiet shushing noises as if Hailey were a very little girl. The tears didn't abate, and Abby looked up to search out Melody. The older woman was still standing at the stove, and when Abby caught her gaze, it seemed to her as though her mother had been crying for hours. Her eyes were red-rimmed and weary. Broken.

"What should I do?" Abby asked wordlessly.

Melody shrugged as if to say, "I've been asking myself the same question for thirteen years."

It seemed like ages passed, but Hailey finally calmed down, though even long after her sobs had subsided, she continued to hold on to Abby. For her part, Abby never slackened her grip, never stopped rubbing and hushing and doting, and at some point her actions became more than simply mechanical.

When Abby's arms were tight around her sister in something other than obligation, it occurred to her that her ministrations were more for herself than Hailey. Against all odds, *Hailey* was helping *her*, not the other way around. For the first time, Abby felt able to grasp the depth of Hailey's desperation—her hands were curled around all one hundred pounds of it. Abby could admit that Hailey was not well.

Hailey was not well. It was an alarming thought. And yet it was freeing somehow, too, like someone had opened a window and the breeze was cool and cleansing. It was true, Abby knew it, and somehow accepting Hailey's illness made it easier to accept Hailey.

When Hailey whispered against Abby's collar,

167

"Do you love me?" it was easy for Abby to respond.

"Yes," she said, her voice low but fervent. "I do."

Hailey pulled away and pinned her older sister with a look so scared and insistent that Abby's breath caught in her throat. "Promise you'll take care of me," Hailey said, her voice crumbling around the raw edges of her fear.

Abby didn't know if Hailey was simply afraid of the side effects of the new medication or if her oversensitive spirit trembled with a deeper foreboding, but she was seized with the desire to answer so definitively that Hailey would never doubt her devotion. But then the young girl smiled a crooked smile, a hint that maybe she was only joking around, and Abby was left wondering if she was serious or not.

Abby had intended to say, "I promise." Instead, she smiled back hesitantly and assured Hailey, "You're strong. You don't need anyone to take care of you."

Then Melody brought her a glass of water, and Hailey tipped a lone pill from the translucent, amber-colored bottle. She took it, and Melody and Abby watched her swallow.

ⓒ *I regained consciousness reluctantly; something deep inside me rebelled against the weight of waking and remembering where I was and why. When I came to, I found myself propped on Hailey's bed. There were pillows stacked behind me and more under my bent knees. Since I was half-lying on the turned-down bedspread, someone had grabbed the plush bathrobe from the hook on Hailey's bedroom door and draped it over me like a blanket. It smelled like her. Like her favorite honeysuckle shampoo and the Calvin Klein perfume she had worn since she was sixteen.*

I moved to push the fabric away and became aware of the fact that someone was holding my arm.

"Hey, she's coming around." He was middle-aged and sparrow-chested, but his eyes were as soft and comforting as his voice. A brief, sad smile crossed his lips. Then he consulted his watch and squeezed his fingers against the slender vessels in my wrist one last time. "Your heart rate is almost back to normal, too."

"I'm sorry," I whispered, surprising even myself by the apology. My voice was raspy and felt unused.

"Nothing to be sorry about. It happens all the time."

"Shock?"

"You're not in shock," he assured me. "You experienced an acute stress response. A little rise in epinephrine that made you panic and hyperventilate. And pass out, but not for long."

"You're not taking me to the hospital?" I didn't mean to sound so disappointed.

But my EMT savior patted my hand gently as if he understood. "No."

There was a hush in the room when his voice fell, and I could hear the movement and bustle throughout the rest of the apartment. "I cleaned the bathroom," I confessed, twin tears racing each other down my cheeks.

"We know. It doesn't look like you tampered with anything important though."

"I didn't."

"It's okay."

"She's my sister," I told him, something in my mind faltering over the words. What was wrong with that sentence? What made me pause? And then I had it: She's *my* sister. *As if she were merely asleep in the bathtub. As if there were still a place carved out for her in my present and future reality. I should have said, "She* was *my sister."*

"We know," he repeated. He zipped a red and white duffel bag and stood. "They're going to have to ask you a few questions. Do you feel up to answering them?"

I pushed myself into a more upright position and covered my forehead with my cool palms. "Yes."

The soothing EMT gave me one last sympathetic look and left the room. Within minutes, he was replaced by a cop in uniform and a medical examiner wearing street clothes. Although they seemed impassive, neither of them perched on the end of the bed or made any move whatsoever to endear themselves to me or put me even slightly at ease. Instead, they shot questions at me and I answered as dutifully as I could.

Name. Address. Date of birth. Home, work, and cell phone numbers. Relationship to the deceased.

"What made you come to her apartment?" the officer asked.

"We were supposed to have lunch. When she didn't show up . . ." I stumbled. "She slit her wrists." I didn't mean to say those brutal, horrible words out loud; they came of their own accord. When I heard them spoken so bluntly, I shuddered.

It wasn't as if they needed me to ascertain the cause of death, and the men tactfully ignored my less-than-helpful observation.

"She probably took pills, too," the examiner informed me. "It's almost impossible to commit suicide by slashing your wrists. The cuts would have to be longitudinal. Otherwise the blood vessels simply draw back into the muscles and . . ." He trailed off, realizing the impact his monologue was having on me. Changing his tactic, he asked,

"Did your sister take any prescribed medications?"

I closed my eyes. "Sometimes. If she felt like it. I know she was just prescribed a new tricyclic anti-depressant. SSRIs didn't work for her. I think it was Tofranil, 300 milligrams a day. And lithium bicarbonate when she was manic. Those are the ones I know about."

"That'll do." The police officer sighed. "Where can I find the pill bottles?"

"She kept them in her purse. It's black. It should be on the counter by the door."

The two men turned to leave, but the examiner stopped just inside the room and asked me one last question. "Had she ever been suicidal before?"

It was my turn to sigh. I didn't want to withhold any information, but I also didn't want to get into specifics. "Hailey's been on and off medication for thirteen years. If she overdosed, it was entirely intentional."

His look betrayed that he wasn't surprised. For a moment I thought he was going to try to say something to comfort me; his lips parted and then closed, parted and closed. But all at once he thought better of it and tipped his head in a salute of sorts, a brief nod of acknowledgment, as if in some small way he shared my sorrow at the senselessness of it all.

I bowed my head in return and found that I couldn't bring myself to pick it back up. I knew he

172

was gone when I heard the soft click of the closing door, and I found myself alone, staring at the mint-colored piles of the terry robe I had bought her for Christmas.

VII

ᏨᏨ HE CALLED EARLY the next morning.

"You up?" The voice was gritty and unmistakable. It sounded to Abigail like the same sand she had been covered in yesterday lined his gristly throat.

"How did you find me? How did you get my number?" she demanded. Part of her was indignant that he assumed enough familiarity to track her down, but the rest of her was too drowsy to feel overtly alarmed.

"I used my superpowers of deductive reasoning and figured out that 'The Sun—' was actually the Sunny Grove Inn and RV Park. It was a stroke of pure brilliance," he said dryly. "Then I called the front desk, and when I described you, Jane patched me through. She said you were up by this time yesterday."

Abigail rubbed her eyes with the back of her hand, burrowing deeper under the covers. It was definitely creepy that he had found her. But then again, she had more or less told him exactly where she was staying. In a small town like Revell, it couldn't be too hard to find someone. Anyway, it wasn't in Abigail's nature to be afraid of people. She was cautious, not panicky.

"You up?" he asked again.

"Yes," Abigail lied.

"Good. I'll meet you for breakfast."

"Pardon me?" Abigail rolled onto her side and squinted at the alarm clock on the bedside stand. The numbers were blurry, so she grabbed her reading glasses and tried again—6:30. She stifled a moan. "I don't think—"

"There's a truck stop just up the road that serves the best breakfast in Revell. Meet me there in half an hour."

Abigail flopped back on her pillow, chewing her bottom lip as she tried to think of an excuse. Who was this guy? What made him think she would agree to meet him? How could she be sure that he wasn't some psycho stalker?

The irony of it hit her without warning. *She* was the stalker. After all, she was the one who had flown thousands of miles to track down a man she didn't even know. She was the one who had left her life behind to chase Tyler. This aging dog lover seemed innocent enough. Besides, it was broad daylight and he didn't even know her name. But then again, she didn't know his name either.

"I don't even know your—"

"It's just south of Main Street at the highway junction," he said, cutting her off. Abigail didn't know if he intended to do so or if he was simply, like her, a poor phone talker. "It's attached to the Husky. Nan and I will be there if you want to come."

Click.

Abigail realized he had meant to interrupt her. She stared at the phone for a minute and then slammed it down on the cradle in frustration. He was bossy, arrogant, and overconfident. And those were just her first impressions. But although he aggravated her, she knew that she would go and see him anyway. What did she have to lose? In spite of his obvious shortcomings, he appeared to be harmless: that feminine sixth sense that usually snaked warning fingers up her spine when she was an object of prey was nowhere to be found. Besides, she hoped to stay in Revell longer than a few days, and he had said that he might be able to work something out. Abigail was willing to try anything.

But if she was going to meet him, it was going to be as much on her terms as she could manage. Abigail took a long shower and then took her precious time getting ready, though she certainly wasn't getting ready for him. It was merely a good way to stall. He could wait; she was not going to rush for him.

When she was finally set to go at quarter after seven, Abigail found the Husky easily enough. The blue and white sign sported an instantly recognizable large, furry dog that seemed distinctly out of place in such a hot climate. Abigail almost felt sorry for him in his winter coat—her own bare arms were already prickling in the morning sun.

The gas station was surprisingly full at such an

early summer hour, and Abigail drove around back in search of a parking space. She found an open spot against a sagging clapboard fence that chopped the hill behind it in half. A small knot of tumbleweed clung to a cracked board, and Abigail reached up to free it. But then she didn't know what to do with the weed and ended up tossing it back over the fence, where it rolled down the hill and caught itself on the same board she had just released it from.

Abigail glared at the tumbleweed, loathing it for the way she was suddenly reminded of Hailey. No matter how many times she had offered her sister freedom, Hailey always returned to a place of bondage. Always. Regression seemed to be a habitual, almost-fundamental aspect of her person. The rush of unhappy memories just about forced Abigail back into the car. But then she shrugged off all thoughts of Hailey and turned from the fence before she could change her mind.

The diner looked dark and greasy—Abigail had an intrinsic dislike for restaurants attached to gas stations. She avoided the shadowed door and made her way around to a tiny cement patio with plastic tables and chairs. There was a low, concrete wall that doubled as a long planter around the enclosure. Unfortunately, the zinnias and balsamroot didn't do much to discourage the dreary atmosphere. But amidst the sun-faded tables and cracked chairs, Abigail saw a lone patron and recognized a yellow tail held high in summons—her breakfast date was outside, not in.

His back was turned to her, but Nan was facing the parking lot and gave a high yelp followed by an insistent whine when Abigail came into view.

"Stay," the man commanded. To Abigail he said, "You're late."

She ignored him and crossed the table so that they were face-to-face. Sticking out her hand, she introduced herself. "Abigail Bennett," she said, pronouncing her surname the way her French ancestors had. No use broadcasting her real name in a town as small as Revell.

The man put down his sandwich, wiped his mouth with a crinkled paper napkin, and finished chewing. Then he brushed his right hand against his jeans and shook hers. "Eli Dixon," he announced and immediately went back to his food.

Abigail was glad that he did because she was certain her forehead wrinkled in confusion. That name. She knew that name from somewhere. It provoked an unspecified hesitancy in her—she was tempted to back away, make some excuse, and never see him again. Why? What could he possibly mean to her?

Then all at once she had it. Her mouth fell open the tiniest bit, and she took a step back, though she didn't flee like she wanted to. He was Tyler's uncle! Jane had mentioned him by the pool, though she had called him Elijah.

179

He was still eating and more or less ignoring her, punishing her no doubt for being late. Abigail was free to study his profile and determine whether or not she could go through with the strange meeting he had initiated. As far as she could tell, there were no similarities between Tyler Kamp and his uncle. *Distant relation,* she figured, though just thinking about Tyler made an indiscriminate anger rise up in her chest. Maybe Elijah could sense it. Maybe he would see the intensity in her eyes and somehow *know*. But that was impossible.

Abigail reached for a chair and forced herself to sink into it. "It's nice to meet you, Mr. Dixon," she said. Her voice was almost normal.

"Don't call me that," he snapped.

"Elijah?"

"Eli. Isn't that what I told you? Nobody calls me Elijah."

Abigail was about to inform him that at least one person called him Elijah, but she bit her tongue.

"Eat your breakfast. It's getting cold." Eli pushed a plate across the table to her and tossed her a napkin that looked like it had already been used.

Abigail studied the sandwich for a moment before carefully asking, "What is it?"

"A BELCH."

She snorted. "Excuse me?"

"Bacon, eggs, lettuce, cheese, ham," he barked. But though he was trying to sound harsh, Abigail saw a smile play at the corner of his mouth.

"Mmmm . . . ," she murmured. "Sounds delicious."

"It is, but you need a little mayo and a lot of ketchup." Eli sent packets of the condiments spinning across the plastic tabletop toward her.

Abigail caught them before they slid off the edge and deposited the foil-wrapped delicacies in the center of the table. "No thanks. I think I'll take my BELCH naked."

"Suit yourself." Eli tipped his head in acknowledgment and took a long swig of his oily coffee.

Abigail gingerly nibbled her sandwich. It was greasy and way too salty, but she had to admit that there was something indulgent and homey about digging into such a calorie-laden treat. Whoever created this sinful extravagance obviously wasn't concerned about low-carb, low-fat, low-sodium, low-taste diets. Abigail decided that for one morning, she wouldn't be concerned either.

While Abigail ate, Eli maintained his silence. He seemed mildly pleased that she had come to this peculiar breakfast rendezvous and content to simply watch the sun somersault slowly up the sky. Their lack of conversation was not unfriendly, and Abigail gradually relaxed enough to realize that for now at least she had nothing to fear in his uncomplicated, straightforward presence.

When Eli saw that she had all but given up on her sandwich, he said, "I have a job for you."

"What makes you think I want a job?"

Eli stared at her. "Guess I misread you." Then he abruptly pushed back his chair and stood. "You can leave the tip," he told her before turning away.

"N-no," Abigail sputtered, shocked by his sudden change of attitude and upset that things had turned around so quickly. "Wait. I . . . I would like to hear about this job."

He swung around to her almost begrudgingly and didn't make a move to sit down again. Instead, Eli gripped the back of the chair he had just vacated and studied Abigail as if the interview had already begun and he was less than impressed by what he saw in her. "Look, finding good, stable help around here isn't easy. I don't intend to bend over backward for you only to have you play games with me or leave me high and dry when I need you the most."

Abigail blinked at his passionate tirade, convinced that hiring was a sore spot with Eli but unaware of anything she could say to calm him down. What did he expect her to do? Jump up and down, proclaim her never-ending gratitude, and blindly take his mysterious job on the spot?

"Do you want a job or not?"

Feeling pressured to answer definitively and afraid that this might be the best, the *only*, offer that she would receive, Abigail nodded, albeit a little tentatively. "Yes."

A look of satisfaction passed over Eli's face for a second. He sat down with a smug grunt. "I own a winery and I'm shorthanded by at least two workers. Your hours will be long and your job description will be varied. Have you ever waitressed before?"

"Um, no," Abigail said, afraid that anything she said or didn't say could send him packing again. How much should she disclose? How much did he have to know? But she had to tell him at least part of the truth. There was no way she could keep one thing a secret. "And, uh, I should tell you that I'm not . . . um, I'm not Canadian."

Eli fixed her with a condescending glare. "You poor thing. But if you're worried about the legality of our arrangement, let me assure you: you're not the first and you won't be the last. In fact, you're not the only nonresident worker I'm employing this summer."

Abigail shrugged.

"Because of your . . . *status*," Eli continued, "I can't offer you the same salary and benefits as my citizen workers. I'll pay you a dollar shy of minimum wage, cash, plus if you need a place to stay, you can bunk in a trailer on the property."

"Roommates?" Abigail tried to ask nonchalantly.

"No, it's recently vacated." Eli sounded disgusted. "Anyway, there's no running water, but you can have access to the full bathroom in the service shed. It'll be your job to clean it, and I charge a loonie a shower."

Abigail's head swam.

"And no trashing the trailer, though you don't seem the type."

"I'm not."

"I didn't think so." Eli stood a second time, but this time he whistled and Nan rose, too. The dog stretched and yawned, then pawed Eli's hand for a pat. "My winery is called Thompson Hills. It's on the highway just past a fruit stand called Mack's—"

"Sweets. On the left, opposite the water," Abigail finished.

A frown furrowed Eli's brow; then he smiled thinly at her. "I'm glad to hear our reputation precedes us." He turned to go.

"When do I start?" Abigail called after him.

"Tomorrow."

"What time?"

"Six a.m."

"What should I wear?"

"Something nice."

"Why are you doing this?" Her final question surprised even Abigail. She hadn't intended to ask, but now there was no taking it back—Eli had heard her and he stopped dead in his tracks.

He shot over his shoulder: "Because you look like you could use a little help."

After he was gone, Abigail sat at the table for a long time. Was it that obvious? Was her desperation written so clearly across her face? The thought of her own vulnerability—so advertised, so blatant—was leveling. Abigail was used to being the strong one: sensible, composed, dependable, consistent. Her high school graduating class had even voted her most likely to succeed, and what else were successful people but the polar opposite of desperate? Who was this woman she had become? Needy, anxious, transparent . . . So unmistakably helpless that a man like Eli Dixon could spot her poverty of spirit from across a beach and intervene in a way that was both intrusive and auspicious.

Abigail was still deciding whether or not she considered Eli's interference propitious. It was true that she needed to find a way to get close to Tyler, and she believed the only way to do so was by remaining in Revell. The bottom line was that in order to accomplish those two things she had to find a legitimate reason to postpone her stay in British Columbia. But she hadn't planned on being *that* close to Tyler. The very thought of him made the sun seem too bright, the tabletop too white. Abigail squinted against the brightness and hated herself a little for being someone she hardly recognized.

When Hailey died—*no*, when Hailey committed suicide—Abigail felt every semblance of self tremble away. It was like she had been rocked by an earthquake, a real fault-line grinder, 8.0 on the Richter scale at least. The walls of her identity proved to be poorly constructed, and as pieces of her crumbled and fell, Abigail was left wondering how she would possibly find the strength to go on when nothing was left but the bare frame of the woman she had once been.

Suddenly nothing made sense. Johnson, McNally & Bennett was little more than a time drain that—rather oddly it seemed to her—broadcast her name from their classy letterhead. Why? What difference did her job make anymore? Even her relationships seemed meaningless. Though her friends called, sent flowers, and insisted that she would make it through the horror, Abigail drew away so completely that eventually the phone stopped ringing. Worst of all, the sharp vein of ambition, the seam that sewed continuity into her life by incessantly prodding her on to the next thing, collapsed and unraveled, another victim of the natural disaster that was Hailey.

Abigail was left with one small shred of self that seemed to be the final fragment that held her together: a clear and burning desire to bring Hailey's incomplete life to some sort of understandable conclusion. Her impetuous decision to leave everything behind and do everything in her power to make that happen was both monumental and uncharacteristic.

Remarkably, in addition to considering Abigail a surefire success, her classmates also nominated her least impulsive. For Abigail, impulsivity proved to be a learned trait.

• • •

Abby graduated high school with honors. She wasn't valedictorian, nor was she nominated (or even given a second thought) for prom queen. But her name carried with it a certain respect, and her smile was readily returned by everyone she met, including teachers, classmates, her friends' parents, even college reps.

A GPA of 3.9 and an ACT score of 32 did much to pique the interest of many local and state colleges and universities. In the beginning, Abby applied indiscriminately, filling out application forms to each and every institute of higher learning with a nice campus, a good-looking recruiter, or a scholarship that seemed an appropriate match for her accomplishments. But when acceptance letters started pouring in, it was time to get serious. Time to make the decision that had plagued Abby for years: should she stay or should she go? Could she cut and run like she had hoped and planned for ages? Or did she have a responsibility to her family, to Hailey?

The truth was, for the first time in longer than she could remember, Abby wasn't completely bent on leaving. This unexpected change of heart was due primarily to the fact that Hailey had leveled off somewhat in the weeks after she was put on Ritalin. Abby had heard horror stories about kids becoming unrecognizable to their families when the medication began to leave its mark on the impressionable psyches of young patients. She had heard that the effects could be positively altering and certainly not worth the high toll they extracted. But just as Abby and Melody had tried to promise, Hailey did not seem to be responding to the meds in horrible ways. In fact, in the wake of the medication victory, life at the Bennetts' became almost pleasant.

Of course, there had been a couple weeks of storms as Dr. Madsen tinkered with her prescription, upping the dosage when it seemed ineffective and then cutting back when Hailey's withdrawals became almost alarmingly severe. But they had found a happy medium at some point, and suddenly Hailey's days seemed more or less normal with only a fifteen- or twenty-minute bratty, tear-filled crash in the evening when the Ritalin began to wear off.

The ensuing sense of normalcy perpetuated a side effect that Abby could never have anticipated: a friendship started to cultivate between the reluctant sisters. For Abby, it was as if someone had chiseled the sharp edges off Hailey's raw personality, and the subsequent softness of spirit was both refreshing and startling.

In many ways the troubled girl began to appear happily reminiscent of the gently captivating woman Melody had been in her younger years. Though Abby couldn't claim to remember the woman her mother had been when Lou had fallen so deeply in love with her, at times there was something nostalgic in the air, as if the new angles and depths now evident in Hailey were a reminder of simpler days. Lou would catch his aging bride in a sweet glance, his lips curled uncharacteristically heavenward and his delight a palpable thread in the room linking them all together, drawing them close.

While Lou and Melody relished the fledgling harmony in their family, Abby found herself mesmerized by her sister. She became aware of the subtle motivations that had contributed to Hailey's instability and which now made her seem complex and even thoughtful. All the posturing, anger, unpredictability, and violence were finally unveiled as a carefully constructed but poorly implemented defense mechanism. Abby realized that Hailey envied her and probably always had.

Though she hated to admit it, Abby had spent the better part of her young life resentful of Hailey. The blonde pixie was—and always had been—like quicksand, clutching at and eventually claiming anyone who came near her. And yet learning that her sister harbored an inconceivable jealousy toward her lanced Abby with a double-edged blade of satisfaction and sorrow. She was strangely pleased that Hailey perceived her as someone to be envied, but she was also filled with sadness at the irony of their juxtaposition. At the tragic intersection of their shared fears, Abby felt a fierce sense of unity. *It is us against the world,* she thought. *You and me: loving and hating, attacking and defending, but ultimately together. Sisters.*

In honor of her growing understanding of her sister, Abby went so far as to offer Hailey a ride to and from school for the month of May. It was the last month Abby would ever darken the halls of Newcastle, and she was feeling benevolent, maybe even somewhat euphoric. Hailey was a student at the middle school, and though the high school was in a separate building, they shared a campus. Driving Hailey to school was a small token, an offering that not only got her out of the long bus ride but also elevated her status from some unrecognizable junior high kid to *Abby's sister.*

That spring Abby had embarked on an unanticipated relationship with the senior class president, a boy whose allure was apparent to every single girl at Newcastle. With peace at home, a summer fling on the horizon, and the new, promise-filled life of college mere months away, Abby felt herself relax in a way that she had never been able to before. Life wasn't just good; it bordered on extraordinary.

Senior exams took place a full two weeks before the rest of the school wrote their finals, and on the day that Abby took her first test, she arranged for one of her friends to drive Hailey home after school. Abby knew her exam would stretch past the end of the school day, and she wanted to take advantage of the excuse to stick around and talk to the guidance counselor about a small liberal arts college she had discovered. She didn't want to make Hailey wait, nor did she feel comfortable forcing her sister to take the bus after she had gotten used to a five-minute commute rather than an hour-long bus ride.

But Abby also didn't want Hailey waiting around for her. Danny, the boy she could almost truthfully call her boyfriend, had promised to take a walk with her when she was finished. The Newcastle Public School campus boasted a two-mile walking trail that meandered through several acres of unused property, and Abby knew of a little knoll off the beaten path that featured a high enough vantage point to survey the miniature rows of infant crops stitching patterns into the surrounding patchwork quilt of fields. She couldn't wait to take Danny there.

When Abby emerged from the high school just after four o'clock, the May sun was warm enough to make welcome the cool, southerly breeze. She jogged across the mostly empty parking lot, expecting to see Danny lounging on the hood of her car. But he wasn't there. Nor was he napping on the backseat with the window rolled down. Abby tossed her backpack into the car and looked around. Shading her eyes from the afternoon sun as a frown plucked at her mouth, she couldn't help but wonder if she had misunderstood Danny or if he had gotten sick of waiting and found another way home.

Then she caught sight of his backpack abandoned in the grass at the edge of the parking lot. It bore a distinctive cluster of used ski-lift passes—mementos of Danny's winter vacations spent at his grandparents' home in Montana—so she was sure it was his. Abigail grinned and all but skipped over to the trailhead, convinced that Danny had instigated a playful game of hide-and-seek.

Abby wandered for almost five minutes, sticking to the main trail as she plotted to overtake Danny by stealth. Rather than allowing herself to be hunted, she intended to turn his plan around on him: Abby would scare him half to death, and in the wake of their flirtatious laughter and mischievous teasing, he'd kiss her. She could almost feel his hand on her cheek.

It was at the turnoff to the lookout where she had hoped to take him that she finally glimpsed Danny's unmistakable navy and gold varsity jacket through the trees. As far as Abby was concerned, the team jackets were sort of silly, like some nostalgic throwback to an era when girls were called dolls and they pined for the chance to wear their boyfriend's oversize, number-laden coat. The jackets seemed emblematic somehow, though rather than making Abby feel a shudder of

Newcastle Falcon pride, she felt like a hick girl from a small town. Which she was. But she didn't care to be reminded of it.

Yet, spotting Danny like she did, the desire to have his coat heavy across her shoulders and spiced with the scent of his cologne, his soap, even the hint of his sweat, surprised Abby. It was cool in the shade of the trees. Maybe he would offer it to her. The thought of it almost made Abby call out to him.

Something stopped her. Or rather someone. It struck Abby that Danny was not alone. His head was inclined toward someone ahead of him on the trail, though his body blocked whoever it was from sight. Instinct made Abby stop, and while she didn't go so far as to hide behind a tree, she also didn't make any move to reveal herself.

Danny was definitely talking to someone. The trees partially blocked him from view as he stood farther down the path and around an s-curve bend, but Abby could see that he was gesturing and nodding. She could hear the rise and fall of his voice even if she couldn't make out the words.

Then Danny laughed and the sound was so bright and happy that Abby's hesitation withered. Whoever he was with was a friend, and though she considered three a crowd this lovely afternoon, she would make the best of it. There would be time to be alone later. Abby started toward Danny with an impulsive grin. *He's a summer fling,* she reminded herself. But she also had to admit that she liked him more than enough to carry her through the summer.

Knowing that Danny wasn't alone ruined Abby's plan to surprise him, so she raised her hand in salute and was about to call a cheerful greeting when Danny's companion stepped into view. Abby stumbled, shocked to see Hailey's distinct, blonde head lift to face her sister's boyfriend. Confusion wrinkled Abby's forehead, and for a second time she froze on the trail.

What was Hailey doing here? Why hadn't she taken the ride that Abby had arranged? And how had she convinced Danny to wander through the parkland with her? Abby shook her head, trying in vain to clear it. "It's not what it looks like," she whispered in an attempt to convince herself.

But it was hard to deny what was right in front of her face. Hailey had shot up in her junior high years, and she was already a few inches taller than Abby. Her slim frame and unexpected height made her almost statuesque, and though she was only thirteen, she could have easily passed for seventeen. Completing the striking picture was Hailey's golden wave of softly curled hair, her eyes the color of a spring thundercloud, and skin so smooth and perfect it rivaled some airbrushed makeup advertisement. Any boy alive would have found Hailey irresistible. And it was obvious that Hailey had Danny in her sights—

especially when she placed her hand on the center of his chest.

For a moment it looked like she was only feeling for his heartbeat. Even from a distance Abby could see that Hailey's touch was light, almost hesitant. But then she rose slightly on her tiptoes, pressing Danny's chest for balance, and brushed his cheek with her own. She didn't kiss him; she just skimmed her cheek against his as if it was all she dared to do. Danny's shoulders went rigid, but instead of backing away he stayed there with her against him.

Abby didn't gasp. She didn't cry or scream. Her heart didn't break in two. It was with a keen sense of futility, a resigned acknowledgment of the inevitable that she watched Hailey gain confidence and turn her head to attempt an awkward kiss. It didn't matter that Danny sprang back as if Hailey had stung him. It didn't matter that Hailey herself looked mortified, that she covered her face with her hands and groaned loud enough for Abby to hear.

What mattered to Abby was the dark, viscous venom that betrayal was pumping through her veins. Not Danny's betrayal. Hailey's. It was the betrayal of all the things Abby had hoped for and was slowly starting to believe. It was the betrayal of the woman whom she had begun to love as a sister. It was unforgivable.

Abby spun on her heel and ran.

• • •

That night Abby hauled out her acceptance letters and settled on South Seminole College in Florida. She had been granted a small scholarship, but she wasn't going to South Seminole for the money or even for the beautiful Florida sunshine. She was going because her college of choice was nearly two thousand miles away from Newcastle, Minnesota.

Nearly two thousand miles away from Hailey.

ଊ *Walking away from Hailey's apartment was one of the hardest things I have ever done. I didn't want to be around when they removed her from the building—I had seen her leave under different circumstances too many times before.*

Somehow it seemed cruel that this time she would not be floating down the two flights of stairs, sunglasses already in place across the bridge of her lightly freckled nose and long legs made even more slim and glamorous by a pair of heels. I didn't have to close my eyes to imagine her perched almost precariously on top of those distinctive stilettos, looking as elegant and haughty as a Hollywood diva. And I didn't have to wonder at how she would feel about being crammed in a black bag and rolled into the elevator by men who were incomparable to the handsome sort of men she usually kept company with.

The whole thing began to feel illusory to me, like a staged production or a dream in the last moments of sleep, those final few realistic still frames of fantasy that take place only seconds before waking up. When I felt strong enough to push her robe off me and stand up from her bed, I actually pinched myself. Like some girl in a movie, I pinched my arm and felt the pain of it and knew that I wasn't sleeping.

So I left. A very nice police officer with russet hair and rosy cheeks to match held my arm just above the elbow and walked every step with me from the door of Hailey's apartment to the door of my car. He didn't make conversation, nor did he offer his condolences or try to be understanding. He just held my arm in his strong fingers as if it was enough, and for those few minutes it was. We arrived at the car and I wanted to hug him. But I didn't. I clicked the door locks off and climbed into the sauna of my Passat. It was stifling and I gasped, but he didn't even notice; he was already halfway across the parking lot with his back toward me.

I turned the car on and cranked the air-conditioning but found it too cold almost immediately and switched it off to roll down the windows instead. The fresh air was oppressively pure in contrast to the suffocating closeness of her apartment, and I drank it in ragged little gulps.

Though I didn't want to admit it, it was a little frightening being alone. There was no one in the car but me, yet I felt assaulted by insubstantial ghosts and grim demons that picked at and plundered my soul. One of the responders had offered to call my priest (rabbi? guru? spiritual leader?), but I declined. Even if there were someone—maybe an older, kindly man whom I respected and admired—I wasn't ready to talk. Certainly not now, maybe not ever. It came down to me and I knew it.

I had to do this alone with no one for company but the phantoms of all I should have done.

The crumpled envelope of the note she had left behind was poking into my lower back. I was well aware of it and had been from the moment I grabbed it off her nightstand, but it took me many long minutes to gather the courage to pull it out. Was I ready to know what she had to say? Would I ever be? The truth was, although I contemplated dropping it in the nearest Dumpster and forgetting that it even existed, I knew that I would not be able to leave the parking lot of the apartment complex until I had opened her letter.

It was just a run-of-the-mill white envelope with my childhood nickname written across it in black pen. Hailey had never gotten used to calling me Abigail, even when I threatened her by tightening my purse strings. Was she taunting me with those four letters? Or was she hoping to remind me of a happier time? It didn't matter. I tore into the envelope and discarded it on the floor of the car. Carefully unfolding the blue-lined paper, I squeezed my eyes closed for a second and then began to read.

There was no address, no introduction. There were only two short lines in the center of the paper:

I don't blame you.
I don't blame Tyler.

She may have intended her cryptic letter to acquit us before we had a chance to condemn ourselves. But it had the opposite effect on me. All I could think was, I do. *And,* I do.

VIII

આ ABIGAIL TIED UP a few loose ends and did what she could to temporarily transplant herself in Revell. It wasn't hard to do, and in some ways she couldn't shake the feeling that everyone she knew had been holding their breath as they waited for this exact thing. They had been eager for her to take some time to herself, to grieve.

After the news of Hailey's suicide first came to light, Blake and Colton had been more than solicitous. They had sent Abigail bouquets of exotic flowers as if a pair of bright birds-of-paradise could lift her spirits and insisted that she take as much time off as she needed. But she didn't want time off. At least, not at first. She wanted to work. She wanted to forget. Unfortunately her memory proved to be all too accurate, and by the time a plan solidified in her mind—a plan to find Tyler and put whatever small thing she could to right— her partners were all but begging her to leave.

In the beginning, when Tyler was nothing more than a name connected with a vague and tenuous recognition, Abigail had tried to contact him. Her fingers trembled over the digits that comprised his cell phone number, and when the line rang twice, she froze in fear and anticipation. But then a recording beeped to life, and she learned that his number had been disconnected. It was the same with his e-mail address, or so she assumed. Abigail had tried to e-mail him; the note was short and imprecise, a generic one-line test to which he never responded. A few days later she tried again, but this message too was lost in cyberspace.

Collecting Tyler's contact information from Hailey's phone signaled a major shift in Abigail's priorities. With each failed attempt at communication, a small piece of her poise dissolved and fell away until her productivity and even her attention were vastly compromised. The extent of her distraction did not go unnoticed at Johnson, McNally & Bennett.

"Go," Colton told her almost harshly. "Take a vacation; join a support group; spend some time with your dad. Don't worry about us. Your job will be here whenever you get back."

Abigail didn't know if she found that thought comforting or threatening. But she did everything she could to transition her clients into Blake's and Colton's more than capable hands, then promised herself she wouldn't be gone long. She had every intention of picking up where she had left off, of using the indulgences earned by her upcoming atonement to buy back the life she had become so comfortable living. However, the truth was, when she left her office for the last time, she looked at it long and hard as if she wanted to memorize each and every detail. She didn't know when, if ever, she would return.

As for her friends, Abigail's relationships were somewhat limited and rather shallow. She hung out mostly with two women who worked in the same block of upscale offices that housed Johnson, McNally & Bennett. Sarah and Elle were both cosmetic dentists, professionals like Abigail and too focused on their blossoming careers to commit much more than the occasional dinner out or early morning jog to a relationship with Abigail. Other than more flowers and a few awkward messages on the answering machine, Sarah and Elle didn't have much to offer Abigail when Hailey died. Abigail accepted those friendships for what they were: temporary and one-dimensional. Dealing with the suicide of a sister blurred the parameters of a trio that was supposed to be lighthearted and fun. By the time Abigail left for Canada, nothing much remained to try to salvage between the three of them.

The only other thing that tied Abigail to Florida was Lou. But Abigail's father was already well established at the Four Seasons Manor Home, and his nurses knew better than to expect a lot from Abigail. Making the necessary arrangements to stay in Revell consisted of two short phone calls: one to Marguerite, the secretary at the accounting firm, and the other to the Four Seasons. Abigail kept both conversations vague—"I need a few more weeks"—and wasn't surprised when no one fussed or complained.

After she clicked the End button on her phone a

second time, Abigail couldn't help but feel cut loose. She was floating into a half-life, a charade that she could have never imagined playacting in. There was only one last thing to do. Cutting herself off from the rest of her life required Abigail to turn off her phone and toss it in the bottom of her luggage. The little device thudded against the sides of her suitcase and Abigail knew she was officially unreachable. With an air of determination, she donned a thin smile, put on a pretty outfit, and dived right in.

When Abigail drove up to Thompson Hills just before six the next morning, Eli was waiting for her on the wide front steps of the main building. He was leaning against the open door of the stately structure and smoking a cigarette. The sun was a sliver of light on the horizon, and it bathed the winery in a creamy early morning glow that was accented by the orange disk of Eli's burning cigarette when he inhaled. Abigail found it a little unsettling that he watched her closely as she parked her car. He didn't take his eyes off her for a second as she collected her purse and started across the parking lot toward him.

"That a rental?" Eli called when Abigail was within earshot.

"Yes," she answered. "That a cigarette?"

"What does it look like?" Eli replied, dropping the last inch of the savored du Maurier at his feet.

He ground the cigarette to ashes and then kicked the remainders into the bushes beside the step.

"You'll get lung cancer, you know." Abigail said it just to annoy him.

But Eli laughed. "I quit years ago."

Raising her eyebrows, Abigail indicated the butt he had discarded a moment before.

"Oh, that doesn't count," Eli scoffed. "I have three-quarters of a cigarette every morning. No more, no less. It's just enough to remind me of what I'm not missing."

Skepticism etched itself across Abigail's face.

"Besides, I'd be more concerned about you and your rental car. Those companies will bleed you dry. How long they been tapping you?"

"Less than a week," Abigail admitted.

"You better ditch that car, 'cause I'm not paying you enough to keep it." Eli turned abruptly and headed into the building.

Abigail wasn't about to tell him that she had more than enough money to pay for her ridiculous rental car, so she merely followed him inside the cool interior of the winery.

Much to her surprise, Abigail found that the central great room, the same tasting room where she had eaten brunch only days ago, was buzzing with people. There were probably fifteen or so men and women milling around, pulling tables together and overturning stacked chairs to make an enormous banquet table. The laughter, the cheerful feel of the room was disconcerting to Abigail. She had expected anything but the partylike atmosphere of the winery at 6 a.m. on a weekday. Was this a private celebration? Was Eli expecting her to wait on all these people? Dread filled Abigail at the thought.

Just as she was about to grab Eli's arm and quietly demand an explanation, he whistled sharply and the whole room stilled. A few people dropped into chairs, but the rest froze where they were and turned as one to Eli.

"This is Abby," he introduced, loud enough for the entire room to hear.

"Abigail," she corrected instantly. She was horrified that all those people were looking at her, but still she couldn't let him introduce her as Abby. She hadn't been Abby for over a decade.

Eli glanced at her, obviously put out that she had reproached him in front of everyone. But he obliged her and said, "This is *Abigail*." She chose to ignore the edge in his voice.

A few people waved, but mostly they just stared at Eli and waited for more instructions.

"Where's breakfast?" he asked. "Whose turn is it?"

"Meg and Natalie," someone answered.

And then there was a scuffle of activity as two young women emerged from the kitchen behind the bar at Abigail's left hand. They were each carrying a huge pan of sticky buns that were obviously straight from the oven. The aroma was divine, and the group began to moan in anticipation as the women approached the group. Abigail saw someone set a few stacks of mismatched plates and two old coffee tins full of silverware at different intervals along the makeshift harvest table. Everyone found a seat, including Eli, who had already abandoned Abigail to her own devices.

"Over here!" A voice rang out above the chatter, and Abigail looked up to see a cute girl with short, tomboyish hair pull out a chair and motion her over.

Abigail smiled gratefully and took her place at the table next to the woman.

"I'm Paige," she said, dipping her head toward Abigail since the room was already quieting down.

"Nice to meet you," Abigail whispered back. "What's going on?"

Paige looked meaningfully at Eli, who was now standing at one end of the table, head bowed and hands folded. She did the same and Abigail followed suit.

When Eli began, "Our Father in Heaven," Abigail gulped down her breath and held it. She hadn't heard that prayer since her childhood, since the days when Lou sat at the head of his own table and boomed out the Lord's Prayer as if the louder he recited it the more likely God would hear it. Abigail found that she still knew every word. By the time Eli made it to the end, she was mouthing along with him almost against her will. *Lead us not into temptation but deliver us from evil. For the kingdom, the power, and the glory are yours now and forever. Amen.*

Everyone echoed *amen* with varying degrees of intensity, and then the table jerked back to life. Abigail was left trying to shrug off the remaining sense of unrest that Eli's prayer had draped over her shoulders. But she barely had time to think about it—someone started cutting the rolls and plopping one caramel monstrosity on each of the plates. Before she knew what was happening, Abigail had breakfast in front of her as well as a mug of the strong, black coffee that two guys were passing around.

"We have breakfast together every Monday morning," Paige explained in response to Abigail's implicit question. "Eli has us take turns making it, and he uses the time to—" she assumed a deep, stern voice—"prep us for the big week ahead."

"There's a big week ahead?" Abigail asked.

"There's always a big week ahead during tourist season. But it depends on what you're doing. What did he hire you for?"

"I don't know," Abigail admitted. "He didn't really tell me."

"Well, Thompson Hills is an estate vineyard— that means it's a winery *and* a vineyard," Paige said, her tone sprinkled with mock condescension. "You'd be surprised how many wineries actually buy their grapes from separate vineyards. Appalling, eh? Anyway, you'll either be farming with Josh Ellens—he's the grower, our viticulturist—or you'll be working with Eli."

"What does Eli do?" Abigail asked around a bite of caramel roll.

"He's the owner, general manager, winemaker, and cellarman. Basically, he does everything, including drive the rest of us crazy."

Abigail frowned. "That bad?"

"Yes," the girl on the other side of Abigail hissed. Then she bit her lip self-consciously. "Sorry. I didn't mean to eavesdrop."

"You weren't. It's not a private conversation." Paige motioned between Abigail and the pretty brunette with her fork. "Abigail, meet Natalie. Natalie, Abigail."

The two girls shook hands, and Abigail realized with a start that Natalie had been her waitress when she first came to Thompson Hills.

Apparently the same thought struck Natalie because she snapped her fingers and grinned. "I know where I've seen you before. I think I waited on you last weekend."

"Got me," Abigail said, putting up her hands.

Natalie regarded her with narrowed eyes. "You had the . . . the fruit platter and a mimosa."

"You're right."

"Don't be impressed," Paige interrupted. "That's what she recommends to everyone."

"And the smart clientele always take my recommendations," Natalie joked.

Abigail was almost beginning to enjoy her conversation with Paige and Natalie when Eli stood and clapped twice.

Everyone shut up instantly and gave the older man their full attention. The transformation from lively chitchat to utter silence was so complete that Abigail hardly dared to swallow lest she make too much noise.

"Vineyard crew is dismissed," he said directly. "Josh will meet you at the service shed."

A handful of people crammed the last bites of breakfast into their mouths and then shoved back from the table. Abigail noticed that the group of workers wasn't limited to men, and she wondered if she was supposed to join them when she looked down at her understated taupe sweater and remembered that Eli had told her to wear something nice. Surely he didn't mean for her to be a part of the vineyard crew. A glance around the table reassured her that the remaining employees were smartly dressed, the men in chinos and collared shirts, the women in skirts or something equally pretty and feminine. It also struck her that Tyler was nowhere to be seen. Had she missed him when he rose to join the vineyard workers? Or was he gone again? Was she sitting at Eli's improvised family table in vain?

Abigail felt a band of disappointment settle

around her heart, and she struggled to make it beat past the feeling of failure that threatened to dam her chest. She was trying to formulate a casual question about Tyler's whereabouts when Eli looked past her and settled his features into a dour smile.

"About time," he said to someone just over her shoulder.

"Sorry, I couldn't find the chardonnay-viognier. It wasn't where you said it would be."

Abigail felt something slide past her and turned to see Tyler's handsome profile only inches from her face. He settled a wooden crate on the table directly in front of her and then shot a flirty grin at the girl across from him.

Eli began removing the bottles from the crate, surveying the labels and appearing to take a mental tally as he spoke each name aloud. "Chardonnay, cabernet, pinot noir, sauvignon blanc, merlot . . ."

Abigail barely heard him. Tyler was still close enough to touch.

"How many is that?" Eli asked, losing count.

"Five," Tyler said. "The chard-viognier is the sixth." He produced it from behind his back and handed it to Abigail with a flourish. "You must be the new girl," he whispered, arresting her with a gaze so intense she blinked to break eye contact. It didn't even cross her mind to respond. She just sat like stone as he threw her a wink and then settled into a chair on the other side of Natalie.

"We have a new white," Eli said, taking the bottle from Abigail's hands. "Josh tried a viognier grape a number of years ago, and our first harvest didn't go too well. So we blended it. I think the end result is quite fine. Natalie, glasses."

Natalie jumped up from the table and came back carrying a tray of tulip-shaped glasses with delicate stems.

Abigail watched her go, then tracked her progress as she set a wineglass in front of every remaining person at the table. Following Natalie, even if only with her eyes, helped Abigail live with the knowledge that there was nothing between her and Tyler but an empty chair. She focused on Natalie's movements, resolutely ignoring the growing suspicion that Tyler was studying her.

"Someone tell me about our chardonnay," Eli demanded, extracting a small corkscrew from his pocket and turning it into the neck of the bottle in his hands.

"Oak-scented and dry," someone offered.

"Buttery."

"Hints of vanilla, pear, and toast."

From the corner of her eye, Abigail could see Tyler open his mouth. "Full-bodied, long-legged, and . . . *sensuous*," he said, his voice exaggeratedly mellow and deep.

A few guffaws erupted around the table, but Eli put a stop to them with a hard look. "Thank you, Tyler. Your observations are . . . *insightful* as always." Getting back to business, he shot out, "Food pairings."

"Lobster, white meat, or salmon."

"Cream sauces and Italian food."

"Goat cheese."

"Predictable," Eli muttered, finally popping the cork and lifting the bottle so he could sniff it. "Surprise me."

"Japanese," Paige called out. "Chardonnay goes great with sushi."

"Good," Eli said, and there was a hint of pride behind his begrudging compliment. "Now, what do you know about viognier?"

The table remained silent and Abigail took the opportunity to look around. When her gaze slid over Tyler, she was stunned to find that he was still looking at her.

He smiled faintly and then directed his attention to Eli. "We don't know anything about viognier, Uncle. Enlighten us."

Eli rolled his eyes to the ceiling but complied. "Viognier is a powerful wine, very complex and best known for its aroma rather than its bouquet."

"Bouquet?" Abigail murmured without thinking.

"The scent created by the winemaker during fermentation and aging," Paige whispered back hastily, keeping her head turned toward Eli.

"Aroma?"

"The naturally occurring fragrance of the wine." Paige's voice dropped even lower as Eli's eyes swept over her. "Determined by the type of grape and *terroir*."

Abigail furrowed her brow in confusion, but before she could ask another muted question out of the corner of her mouth, Eli continued. "It's quite dry but more creamy than acidic and perfectly paired with a good, bold chard." He poured an inch of the golden wine into the nearest glass. "I'll let you taste for yourselves. Let's see if you can pick out the fruit."

He wandered up one side of the table and down the other, measuring a bit out for everyone. There was just enough to go around. Abigail could see the dregs of wine like liquid sunlight sloshing about in the translucent bottle.

All over the table, people picked up their glasses by the stem, swirling the contents and scrutinizing the wine inside. Though Abigail had enjoyed a glass of wine before, she certainly wasn't a connoisseur and she had absolutely no idea what to do. Thankfully, Paige bumped her arm and raised her eyebrows as if to say, "Like this." Abigail copied her every move, holding the glass to the light so she could first examine it. Then, taking her cues from Paige, she breathed deeply of the wine, swished, sniffed again, and finally sipped. The wine was distinctive and rich on her tongue but also unexpectedly sweet and smooth. Like Eli had suggested, Abigail could sense a hint of fruit, but she couldn't quite place it. She took another sip.

"Good grief, Abigail!" The harsh words sliced through the room.

Abigail swallowed almost guiltily and met Eli's shocked stare. "Don't swallow it, girl! You'll be drunk before we open the third bottle."

Chastened, Abigail watched as Paige lifted her empty coffee mug and spit a mouthful of wine into it. Around the table the others did the same.

Eli sighed heavily through his nose and turned with deliberate disdain from Abigail. "Aroma?"

"Pineapple?"

"Tangerine?"

"Apricot!"

"That's it: apricot. Overripe apricot."

"And oranges."

"Orange *blossoms*," Tyler corrected.

The room burst into laughter as if relieved to have something to giggle out loud about. Abigail had watched a few people bite their lips when Eli admonished her, but there wasn't time for her to be humiliated. She wasn't permitted to swallow the wine, but she forced herself to swallow a lot of other things: her pride, her uncertainty, her apprehension.

By the time the final bottle had been decimated and Abigail had tasted and spat out six different varieties of wine, her head was spinning and she was exhausted. Thompson Hills opened to the public at eleven o'clock, and she was expected to be a veritable wine expert, handing out samples and answering questions about vintage and tannins, legs and food pairings.

"You okay?" Paige asked when Eli dismissed his workers and they started to dismantle the thrown-together tables.

Abigail smiled ruefully. She wanted to say, "I'm a partner in a well-known and widely respected accounting firm. Recommending a silly little bottle of wine should be a piece of cake." But she didn't say that. Instead she complained, "Can't there just be two kinds? You've got your white—" she raised one hand, palm up—"and you've got your red." Abigail held up her other hand. "Keep it simple."

Paige laughed. "Oh, you'll fall in love before you know it. You'll never be able to drink the cheap stuff again."

"Can't I just label bottles or something?"

"You will at some point or another. Eli keeps one or two people in the cellar with him. But believe me, you'd rather be in the tasting room for now."

Abigail wasn't too sure about that. And though she couldn't tell whether Eli was regretting his earlier degrading display or if he was simply making sure that she didn't screw up too bad, she almost moaned in relief when he instructed Paige to take the "new girl" under her wing for the day. At least she wouldn't make the horrifying mistake of recommending the cabernet as a complement to chocolate fondue. "The wine should always be sweeter than the dessert," Paige had muttered desperately when Eli pinned Abigail with that exact question in front of everyone.

Hours later, after the tasting room was ready for guests and the employees were looking uniform with starched white aprons over their fashionable outfits, Abigail approached Paige with a weary smile. "May I please use the bathroom, Miss Paige?"

"We call it a washroom, Yankee," Paige teased. She consulted her watch. "But yes, you may. Doors open in about five minutes, so make it snappy. Eli usually sulks around the kitchen for an hour when we first open. He's been known to stomp out and yell at us in front of customers."

"Sounds frightening," Abigail mused.

"It is."

Abigail slipped into the cathedral-ceilinged entryway of the building, her high heels clicking loudly with each step on the tile floor. She remembered seeing a discreet sign for a public restroom near the entrance, and though Paige had told her that there were employee bathrooms just beyond the kitchen, she was looking forward to a brief respite before the chaos of the rest of her day.

The washrooms were behind a curving wall of stacked stone slabs that were slick with trickles of water from a gurgling but understated cascade. Abigail paused to admire the engineering behind the basinless waterworks when she felt someone move in close behind her.

"I needed a little peace and quiet," she quickly explained, expecting Paige to inform her that the public restrooms were not for employee use. But then it hit her that she hadn't heard Paige approach. She stiffened. Only a man's shoes could be noiseless on the granite floor.

"Tell me about it."

The voice was definitely not Paige's, and Abigail turned slowly, fearing who she would find.

Tyler was even closer than she had anticipated, close enough for Abigail to pick up his musky cologne. She breathed shallowly, sure for a moment that he knew who she was and had guessed why she was here. But that was impossible. *Impossible.* Abigail had to force her mouth not to form the word.

"It's Abigail, right?"

She nodded once, stiffly.

The corner of his mouth pulled up in a brazen smile. "I didn't catch your last name."

"Bennett," Abigail whispered, hoping her French intonation was believable. Since Hailey used her last name when it suited her and made up interesting alternatives when it didn't, Abigail wasn't sure if Tyler knew Hailey as a Bennett or not. But she hoped that softening the consonants and elongating the vowels would make it sound different enough that he wouldn't notice. Tyler certainly wouldn't see any similarities between Hailey and her older sister. Besides, Abigail could easily pass for French and Hailey was anything but. All the same, her heart paused as she waited for him to respond.

Tyler didn't flinch. "You look tired," he observed, taking a small step back. "It gets better, I promise. Or maybe you get better. You get used to it." The bravado of his roguish exterior shimmered, and Abigail thought she could detect a hint of self-consciousness, an almost-boyish diffidence that she was sure had been irresistible to her sister. But then just as quickly as it flashed to the surface, it was gone. Tyler tossed a lopsided smile at her and cocked his eyebrow in a carbon copy of the same look he had thrown the girl across the table. "At least you've already figured out never to use the employee bathrooms. Smart. I like that in a woman."

The way he said *woman* made Abigail distinctly aware of her femininity. She felt so bare, so on display and at the mercy of his appraising eyes that she didn't say anything in reply. She couldn't.

But it didn't matter; Tyler wasn't trying to make conversation. He gave her one last calculated grin and then turned and strode across the entryway. "See ya around!"

In the bathroom, Abigail realized that she was trembling. She turned on the cold water tap and thrust her wrists under the icy stream. There were dots of sweat prickling along the back of her neck, underneath her heavy hair. The heat was intense, uncomfortable. She felt she could have cried of it.

Being here, being so close to Tyler, to the only other person that Hailey had fingered in what Abigail considered her accusation, was excruciating. Living with herself was hard enough. Living with Tyler was something she wasn't sure she could do. Just the thought of it dislodged something in Abigail's mind that made her heart pound painfully in her chest and her eyes spring to the mirror so they could seek out the woman who had birthed such nonsense in her subconscious. She stared at herself for a long time, begging the brown-eyed girl to say it wasn't so, to rebuke the demons that suggested such things. But it was no use.

What could cover the sin of Hailey's spilled blood? What sort of penance could cancel the debt that her life demanded? And what really had Abigail hoped to accomplish in finding Tyler? Did she plan to secure his heartfelt apology? force him to pledge his undying devotion to a woman already dead? beg him to do the impossible and rewind the clock, change his mind about leaving so Hailey wouldn't feel so abandoned? hopeless? alone?

Abigail knew that her motives in coming to BC had much more to do with revenge than reconciliation. She knew the stories; she knew that even the Bible had demanded an eye for an eye, a tooth for a tooth. And she knew that the crime of murder carried with it a toll so heavy that the perpetrator's life would never, ever be the same. Though Abigail couldn't lock Tyler up for life, she could change his life.

She could *take* his life.

There. The girl in the mirror had admitted it.

I could kill Tyler Kamp. Abigail mouthed the words, and as she did, she began to sob.

Hailey sobbed like the world would end when Abby announced that she was leaving for Florida. She sulked for days, and it seemed for those long hours as if the medication that had restored such harmony to the Bennett home was nothing more than a placebo. The desperate look that had haunted Melody's eyes returned almost overnight. And Lou began to draw deeper into himself again, retreating from the family and spending his evenings on the couch with the remote in one hand and a Pabst Blue Ribbon in the other.

Though she promised herself she would not feel guilty, Abby had to work hard to maintain her composure and not give in to the general con-sensus that life could not go on without her steadying presence. *Too bad,* she thought. *I'm not Hailey's mother. It's not my job.* And yet she also had a difficult time imagining how the household would continue to plod along without her. Melody was fragile, Lou distant, Hailey unpredictable. But Abby pushed those thoughts to the edges of her mind. She couldn't remove them entirely, but she could suppress them.

A few days after Abby's announcement, Hailey tracked her sister down to her bedroom and stood in the doorframe as if she would physically prevent her from leaving.

"Why?" Hailey demanded, an edge of anger sharpening the challenge in her voice.

Abby didn't say anything. Pretending that Hailey wasn't even there, she just went back to stacking and restacking the contents of her dresser drawer. She wasn't leaving for months, but after her decision to attend South Seminole, she suddenly felt an urgent need to get her life in order. How does one pack up eighteen years of living and condense it into a few choice memories and a trunk full of necessities?

"I asked you a question," Hailey spat out, refusing to be ignored.

"Because I'm eighteen," Abby said calmly, quietly. She didn't even turn around to regard her sister but focused on her drawer, removing a balled-up pair of socks with holes in the heels and tossing them in the garbage. "Because I need my own space. I need my own life." She didn't say "without you," but Hailey caught the implication anyway.

"You saw . . . ," Hailey began. Then she quickly changed her tactic, unwilling to admit to anything that she didn't have to. "Why do you hate me?"

Abby growled impatiently. "Don't be so self-absorbed. What makes you think I'm leaving because of you?"

"See?" Hailey's tone rose in intensity. "You didn't even deny it. You *do* hate me."

"I do not hate you."

"You're only saying that because I made you."

"Hailey—"

"You *loathe* me. You *abhor* me. You wish you could eradicate my very memory from your mind."

Abby unearthed another pair of worn socks and threw them straight at Hailey's head. "Grow up."

"Would you like me better if I did?"

Rolling her eyes, Abby left the drawer and went to grab her sister. Seizing her by the arms, she pulled Hailey over to the bed and pushed her down on it. She didn't intend to be so forceful, but with Hailey looking up at her in a mockery of total innocence, she felt herself begin to seethe. Emotions that she thought she had buried were far closer to the surface than she had realized. Before Abby knew it, her finger was an inch from Hailey's nose and she was muttering through clenched teeth, "You kissed my boyfriend."

Shock rippled across Hailey's face, and she shook her head. "I did not. I would never do that. I—"

"Oh, shut up!" Abby yelled. "You did, too! I saw you." Taking a jagged breath, she straightened and put her hands on her hips. "I can't believe you did that." She spun away and added, almost as an afterthought, "But that's not why I'm leaving."

"I don't know what you *think* you saw, but I didn't—"

"Stop lying," Abby whispered acidly.

Hailey chewed her bottom lip in concentration, her eyes inviting Abby to defy her. It was a lose-lose situation, Abby knew. When Hailey dug herself into a lie, there was no convincing her that what she so firmly contended was anything less than the god-honest truth. Abby didn't know if her sister was delusional at times, or if she was so pathological that she could convince herself of anything that suited her purposes. Either way, it was a battle that Abby couldn't win, so she threw her hands up in defeat and turned back to the drawer.

"You can't go all the way to Florida because of something you *think* you saw," Hailey reiterated.

Abby sighed. "I told you, I'm not leaving because of . . . *that*."

The bedsprings creaked and Abby could tell that Hailey had lain back, propping herself against the sky blue pillows. "Then why?"

How could Abby explain it? How could she tell Hailey that the pressure of being her sister—and her surrogate mother, her counselor, her punching bag, her scapegoat—was deflating her spirit? Abby felt like a mortal wound had been inflicted on her person the day Hailey was born. It was a small lesion, but Hailey pressed on it and it oozed a little every day. Abby lost herself little by little, bit by bit, until she was sure that there would be nothing left.

But she didn't try to explain that. She said, "I told you. I just need some space."

Hailey didn't respond. In fact, it was so silent in her corner of the room that after a moment Abby turned to see if her sister had fallen asleep or maybe even left the room. She hadn't. Hailey was sunken against the pillows, head tilted back and eyes fixed unwaveringly on Abby. Her lips pulled into a misleadingly gentle smile when Abby caught her gaze.

"I won't let you leave," she said. Her words were so measured and calm that Abby had to stifle a shiver.

"We'll see about that," Abby countered. Then she abandoned the drawer and left Hailey alone, lounging on the bed and watching her retreat with a knowing look.

Like Hailey's first near-death experience, her second suicide attempt wasn't really a suicide attempt at all. After leveling her threat at Abby, Hailey slipped into the bathroom and found herself a small bottle of ibuprofen. It was brand-new, and the neck was still encased in plastic. Hailey ripped through the perforated seal, plucked out the bit of cotton, and downed the entire bottle between sips of Diet Coke. The pills had a slippery, orange coating, and by the time she was done, her tongue was stained fluorescent orange.

When the pills were gone, Hailey curled up on the floor of the bathroom with the door propped open and the bottle in her hand. She had a stomachache, and if she wasn't imagining the side effects, she felt slightly dizzy and her vision seemed blurry.

As it was nearly suppertime, Melody found her within ten minutes. She screamed, her voice echoing through the tiny house: "Help! Someone call 911!"

Lou bounded up the stairs two at a time. He assessed the situation in a fraction of a second and scooped up Hailey in arms that were no less strong than they had been twenty years before.

The ride to the hospital was tense, though Abby tried to convince her parents that an ibuprofen overdose was only rarely fatal when caught early. Damaging if left untreated, yes. But not necessarily fatal. Lou and Melody didn't seem to be much comforted.

At the hospital, the ER doctor induced vomiting and then treated Hailey with activated charcoal. He also ran a few basic labs: arterial blood gases, electrolyte levels, and liver function. When everything came back okay, Abby thought Hailey would be released and they would all be able to go home and begin again the process of forgetting.

But as the doctor studied Hailey's chart, his brows crept closer and closer together. "I want to keep her for observation," he said.

Abby knew what that meant: Dr. Madsen would be getting a call.

Though it broke her heart to do so, Abby threw her South Seminole enrollment package in the garbage. She registered at the local tech school, signing up for entry-level classes that would easily, hopefully, transfer to a larger college in a year or two. When Hailey stabilized a bit.

If Hailey ever stabilized a bit.

My head was pounding so furiously that I drove straight to Starbucks and ordered a grande hazelnut latte with an extra shot of espresso. "Skinny, no foam, and a sprinkle of cinnamon, please." The words came automatically. I didn't even have to think about what I was saying, what I was doing. But when I pulled up to the drive-through window and fumbled in my purse for money, it hit me that I was ordering a specialty drink while my sister was being taken to the morgue.

I nearly vomited. Bile rose up in my throat so suddenly, so unexpectedly, that I actually slapped a hand to my mouth.

"Four sixty-seven," the barista called cheerfully through the open window.

The sound surprised me and I spun toward him.

The standard-issue smile that he had pasted to his face disappeared in an instant. "You okay?" he asked, the hesitancy in his voice matched by the intentional step he took away from the window.

I closed my eyes and nodded, slowly lowering my hand from my mouth. Parting my lips the tiniest bit, I realized that it was safe. "I'm fine," I managed. Then I grabbed a bill from my wallet and thrust it at him.

He took the money and passed me my coffee, his

fingers around the very tip of the cup as if he didn't dare touch me. As if my sorrow were contagious and he could become infected through casual contact.

The coffee cup was hot in my palm—he had forgotten to put a sleeve around it. But instead of complaining, I drove away. I heard him yell something about change, but I didn't care whether I had given him a five or a fifty. It was ridiculous, but I didn't want my change or my receipt. I didn't even want my coffee; I wanted to pour it out the window, remove any evidence of it so I wouldn't have to admit that I had indulged in an act of normalcy when the world was so obviously anything but.

Though I didn't dare to even glance at it, Hailey's letter was open on the seat beside me, faceup, accusing me of things that I could never seek forgiveness for. A part of me regretted ever opening it. As always, she had changed everything. I didn't see how life could ever be commonplace again. How could I drink lattes, go to work, meet my friends for a Saturday jog on the beach?

Suddenly furious, I slammed the steering wheel with my fists. I did it again and again until my hands tingled with the ferocity of my misery. The car swerved a little, and the driver of the SUV in the lane beside me tapped his horn and made an obscene gesture. I glared at him and accelerated, too angry to care that I was being uncharacteristically reckless and too blinded by my emotions to even realize where I was going.

I drove instinctively for fifteen minutes before pulling into the parking lot of the Four Seasons Manor Home. The long shadows of the palm tree–lined driveway striped across the road and made me feel like I was the villain in an old black-and-white movie, blurred in the fuzzy frames and trembling on a rickety reel.

"Help," I breathed, not knowing exactly who I hoped would come to my aid. "I can't do this."

But I had to do it. Lou had no one else.

IX

CR BEFORE THE END of her first day at Thompson Hills, work proved to be so all-consuming that Abigail barely had time to think, much less contemplate, the atrocities her wounded heart seemed willing to ponder. She excelled in the art of pushing things down deep, and that's exactly what she did—forcing all the thoughts and feelings she couldn't quite bring herself to face into hidden recesses where they could ferment in the darkness and silence. They lurked there, hushed but waiting, and while Abigail agonized inside, she seemed to flourish on the outside.

In spite of all the things she had heard about the incorrigible Elijah Dixon, Abigail actually enjoyed working at Thompson Hills. She caught on quickly to the wine jargon and found that when she was in the tasting room, the only thing she really needed was confidence. Most of the people who darkened the doors of the winery knew little to nothing about wine and came only because the Summerlands seemed synonymous with chardonnay. Or pinot noir or merlot or whatever—the names weren't important; the nicely labeled bottles were. Tourists invariably went home with two souvenirs: sunburns and wine. So Abigail learned early on to smile wide and tell her customers what to think.

"It's nice and rich on your tongue," she'd say. Or,

"Notice the lingering sweetness after you swallow." And they would nod seriously and buy a bottle or two of each at twenty to thirty dollars apiece.

Abigail also learned that Eli had, for incomprehensible reasons, set her apart from most of her coworkers. Nearly everyone she met on the first day worked a scant thirty-hour week. But Eli had made it clear when Abigail left on Monday afternoon that her hours would be longer.

"I want you back at six tomorrow morning," Eli said, stopping Abigail just as she was about to leave the winery.

It had been an exhausting day, and Abigail turned to him slowly, too tired to argue but curious just the same. "Paige said that Monday and Saturday are the only 6 a.m. days. Tuesday through Friday we start at ten."

"Not for you," Eli informed her. "I need barrels washed in the cellar and bottles filled and labeled. I can't do that all by myself."

Abigail stared at him, deciding if she should complain, but she simply didn't feel like it. "Fine. I'll see you in the morning." But as Eli strode off, Abigail felt compelled to utter something that she normally would have only wondered about. "Why me?"

" 'Cause you're new and I can still stand you," Eli called without slowing his step.

Abigail could only laugh.

For the rest of the week, Abigail arrived at Thompson Hills as the birds were trilling their daybreak tunes and stayed until late in the afternoon. Her mornings were spent hosing out giant oak barrels so they could be filled with new wine. It was a dirty job, and Abigail was inevitably soaked by the end of the morning and in desperate need of a shower before taking her place in the charming tasting room upstairs. When midweek rolled around, her fingers were even stained a pale burgundy around the nails. Watered-down or not, the wine seemed to get everywhere, marking her hands and blooming in faded patches across her clothes.

The first day Abigail hadn't thought to bring an extra set of clothes and had to run back to the Sunny Grove to clean up and change. After that, Eli showed her the small locker room in the service shed and instructed her to shower on the premises.

The bathroom had a concrete floor with a filthy, plastic drain at the concave center that was clotted with dirt and grass. Abigail longed to take the hose from the service shed and spray down the entire room—mirrors, toilet, shower, even the ceiling—but the bathroom wasn't her responsibility. Yet. Instead, Abigail showered with her flip-flops on and then dressed quickly and made a beeline for the gorgeous guest bathroom at the winery entrance. She finished getting ready there, and if Eli knew about it, he didn't say anything.

Abigail didn't mind the setup, though she avoided the same sink and mirror where she had confronted all she seemed capable of when it came to Tyler. For some reason, she couldn't bring herself to look in that mirror, even in passing. It was almost as if her obsessions were trapped in the curving glass above the middle sink, and as long as she avoided it, she could put off dealing with her demons. *Mirror, mirror on the wall* . . . And she knew there was a wicked witch inside. Abigail was more than happy to lower her eyes when she passed and pretend that she had forgotten what she had said.

Abigail knew she was many things, but in all her life she had never counted herself capable of even seriously contemplating what she had admitted to her own reflection. *Murderess*. The word haunted her. It was soft, sibilant, almost sensuous, like the warning hiss of a deadly but terrifyingly beautiful snake. She couldn't deal with it, not really. So she decided that her bathroom confession was nothing more than a result of her anger chasing itself to the farthest possible conclusion. Backing away from that dark, unholy dead end was the only logical course of action.

By the time Friday rolled around, Abigail was used to her temporary pattern of life. In fact, she was so busy, so immersed in the facade she had constructed that she felt as if her life, her real life, had ceased to exist. This was her new reality: Thompson Hills, wine, Tyler.

Though she hadn't said even two consecutive words to Tyler yet. Sometimes he led tours of the winery, and she only saw him as he passed through the main room with camera-carrying guests in tow. Other days he stood behind the bar on the opposite side of the tasting room.

Paige, Natalie, and Abigail had more or less claimed the counter on the south side, across from the kitchen. It afforded the best view of the deck, and beyond the cedar railings the vineyards gave way to orchards that shimmered darkly against the blue of the lake in the distance. When traffic was light in the winery, the girls leaned against the counter and talked, admiring the landscape. Tyler and the four other regulars were relegated to the bar by the kitchen and took turns as tour guides. As the most recently hired, Paige and Abigail could beg off tour guide duty for a couple more weeks at least. And Natalie acted as their supervisor, showing them the ropes and filling in the gaps when their inexperience was obvious.

Since she was a newbie, Abigail also knew enough to keep her mouth shut about Eli's offer of the trailer on the property. She couldn't imagine that anyone else would want to stay at Thompson Hills, yet she didn't make the invitation public knowledge. She hadn't even seen the trailer, but Eli had asked her one morning while they were working in the cellar when—*if*—she was moving in. Since Abigail had already promised to pay Jane for the entire week at the Sunny Grove, they decided that Saturday morning she would bring her things over to Thompson Hills. Not that she had anything more to move than a suitcase.

In anticipation of her relocation, Eli even gave Abigail Saturday off. She had already put in almost fifty hours her first week, but Eli implied that her complete lack of waitressing experience would only muck up the entire day and that was why he wasn't requiring her to work. Abigail couldn't help but suspect that his gesture was actually a feeble attempt at kindness, though she didn't bother to aggravate him by saying so.

When Abigail went to settle her bill at the Sunny Grove on Saturday morning, Jane acted as if it was hard to say good-bye. "You're kind of fun to have around," she said with a grin. "I like the brooding, thoughtful type. You going home?"

Abigail paused, not sure how much she wanted to share with the nosy proprietor. "We'll see," she finally said.

"You're staying!" Jane accused, a glint in her eye. "You love it here. You can't leave." She gasped. "You've found a *job*!"

Shaking her head, Abigail took the credit card receipt from under Jane's fingers and signed it.

"Come on, tell me."

Abigail held her tongue and waved good-bye.

"Well, at least come back sometime and let me

take you out for ice cream," Jane cajoled. "Coffee? Wine?"

The last suggestion made Abigail smile. "We'll see," she said again.

"Good luck to you!"

"Thanks," Abigail replied, but Jane had already turned back to her TV.

It was after 10 a.m. when Abigail pulled up to Thompson Hills. She prayed that her coworkers were too busy with brunch customers to detect her unmistakable orange Kia as she pulled slowly through the crowded parking lot and continued on to the back of the property.

Abigail had noticed the dusty gravel service road that wound past the machine sheds, but she had never paused to wonder where it led. But now, following Eli's instructions, she took the deeply rutted path and drove alongside the vineyards, away from the main buildings of the winery.

The road eventually rambled all the way to the edge of the estate, where the rows of grapevines bowed beneath the branches of a sprawling cherry orchard on the far side of the gravel lane. Eli had told Abigail that his house was off the beaten path, but she hadn't realized just how much he liked his privacy until she had spent nearly five minutes looking for his humble abode.

Just when she was sure that she had misunderstood his directions and was nowhere near where she was supposed to be, the road rose sharply and a small log cabin came into view. It was simple but appealing, almost quaint-looking on the top of a hill. Windows lined the entire east side, stretching from the floor to the second-story ceiling and reflecting the brilliant midmorning sunshine. Abigail peeked in her rearview mirror and appreciated that the view from those windows would be spectacular—the peaked roofs of Thompson Hills were a lovely interruption amidst all the green.

But Abigail wasn't staying in the pleasant little cabin. She was staying in the sun-scorched monstrosity beside it. The so-called trailer was actually an old motor home that Abigail was convinced could no longer motor anywhere. Below the shaded windshield it was just possible to make out the letters *N* and after a few spaces *gator*. *Navigator?* Abigail guessed with a shudder. The ugly heap of metal looked like it was ready for the wrecking yard, not a grand adventure.

Heaving a frustrated sigh, Abigail parked beside the Navigator and shut off her car. "Home sweet home," she mumbled, climbing out of the car so she could get a better look. Nope, it didn't improve any on closer inspection. In fact, it seemed even older and grimier than Abigail had first suspected. She wasn't sure she could set foot in it, never mind live in it.

"Not much to look at, is she?"

Abigail whirled around in time to see the screen

door slam behind Tyler as he stepped out of Eli's cabin. She struggled to hide the shock that she knew had exploded in crimson across her pale cheeks. Adrenaline made her feel unnaturally hot, and she touched the fingers of her right hand to her neck in an instinctive act of defense. He had said something. *What had he said?* "Uh-huh," she muttered weakly, hoping that it would be enough. Then she looked back at the motor home so she didn't have to face him.

"It's not much better on the inside," Tyler assured her.

Abigail didn't see Tyler come to stand beside her, but she felt him. They surveyed the Navigator for a few moments without saying anything, and Abigail was grateful for the chance to collect herself. For the chance to breathe. Just breathe. In and out, in and out, as if she could control the situation by controlling herself. As if Tyler was just a guy and she was just . . . Abigail.

"Hey, don't look so depressed."

Though she tried not to, Abigail jumped the tiniest bit when he spoke. She forced herself to glance sideways at him and even contemplated faking a laugh, but she wasn't prepared for such extensive theatrics. Nor was she prepared to find that Tyler was studying her with what seemed to be a mixture of skepticism and concern mingling in his eyes. Skepticism she could understand; she definitely acted strangely around him. But concern? Maybe she was misinterpreting the troubled slant of his eyebrows.

Before she could contemplate it further, Tyler lifted his hand, fingers slightly fanned as if he planned to trail them down the length of her bare arm. Abigail was close enough to feel the heat from his body, and the strong lines of his long hand seemed chiseled from a perfect slab of warm sandstone. She couldn't stand the thought of him touching her. She took a step back.

Tyler looked away and used his raised arm to motion grandly at the motor home. "At least it's clean."

Abigail noticed for the first time that he was holding a blue bottle of Windex and a half roll of paper towels. "You cleaned it?" she asked, finally capable of stringing three words together.

Tyler shrugged. "I have the morning off."

"But . . ." Her voice faded. She didn't know what else to say.

"It's not perfect," Tyler rushed to explain. "But I used the Shop-Vac on the carpets and scrubbed through the dust on the windows. You can see out at least."

Abigail was still struggling to find words. "You didn't have to—"

"I know. Look, I didn't touch the kitchen area or the bathroom. Not that you can really use them anyway. There are no hookups out here, obviously."

"Okay."

"As for a bathroom, there's a little mudroom around the back of the house with a sink and toilet. There's no shower, but Eli said you'd be using the one in the service garage."

Abigail thought about the drive back to the winery and was grateful that she would at least have access to a bathroom nearby.

Tyler seemed to read her mind. "It's actually faster to walk to the winery." Pointing out over the hills toward the curving vineyards, he crossed slightly in front of her. She could smell the mineral undertones of his warm skin, and if he were a different man and she were a different woman, she would have leaned in and looked down the line of his well-formed arm. "You can walk back as the crow flies instead of going all the way around the property. It's less than half a klick to the tasting room—five minutes, tops."

"Do you live here?" Abigail asked suddenly.

"Yeah, I don't call Eli *uncle* just for the fun of it." Tyler's smile was quick and brilliant, but it faded just as abruptly as it appeared. "I moved in with him a while back."

It surprised Abigail that she actually wanted to know why. She wanted to know what had wiped the smile off his face so completely. But Tyler had already changed the subject.

"You know," he said, stuffing the roll of paper towels under his arm and switching the cleaner to his left hand, "I don't think we've properly met." He reached out for her.

Abigail realized that her own hand still fingered the sharp line of her jawbone. Clearing her throat self-consciously, she lowered her arm to let Tyler wrap her hand in his. But at the last second she simply couldn't do it. She whipped away from him and sneezed into her hands. "Sorry," she whispered, shrugging, hoping her little act was convincing.

Tyler gave her a strange look, but eventually he shrugged, too. "I'm Tyler and you're Abigail. I know your name, but it's nice to meet you officially."

"Yeah," Abigail managed, unable to echo his sentiments; it was not nice to meet Tyler. She wished he'd stop staring at her, but he seemed determined to make her uncomfortable by holding her gaze longer than necessary.

"I can't quite put my finger on it, but you seem familiar somehow." Tyler tilted his head back and pressed his lips together as if trying to remember.

"You served me brunch at the winery a week ago," Abigail confirmed. Her tone was even, her look steady. Nothing in her face indicated that there was any other point of connection between them.

"No." Tyler shook his head. Abigail's heart stuttered painfully, but before she could really panic, he continued, "I didn't serve you. I just settled the bill."

Relief carved a thin smile across Abigail's face. Tyler appeared to assume the expression was a direct result of his charms. He let go of her eyes slowly, his brows narrowing for a second before he glanced away.

"Tell you what," he said, turning back to the motor home, "I'll run an extension cord from the house so you can have light at least. The main hookup is shot, but we can plug in a lamp."

Abigail hadn't planned on this unexpected kindness. She hadn't prepared herself for the possibility that Tyler would be anything other than a callous heartbreaker, a seedy womanizer with a proclivity for narcissism. This sort of Windex-wielding selflessness didn't fit her preconceptions at all. Was this the beginning of a slow seduction? Was Tyler trying to win her over by playing the part of a gentleman? Or was something else going on?

"Did Eli make you do this?" Abigail blurted, thinking that was the only viable explanation.

Though he had exuded an air of contentment and calm only a moment ago, everything changed in an instant. Tyler's chin inched up defensively and his shoulders squared. For a moment he appeared exactly how Abigail had pictured him in the days before he became her waking obsession: he was defiant yet haughty, irreproachable and arrogant. Above all, he seemed appalled that someone would question him.

But then again, maybe he was just hurt.

"No," he said, clipping off the word abruptly. Then he thrust the cleaning supplies at her. "Guess you can finish up now that you're here."

Abigail took the bottle from him, but they fumbled over the paper towels and the roll dropped into the dust at their feet.

Tyler bent to retrieve it at the same time Abigail did. He stopped, raised his hands, and backed away. "Looks like you have things under control."

She nodded and watched him leave, kicking up dust as he went and never once looking back.

After Hailey forced her older sister to stay in Newcastle and forfeit her unrealistic dream of freedom and Florida, Abby didn't look back. At least, she tried not to.

The decision to stay was less the result of obligation than it was an act of intention. Of resignation. *She needs me,* Abby reasoned. And hidden in the agony of that unasked-for duty was a small seed of entitlement. Abby was well aware of Hailey's codependency, and though her need was exhausting, there was also something strangely empowering about being the hero. She wouldn't admit it to a soul, but some part of Abby couldn't help but like feeling irreplaceable.

For a while, Hailey almost seemed to reward Abby for her decision to stay. She was polite and solicitous to Abby, giving her a wide, respectful berth that afforded her a little room to breathe. Danny was never mentioned by name again, though once when Melody asked about that "nice young man" Abby had been seeing, Hailey gave her such a verbal roasting her mother never interfered in her daughters' love lives again.

The tirade surprised Abby, for it bordered on an admittance of wrong on Hailey's part. Why should she dislike Danny so vehemently? so openly? But Hailey was oblivious. Instead of catching her obvious slip, she caught Abby's eye and gave an almost-imperceptible nod. Abby took it to mean that Hailey thought they were conspirators and she had just taken a courageous stand against their nemesis, the evil but heartbreakingly handsome villain.

If there's a villain, Abby thought, *it's you. It's always been you.*

But what was done was done, and Abby didn't care to give any more thought to what had happened or why. Her role in the family was so clearly defined she only caused herself and everyone else unnecessary heartache by disrupting the order of things.

By fall, life had entered a predictable holding pattern for the Bennetts. Abby had classes at the community college on Mondays, Wednesdays, and Fridays, and she worked as a part-time bookkeeper and administrative assistant at Newcastle's only dentist's office on Tuesdays and Thursdays. Since she lived at home, she studied in the evenings and didn't have to worry about details like laundry, cooking, or a life.

Abby tried hard not to think about how different things would have been if the threat of Hailey's imminent, self-inflicted death didn't hang over her head. She tried not to be resentful. Sometimes it worked.

Two things that helped Abby in her quest to be understanding of her sister's needs were Hailey's most recent diagnosis and her confirmation.

Shortly after Hailey overdosed on ibuprofen, Dr. Madsen came to the conclusion that she suffered from more than simple ADHD. Depression was added to her list of ailments, and Dr. Madsen introduced a second pill to Hailey's daily regimen.

Though Abby wasn't at the appointment when Dr. Madsen explained the possible side effects of Hailey's new prescription, Melody outlined everything for her eldest daughter in terms that were both comprehensive and serious. "Panic attacks, anxiety, aggressiveness—"

"We've been there before," Abby muttered.

"Be serious."

"I am. This is supposed to *help*?" Abby asked incredulously.

Melody pursed her lips and fluttered the papers. "There's more, but we're most concerned about new thoughts of suicide."

"Suicide?" Abby was indignant. "Isn't that exactly what we're trying to avoid?"

"You're not a doctor," Melody said. She squeezed her eyes shut and sighed. "I trust Dr. Madsen."

"I do too."

"We're a Prozac family now." Melody smiled faintly, attempting to lighten the dark cloud that had settled over them.

"Prozac? That's so cliché," Abby teased, trying to meet her mother halfway. But she took the papers from Melody and studied every word so she knew exactly what to watch for in the coming days and weeks.

Thankfully, on the new medication Hailey's suicidal tendencies seemed to dissipate rather than increase. Abby thought her sister seemed a bit dazed at times, wide-eyed and not quite vacant, but placid to be sure. It was okay for the time being; everyone was just happy that a transitory calm had once again been achieved. And though Abby secretly hoped for a continuation of the blessed monotony they had experienced all summer, when the leaves began to change in September, Hailey announced that it was time for her confirmation.

Abby's confirmation had taken place when she was thirteen years old, and she had participated in the sacrament not because she comprehended it but because her parents made her. She couldn't really claim to grasp what was happening, that the sign administered in her baptism was now being sealed by her confirmation. All the talk about grace and the safeguarding of the Holy Spirit were merely words that filled the six hours of classes she had to take before the bishop could perform the sacrament. When he anointed her head with the aromatic oil and breathed on her cheeks, she didn't feel a rush of holy awareness. She only felt a tinge of concern about the greasy mark on her forehead.

The truth was, the Bennetts attended church regularly, but they were far from devout Catholics. Lou was a relatively new convert who went through the motions because it seemed like the right thing to do. Melody's grandmother had tried to raise Melody in the Catholic church, but her experiences at Mass were limited to the times the imposing Mrs. Van Bemmel could lay hold of her before her parents whisked her off to some more exciting Sunday morning activity. But since Melody's childhood experience was all she knew of church, St. Mary's was the only logical home for them.

Most of the time they were simply conscious of a vague understanding that the world was filled with right and wrong, good and evil, and they wanted to be on the winning side. Baptism, first communion, confirmation, and even the stoic books of written prayers were oddities that they could barely wrap their minds around. Once Melody had tinkered with a pretty beaded rosary because it reminded her of her grandmother. Following Mass the Sunday after she bought the rosary, someone teased Melody that it wasn't a necklace. The slender décolletage ornamented by the beads flushed. Melody removed the rosary and never wore it or touched it again.

So when Hailey announced that she was ready for confirmation with an uncharacteristic enthusiasm, faith took on an entirely new meaning for the Bennetts. Lou contacted Father Timothy at once, and although no one else in his small parish seemed ready to partake in this particular sacrament, he set aside six consecutive Saturday mornings for Hailey's personal instruction.

While Hailey faithfully attended the mandatory classes, Melody rushed to research confirmation. "Did you know that some bishops confer a confirmation name?"

"Excuse me?" Abby was sitting at the kitchen table, poring over a finance textbook and trying not to listen too closely to her mother.

"It says here that sometimes a confirmation name is given when a child is confirmed."

"Hailey's not a child."

"You know what I mean."

Abby didn't feel like participating in this particular discussion, but Melody was keen to share her newfound knowledge with someone. "What's a confirmation name?" Abby asked dutifully, stifling an inward groan. She turned back to her books.

"It's generally the name of a favorite saint. It's representative of the continued path of Christian initiation and the strengthened link to the church."

"Hmmm . . . ," Abby muttered, entering a number in her workbook ledger.

"It has something to do with the impartation of the Holy Spirit."

Abby grunted.

"And it makes me think about the . . . the corporate aspect of our faith," Melody went on, and it seemed to Abby that she was trying to fit what she was learning into the flimsy framework of belief that she had built over the years. "You know, our *togetherness*."

"Togetherness," Abby echoed.

"Do you know any saints?"

"Not personally."

"Abigail Rose," Melody chirped.

After a moment Abby commented, "I never got a confirmation name. Maybe I could go by Mary Martha. Or Martha Mary."

Melody looked up from her papers and fixed Abby with a solemn gaze. "It's different with you," she said quietly.

Abby watched for a moment as her mother struggled for words. But Abby was anxious to steer the conversation back toward less dangerous ground, so she waved her hand dismissively before Melody could continue. "I know." Then she added, "Find a good one."

Melody smiled faintly. "Thanks, Abby."

Initially, Melody set out to discover a saint that would hold personal meaning for Hailey's tumultuous life. But the more widely known saints didn't seem to quite encompass everything about Hailey. Eventually, Melody found that there was a patron saint of mental illness and thought that Saint Christina the Astonishing presented her with the possibility of a lovely name. After all, Hailey Christina just rolled off her tongue. But on further investigation, the astonishing saint seemed merely disturbed, and Melody's fervor faded entirely when she unearthed Saint Zita, the patron saint of lost keys, and Saint Magnus of Füssen, the patron saint of caterpillars. The idea of a confirmation name was abandoned, but none of the excitement was diminished.

Abby was the only one who didn't catch the confirmation spirit. It wasn't that she begrudged her sister the attention or even that she was skeptical of her budding devotion. In fact, Abby was grateful that Hailey had found something to hold on to. She was somewhat envious that Hailey had stumbled on a point of connection, a launching pad from which to reach for something larger than herself. In many ways, Abby longed for the same thing. What kept her from embracing Hailey's newly conceived faith was the step before the impending confirmation: the sacrament of reconciliation.

The memory of her own act of reconciliation

before confirmation was somewhat foggy and indistinct. But Abby remembered Father Timothy questioning her about unconfessed sins and the rush of understanding that flooded over her when she realized that she was supposed to feel guilty for the things she had done. It was one of her first experiences with the double-edged sword of shame and culpability that would pierce her so often in the years to come. However, at that point guilt was an imprecise emotion for Abby, and instead of giving his question adequate thought, on the spot she came up with a short list of jealousies, white lies, and examples of disobedience. He had laughed gently and directed her to the confessional for a time of rededication. Abby did as she was told and tried to be penitent for things that seemed inconsequential.

But Hailey was an entirely different story. What litany of transgressions would she be held accountable for? What list of sins would stand between her and the grace that she suddenly seemed so eager to receive? Confession was something the Bennetts avoided when they added religion piecemeal to their lives. How would Hailey deal with it now, and more importantly, would it leave scars?

But for all her worrying and wondering, as far as Abby could tell, Hailey's reconciliation went just fine. If there were any residual insecurities or feelings of inadequacy or shame, Hailey certainly didn't let on.

And at Mass one Sunday in late October, Hailey stood for her confirmation. Her Sunday school teacher kept watch beside her, and Hailey seemed downright blissful when the bishop murmured, "Be sealed with the gift of the Holy Spirit." She even sighed when he breathed on her.

Abby was stunned to feel her chest tighten at the sight of that bowed head, and she even went so far as to let her soul whisper a fumbling, flightless prayer for her troubled sister. "Keep her safe, Lord. Keep her safe."

The night Hailey was confirmed, Abby stole down the hall after midnight and peeked into her sister's dark room. The door was open just a crack, and Abby could hear Hailey rustling the sheets as she rolled over. Abby couldn't tell if she was awake or not, and she didn't want to rouse her if she was asleep. She lingered in the doorway and listened, waiting for the slightest indication that Hailey was stirring.

When she caught her sister whispering to herself, Abby pushed the door open with her toe.

"O my God, relying on thy almighty power and infinite mercy and promises, I hope to obtain pardon of my sins, the help of thy grace, and life everlasting, through the merits of Jesus Christ, my Lord and Redeemer. Amen."

Even though Abby had wished for some sign of life from Hailey so she could slip inside the room and talk, something about hearing Hailey's simple prayer stopped her cold. *"Pardon of my sins,"* Hailey had said.

Abby knew the prayer. She had learned it in Sunday school as a child. If she remembered correctly, it was called Act of Hope.

Suddenly Abby realized why Hailey's confirmation and her unpretentious act of hope gnawed at her spirit and made her uncomfortable. As a little girl, Abby had learned that someday everyone would stand before the face of God and be held accountable for the sins they had committed. Knowing she was a bold-faced sinner—a rotten, fickle, faithless lout—was something Abby could accept. But as much as she hated Hailey sometimes, as much as she resented her and blamed her for the things that went wrong, Abby had a very hard time believing that Hailey could be held responsible for the acts of a broken mind. How could God possibly fault her for the way he had made her?

Rather than going to sit beside Hailey as she had planned, Abby noiselessly pulled the bedroom door shut and made her way back to her room.

Though she had thought it a thousand times before, with culpability and lies and now faith steadily building impassable roadblocks between them, Abby was convinced that she had never been further away from her sister.

Lou's hand was warm and soft when I reached for it. The nurse at the triage desk had informed me that he was asleep, but instead of waiting in the atrium like I usually did, I went straight to his room and sank into the chair by his bed. I was glad that he was sleeping. Not only did it afford me a bit more time, I was also able to do something that I hadn't done in years. I was able to look at him. Really look at him.

I took in the fine wisps of downy white hair that clung to his mottled head in a feathery semicircle above his ears. I studied the delicate creases of skin that lined every inch of his broad face in deep folds like wrinkled crepe paper. I held his hand and my eyes consumed it, devouring the long fingers that had been so tough, so powerful, when I was a little girl.

I wasn't angry at him, not anymore. In fact, with his mouth slack in sleep and his chest sunken and hollow beneath the line of his clay-colored blanket, I pitied him. I remembered the days when he was formidable, a man to be reckoned with, and I felt a twinge of compassion for him.

For a moment I feared that this would break him. I worried that he would wake, I would tell him, and he simply wouldn't be able to go on. That he'd leave me alone in the world.

It was a selfish thought. Me. Alone. There were other things to agonize over, more important troubles at hand. But weren't there always? Was there ever a time in my life when I was able to grieve for myself? worry about my own sorrows? spend a sleepless night contemplating something, someone other than Hailey?

He woke up coughing, hacking and choking as if his last cigarette were hours, not decades ago. I let go of his hand quickly and sat back in my chair, clearing my throat so I wouldn't startle him with my presence. Lou's eyes flicked to me, but his coughing fit was far from over and he looked away immediately, clutching great handfuls of his blanket with blue-tipped fingers. I waited for it to pass, not daring to touch him.

When Lou could breathe again, he fell back against his pillows and glared at me. "Why didn't you help me?"

It crossed my mind that I should defend myself, remind him of all the other times I did reach out to help and he batted me away. But it wouldn't do any good. He either wouldn't remember or he wouldn't care. I knew exactly how he would respond if I stuck up for myself: he'd say that he had wanted help this *time; couldn't I see that? My complete inability to know what he needed and when he needed it was a road we had traveled down a hundred times before. I couldn't let him drag me down it again. Not today.*

I leaned forward and met his gaze with far less ferocity and far more fear than I meant to. I laid my palms on his bed, being careful not to touch him but mindful that my hands were close enough to reach if he wanted to. An offering.

"Dad," I said, and though I tried to be collected, my voice broke on the word. I tried again. "Dad, she's gone."

The words were stark, definitive. And he knew exactly what I meant. He had steeled himself against those very words for years. When I said them, when he finally knew that he had not prevailed in beating his sweet Hailey to the grave, something inside him burst. The leaky dam that held back all his worst nightmares fractured and split. I watched it happen in the golden brown sunset of his broken eyes.

Lou crumpled. He seemed to deflate as he exhaled in one lingering, low moan. Then he shook with noiseless sobs, wordless groans.

I stood and boldly wrapped my arms around his brittle shoulders. I held him and he didn't push me away. Maybe he didn't have the strength.

We cried, but we didn't cry together.

X

CR THANKFULLY THE NAVIGATOR wasn't as bad on the inside as the exterior suggested. Either Tyler had done an admirable job of cleaning it, or it had been well kept for years even as it languished on blocks in Eli's tiny yard.

Abigail suspected that someone frequented the old trailer. Someone who paid careful attention to the soft suede duvet on the queen-size bed and who took the time to seek out wildflowers for the rough-cut, rectangular glass vase on the small table behind the captain's chair. But Abigail didn't ask. It wasn't her place, and even if she wanted to, she couldn't Tyler had disappeared in a faded blue pickup with a lift kit and fat off-road tires only minutes after he left her standing alone in front of the trailer.

It took Abigail a grand total of ten minutes to get settled into her new home. After she snooped around a bit, she hung her clothes in a miniscule closet and lined up her shoes by the door. Her toiletries stayed in a canvas bag that she hung on a hook next to the sink for easy access. Then she opened all the windows except for the one in the bathroom since the screen was missing. It wasn't like she could use the bathroom anyway, Abigail reasoned, and she closed the bathroom door altogether.

Once she was situated, Abigail did the only thing that made sense to her: she went for a run. She wished she had a destination in mind, a place to go or a friend to visit, but just as suddenly as she craved a connection, she was grateful that she didn't have one. Friends were not what Abigail sought in BC, and she decided it would be much better for her if she avoided any ties that would have to be severed when she left. She made a mental note not to take Jane up on her offer of ice cream. And she also determined to step back from the relationships she was beginning to foster at the winery. Paige, Natalie, and the rest of her coworkers were nice, but she had to keep her wits about her.

For some reason, with her feet slapping the hard-packed earth in flawless rhythm, Abigail found she was able to think about things that she couldn't contemplate when her body was still. Why was she here? What had brought her across the continent to some small town in the middle of nowhere, some inconsequential speck on a map?

Her obsession had started with a dozen little things. A used tube of men's deodorant that stained her fingers with the scent of cloves and wood. A worn paperback novel, some spy thriller that was utterly absurd in Hailey's apartment when Abigail knew that her sister didn't read—and if she did deign to crack the spine of a book, it would not feature a pool of glossy blood on the cover. Then there was a men's Fruit of the Loom T-shirt, size large, in the laundry hamper and athletic socks under the bed. He was everywhere, imprinting Hailey's apartment, her life, with the outline of himself.

It drove Abigail crazy. When her relationship with Hailey was tenuous and interrupted, this man, a *stranger*, kept a case of Samuel Adams in Hailey's refrigerator and slept beside her at night. Abigail's contact with her sister was inconsistent and sprinkled with long days and weeks of separation when she didn't know where Hailey was or with whom. But *he* lost socks under her bed and threw his laundry in with her size-four jeans. Did he watch her decline and do nothing about it? Had he *caused* her decline?

The unanswered questions stacked like evidence against the man Abigail couldn't stop herself from hunting down. She wanted to slap the seductive grin right off his face. She wanted to wrap her fingers around his neck and squeeze the answers from him. She wanted to know *why*.

Abigail shuddered and picked up the pace, forcing herself to clear her mind and focus on her feet, her perfectly regular heartbeat. She could only see the next step in front of her. And murderous thoughts aside, she wasn't stupid. Abigail had no intention of marching up to Tyler and doing something violent. Just skimming against such ideas made her feel faint; she stumbled on a clod of dirt and almost pitched headlong into a weedy ditch. *First things first,* she thought. *One step at a time.* It was time to take a step or two toward Tyler.

As far as Abigail could tell, there was only one way for her to get close to him.

Late Saturday night, Abigail picked her way across Eli's lawn and knocked on the side door of his log cabin. All the lights were on, and Abigail could make out the iridescent shimmer of a television screen reflecting on the glass of his many windows. Tyler hadn't come home all day and Abigail knew Eli was alone.

"The winery is closed on Sundays," Eli informed Abigail when she asked him what hours she was scheduled for the following day. He scrutinized her with one eyebrow cocked, as if he couldn't believe that she would even ask such a ridiculous question. "Church, girl. Don't you go to church?"

"I grew up Catholic," Abigail said, avoiding the present tense.

"I like Catholics."

Abigail wasn't surprised. Somehow the liturgy, the order, and the eloquence of high church seemed to fit Eli. His inflexible exterior and love for discipline seemed well suited for what she remembered of the religious experiences of her youth. Abigail could easily picture Eli on his knees with his back rigid and forehead pressed against the smooth wood of the pew in front of him. There had been many formidable men like Eli at St. Mary's.

"So you grew up Catholic," Eli repeated. "What about now?"

Abigail stalled, thinking of the handful of times that she had allowed a friend to coerce her into a theater-styled megachurch. Everyone carried a Bible and swayed to the beat of a rock band. She had been painfully uncomfortable. Then there was an Anglican church where she felt more at home but where memories of her childhood seemed frustratingly close to the surface. And once or twice she had attended a Presbyterian church. . . . "Nondenominational," she improvised.

"Me too. Come with me tomorrow."

Flustered, Abigail struggled to come up with an appropriate response.

Eli let her off the hook by waving his hands in front of him and shooing her back to the trailer. "Didn't expect you would. But I did have high hopes for you."

Abigail didn't know whether to be insulted or relieved. Either way, she had no intention of accompanying Eli to church. She had the Gideon's Bible waiting at the bottom of her bag, and she figured that was a big enough step for now.

Though she had expected to toss and turn all night long, Abigail slept hard and deep. She woke only once, and that was because she had left the windows open and a cool breeze was chilling the exposed skin on her neck and arms. As she slid the windows closed, Abigail was shocked to see

Tyler's pickup parked next to the house and glowing faintly in the moonlight; she hadn't even heard him come home. It unsettled her to know that she was so oblivious to the world in her sleep. She double-checked that the trailer door was locked, but she wasn't much comforted by the flimsy bolt on the rickety screen door.

Abigail was wide-awake well before 6 a.m., and she didn't even try to fight back the day by staying in bed. Slipping into a pair of running shorts and a light sweatshirt, she threw her canvas bag over her shoulder and started off across the vineyard toward the service shed for a shower. Usually she started the day with a run, but boredom had forced her into her running shoes twice yesterday, and Abigail noticed that she was getting scrawny. A slight change in diet or an increase in her physical activity threatened Abigail with downright wiriness. If she hoped to attract Tyler's attention, she knew that maintaining some semblance of a feminine figure would be helpful.

The vineyards were so quiet and peaceful on a Sunday morning that Abigail couldn't stop herself from wandering the rows of grapevines and enjoying the gradually warming air. Since Abigail was short, the arbors reached just over her head, and all along the shady paths she stopped to admire the miniature fruit beginning to unfold beneath the generous grape leaves.

Each cluster of grapes was a tiny green preview

of the impending harvest. It reminded Abigail of the full-color poster of the stages of pregnancy in her doctor's office. The ten-week old fetus was shown actual size, and Abigail had touched her palm to the picture, closing the child in her hand and marveling that it had ten fingers, ten toes, and two exquisite little eyelids closed over sleeping eyes. A perfect replica of the finished product. Each little bunch of grapes was exactly the same: a precise foretaste of what was to come.

By the time she had finished meandering and showering, Eli's car was missing from its parking spot between Tyler's truck and the house. *Early church service,* Abigail mused. But then she remembered that it was exactly a week ago that she had met Eli for breakfast at the Husky. She could picture him sitting there with Nan now, and she wondered if he was alone or if he had found another lost soul he could help against her will. Though he was certainly rough around the edges and nowhere near easy to handle, Abigail felt an unexpected surge of tepid warmth toward him. He had reached out. Not many people were willing to do that.

Since she had no desire to dive back into the narrow confines of the old trailer, and since she was convinced that Tyler was the type of guy who ascribed to a motto of late to bed, late to rise, Abigail threw her bag on the hood of the Kia and climbed up beside it. Kicking off her flip-flops, she stretched out on the warm car and laid her head back against the windshield, closing her eyes and letting the breeze skim over her bare legs. The early morning air was nothing less than glorious. If she turned her face toward the sun and held herself very still, Abigail found that she could, moment by moment, clear her mind entirely and think of nothing but the light on her face.

The sound of the cabin door slamming startled Abigail. She bolted upright, crossing her legs at the ankles and shading her eyes from the sun. Watching Tyler stride across the lawn toward her forced an uncomfortable sense of déjà vu to prick at Abigail's consciousness. Was he always accompanied by slamming doors?

Tyler walked toward Abigail purposefully, his lips pulled in a tight, obligatory smile and a mug in each hand. He didn't seem happy to be narrowing the space between them, but he did seem determined to be civil. Abigail pressed her hands to the hood of the car and readied herself to do the same.

"Eli says we gotta get rid of that car," he said, skipping right over the regular niceties of hello or good morning.

Abigail's brow creased in confusion. "Excuse me?"

"The Kia," Tyler indicated, tipping one of the mugs toward her rental car. Abigail saw the steaming coffee inside nearly slosh out, and her mouth began to water.

"But I need a car," Abigail said.

"According to my infinitely wise uncle, rentals are too expensive. Besides, he really only uses his car on Sundays. He says you can borrow his if you need to go anywhere, and when the summer is over, he'll drive you back to Westphalia to get another rental."

"When the summer's over? I don't know if I'm planning on sticking around that long."

"Whatever you do, don't tell my uncle that," Tyler warned her.

Abigail was speechless. She stared at Tyler, trying to come up with a reason to keep her car. So what if the rental was expensive? Her annual salary was more than enough to cover a few weeks of renting the silly compact she was currently sitting on. But she couldn't tell Tyler that. *In my real life I'm an accountant. Don't worry about me.* Just the thought made a genuine smile tickle at the corners of her lips.

When Abigail smiled, something in Tyler's demeanor changed. His face loosened somehow, and his gaze slid away from her face to take in the rest of her. She was suddenly and mortifyingly self-conscious. Her running shorts were almost covered by the thin sweatshirt she had tossed on before leaving the trailer, and her bare legs and feet seemed on display as she perched on the hood of the orange car. Tyler didn't seem to mind. Though he wasn't leering, Abigail could easily read the appreciative slant in his eyes.

Feeling exposed, she raised a timid hand to play with the damp curls at the nape of her neck and watched as Tyler's gaze followed the arc of her arm. Abigail's heart thudded. She was practically half-dressed and still damp from the shower. It was obvious that Tyler found her early morning look sexy.

But that was what she wanted! Abigail had to remind herself that if getting close to Tyler was the objective, this was the best possible way to do it. And while she imagined that because Tyler had loved Hailey, Abigail herself would be the farthest thing from his type, it seemed that she wasn't going to have a problem securing his attraction. Working hard to stifle her feelings, Abigail pulled her legs beneath her and circled her fingers around her ankle. She bit her bottom lip and hoped she looked coy, not afraid.

"Okay," she said finally. "I could . . . I could use the extra money."

"Good." Tyler seemed relieved that they were more or less getting along. He took a step toward the car and splashed hot coffee on his hand. Biting off a mumbled profanity, he grinned at Abigail and handed her the clean mug. "Look out—it's scalding."

"Thanks." Abigail took the proffered coffee in both hands and inhaled the slightly bitter scent. "I've been craving a cup."

Judging by the glint in his eye, this pleased Tyler

immensely. "Enjoy it," he told her, wiping his coffee-splattered hand on his jeans. "And be ready in half an hour—we're taking that car to Westphalia this morning."

"B-but," Abigail stammered, trying to think of a way out, "I have to return it to the same rental car agency."

"You will. There's a depot there."

"But how did . . . ?" Abigail didn't even have to finish her question.

Tyler indicated a gaudy bumper sticker on the Kia's fender that broadcast the company logo, then tapped his temple with two fingers. "Brains run in the family," he joked.

Abigail was effectively stuck. She could see no apparent way out of this little road trip with Tyler. Eli was at church, the winery was closed, and she had no believable excuse. Taking a sip of coffee to buy a few extra seconds, Abigail realized that though she didn't want to be alone with Tyler, maybe this scenario would prove to be advantageous. *Providential,* she thought, the word unexpectedly cut loose from some forgotten corner of her mind.

"How far is it to Westphalia?" she asked.

"About an hour straight north. I'll drive my truck and you can follow me in the Kia." Tyler winked in the infuriating, playful way that was beginning to drive her crazy. "Tell you what: I'll even give you a lift back to Thompson Hills."

"How gentlemanly of you." Abigail rolled her eyes.

But Tyler wasn't deterred in the least. Laughing, he watched her take another drink of coffee. "And just so you know, bringing the car back was Eli's idea. But the coffee was mine."

Abigail didn't have a chance to acknowledge his apparent thoughtfulness or the allusion to her accusation of the day before. The second the words were out of his mouth, Tyler saluted her with his mug and took off, calling to her as he walked away, "Half an hour!"

Abigail changed clothes quickly, tangling herself in three different outfits before she settled on a pair of jean shorts and a simple cotton shirt. Her tiny closet contained only a handful of dressy outfits and even less that could be considered casual, so she didn't have much to choose from. Something told Abigail that trying too hard would give Tyler the wrong impression, but she also didn't want to slob out completely and kill any mild interest that he had in her. It was a delicate balance to walk, and Abigail fought to suppress the way her stomach churned when she thought about what she was doing. The only way to survive the coming weeks, she decided, was to put on her identity like a costume, to become a different woman—a woman who was strong and capable and smart. A woman much like the girl she used to be.

The road to Westphalia curved gently along the

lake, but Abigail couldn't enjoy it because she was so focused on the muddy tailgate of the Toyota Tacoma in front of her. Tyler drove fast, making the cab of his truck tip on the corners and causing dried chunks of dirt and grass to spin off his tires in unpredictable bursts that exploded on Abigail's car. It annoyed her so much that she wondered if she'd be able to be polite and charming on the way home. If it wasn't for her intention to get to know Tyler better, Abigail would have given him a piece of her mind the second she hopped out of the Kia and then paid a taxi to drive her home.

When they finally arrived in Westphalia after well over an hour of driving, Abigail followed Tyler down side streets and through the touristy district of the small city until he pulled up in front of a rental car depot. It was one large building with at least five different companies listed on the sign, including the agency Abigail had booked her car through. However, the windows of the office were dark and the parking lot seemed abandoned.

"Looks like they're closed on Sundays!" Tyler yelled. His truck was still running, but he had opened the window to lean out and shrug innocently at Abigail.

Irritated, she ignored him and drove right up to the office, looking for a night box or instructions on how to return a car after hours. There was a metal mailbox near the front door with a narrow slot just big enough for a packet containing the rental agreement and a set of keys. Abigail had contracted the car for three weeks, so she found a pen in her purse and jotted a note explaining that she didn't need it anymore. She included her contact information in Florida as well as her cell number, then drove to an empty parking spot right near the door. Writing the stall number in bold strokes across the front of the packet, Abigail stepped out of the car and locked it. She dropped everything in the box and made her way to where Tyler was waiting.

"You're just gonna leave it?" he questioned her.

"What would you have me do?" Abigail climbed into the cab of his pickup, trying to hide her reluctance. "We drove all this way. Besides, people drop off rental cars after hours all the time."

"They might charge you for it."

"They absolutely will." Abigail stifled a sigh and stared stoically out of Tyler's windshield. She didn't care a bit about the money; it was Tyler who was making her weary.

But Tyler didn't pull away from the curb once Abigail was settled inside the truck. She became aware that he was staring at her, and though she hesitated to do so, she turned toward him with what she hoped was a believable smile. "What?"

"Have you had breakfast?"

Abigail glanced at the digital clock on his dashboard. "It's almost noon."

"Well then, have you had lunch?"

He knew the answer to the question, and she knew exactly where this conversation was going. "No," she said.

"Can you stomach hot dogs?"

Abigail wrinkled her nose in confusion.

"Not everyone likes hot dogs, but I'll take that as a yes." Tyler swung a wide U-turn in the middle of the empty street and headed east toward the lake. "A quick snack on the beach before we head back to Revell," he explained.

Tyler turned his attention to the road, and the cab filled slowly with the sort of suffocating silence that made Abigail's chest clench. It was too hard to sit with Tyler beside her and let the stillness conjure demons that she didn't want to face. She was shocked to find that for some unfathomable reason, she wanted to talk about Hailey. Tyler knew her—this smug, self-satisfied man sitting beside her knew the beautiful girl who existed now only in Abigail's already-fading memory. Abigail wanted to press him, to make him tell her things about her sister that she hadn't taken the time to learn when she was alive. Her name was on the tip of Abigail's tongue, but the taste was sharp as acid. It stung.

Frantic to fill the quiet void and banish thoughts of Hailey, Abigail clutched at the first thing that came to mind. She held on tight and let the present pull her sharply from the past. "Does it bother Eli that you didn't go to church with him this morning?"

"Nah, he doesn't care what I do with my Sundays. He just doesn't want the winery open."

"Doesn't that hurt business?"

"Sure it does, but Eli doesn't care. Thompson Hills is a relatively small operation, and Eli has no desire to expand it."

Abigail did not ask why Eli wasn't motivated by the all-too-familiar concept of bigger equals better. Her boss struck her as a rather simple, uncomplicated man. It made sense to her that he balked at the idea of changing anything. In a way, she admired him for it.

"You're cleaning barrels these days, aren't you?" Tyler asked.

"Yeah. Messy job."

"Well, our storage bins are nothing compared to what the big wineries use. Their barrels are steel or even plastic, and they hold so many liters you have to climb inside to wash them out by hand. Then they have these little sprinklers that you set in the tank to disinfect it with a special cleaning solution. Our small operation is kind of homespun in comparison." Tyler shook his head as if he didn't quite understand. But then he laughed and said, "Eli likes things just the way they are. He wants to be involved in every part of his winery."

Abigail nodded, watching the intermittent traffic through the fractured veins intersecting the pickup's cracked windshield.

Tyler glanced at her before looking both ways

and coasting through a stop sign. "My uncle likes things uncomplicated. Straightforward."

Something in Tyler's voice made Abigail turn. He was finally giving the road his full attention, and she was free to just take him in. Abigail didn't have to wonder why Hailey had found him so attractive. Tyler was gorgeous. And though she hated to admit it, he stirred up so many emotions in her she didn't know how to begin to unknot them. Fear, uncertainty, and anger were the most prominent threads, but here and now, sitting so close to him as a secret little smile pulled on his lips, Abigail felt something else rising in her. It was buoyant somehow, a sort of dizzying vertigo that filled her head and pressed against the backs of her eyes as she stared over the edge of something that she didn't understand.

"Are you like your uncle?" Abigail asked slowly.

"Nope," Tyler replied, still staring straight ahead. But then he grinned, and Abigail whipped her head back to the road as if she had been caught in the act of doing something wrong.

Tyler ignored her obvious discomfort and put his hand on the seat between them. He snaked his fingers toward her legs and stopped mere inches from the curve of her thigh, then picked at what looked like a cigarette burn in the charcoal fabric. There was a suggestive undercurrent in his voice when he said, "I tend to like my life much more messy."

Hailey managed to stay relatively mess-free for almost a year after her confirmation. Or so it seemed to everyone around her.

She transitioned to high school rather well and managed to channel much of her energy into the healthy outlets of soccer in the fall, basketball throughout the winter, and softball when spring rains thawed the ground. The medications were second nature and the appointments with Dr. Madsen were habitual, but from the outside looking in, they seemed to be a far cry from the colossal experiences that they had been in years past.

Everyone in the Bennett house fell gratefully into their prescribed roles for this new chapter of their lives. Especially Lou. He had partially retired years earlier, but when Hailey entered high school and found her identity as an all-around athlete, he finally sold his gaudy pickup and signed over the rights to his Handy Lou logo and the memorable phone number. Melody cried a little over the end of an era, but Lou was elated. For the first time in his life, the handyman became the full-time and fully devoted father of a seemingly whole and healthy daughter. He didn't miss a single one of Hailey's games.

Abby missed most of them. Her daydreams of post–high school autonomy evolved into a daily reality, and she was not about to give it up. With her sister on the right track at last, Abby could hour by hour and day by day untangle herself from her stifling familial role. And that's exactly what she did.

Hailey went to confession once a week. Abby stopped going to church. Hailey spent her weekends in uniform, sweating out her aggressions on a field or a court. Abby loosened up for one of the first times in her life and spent her Fridays playing pool with a short parade of different boyfriends—most of them didn't know how to play pool, but they did know how to kiss. Hailey shifted into the role of a good daughter, and Abby happily took her place on the outskirts.

It wasn't that Abby was particularly bad or that Hailey became a saint overnight, but Lou and Melody transferred the source of their worry from younger daughter to older. In truth, it was a welcome transition. Abby's young adult blunders were so normal, so blessedly average and ordinary, that when Abby routinely slipped into the house after 2 a.m. on weekend nights, Melody only rolled over in her sleep, half-annoyed but mostly thankful to know that her daughter was finally home. Lou didn't even stir.

I should have gone to Florida, Abby thought on a dozen occasions. *Hailey would have been just fine without me.*

But by the spring of Hailey's freshman year, Abby knew that peace had been an illusion. She knew that Hailey would not have been just fine without her. Not at all.

The first time she caught a glimpse of the old Hailey, the frantic young woman who had all but disappeared after her last suicide attempt and her older sister's compulsory decision to stay in Newcastle, it filled Abby with such a fast-bleeding dread it stunned her. Abby felt as if she were perched on the peak of a mountain, looking down at the depths that were to come with a mixture of raw fear and bottomless loathing. Somehow the continual uphill climb of months past had caused her to forget how far they had come, how far Hailey had come. It was a long way down.

It was the weekend after Hailey's fifteenth birthday when Abby first doubted that her sister was as steady, healthy, and well as she seemed to be. Hailey's newfound stability had caused her parents to relax their anxious hold on her, and they didn't stop to question anything when their youngest daughter asked permission to attend a small get-together at a friend's house. She was smart enough not to call it a party, and since Lou and Melody had never had trouble with an adolescent Abby, they didn't think to ask.

Abby was oblivious about the arrangement. She didn't see her sister leave the house early or come home late. She didn't make a mental note of the way Hailey's tank top dipped dangerously low beneath a gray hoodie that could easily be discarded the moment she walked out the door. But when Abby herself crept home well past midnight and tiptoed to the bathroom to brush her teeth and get ready for bed, she almost tripped over Hailey huddled in the darkness.

"What in the . . . ?" Abby muttered, stumbling headlong into a warm body crouched in the pitch-black bathroom. Her heart leaped into her throat, and although she couldn't utter another word, she automatically edged the door closed with her hip and flicked on the bathroom light.

Hailey was rising from the floor, one hand over her mouth and a wicked grin glinting in the narrow slits of her squinted eyes. Without looking away from Abby, she reached over and flushed the toilet. The lid was down and Abby couldn't see anything in the porcelain bowl, but an unmistakable acrid scent hung in the air.

"Are you okay?" Abby asked in confusion. The lump in her throat made her whisper barely audible. "You scared me half to death."

Nodding, Hailey turned on the tap and swung the handle all the way to the right, as cold as it would go. "I'm fine," she said. And then she began to giggle.

All at once, Abby knew why Hailey was sneaking around the bathroom in the middle of the night, why the room smelled sickly sweet, why Hailey seemed to teeter from heel to toe and back again. She was close enough to touch, and Abby grabbed her shoulders, ignoring the running faucet and spinning her sister around in one firm movement.

"What have you done?" Abby growled.

Water dripped from Hailey's hands and formed droplets on the wet skin of her lovely face. She giggled again and blinked water from her eyes. "Hey," she moaned, drawing out the word. "Hey, come on. Cool it."

Alcohol was rife on Hailey's breath, and Abby pushed her away in disgust. But she didn't leave. Blocking the door with her body, Abby crossed her arms in front of her and confronted her sister. "You're insane. Dad is going to skin you alive."

Hailey leaned over the sink again, splashing her face with abandon and splattering the mirror. "Uh-uh," she hummed in a singsong voice that was just a smidge too loud to ensure the rest of the house would remain asleep.

Abby turned off the tap with a yank. Throwing a hand towel at Hailey, she whispered, "Be quiet, you idiot. You'll wake them up."

"Dad was awake when I got home," Hailey said, her voice muffled by the towel but still too loud. She dropped her hands from her face and fixed Abby with a disbelieving look. *"He didn't even know."*

He knew, Abby thought. *He just didn't want to face it.* To Hailey she said, "What in the world do you think you're doing?"

"Having fun."

"You're fifteen."

"I feel eighteen," Hailey shot back. She put a hand on her slim waist and struck a pose far too seductive for her young age.

"I don't care what you feel like." Abby gripped Hailey's chin in her hand and said, "You're sleeping in my room tonight. This is not over."

Hailey put a finger to her lips and widened her eyes conspiratorially. "Like a secret sleepover," she slurred.

"No, not like a secret sleepover. You're sleeping on the floor. And when you sober up, I'm going to strangle you."

Hailey didn't throw up again that night, but she did more or less pass out on the floor the moment Abby dropped her there. Abby didn't even bother to get her a pillow; she figured the hard floor and scratchy carpet were a just consequence for coming home drunk. Though an uncomfortable night and a stiff morning were only the beginning of what Abby had in store for her.

Abby heard her parents get up around seven thirty the next morning, and she dragged herself out of bed so that she could cover for Hailey. Her actions seemed sisterly, but she was really trying to preserve the situation so she could handle it on her own. Abby knew that if her parents learned what Hailey had been up to the night before, Lou would defend his baby and Melody would just cry.

They'd worry and fret, then sweep everything under the rug like they always did. Abby wasn't about to let that happen this time. Not when so much calm and constancy hung in the balance. And certainly not when she had forfeited her own future, her own dream of freedom and Florida to stay home and safeguard her sister from this exact sort of thing.

Lou and Melody bought Abby's story about Hailey feeling ill in the middle of the night because they wanted to. Melody even made a tray for Hailey: a piece of buttered toast, a few dry crackers, and a small glass of 7UP that she let stand on the counter until it was room temperature and the bubbles were gone.

"Should I bring it to her?" Melody asked, lifting the tray from the counter and seeking permission from Abby with her eyes.

"No. She's still sleeping. Let her sleep."

Melody lowered the tray slowly, letting her fingers linger against the edges as if she were imparting a blessing over the food. "Let her sleep," she echoed.

After breakfast, Lou and Melody took off to the grocery store, and Abby mounted the stairs to wake the hungover Hailey. But before she left the kitchen, she threw Melody's lovingly prepared sour-stomach breakfast in the garbage and poured the pop down the sink. No free handouts. Not this time.

Stomping down the short second-floor hallway, Abby banged her bedroom door open and flicked on the lights. "Wake up, Sleeping Beauty," she called, her voice thick with irony. Then she pulled the curtains open and flopped down on her bed, throwing a pillow at Hailey's prostrate form. When she didn't move, Abby gave her back a little nudge with her pointed toe.

Hailey groaned and rolled into a fetal position, grabbing her head in her hands. "I have a headache."

"I'm sure you do. Too bad. Get up."

"No," Hailey complained. "You can't make me."

That was enough to annihilate Abby's short fuse. Bending over, she gripped her sister under the arms and heaved her into a sitting position. "Get up," she commanded again.

Rubbing her face and glaring at Abby, Hailey scooted away from the bed until her back was against the wall. She slouched there and glowered at Abby with swollen eyes. "What's your problem?"

"You," Abby spat out cruelly. But Hailey cut such a pathetic form huddled in the corner that she regretted the insult immediately. Her anger leveled out a bit, and she sank to the floor so she could walk on her knees to Hailey. "What are you doing?" she asked, so desperate and furious her voice cracked.

"What do you mean?" Hailey drew into the corner a little more.

"You know exactly what I mean. You've had such a great year. Why would you chance ruining it?"

"By drinking?" Hailey asked as if she still didn't understand.

Abby threw her arms up in exasperation. "Yes, by drinking." And then she caught sight of a small bruise at the nape of Hailey's neck. Reaching over, she yanked down the collar of Hailey's pink pajamas and gaped. "You have a hickey?" she demanded in an entirely different decibel.

"Chill out." Hailey pushed Abby's hand away and realigned her pajamas to cover the mark. "It's no big deal."

"No big deal? *No big deal?*" Abby hurled herself to her feet so she could pace the room. "Do you have any idea what you're doing?"

"Having fun?"

"No!" Abby yelled, spinning around. "You're ruining everything! Again!" Her words hung heavy in the air.

Hailey stared at Abby in shock, her look betraying that her worst fears had just been confirmed. Cracks appeared in her tough exterior, and she quickly closed her eyes before Abby could see the damage that she had done.

"Hailey," Abby started, "I shouldn't have said that. I didn't mean it."

"Yes, you did," Hailey whispered.

"No, I didn't. I'm just angry—"

"You don't understand."

Abby towered over her sister, but she didn't dare sit down. "What don't I understand?"

Hailey paused.

Though she had to fight the urge to keep talking, Abby waited. She examined the jagged line of the part on Hailey's head and traced it back and forth, back and forth. She noticed the tangles, the stringy clumps of hair that needed hot water and a good shampoo. The peculiar jumble of Hailey's reticence and this small, mundane sign of her basic need troubled Abby. She wished she could give her little sister one do-over. One chance to go back and make the right decision the second time around.

"What don't I understand?" Abby prodded.

"It's too hard," Hailey said suddenly. "I can't do this. I can't pretend. I can't hold it in. I know you all want me to be good—"

"You *are* good," Abby interrupted.

"Shut up!" Hailey scowled at Abby. "You all want me to be good and I just *can't*. Sometimes I just get so angry . . . and so sad. . . ."

Abby waited a few breaths before lowering herself carefully to the floor. "But you've been doing so well," she said, trying to urge Hailey on.

"No, I haven't."

"Yes, you have. You've had such a great year. You're on all those teams . . . and you got confirmed last fall. You even go to confession. Not many people do that."

"Not many people have to."

Abby didn't know what to say. The sisters sat in silence for a while, Hailey hugging her knees and Abby inexplicably wanting to hug Hailey, even though only minutes before she had wanted to throttle her.

"Help me understand," Abby finally said. "I want to understand."

Hailey met her gaze and looked deep, apparently probing her to see if she truly meant what she said and if she could handle it. She seemed more or less satisfied, but before she began to talk, she laid her cheek on her knees and looked away from Abby.

"The meds help," she started, staring at the wall. "So does soccer. And basketball, but softball is a bore. I hate it. I only do it because Dad likes to watch me play."

"See," Abby ribbed gently, "you are good."

Hailey ignored her. "But what I *do* and the way I *feel* are usually two very different things." She grappled for the right words.

"Yeah," Abby murmured, hoping it was enough encouragement for Hailey to go on.

"Sometimes I feel this weight on my heart—like, I can physically feel it—and it's so heavy I'm surprised that I can even sit up. And sometimes I just . . . I just want to hurt someone." Hailey swallowed so hard Abby could hear it. "I want to hurt myself."

No, no, no, Abby screamed wordlessly. *Not this again!* But she tried to keep her face neutral, tried

288

to keep listening instead of analyzing so Hailey would continue to talk.

When Abby didn't say anything, Hailey went on. "But then there are times I feel good, too. Like when we almost went to state for basketball, I was high for a week. I thought I could win all those games by myself if they'd just get everyone else off the court."

"So you cling to those times," Abby said, unable to contain herself anymore. It was so black-and-white to her, so easy to determine the cause of the problem and then root it out. Why couldn't Hailey kick this thing? Why couldn't Hailey just be normal?

"It's not like that." Hailey cupped her head and whimpered. "My head hurts so bad."

"Then don't ever do this again."

"It was worth it."

Abby blinked, wondering if she had heard right. "Excuse me?"

"I said, it was worth it." Hailey pierced Abby with a look so severe it stung.

"Why?"

"Because it stopped the itching for a little while."

For some reason this scared Abby more than anything she had heard so far, and it was with serious trepidation that she questioned, "Hailey, honey, what do you mean?"

"I itch," Hailey whispered.

The moment of silence when Hailey closed her perfect lips was so tangible, so full and weighted that Abby felt it pressing against her, pushing her down.

"Like, I feel like I'm going crazy, you know, but I don't want anybody else to know that I feel this way. And I just . . . I just have to do something about it." Hailey's voice dropped even lower. "I have to scratch it."

Abby didn't even have to ask.

Without any explanation, without any attempt to prepare her sister, Hailey stretched out her legs and lifted her shirt with trembling hands. The beautiful skin of her shapely legs was perfect; the clean lines of her fine arms were unmarked. But beneath the thin T-shirt she slept in, Hailey's skin was intersected with crisscrossing lines and gouges, shallow cuts and cherry-colored scratches that were as horrifying as they were gruesome.

It could not have hit Abby any harder if Hailey slapped her full in the face. She doubled over, instantly sickened and terrified of the woman-child before her. The girl she didn't know.

"It stopped the itching," Hailey said again. "When I drank and when he kissed me . . . I loved it."

Abby made her own appointment to see Dr. Madsen. She showed up at his office ready to lambaste him for missing the signs, for not realizing that Hailey wasn't doing well at all—that the troubled girl was just doing everything in her power to contain herself, with unacceptably dire consequences.

But rather than becoming defensive like Abby anticipated, when Dr. Madsen heard what Abby had to tell him, his shoulders fell and he buried his face in his hands. For a moment, Abby was sure he was crying. Then he looked up, and Abby could see that while he wasn't shedding any tears, his soul was wracked with the misery wrought by his oversight. By his inability, after all these years, to truly know Hailey.

"She's a very good liar," he said quietly.

"I think we've all become quite adept," Abby agreed.

When Dr. Madsen informed Abby that he had no choice but to tell Lou and Melody, she knew it was the right thing to do, even though she didn't want to disrupt their happy reverie. But even more than she feared her parents' reaction, she worried about Hailey's. She was sure Hailey would hate her and that their relationship would go through yet another nearly fatal trauma. However, now that Abby had told Dr. Madsen, the decision was out of her hands. Besides, the desire to see Hailey whole and healthy outweighed Abby's concern over her sister's reaction.

Within the week, Lou and Melody knew, and Hailey was admitted to Sacred Heart Hospital, an hour's drive from Newcastle. It was amazing to Abby that Hailey went willingly—she didn't say much, but then again, she didn't go off the deep end either. Abby took that as a very good sign. A hopeful sign.

Hailey was in the pediatric psychiatric ward at Sacred Heart for five days. In the end, her team evaluation unearthed a new diagnosis entirely. She was not merely ADHD or depressed or even a combination of the two. The final verdict: bipolar disorder NOS (not otherwise specified). Hailey could have had bipolar I or II, or cyclothymia, but since her symptoms were somewhat unclear, it seemed best to lump her in the unspecified category and wait for further evidence to emerge.

Lou and Melody treated the diagnosis like the worst-case scenario, but Abby was encouraged that bipolar disorder seemed slightly less threatening than some of the other possibilities the doctors were exploring.

"At least we're not talking about borderline personality disorder," Abby said, her voice unnecessarily low in the empty hospital hallway. Just the name sounded ominous and she stifled a little chill.

"Or schizophrenia," Melody added. She tucked her bottom lip beneath her teeth for a moment. "What exactly is schizophrenia again?"

"It doesn't matter." Lou glowered at them both, seemingly indignant that his wife and daughter could even entertain thoughts of Hailey's diagnosis being less devastating than he imagined it. "Neither of those disorders can be accurately diagnosed until she's older anyway. We won't know anything for sure until she's nearly thirty."

"We know that she's our daughter, Lou. We know that they are doing everything they can to help her."

"She has a severe form of bipolar disorder," he stated, assigning each word the gravity of a death sentence.

"There's a lot they can do," Abby insisted, refusing to let him sulk. "There are many manifestations of the syndrome that she doesn't exhibit."

"She's not violent," Melody joined in, but her voice broke over the words.

Abby watched a tear slide down her mother's cheek, and she was seized with a longing to wipe it away. But the act felt too intimate, too close, so Abby had to content herself with reaching for Melody's small hand. When she did, the older woman bridged the distance and, tangling Abby's fingers in her own, held on for dear life.

"Her rages are controllable," Abby said, squeezing her mother's hand.

"Psychotic mania," Lou reiterated. "Acute depression. Don't you understand what that means? Don't you get it?"

Though Abby wanted to scream at him for being so negative and cynical, she also couldn't help but hope that his pessimism was nothing more than a high wall that he could hide behind. "We're going to be okay," she whispered. Then she held out her other hand, and after a long moment, Lou took it.

Melody took a step in, and so did Abby. When Lou didn't move to meet them, they shuffled forward again. Melody let her forehead rest on Lou's chest, and Abby let her cheek fall against her mother's shoulder. They bent together, the three of them, a tiny fortress in the middle of a storm.

Abby stood like stone and took it all in: the feel of her parents' hands in hers, the proximity of their bodies, the sigh of their breath in a tumbling rhythm of quiet song. There was a meditative quality to their closeness, as if they could corporately will Hailey better. Abby didn't want it to end, but suddenly Lou pulled away in one firm, decisive motion and dug in his coat pocket.

Producing a tin, he held it out and asked, "Gum?" The spell was broken.

Hailey left the hospital with a whole new batch of medications. In addition to her antidepressants and stimulants, a mood stabilizer was added to level everything out, and a strict regimen of psychotherapy and cognitive behavioral therapy joined her weekly routine. Even Lou and Melody had a role to play. Dr. Madsen spent time with them explaining therapeutic parenting and even suggested that the entire family join a multifamily support group. Or maybe start one since there wasn't a group within a two-hundred mile radius of Newcastle.

During the entire process Abby doted on her sister. She loved her with all the energy and enthusiasm her battered heart would allow, and then she made room for her family to begin the process of working through their altered life. It was promising to see Lou and Melody take their daughter's illness seriously once they got over the initial shock of the charade that Hailey had been pulling off so admirably. In some ways it seemed like now that they had a specific task to set their hands to, they were more than willing to dig in up to their elbows and get dirty. There seemed to be a light at the end of the tunnel.

And as Hailey's mother and father took over their respective roles, Abby did what she had been waiting years to do: she left.

When the school year ended and summer stretched before them—full of promise now that Hailey's illness had a name and her medications were finally balanced—Abby resurrected her South Seminole brochures and reapplied. This time, she didn't tell a soul.

Of course, everyone instinctively knew what she was doing, but no one mentioned it. There was a shift in the air, a significance to everything Abby did in her final months at home that it was impossible not to realize that life as the Bennetts knew it was about to change. But Abby maintained her silence and so did everyone else. It wasn't until two weeks before Abby was scheduled to board a plane for Florida that Hailey sought out her older sister to say, "It's okay."

Abby knew exactly what she meant.

At Hailey's request, the day before she left for Florida Abby accompanied her sister to confession. It was the only thing Hailey requested of her, the only small sacrifice she petitioned for even though she knew that Abby would have granted her a wish of far greater proportions.

Though nobody really went to confession anymore, Hailey had attached herself to the ritual as if it could single-handedly assure her salvation. It became a weekly habit for her, an act of penance that held the power to erase anything and everything that had happened in the days between. Abby found it archaic and depressing, but Hailey seemed so fixated on the idea of taking her along that Abby couldn't find it in her heart to say no.

The day of the sisters' communal confession dawned warm and still, the sort of perfect late summer morning that hinted of the temperate autumn to come. It broke Abby's heart somehow— the perfect, clean scent of the air, the way the light filtered through the leaves in fleeting blessing, the soft pad of Hailey's feet as her flip-flops slapped the cracked cement sidewalk. Everything seemed intentionally staged to punish her for leaving. It was as if the whole world were rebuking her for this act of abandonment. And it was with a sober, heavy guilt burdening her soul that Abby fell in step behind Hailey and watched her narrow frame part the lovely day as she walked toward the white-washed church.

Abby was well behind Hailey by the time the fine girl floated waiflike up the wide steps of St. Mary's and disappeared into the church like the reincarnation of one of the saints. Abby followed, sickhearted and brick-footed, but prepared in her own doubting way to say the words that she was furiously trying to make herself feel. *Father, forgive me, for I have sinned. . . .* Then what? Where did her list of transgressions begin and end? How could she do penance for things that she wasn't convinced were wrong?

The holy water was lukewarm, and Abby thought the bowl was empty until she lifted her hand and saw droplets at the tips of her fingers. She made the sign of the cross instinctively, touching her T-shirt over her heart and leaving a wet imprint with her middle finger, a mark at the center of her chest as if to say: *Here. It is here.* But Abby felt as if the quickly disappearing indication was wrong: her heart existed in many more places than simply the cavity behind her arching rib bones.

Abby pulled back when they were inside the sanctuary, hemmed in by rows of straight-backed pews and pinned beneath the sorrowful stare of the crucified Christ. She motioned Hailey forward and sank onto the last bench, afraid to let her back rest against the smooth wood. *What am I doing here?* Abby thought, avoiding the tear-streaked face of the Savior behind the ornate pulpit. Of course, the sad, brown eyes of Jesus were cast heavenward; she didn't have to meet them to address the accusation she was sure she would find there, but Abby couldn't bring herself to look at the statue at all.

Instead, she thought of Hailey. She focused on her broken skin, the cuts that lined her silky abdomen with scars that testified to the turmoil in her damaged mind. Abby imagined what her sister was saying to the indistinct outline of Father Timothy as she knelt on the padded bench beneath his soft profile in silhouette. *I've betrayed myself. I lust after something, anything that will make me forget. I'm filled with wrath about my illness.*

Abby could understand the wrath. She felt it acutely herself.

When Hailey finally stepped out of the confessional booth, fingering her pretty rosary and training her eyes on the floor, Abby slid to her knees as if in prayer. "I'm sorry," she whispered, because she knew even then that she would not follow her sister's lead. She could not bring herself to partake in the simple act of faith that the confessional represented. Forgiveness first required a contrite heart.

Hailey knelt at the altar, head thrown back so she could search the face of the statue that Abby worked so hard to avoid. Her long, blonde hair was in a ponytail, a white flame of dedication that matched the blue gold burning of the candles before her. Abby thought her so beautiful in that moment, such a pure and lovely pilgrim that she could have wept for the sight of her young sister rapt in devotion.

Minutes later—it could have been hours—Hailey rose, her face approaching a sort of provisional peace and her eyes wide and bright. She walked purposefully to where Abby sat.

"I'm done," Abby said quietly before Hailey could encourage her to step behind the dim curtain and say things she didn't want to say. She stood and walked to the back of the church, ignoring Hailey's confused look and shoving her way out of the carved, wooden door before anything could stop her.

"Abby—"

"You know," Abby interrupted before Hailey could continue, "I think I'm going to go by Abigail from now on. What do you think?"

Hailey just stared at her.

"I think a new life deserves a new name."

Hailey still didn't say anything, and they walked the few blocks home in complete silence.

As they navigated the fractured sidewalks of Newcastle, Abby tried on her new name like a mantle. *Abigail.* It was perfect. Not only did it sound older and more sophisticated, Abby also remembered from her mother's research that some argued there was no saint Abigail. Her namesake, the beautiful, clever wife of Nabal, was considered for canonization but ultimately overlooked by many because although she was spiritually astute, Abigail was ultimately selfish. Sure, her quick thinking and skillful negotiation kept King David from taking vengeance on her husband and eventually made her the wife of that same king, but her motivations seemed based on self-preservation. Above all, she acted in her own best interest.

Abigail Bennett could relate.

CR At some point I gave up trying to comfort Lou and went to get the nurse. I had told her what happened before I went in to see him, and she was prepared for the worst. Without a word, she brought him a tiny pill in what looked to me like a mini muffin cup. Candy, I thought. They make it look like candy so it's easier to swallow. Somehow that made it harder for me to swallow.

Lou was equally unimpressed with her efforts. At first he batted her hand away and growled fiercely, though I knew he was simply incapable of articulating everything he felt. I almost told her to forget it. I'd stay with him: I'd mourn with him and calm him down on my own. But that was impossible. He didn't even want me here.

"Dad," I coaxed, "take the pill. It will make you sleep."

He turned his head from us and buried his face in his hands.

"Dad," I said, firmer this time, "if you don't take the pill, they're going to have to inject you with something."

My father has always been a man's man, but he has never been a needle man. When I mentioned an injection, he stiffened. The nurse held out the pill again and this time he took it. With obvious reluctance, he tipped it in his mouth but refused the water she offered. He struggled to swallow for a moment and tilted his head back as if that would help. I watched a tear slide into his ear.

The nurse moved toward me as if she intended to fold me in a quick, supportive hug. But she stopped short, lifting her arms awkwardly and giving me a sympathetic look and a helpless shrug instead. Then she shuffled away with an apologetic air, leaving me alone again with Lou.

He was curled on his side now, facing away from me with his hand across his face so I could only see the chrysalis of his ear. I spoke softly, afraid of damaging that exposed organ, so bare and vulnerable to hearing things that could wound so deeply. "I'm going now. If you need me for anything, the nurses have my cell number. I can . . . I can be here in no time. Okay? Dad, okay?"

Lou didn't say anything. He didn't make any indication at all that he had heard me.

Should I tell him that they were going to do an autopsy? That it was standard procedure for suicides? As quickly as the thought entered my mind, I dismissed it. Lou did not need to know that Hailey would be cut, that she would be more or less filleted on a slab of cold, hard metal. The thought was so stark, so staggering, I grabbed the rail of Lou's bed to steady myself.

"We'll have to . . . to figure out . . ." I couldn't finish. He didn't want to hear about funeral arrangements. He didn't want to hear about the

responsibilities that had been thrown on us—on me. "I can't do it," I whispered.

Lou gave no signal that he had heard me.

Giving up, I leaned over to kiss the spot where his cheek would have been if it weren't covered with his hand. His knuckles looked soft; his veins were thick and protruding like intersecting rivers bursting their banks beneath the thin film of his skin. I kissed my fingers and pressed them to the spot.

"Bye, Dad. I'll be back soon." My heels clicked all the way to the door, but when I reached the threshold, I stopped. I turned and watched him for signs of life, but he didn't move.

XI

ᘛ ABIGAIL TRIED TO keep her new living arrangement a secret, but by the time the staff of Thompson Hills gathered for their traditional Monday morning breakfast, everyone seemed to know.

"You're living with Eli?" Paige asked, shock and disbelief widening her already-large eyes to alarming proportions.

"No," Abigail choked out emphatically. "I am *not* living with Eli. There's a trailer on his property that he's letting me crash in for a while."

Paige raised a quizzical eyebrow but didn't say another word.

Abigail sighed. She knew there would be questions about her sudden appearance in Revell, but she didn't relish the lies she would have to tell in order to preserve her relative anonymity. Mostly she knew from past experience that constructing a tower of lies was much like building a castle of cards—one false move, one poorly timed twitch and everything came crashing down. Abigail didn't feel capable of maintaining such a complex pretense. A part of her had hoped that everyone would just accept her presence and leave it at that.

"I came to the Summerlands on a whim," Abigail finally admitted. "When I got here, I didn't have a place to stay, so Eli offered me the trailer and I took it."

"You're crazy," Paige said with a crooked smile. "You couldn't pay me to stay with Eli."

"I'm not staying with Eli!"

"In his trailer, whatever. You know what I mean. Don't get all defensive, eh?"

"I'm not defensive."

Paige took a large bite of the rubbery egg casserole that was posing as breakfast. "So where are you from?"

"Minnesota," Abigail said. At least that wasn't a lie. It wasn't quite the whole truth, but Abigail figured the penance for such a tiny fib was next to nothing.

"What in the world brought you up here?"

"Family matters." Abigail bit her lip. Another perfect but incomplete truth.

"Preach it, sister. That's why I'm here, too. Grew up in Vancouver, but it's too rainy and way too close to my stepmom for my liking." Paige forked another bite but stopped before putting it in her mouth. Discarding it on her plate, she said loudly, "The guys should be banned from cooking forever."

There were cheers and murmurs of assent around the table.

"We don't want to cook anyway!" someone yelled.

Paige rolled her eyes and shoved her plate away

from her with a grunt. "How old are you?" she asked Abigail.

Abigail laughed. "That was out of the blue. How old are *you*?"

"Twenty-three. I'm one of the youngest here."

"Twenty-nine," Abigail said, matching disclosure for disclosure. She figured two years younger than her actual age was both believable and appropriate for the age range of workers at Thompson Hills.

"No way. You are not twenty-nine."

"Yes, I am," Abigail argued, afraid that Paige could tell she was lying. Why hadn't she told the truth? This was one extra falsehood she didn't need the headache of remembering. So what if her coworkers knew that she was thirty-one?

"We thought you were going to be the new baby," Paige explained, misunderstanding the look that crossed Abigail's face. She leaned over to one of the guys who had prepared the unfortunate breakfast. "Pay up," she said, smacking her hand on the table to get his attention. "She's over twenty-five."

"No way." He raised his eyebrows at Abigail. "Is this true?"

Abigail nodded. "I'm afraid so."

"I think you two are scheming to get my money," the guy complained as he reached into his back pocket and withdrew a crinkled ten-dollar bill from his wallet. "Now don't spend that all in one place," he warned Paige.

Tyler was watching the exchange with obvious interest. "You don't look twenty-nine," he told Abigail.

"I think it's rude to ask a woman her age, never mind spend time dwelling on it," Abigail responded, trying to sound haughty. All the personal questions were starting to unnerve her. She was anxious to shift the conversation away from herself and her reasons for being in BC. "How old are you?" she grilled Tyler.

"I'm twenty-nine, too," he replied amiably.

"Thirty at the end of the summer," Eli broke in from the opposite end of the table.

"And I expect a huge surprise party," Tyler said, raising his finger and leveling it at everyone in turn.

"I thought you were going to be gone by then," Eli mumbled.

All at once the tone at the table struck a discordant note. Abigail glanced from Eli to Tyler and back again. She felt like she had been thrust into a preexisting awkwardness, something that had a long history and an even longer list of mitigating circumstances. By the way her coworkers turned to their food and averted their eyes from both Tyler and Eli, Abigail suspected that the tautness in the room was all too familiar.

"I don't know." Tyler looked pointedly at Eli before letting his gaze fall to his plate. Abigail couldn't help but notice the change in his demeanor, the way he couldn't meet Eli's direct stare.

The moment stretched out awkwardly; then Eli took a deliberate mouthful of the bland eggs. The whole table seemed to exhale when Eli didn't press his nephew further, and gradually people struck up their own conversations again.

When the vineyard crew was dismissed, Abigail rose gratefully to start clearing the table. She wanted to put as much distance between herself and more inconvenient questions and probings as possible.

Abigail had overheard Eli tell someone that there would be no wine tasting today. Instead, they were all going to walk the grounds and learn how to give tours. Of course, some of the workers had been giving tours for weeks already, but Eli was very particular about what was shown and what was said, and he took it upon himself to give refresher courses every few weeks. Abigail was actually looking forward to putting the unsettling morning behind her and learning more about Thompson Hills.

The tour began at the remarkable entrance to the winery. Eli had designed the excursion to be a cozy, laid-back affair with casual tours being led by two workers who alternated escorting groups every half hour. There was no formal sign-up sheet and no fee for the tour. Anyone who wanted to go simply had to show up in the entryway either at the top or the bottom of the hour. Sometimes nobody showed up, and the designated tour guide was free to roam the tasting room, clearing tables as needed and answering questions about Thompson Hills's wine.

Abigail anticipated the chance to learn more about Eli's passion. It was obvious to her that he took his estate and his wine seriously, and she was interested to find out everything she could. Learning about Eli somehow spilled over into learning about Tyler, about their family and their ties. For some reason, Abigail couldn't shake the feeling that, apparent coolness aside, Eli played a more prominent role in Tyler's life than his stepfather, Murray.

Eli began by leading them out of the winery and into the vineyards below the expansive tasting room deck. From this side of the building they could see the lake in the distance and the sweeping curve of the desert valley beyond the water. The rows of grapevines ran east to west, cutting straight, regular columns into the earth and offering unobstructed views of the valley when Abigail stood between the arbors. Everything was set up for the tourists here. Each row boasted a different variety of grape so visitors could see the differences for themselves. Meticulously hand-painted wooden signs adorned the rows, indicating the type of grape and its characteristics.

There was even a whitewashed arch over a wrought-iron bench strategically positioned for enjoying the vista.

"Terroir," Eli began when everyone was gathered within earshot. He bent over to scratch out a fistful of dirt from the base of one of the vines. "Learn how to say it and learn what it means."

"We all know how to say it and we all know what it means," Paige muttered from her spot at Abigail's elbow. *"Terroir,"* she mimicked, trying out a different accent, a different pronunciation on each variation: *"terroir, terroir, terroir."*

"I don't know what it means," Abigail hissed.

Paige gave her a crooked smile and whispered enigmatically, " 'Somewhereness.' "

"It's the soil," Eli continued, "the sun, the rain, the wind, the earth below. It's everything that happens from the tip of the highest leaf to the point of the lowest root and all the places between."

"He can wax poetic about this for hours," Paige mumbled, stifling a yawn. But Abigail was mesmerized.

"Terroir is the uniqueness of the where. Where the vine is planted and what is enacted upon it throughout every stage of its life will ultimately determine the end result of the wine. In a way, you could say that *terroir* is home. And our home is a very special place indeed to raise fine, complex, maybe even extraordinary grapes that will someday become extraordinary wine."

It was obvious to Abigail that as far as Eli was concerned, the vineyards were much more than simply a place to produce fruit. She couldn't claim to understand, but something in his words breathed air into a darkened corner of her being. She realized that she had been holding her breath, trying to hear Eli over the quiet buzz of voices. Apparently everyone else found Eli's instruction boring. She leaned in a little closer.

"The best part?" Eli asked rhetorically, dropping the soil and leaning over to find a diminutive cluster of pea green grapes. "The vines that suffer the most, the vines that struggle amidst demanding *terroir* and experience drought, erosion, and every difficulty imaginable often produce the best wine. They have to be strong and imaginative, willing to put down deep roots to extract what they need to survive. The end result is full of unexpected undertones and delightful nuances."

Abigail was sure she wouldn't have the palate to discern the different tones and shades of survival that Eli seemed so eager to discuss, but listening to him talk made her want to try. She wished he'd brought a bottle of wine along for their tour.

As they moved along, Abigail studied the gnarled vines that snaked out of the earth and thrust jade hands heavenward. If they could speak, what manner of tale would they tell? a love story? a tragedy? one of brokenness? or one of life abundant?

"This is my favorite part of the tour," Tyler whispered, coming up behind Abigail as Eli went on about soil conditions, moisture, and sunlight. "All you have to do is read from the signs and then let people wander around and take pictures for a few minutes."

"Mm-hmm," Abigail murmured, not taking her eyes off Eli.

"Besides, the view is spectacular."

Abigail was about to nod her assent and once again give Eli her full attention when it struck her that Tyler wasn't looking off over the lake. He was facing the opposite direction. Abigail turned, trying not to be conspicuous, and followed his gaze. Behind them, the winery rose majestically. Flanking the remarkable building, two wide, curving staircases coiled up to the huge deck, and the steep-pitched, tiled roof glared in the hot sunlight. It was a sight to behold. But a glance at Tyler told Abigail that he was looking past the architectural lines and angles to the open glass doors of the tasting room beyond. There, framed behind the pillars that vaulted two stories high, was the bar where Abigail always stood, perfectly visible and strikingly accentuated as if the designers had intended it to be a focal point from the vineyard.

"Of course," Tyler said, "the scene improves considerably when a certain someone is standing behind the bar."

Abigail started to feel herself bristle. Tyler

watched her? What was he saying? But before apprehension could overwhelm her, Tyler bumped her with his shoulder and grinned. He was teasing her.

"Shut up," she said through clenched teeth.

Though Abigail knew she should take advantage of Tyler's subtle flirtation, she couldn't quite bring herself to do it. For the rest of the tour, she stuck close to Paige and pretended that she was intently absorbing every word Eli had to say. There were enough people around that Abigail didn't have to work too hard to keep Tyler at a distance.

Near the end of the morning when they were talking about the aging process in the cellars, Abigail saw Tyler take a few intentional steps toward her. But Paige stepped in between them. Though her interference was accidental, Abigail warmed to her a bit more because of it.

Hours later, the winery was teeming with people and Abigail didn't have time to think about Tyler anymore. She was so busy uncorking bottles, pouring wine, and chatting with customers that she almost forgot about Tyler's allusion and his tour guide vantage point from the vineyards below.

But at one point in the afternoon there was a lull in activity, and Abigail felt an uneasy prickle scurry up her neck. Someone was watching her. Unable to stop herself, she peeked past the wide, sun-drenched deck, trying to appear casual instead of intentional. Through the open windows, it was impossible to miss Tyler standing at the edge of the vineyard. He was surrounded by a small group of people who were occupied with the view, their backs turned to the winery. Not Tyler. He was staring straight at her, and when she caught his eye, he winked and waved.

"He's got a thing for you," Paige informed Abigail as she squirted orange-scented oil on the mahogany counter.

"Excuse me?"

"Tyler. I think he's got his eye on you."

"Yep," Natalie agreed, turning from her task of hanging the clean wineglasses by their delicate stems. "Definitely."

Abigail squeezed her eyes shut for a second, wondering how this should be played. What should she say? Feign interest so Paige and Natalie could spread the rumor that she would respond positively to any advance Tyler made? Or convince them that she had no intention of encouraging him in any way? "What makes you think that?" she finally asked, hoping she'd find a way to squelch the discussion quickly.

"Oh, it's obvious. You're the new girl."

Paige and Natalie laughed as if nothing could be funnier.

"Sorry," Paige explained, "it's just that he's been through every one of us now."

"You're kidding, right?" Abigail was unable to muffle the disgust in her voice.

"Not really." Paige handed Abigail the cleaning solution so she could do the far side of the bar.

"Tyler's just such a player," Natalie chimed in. "He's a nice enough guy, I guess. But he's also an incurable flirt."

"He thinks he's Don Juan." Paige rolled her eyes.

"Casanova." Natalie giggled.

"He's good-looking. I'll give you that."

Abigail watched the exchange, forgetting about the bottle in her hand. "Why is he here?" she asked. It wasn't until after the words were out of her mouth that Abigail realized it was possibly a risky question to pose, one that could indicate she knew more about Tyler Kamp than she let on. Why shouldn't he be here? But Abigail couldn't bury the fact that she knew Tyler had been happily living in Florida only a few months ago. She knew he had been at the brink of putting down roots with her sister. And now she could add to that knowledge the certainty that Tyler and Eli were hardly the best of friends. What had made him move back to Canada? Why now? Why here?

Paige gave her a funny look. "He's working for his uncle," she said as if it was the most obvious thing in the world.

"I heard that his mom died," Natalie offered, glancing around to make sure that everyone else was too far away to hear.

"What does that have to do with anything?"

"Well, I think he came back here to be close to his family," Natalie theorized.

"His uncle, you mean? I think you're giving him too much credit," Paige protested. "It's obvious that Tyler and Eli aren't on the best terms."

Natalie shrugged. "Whatever. I just don't think he's as bad as you make him out to be." She aimed a sly look at Abigail. "Besides, what if the new girl starts dating him?"

"Unlikely," Abigail said, suddenly feeling the weight of the bottle of cleaning solution in her hand. She squirted some on the counter and grabbed the cloth to buff it out.

"I don't know," Natalie went on. "He seems more . . . purposeful with you. He flirts with the rest of us, but he watches you."

"That's comforting," Abigail said sarcastically.

"That's creepy," Paige muttered.

"Oh, chill out. You're making way too much out of this."

Abigail nodded emphatically.

She was thankful when Natalie added, "I'm done and I'm out of here. See you guys tomorrow."

People filtered out of the winery, and by the time Abigail was ready to go, the sprawling building was nearly empty. Without her little orange Kia waiting for her by the trailer, Abigail could hardly stomach the thought of going home. *Home,* she thought. *What an unsuitable name for that miserable heap of metal.* The truth was, just the idea of

317

going back there and being confined by her inability to go where she wanted to go made Abigail feel claustrophobic. Why had she let Tyler talk her into getting rid of the rental in the first place? Why had she let Eli decide what she should and should not do?

Abigail was in a sour mood when she grabbed her purse from a hook in the winery kitchen and set off for the trailer across the fields. "Granola bars and apples for supper again," she groaned, mentally going through her small stash of food and realizing that she didn't have much left. She'd have to borrow Eli's car the next break she got.

Cranky about her measly rations, her relative confinement, and Tyler's inexplicable interest in her, Abigail marched out of the winery and made it halfway across the parking lot when she heard someone call her name. She knew instantly that it was Tyler, and she didn't even bother to turn around as he jogged up beside her.

"I'll walk you home," he offered, falling in step with her hurried pace.

"Thanks," she said curtly.

"Whoa." Tyler whistled. "Maybe I've changed my mind. What's up with you?"

"Nothing." Abigail berated herself for being so transparent.

"Could've fooled me."

They walked in silence for a few minutes. Tyler stuffed his hands in the pockets of his light khaki cords and took turns watching the uneven path in front of him and peering at Abigail. Even though she could feel his eyes on her from time to time, Abigail stared straight ahead. She didn't trust herself to utter a single word.

Tyler broke the stillness with an artificial laugh. "No, seriously. What's the deal?"

"No, seriously," Abigail parroted, "nothing."

"Well, I'm going to have to call you a liar."

Abigail reached out a hand and trailed it along the papery leaves of the grapevines. She knew she should be happy with the way things were going. She should be thankful that Tyler continued to seek her out and that he tried to get close to her even though she couldn't stop herself from acting peculiarly around him. But after such a long and perplexing day, Abigail simply didn't have it in her to act anymore. She was tired, she was confused, and she was incapable of pretending. She was fully and completely Abigail, the broken woman who had found her dead sister floating in a bathtub only three months ago.

Tyler stopped. Abigail instinctively did the same, but the second she faced him, she wished she could run away like a child fleeing from a nightmare.

"Why do you hate me?" Tyler asked, piercing her with a look so bold she couldn't hold his gaze.

"I don't hate you," she forced.

"Yeah, I think you might. But I can't for the life of me figure out why." Tyler started walking again, and Abigail found that she almost had to jog to keep up. "The rub is," he went on, "I happen to like you."

Abigail didn't know what to say. "That's nice," she finally managed.

"That's nice?" Tyler laughed. "You're a strange one, Abigail."

"Thanks."

"Bad choice of words. You're just . . . different."

"That's original," Abigail snapped.

"Distinctive?"

Abigail moaned. "What are you trying to say?"

"I don't know."

"Are you trying to ask me out?" Abigail posed the question mechanically, without the slightest hint of true emotion.

"Oh, please. Is that what you think?"

"No."

"Good, because I've sworn off women. My last girlfriend was a total psycho."

Abigail felt herself get hot. She didn't mean to grunt, but the impulsive noise made Tyler glare at her.

"Retract the claws, kitty. Don't pretend like you know me."

"I guess I know you don't date *psychos*." The word was hard to say, but it had the desired effect. Tyler instantly looked defensive.

"You don't understand," he said. "She was totally off and on, up and down . . ." He trailed off.

"Why am I telling you this? I don't have to explain myself to you."

Allowing herself the luxury of burying her face in her hands, Abigail fought back a frustrated scream. She was annihilating any small connection she had built with Tyler. "Sorry," she muttered from behind her hands. "I'm just . . . It's been a long day. I'm not myself right now."

Tyler slowed his step and studied Abigail openly. She couldn't meet his eyes, but she felt the touch of his gaze on her cheek. Angling her chin away from him, she watched a line of soft, white clouds rise like foam at the edge of the horizon. Abigail breathed deep and then again. *I can do this,* she told herself.

After they had walked a few paces with nothing but the light breeze for company, Tyler broke the calm by saying, "You're so . . . pensive."

"What's with you and all the adjectives?" Abigail joked weakly. "I'm surprised you even know what *pensive* means." When Tyler didn't respond immediately, she added, "It was a joke. I'm joking."

"You're not much of a comedienne."

"Guilty," Abigail admitted. The word stung somehow.

"You are one complicated girl."

"Complicated?"

"Maybe *complex* is a better fit."

Complex? He *was* trying to pick her up.

"When I look at you, I just know there's a lot going on behind those brown eyes of yours," he finished.

Tyler's face was turned away from her, and Abigail allowed herself the luxury of rolling those brown eyes of which he spoke so fondly. She knew what was going to come next, and it made her want to ball her hands into fists and use them against him, to feel her knuckles break against the hard angle of his jaw. He was going to carry on about how beautiful her eyes were, how expressive and mysterious. Abigail could imagine him using the same lines on a much more vulnerable Hailey. It made her sick.

But Tyler didn't say another word about Abigail's eyes. Instead, he surprised her by spinning toward her and raising a finger almost in accusation. "You're furious and you're sad. And something about you makes me want to know why."

It was Abigail's turn to stop dead. Furious and sad? How could he see that in her? Abigail was livid, but she also had to struggle to choke down something that tasted a lot like fear. How could he know her? She wanted to rage at him and demand that he tell her how he *knew*. *"Don't pretend like you know me,"* Tyler had said. She wanted to shout it back at him.

But Tyler didn't give her the chance. He kept walking.

"Why?" she challenged, watching his back as he drew away from her. "Why do you care if I'm—" she flicked her hands feverishly in front of her—"furious and sad?"

Tyler was already several long strides away. For a second Abigail was convinced that he wasn't going to respond and she almost took off after him. She wanted to spin him around, to make him answer her. It was true that she had struggled with her intentions concerning Tyler, but for one fierce moment Abigail felt a flash of anger toward him that was so fine-tuned everything came into sharp focus. All she could think was, *You killed my sister, you sanctimonious jerk.*

Maybe Tyler heard her sharp intake of breath. Maybe he felt like toying with her. Maybe he hoped to offer her a bit of understanding, a glimpse inside. Whatever the reason, right before Abigail opened her mouth to tell him exactly what she thought of him, Tyler answered her. Without turning back, he called, "I *don't* care. But I can relate."

It wasn't at all what Abigail expected to hear. She didn't move. She just stared at the soft charcoal of Tyler's stylishly wrinkled dress shirt until he disappeared at the spot where the row began to bend.

For the newly minted, twenty-year-old Abigail Bennett, moving to Florida had nothing to do with disappearing and everything to do with *appearing*. She felt like she had been waiting for fifteen years to emerge from behind the long shadow of Hailey. Fifteen years of delaying her own life, of abiding, of remaining, of staying exactly where she was and who she was because the slightest shift of self threatened to tip the careful balance. Abigail hardly knew the person she had become when no one else, including herself, was looking.

The young woman who boarded a plane in Sioux Falls, South Dakota, brought with her nothing more than two huge suitcases stuffed to bursting and one carry-on that was filled with too much empty space. As Abigail marched to her gate, the messenger bag that she had slung over her shoulder thumped her hip with each step, the three essential items inside serving as sharp-edged reminders of all she left behind: there was a small, rectangular tin of gum, a hardcover copy of Kahlil Gibran's *The Prophet*, and a photo that Melody had taken at the Fourth of July picnic. Hailey had printed off two copies and purchased a pair of cheap silver frames for them. She kept one and thrust the other into her sister's hands as she left.

Abigail was far from fond of the picture. She and Hailey were off-center, and though their youthful faces were arresting, something about the casual way Hailey's arm was thrown over her shoulder irritated Abigail. But she stuffed it in her nearly empty bag anyway, discarding it alongside the book that had sat on her bedside stand since she fell in love with Gibran in her tenth-grade English class and the tin of cinnamon gum she had stolen. The ancient container rattled in the bottom of her bag and almost gave her away; Abigail was sure that Lou would hear the distinctive clink and know what she had done.

It wasn't like she planned on taking Lou's tin. It was hardly a premeditated act—it was more of an accident, really.

The whole family had decided to accompany Abigail to the airport, which was an hour's drive from Newcastle. When her bags were in the trunk and everyone was in the car and ready to go, Abigail remembered that her Nike Windbreaker was still hanging on the hook in the mudroom. Lou was annoyed, but she raced back into the house anyway, leaving the car running in the driveway and her family waiting for her.

Abigail swept into the house, took one last, unexpectedly hungry look around, and then snagged her coat. The fabric caught on the old, crooked hook, and when Abigail gave it a hard tug, the coat beneath her Windbreaker fell, too. It was Lou's lined canvas jacket, and his beloved little tin spun out of the pocket and banged the floor with a sharp clang. Abigail grabbed it and the coat, ready to stuff everything back on the hook. But something about the cold feel of the metal in her hand stopped her. She couldn't explain it, but holding the tin in her palm made her knees feel weak, as if she couldn't walk out the door without trembling through every step.

The smudged Altoids tin hadn't held peppermints in years—Lou preferred cinnamon gum and bought it by the ten-pack, unwrapping the brick-like pieces and stacking them with meticulous precision in the flat peppermint container. Abigail could vividly remember when his gum addiction started, when she began to associate her father with the scent of cinnamon gum. It was a week after Hailey was born. It was the week that heralded Lou's decision to finally give up smoking once and for all.

Her father honked the horn in the driveway, and Abigail carefully hung his coat on the hook exactly where it had been. But she dropped the distinctive pack of gum in her bag and zipped the pocket closed.

Although she didn't realize it until years later, Abigail had left Minnesota with a piece of almost everyone she loved: Hailey was in the photo, Lou was in the tin, and Abigail was sure that there were pieces of herself—her hidden self, the self she had always secretly been and would now be able to become—in that beautiful, mystifying book. The only person not represented in Abigail's light but heavy-laden messenger bag was Melody.

Abigail regretted the oversight for the rest of her life.

Florida was everything Abigail had hoped for and more. It was lush and warm, exotic and foreign. The people were tan, and the grocery stores dedicated entire aisles to ethnic foods that Abigail had never heard of much less eaten. There was a pulse about the city of Rosa Beach, an undercurrent of life, of excitement. Though southern Florida didn't match the short list of preconceptions that Abigail had amassed by watching the odd rerun of *Miami Vice* on cable with Lou, it did swing to the beat of a soundtrack that was wholly unfamiliar and undeniably electrifying. She loved it.

South Seminole also exceeded Abigail's expectations. The small liberal arts college was sufficiently pretentious to assure that Abigail felt superior in her new career as full-time student. But South Seminole was insignificant enough to maintain an air of down-home ease, too. Abigail wanted for nothing in her college experience. It was a pleasant mix of culture and intellectual pursuit, casual parties and fast friendships. From nearly her very first day, Abigail sank into her new life with an air of complete surrender.

Melody had made Abigail promise that she would call home at least once a week. It wasn't too much to ask, was it? After all, Melody's first-born daughter had spent twenty years of her life under the same roof as her parents. Their relationship implied a closeness that couldn't be severed with a simple move across the country. Could it?

At first, Abigail was mildly homesick—though incapable of admitting it in light of finally getting what she had always wanted—and good at remembering the promise she had made to her mother. She dialed her parents' number every Sunday afternoon and forced herself to make small talk for half an hour at least. While the details changed from week to week, each time the conversation felt the same to Abigail.

The phone always rang twice. Then: "Hello?"

"Hi, Mom."

"Oh, Abby. It's so nice to hear your voice."

"Abigail, Mom. I go by Abigail now."

"Sweetie, you'll always be Abby to me."

"I'm not—oh, forget it. How are you?"

"Good, we're doing good. We're all good. And you?"

"Good."

"How's school?"

"Good. How's Hailey?"

"Good."

And on and on until Melody inevitably passed the phone to Hailey for more chitchat that skimmed the surface but never went deeper than a short list of what's new and who's who. Once or twice Lou was handed the phone, and Abigail asked her father a series of questions that he answered with vague grunts. Abigail could hear the television on in the background.

On a particularly warm Sunday in early October, Abigail went to the beach with her friends and forgot to call home. When she got back to her dorm room later that evening, there was a message from Melody on her answering service.

"This is a message for Abby," Melody said uncertainly, her concern traveling almost tangibly over the thousands of miles between them. Her voice sounded very far away and tremulous. "Hi, honey. It's Mom. Just wondering if you're okay. We didn't hear from you this afternoon, and we wanted to make sure you were all right. Well, okay. I'll talk to you later, okay? I'll try again. Or you can call us. Bye. Love you. Bye."

"It's after ten," Abigail explained to her roommate as she erased the message. "I'll call her tomorrow."

"Aren't you from Minnesota? It's an hour earlier there."

Abigail shrugged off the reminder and promised herself she'd call the next day.

But the next day faded into the next and then the next until the phone in Abigail's dorm room rang one afternoon nearly a week later.

"Yep?" Abigail quipped when she had clicked on the cordless telephone.

"Abby?"

"Hailey?"

"Well, at least I know you're alive. Thanks for calling, Sis."

"Hey, I'm sorry, okay? It's only been a few days."

"Whatever. Mom's been having a conniption."

"It's only been a few days," Abigail repeated.

"Feels like more than that to us," Hailey complained. "The house feels vacant without you, cavernous. We live for those brief moments of contact when you deign to set aside your incalculably satisfying new life to call us one measly time a week."

"Be serious."

"I am."

For a few seconds nothing filled the line but the sound of Abigail and Hailey breathing in perfect cadence.

"I—"

"You—"

"What?" Abigail persisted. "You go first."

"Nothing, really. I don't remember what I was going to say."

"How're Mom and Dad?"

"Fine."

"How are you?"

"Fine."

This is why I didn't bother calling, Abigail thought.

After that, the habit that Abigail had cultivated of regular Sunday afternoon phone calls fell to pieces. Sometimes Abigail called; sometimes she didn't. Sometimes Melody called. And every once in a while Hailey picked up the phone and took a few minutes to reprimand her sister for not continuing to pull tight the knot of family ties.

Christmas quickly became a hot topic, and Abigail dreaded the conversations that always started with, "It will be so nice when you're home for a month over Christmas break!"

"It's not a month," Abigail reiterated with increasing irritation. "It's three weeks, and I don't even know if I'll be able to be home that whole time." In truth, Abigail couldn't quite deal with the thought of spending any substantial amount of time back in the little second-story bedroom she had occupied for most of her life. It had taken years, but she had finally moved on. She loved her family, but she was happy for now to let that complicated love simmer from a distance.

Of course, Melody and Hailey weren't deterred. They acted like a month with Abigail home was the highlight of their year. And as if they could will her trip into being through earnest prayers and petition, they applied themselves with downright fervor. In the end, Abigail bought a ticket for just over two weeks, intending to fly standby on an earlier flight if she found that life in the Bennett house was something she had utterly outgrown.

Two weeks, Abigail told herself. *I can survive for two weeks.*

Then, less than a month before Abigail was scheduled to return home, the phone rang at five o'clock on a Tuesday morning. Abigail shot awake, glanced at the clock, and grumbled that whoever dared to bother her at such an ungodly hour deserved to be shot. "They can leave a message," she mumbled to her roommate.

The phone stopped ringing.

It started again a second later. Abigail put her pillow over her head and tried to ignore the insistent sound. But after the answering service picked up the second call, whoever was trying to get ahold of room 224 dialed their number yet again.

"Make it stop!" Abigail groaned. But she rolled out of bed anyway and grabbed the phone groggily. "What?"

There was a strange sighing on the other end of the line, a soft, low moan that sounded like static or maybe a bad international connection that hummed vaguely over continents and oceans too far away to be clearly connected. It was obviously some drunk, some psycho. But just before Abigail was about to hang up, she became aware of a rhythm in the sound, a two-syllable whimper that finally became recognizable. Somebody was calling her name.

"Hailey?" Abigail asked, immediately wide-awake now. She dropped to the edge of her bed as if she had been shoved down. "Hailey, is that you? What's wrong?"

"Abby, Abby, Abby . . ."

"Hailey Bennett, you tell me what's going on."

Abigail clutched the phone in two hands. She pressed it forcefully to her ear, trapped it there, because what she really wanted to do was throw it across the room.

"Abby . . ." The word had become an incantation, a prayer almost.

"Hailey, tell me!" Abigail was terrified, but she was ready. Hailey had been suicidal before; her meds had failed her before. Even as she waited for Hailey to pull herself together enough to respond, Abigail was thinking of what she should do. If she called 911 in Rosa Beach, could they patch her through to the crisis line in Newcastle, Minnesota? If she could remember the neighbors' phone number, would they be able to run over? Could she avert this disaster from two thousand miles away?

But the emergency wasn't what Abigail expected. There was nothing she could do to prevent it, nothing she could have done to anticipate it.

When Hailey finally mustered the strength to say the words, they struck Abigail with such force she gasped for breath. She choked so hard that her roommate jumped from the top bunk of their bed and caught her as she collapsed.

"Abby, Mom's dead."

By the time I made it home, it was getting late. My apartment was dim and filled with long shadows. I stood with my back against the door, the strap of my purse barely clinging to my limp fingers, and listened to the hum of the refrigerator. There was a digital clock in the sleek, stainless steel door, and as I watched, it blinked from 8:44 to 8:45.

Eight forty-five. Had it been twelve hours? Had half a day passed since Hailey climbed into her bathtub—fully clothed, with her hair tied back and her makeup in place, her lips full and soft and shining with berry-scented gloss—and pulled the razor across her wrists? It didn't seem real. It couldn't be real.

But I knew it was.

"You're selfish," I whispered into the fading light. As if she could hear me. Where was she? Purgatory? For all her failings, from the day Hailey decided to go forward with her confirmation, she never once stopped praying to and believing in the God she clung to with all her might. Maybe her penance over those years had been enough to cover this one last indefensible sin. Or was Hailey's suicide unpardonable? How could God forgive her if she was unable to repent for this final, deplorable act of transgression? Though I

knew that many would count her past the point of pardon, everything inside me rebelled at the thought of my sister in hell.

"Oh, God," I breathed into the stillness, his name an implicit prayer. "It's up to me, isn't it?"

I had intermittently attended a handful of different churches since the first year I lived in Florida, but something about this staggering circumstance demanded the solemnity of my youth. A Bible and a well-used but recently untouched book of prayers were collecting dust in the bottom drawer of my dresser. I grabbed them both and added to the pile in my arms the glass-beaded rosary that hung from the corner of my armoire mirror.

As I crept back to the living room, I could not help but stoop beneath the weight of my own inadequacies. I believed in God, but I had too many doubts and questions to consider myself very spiritual. What was I supposed to say? What was I supposed to do? A deep ache for my mother emptied me like a long exhalation. She would know.

I sank to the floor in front of my coffee table and laid the books on the spotless glass in front of me. But the rosary I held in my hands, tumbling the edged glass beads between my fingertips as if I could coax the sound of her prayers from their smooth angles. It was comforting somehow, to hold what she had held, to roll the blue green glass against my fingers and hear in my mind the echo of *those words that played a quiet soundtrack throughout my youth. I didn't realize that I was crying until the beads were suddenly hot and wet, almost slipping through my desperate hold.*

Passing the back of my hand over my mouth, my nose, I reached for the prayer book. Mom had written all over it, inscribing prayer requests, reminders, and notes across the empty margins and nearly filling every bit of blank space. When I opened the pages, it released a bit of her, a scent maybe or the remnant of a decade-old memory that made my lips pull into the faintest imprint of a smile.

"I wish you were here," I said and was startled by the sound of my own voice.

On the inside cover of the small, leather-bound book, Mom had copied an eight-step process and labeled it "How to Pray the Rosary." Most people at St. Mary's considered the rosary pretty old-school, but with each year that passed, my mom seemed to sink deeper into the tradition and ritual of her youth. Maybe she began to feel a certain kinship with her grandmother as she aged. Or maybe she felt as if she had no choice but to invoke a higher power.

I ran a heavy thumb over the smudged lines of her penciled words. The Apostle's Creed was followed by Our Father, then three Hail Marys and Glory be to the Father, back to Our Father and through the whole process again. . . . I squeezed my eyes shut, trying to remember. But I didn't. The phrases were jumbled and dim, as if I were staring across a great distance without the aid of my contacts. I would have to read every single one.

Tucking the cross of the rosary in the soft flesh of my palm, I used my forefinger and thumb to pick out a single bead and began. I didn't know if I was praying my sister through purgatory or praying for a miracle. I didn't know if I was wasting the air around me on useless ramblings or if each word had the power to release the very breath of life.

When a decade of beads had passed beneath my hands, I whispered the prayer that my mother had copied in her book: "O my Jesus, forgive us our sins, save us from the fires of hell, lead all souls to Heaven, especially those who have most need of your mercy. Amen. Amen. Amen." I said it again and again and again until it faded of its own accord. Amen.

So shall it be, through the mercy of God. "Be merciful," I whispered. I didn't know if I was asking for Hailey or for me.

XII

ᑫ THE DAYS PASSED QUICKLY, and Abigail became adept at spiraling through the inelegant dance that was her relationship with Tyler. At times she drew close to him, steeling herself to probe for the answers she sought, to learn why he left Hailey and how and when. But then he would come on to her or make some offhand observation that would fill her with such revulsion, she'd pull away to nurse the fury that made the air feel electric whenever he was around.

Abigail wanted to hurt Tyler. She wanted to love him and leave him or make his life miserable or ruin any relationship he embarked upon. Whatever it took to break his heart. To make him pay for what she assumed resulted in the death of her sister. But revenge turned out to be easier said than done, and Abigail found herself illogically frozen. So instead of making plans, instead of calculating with any amount of certainty what she hoped to accomplish in British Columbia, she merely went through the motions. She lived her new life because it was all she could bring herself to do.

Working for Eli meant that Abigail was rarely at a loss for something to occupy her hands or her mind. Her work schedule was rigorous, and Eli made sure that she was never bored when they worked alone together on weekday mornings.

Contrary to his country-bumpkin visage, Eli turned out to be a full-fledged historian, a dabbling philosopher, and a would-be theologian. He had an endless supply of questions and topics hot enough to make Abigail forget herself and get lost in his musings.

Sometimes, while Abigail was busy with her head in a barrel, Eli would abandon bottling entirely and wander over to regale her with his theories and reflections. Leaning against a newly washed barrel, he'd pepper her with questions, then fall into a long monologue about his own belief system, ideas, and speculations.

Abigail wasn't opposed to Eli's loquaciousness. In fact, she welcomed his company and the authoritarian way in which he communicated his opinions. He gave her a lot to think about without asking too much in return. It was just enough to keep her mind planted somewhat firmly in the now, leaving little freedom for introspection into either her future or her past.

"What's with this purgatory thing that Catholics believe?" Eli drilled her one morning late in June. "I learned about it in social studies when I was a kid growing up in Washington, but what with the Reformation and all, you guys don't still believe in that stuff, do you?"

"I'm not a Catholic anymore, so I don't know why you're asking me," she said.

Eli frowned at her. "You're one of the guys. And

you're a former Catholic, so you still count. Spill it: what's with purgatory?"

Abigail ignored him and picked up her hose. Training the nozzle inside the barrel, she depressed the handle and sent a jet of cold water against the cleaning solution–soaked sides. A fine mist rose out of the opening and lighted on Abigail's arms, her cheeks. It made her sneeze.

"Don't think you're getting off so easy." Eli raised his voice over the thunder of water. "I have questions and you've got answers."

"What makes you think I have answers?" Abigail shouted back. "I was a nominal Catholic at best."

"You're a smart girl," Eli countered. "You know your stuff."

Abigail finished up in the barrel and then directed her hose at the floor. She helped the water along its path to the drains in the middle of the slanting cement, making sure she got a little too close to Eli's feet so that she sprinkled him with some of the frigid spray.

"Hey!" he yelled, leaping backward.

"Sorry, just doing my job."

Eli reached over and took the hose from her. He tossed it on the ground and then crossed his arms over his chest in challenge. "You're done here. I need help labeling this morning."

With a shrug, Abigail followed Eli to the counter where they hand-labeled special bottles. There was a machine that did most of the large orders, but whenever Thompson Hills produced a particularly special or rare wine, all the bottles were labeled by hand—Eli's hands. For these extraordinary vintages, Eli employed a graphic designer who made the labels look exquisite, one-of-a-kind.

Abigail surveyed the tall, slim bottles and the flat stacks of newly printed labels. They were adorned in what looked like a pencil sketch of a woman's slender back in blurred, charcoal lines. She was looking over her shoulder and holding a delicate wineglass in her outstretched hand. The glass was just about to tip.

"Pretty," Abigail commented.

"It's our first ice wine," Eli told her. "I'm very proud of it. We even got our VQA stamp of approval, and that's not easy to do with ice wine."

Abigail knew that VQA was the Vintners Quality Alliance and that Eli would never dream of selling a wine that didn't have their sign and seal. Thompson Hills may not have been considered one of the finest wineries in the area, but Eli made a point of doing absolutely everything by the book. But though she knew this small, obscure fact, Abigail had never heard of ice wine before.

"It was an accident, you know," Eli began without waiting for her to question him. "Ice wine, I mean. They say that in the eighteenth century a German vineyard owner was away on business during harvesttime. Well, if he'd had even an ounce of sense, he would've known that he'd come home to a frozen vineyard. Lucky accident though, I guess, 'cause rather than abandoning the crop, he harvested the frozen grapes and processed them anyway. Winter wine."

Eli held up a bottle, letting the light refract through the garnet-colored liquid inside. It did seem icy to Abigail, like the frozen-juice mess of holly berries on the driveway of her childhood home. She remembered how she loved to step on the fallen fruit and how Lou yelled at her for it. The sudden burst of angry red against the snowy, sable-shadowed concrete was worth it every time.

"We'll see how it goes. It's a lot of work." Suddenly he glanced at Abigail. "Maybe you'll be here in the fall and be able to participate in a midnight harvest with us."

Abigail didn't squirm visibly, but a strange look must have crossed her face because Eli's eyes narrowed. For a moment Abigail was sure he knew more than he let on, that he suspected her intentions at Thompson Hills were less than mundane, little more than temporal.

But then it passed. Eli looked away and changed the subject. "Don't think I've forgotten about the purgatory thing."

"Oh, I knew you hadn't." Abigail sighed, though she was actually happy to reclaim the less personal ground of corporate theology. "What do you want to know?"

"Everything."

"There's not much to say." Abigail grabbed a bottle and a label and closely watched Eli's hands go through the motions as she talked. "Purgatory is neither heaven nor hell. It's a place between, where souls destined for heaven go for the purification of their sins. A place of absolution, of paying the price."

"There's a price for sin?"

"It's called satisfaction. Like you've taken something from God, and he has to be repaid. The debt has to be satisfied."

"So purgatory is the place where you go to atone for what you did wrong. It's the step before you're allowed to enter heaven," Eli concluded.

"In a nutshell."

"What about forgiveness?"

"God always forgives the truly repentant, but there will always be consequences for our actions, too. Those consequences have to play out."

Eli cocked an eyebrow at Abigail. "So if I cheated on a test when I was a kid and wasn't caught, I'll have to sit in detention in purgatory?"

Abigail glared at him good-naturedly. "You're being obtuse on purpose. Forgiveness requires true repentance and repentance has to be more than a feeling. 'Penitential acts are the real fruits of repentance,'" she quoted. "Hey, I remembered something from Sunday school!"

Eli grumbled an enigmatic reply, and Abigail couldn't tell if he was laughing with her or at her.

After a moment he muttered, "I knew there was a reason I wasn't a Catholic. Who needs purgatory? I can't help thinking that this life is purgatory—a place to work out our penitence."

"But what if you don't work out that penance on earth?"

"In the case of, say, a sin you were not sorry for?"

"Or one you were unable to ask forgiveness for," Abigail finished, surprising herself. This was dangerous ground, this seemingly innocuous early morning conversation.

"I thought that's what the prayers of the saints were for. Isn't that why you guys light candles and pray for family members who have died? Isn't it your job to help them out of purgatory?"

"It's ultimately up to God. But you're right; it's the responsibility of the living, too." She didn't realize that her hands were inert, clutching the bottle and wrinkling the lovely label until Eli cleared his throat. "Sorry," she said quickly, trying to smooth out the sepia-toned paper.

Eli wrenched it from her and threw it away. "I want my labels perfect."

They worked in silence for a few minutes, Abigail forcing herself to focus on getting a few labels just right. Flawlessly straight. Faultlessly flat. She was struggling to erase the talk of purgatory from her mind, of sins unforgiven and contrition without conclusion, of sins yet to come and unforgivable, when Eli broke the stillness.

"Do you believe in it?"

"Excuse me?"

"Purgatory," Eli clarified. "You said you're not a Catholic anymore. Do you still believe in purgatory?"

Abigail dragged her thumb over the top half of a label, pressing out an air bubble and sealing the seam. "I don't know," she said, unable to stop herself from responding, although all she wanted to do was forget that he ever brought up such a weighted topic. "I guess I'd like to believe that God can see past *what* we've done to understand *why* we did it. Maybe our reasons should count for something." Out of the corner of her eye, Abigail watched Eli regard her.

"I'm a relatively new believer," he admitted, "but this whole purgatory thing doesn't seem very grace filled to me."

"It's not about grace," Abigail said quietly. "It's about judgment."

Though Eli usually loved to talk about things that kept Abigail on her toes, there were some days that he was quiet, lost in his own thoughts, and stubbornly tight-lipped. On those days, Abigail held her counsel and did her job without wavering from her task unless Eli specifically instructed her otherwise. She tried to keep out of his way, but every once in a while he would very intentionally stroke his surly mood by prying into Abigail's personal life.

"What are you doing for Canada Day?" he asked her one morning after they had worked in detached silence for well over an hour.

"Canada Day?" she repeated, completely nonplussed. "When you live in Canada, isn't every day Canada day?"

Eli didn't crack a smile at what Abigail was sure he realized was a joke. "It's Canada's birthday," he said snappishly. "If you're going to live in this country, it would serve you well to learn a little about it."

Abigail didn't apologize for her ignorance—she figured that when Eli was in one of his moods, he didn't deserve her regret—but she did ask Paige about the holiday.

"It's the day Canada was officially recognized by the British government as a commonwealth," Paige recited, her eyes glazing over. Then she perked up. "It's like the Fourth of July without the backyard fireworks."

"We never did fireworks in the backyard," Abigail said, feigning offense. "It was always bottle rockets and Roman candles on the *driveway*."

"Exactly." Paige jabbed the air with a mock angry fist. "But at least we get a day off. A bunch of us are going boating. Do you ski?"

Thinking back to the handful of times that Abigail could claim to have ever set foot on a boat, she found Paige's question almost humorous. "Uh, no," she said, using her tone to convey just how strongly she felt about participating in water sports.

"Baby," Paige teased. "Come anyway. There's a water tube built for two. We'll pair you up with just the right guy and then make sure to toss you on a corner. Insta-romance."

Abigail put her finger to her lips as if to shush Paige. "Enough. You're not talking me into it. I like to keep my feet in the vicinity of dry ground."

"You're missing out," Paige singsonged.

"I don't care," Abigail singsonged back.

Part of the reason why Abigail wasn't interested in Paige's holiday invitation was her suspicion that Tyler would be one of the bodies taking up space on the boat. When it came to Tyler, she tried to walk the careful line between subtle flirtation and avoidance, and Abigail was convinced that spending uninterrupted hours with the object of her obsession would result in the balance being tipped—with potentially devastating consequences.

It didn't help that after their confrontation in the vineyard Tyler had made a point of joining Abigail as often as he could for their daily walk home. He acted like they had never tussled, and on the days that Abigail was feeling strong and capable of being coy and playful, he made no attempt to disguise his growing attraction to her. One evening, he even tried to touch her, to press his fingers against the curve of her waist as he sidled close enough to show her the difference between two varieties of grapes.

Abigail felt the warmth of his hand at her side and jumped as if he had stung her. The look on her face, the shock and revulsion, must have been agonizingly evident because Tyler dropped his hand, spun on his heel, and made some excuse before leaving Abigail alone in the vineyard.

For days he barely looked at her. She didn't know how to mend the rift, and she wasn't sure that she even wanted to. But she did know that being confined in a motorboat with Tyler, barechested and browned by the sun, did not sound like a safe idea. She didn't trust him, and she didn't trust herself.

Canada Day dawned so blisteringly hot that the ground actually breathed a slow exhalation of misty vapor. From her perch slightly above the fields on Eli's small hill, Abigail could watch the early morning fog rise from the sleeping vineyards as if God himself had just taken the lid off the simmering pot of Revell.

Abigail hated to admit it, but in the hushed stillness of the steamy morning, she wished she had taken Paige up on her invitation. Mild fear of boating or no, Abigail couldn't help but long for a little company. The past several weeks had taught her that unoccupied hours were rather predictably filled with dark and troubled thoughts. Sometimes she wished she could just forget everything—Johnson, McNally & Bennett, her life in Florida, her gradually fading father, even Hailey—and just start over fresh in this new reality. This existence without a past to weigh it down and complicate it.

As much as Abigail didn't want to be alone, she wasn't brave enough to call Paige and tell her that she'd changed her mind. Instead, she went on a short jog, took a long, cold shower, and then went to knock on Eli's door right before 9 a.m.

He answered in a wrinkled pair of old jeans and a T-shirt so thin and faded it looked as if he might have worn it when he was Abigail's age. While Eli unlocked the screen door and propped it open, Nan ambled up beside him, yawning wide and looking for all the world as if he were dressed in furry, rumpled pajamas and mildly resented the intrusion.

"What do you want, girl? You have the day off today." Although there was a stern line creasing his already-furrowed forehead, Abigail could instantly tell that he was in a good mood.

"I know." Abigail found herself smiling at his tetchiness in spite of herself. "I was hoping I could borrow your car for a while today."

Under different circumstances, it might have been a bit of a bold request. But living in the trailer had taught Abigail that Eli rarely left the estate. Once or twice a week he took Nan out for a lope down the beach, and on Sundays he went to the diner behind the Husky and to church. Abigail wasn't sure when he did his grocery shopping, but she had to admit that she had rarely seen him eat at all. Eli seemed to subsist entirely on the three-quarters of a cigarette he smoked every day and a daily glass of his own wine.

"You want my car?" Eli asked. "You got groceries yesterday."

"I forgot something."

"You make lists."

"I'm meeting a friend."

"Everyone is going boating."

"I have a hot date."

Eli squinted at her. "Nope, you don't. Try again."

Abigail threw her hands up in exasperation. "I want to get out of here for a while. *You* made me get rid of my car, remember?"

Reaching behind the door, Eli grabbed a set of keys and handed them to her. "You can take the car on one condition."

"Excuse me?"

Eli shook the keys tantalizingly. "It's no big deal. I just want you to pick up some stuff for tonight."

Abigail took the keys. "What are you talking about?"

"It's obvious you don't have plans for today, so I'm going to make you my famous balsamic marinated salmon. We'll slice a few potatoes real thin and throw them on the grill with some asparagus.

Do you like apricots? I'm thinking we'll start with grilled apricots in a mustard glaze and chardonnay. Then the salmon with pinot noir. For dessert, plain, old vanilla ice cream and fresh cherries. What do you think? Shall we try the ice wine?"

Abigail sputtered.

"A simple yes or no will do." Eli dug in his back pocket and produced a couple of twenties from his wallet. "The best salmon is at the IGA on the south side of town. Look for nice, dark pink flesh. And make sure the package says 'fresh' or 'Pacific' or something like that. Sockeye if you can find it. I can't stand farmed salmon."

"Okay," Abigail muttered, finding her voice. Eli could be so compelling, virtually magnetic at times, and it was impossible to fight the pull of his gravity. Not that she wanted to in this case. Salmon? Grilled apricots? Her mouth watered at the thought.

"Do you need me to write the list down? Or did you get all that?" Eli demanded. He added, "Don't worry about the cherries. I'll pick them up. The Warkentin farm is just over the ridge. It might be a bit early for cherries, but I'll find some ripe ones."

"Apricots?" Abigail asked.

"You'll have to buy those. They won't be done until the end of July."

"Okay," Abigail said again.

"Let's do an early dinner. Say four o'clock? I'll start the grill and we can take our time."

A grin flashed across Abigail's face before she could contain it. "Okay."

"You need a thesaurus," Eli remarked, then pulled Nan back by the collar and shut the door without another word.

Abigail laughed.

The IGA was packed with people throwing packages of hot dogs, chips, and buns in green baskets slung over their arms. Abigail was happy to go against the frenzied flow. For the first time in months, she got a cart and meandered through the aisles, leaning against the long handle and inspecting the goods the grocery store had to offer. She bought a fat loaf of still-warm-from-the-oven sourdough bread and a little plastic container of candied walnuts for the ice cream and cherries. In the produce section she picked out a bunch of crisp, slender asparagus and carefully selected five small, heavy apricots with peachy-pomegranate colored skin.

Picking out salmon proved to be a bit more difficult since Abigail had grown up in the Midwest and had never fully developed an appreciation for fish. The thick slabs of sirloins and rib eyes tempted her, but Abigail passed over them and spent no less than ten minutes trying to select the perfect salmon fillets instead. She couldn't decide between two different packages with hunks of salmon like open butterfly wings, so she bought them all. Eli could put the extras in his freezer, she rationalized.

Driving back to Thompson Hills with her back-seat full of such gourmet delicacies was distinctly exhilarating for Abigail. She was looking forward to her afternoon and evening with Eli more than she could have ever anticipated. It felt normal. It felt casual, fun, maybe even comfortable.

Abigail talked Eli into letting her borrow one of the *Wine Spectator* magazines that she saw cluttering up his counter when she dropped off the groceries. He flipped through the stack and pulled out one that broadcast the headline "Ultimate Wine Buying Guide" and told her to study it as if reading the magazine had been his idea.

After a quick lunch of sliced apple and generous hunks of cheddar, Abigail took her magazine and the woven blanket that was folded up on the bench in the trailer and found a grassy spot to relax beneath a gnarled tree. She fell asleep with the magazine opened as far as the table of contents on her chest.

It was the sharp, almost-metallic tang of burning charcoal and the sound of voices that finally roused Abigail from her afternoon nap. She breathed deeply, remembering what she had to look forward to in a sudden wash of anticipation. Stretching lazily, she considered the soft suffusion of robin's egg blue peeking from between the celadon leaves of the aspen above her and savored the moment. The scent, the feel, the sounds . . . It hit her all at once that she heard voices. *Voices?*

Sitting straight up, Abigail twisted around and saw Eli and Tyler standing together over Eli's old-fashioned, bowl-shaped charcoal grill. Their heads were bent together and they seemed to be, at least for the moment, somewhat friendly.

As if he could sense her waking, Eli looked up and called across the lawn, "Good morning, Sleeping Beauty."

Abigail waved weakly. Why was Tyler here? His truck hadn't moved for days, but she hadn't seen him around the house in at least as long. She figured he had decided to crash on the couch at a friend's house or something. She certainly hadn't expected him to be around tonight.

Eli greeted her with a raised blackened pair of tongs that he had been using to poke at the coals. Tyler waved, too, his mouth a tight line of resignation that told Abigail he had been roped into sticking around against his will; he wasn't going anywhere. She groaned inwardly. Why had Eli invited him to stay for their little celebration? The uncle-nephew duo didn't even get along most of the time.

But there was nothing she could do about it now. Abigail reluctantly got to her feet and, with deliberate precision, folded the blanket she had been lying on. She tucked it under her arm, grabbed the magazine, and forced herself to join the men at the grill.

"We've got twenty minutes or so on the coals yet," Eli remarked, closing the lid. "Get her a glass of chard," he told Tyler.

"No thank you," Abigail demurred. "All I need right now is a big, tall glass of ice water."

Eli flicked his wrist at Tyler authoritatively. The younger man turned toward the house, presumably to get Abigail the glass of water she had just mentioned.

"Oh no, Tyler," Abigail called after him, "you don't have to get me water. I can get it myself. . . ."

But he was already gone.

"Let him do it," Eli directed her. "It's good for him to do something for someone other than himself once in a while."

Abigail sank onto the bench of Eli's picnic table with a sigh.

"What is it with you two?" Eli asked without warning. He sat down across from her and put his elbows on the peeling-paint tabletop, leaning in conspiratorially.

"Excuse me?" Abigail murmured, startled.

"What is it with you and Tyler?" Eli repeated. "I can't decide if you're in love with him or if you hate his guts."

"I am not in love with him," Abigail snapped.

"Then it's the other."

"No," Abigail rushed to explain. "*No*. It's not that at all."

Eli stabbed her with a meaningful look. "Honey, when it comes to Tyler, you are either one or the other. There's no in-between."

"What about you?" Abigail shot back. "He's your nephew, but you sure act like you hate him."

Throwing back his head, Eli laughed long and hard. "I love that boy more than my own life. But he ticks me off something fierce. I'm hard on him because I expect more than he's often willing to give. That kid is a mistake waiting to happen, and I'm fighting it with all I've got."

Abigail looked pointedly over Eli's shoulder, warning him that Tyler was coming. Eli just smiled at her and took a small sip of his wine.

Although Abigail had expected the clash and disharmony of three incompatibly strong wills to dominate the evening, the rest of the night unfolded quietly, like a languid song played by an unhurried hand. Eli talked, filling in the stifling pauses that threatened to spread and conquer and disrupt the gentle night with conflict. And it worked. Maybe it was the inviting breeze above the sun-warmed earth. Maybe it was because they had been softened by wine. Whatever the reason, they—all three of them—were so impassive they didn't have the energy to worry about the friction between them.

Tyler tried to be civil and unobtrusive, and

Abigail did her best to be as indifferent to him as she was to the pepper mill at the center of the table. It didn't quite work—Abigail sat almost piously rigid on the picnic table bench—but by the time she forked a bite of Eli's exquisite salmon and let it melt on her tongue, she was at least relaxed enough to truly enjoy the food.

"Amazing," Abigail breathed, sampling Eli's grill fare. "Buttery and soft . . . tangy . . . a hint of sweet . . . I love it."

"Try it with the pinot," Eli instructed.

Abigail lifted the glass and let the wine slide over her tongue. "Perfect."

"If there's one thing my uncle does right, it's salmon." Tyler lifted his glass in a toast to Eli.

Eli cleared his throat and indicated the wineglass he was holding by striking it gently with the tines of his fork. The ensuing hum was so clear and resonant, Abigail knew she was drinking out of the finest crystal.

"Excuse me," Tyler amended. "If there are *two* things my uncle does right, they are salmon *and* wine."

"Hear, hear!" Eli cheered. He lifted his glass with a triumphant flair and held it high over the table. "A toast," he said grandly. "To fine wine, good company, and—" he paused notably—"new beginnings."

Abigail faltered with her hand in the air, drawn down by a glass of pinot noir so deep and rich and lovely that her eyes were relentlessly pulled to the glistening shimmer. It held such weight she could barely keep it from toppling out of her hand.

New beginnings? What was Eli talking about? How could he possibly guess at what she deep down wanted? The chance to start over was a hope she had buried long ago and endeavored to ignore. And that latent wish now lay in shambles—an impossible dream. How did Eli know? Suddenly the night took on a menacing quality; it filled so quickly with a sense of foreboding that Abigail felt regret begin to nip at her consciousness.

But before Abigail could let worry overtake her, Tyler tipped his glass against Eli's and then hers. She watched in confusion as he gratefully took a generous mouthful and then squeezed his eyes closed for the briefest of seconds before swallowing. It looked like he had to struggle to get the wine down; like Eli's toast was more than a toast—it was a hard reality to digest.

Uncertain, Abigail glanced between Eli and Tyler and back again. Tyler was looking into his wineglass as if the answers resided there, but Eli was staring at his nephew. The palpable ache of longing that fled across Eli's face when the younger man took another sip of deliberate consummation was so fierce and raw that Abigail's breath caught in her chest. In that moment she knew without a doubt that the toast hadn't been about her. It had been about Tyler.

• • •

Melody's death had nothing to do with Abigail leaving for Florida, but her elder daughter couldn't help but shoulder at least part of the blame. *I should have known. I should have guessed. I should have stayed. . . .* Abigail abused herself as she retraced her steps back to Newcastle, Minnesota. Back to the place that seemed so intent to hold her fast. And the whole way, she couldn't stop wondering: *If I would have stayed, would she have lived? Would I have somehow known? Could I have stopped it? maybe even prevented it?*

It took Abigail nearly eight hours to secure a flight home, and in that time she was able to piece together what had happened. Mrs. Manning, the Bennetts' neighbor for over thirteen years, had lost her husband a number of months before, and when she learned about Melody's untimely passing, she moved into the Bennett home as if she were family. Abigail called Mrs. Manning collect from the Fort Myers airport no less than a dozen times, numbly giving her flight information and then changing it, and in the moments between business the elderly woman told Abigail everything she knew.

Melody died of a massive brain aneurysm. The initial autopsy results identified that much, but later information revealed that she had suffered a subarachnoid hemorrhage, a cerebral rupture that released blood into her brain and ultimately caused a stroke of such lethal proportions that it would have been fatal with or without the provocation of an aneurysm. Even if she hadn't gone to bed with a splitting headache and bled out quietly, alone in her room, even if Lou had been with her and had raced for the phone and called an ambulance, Melody would have probably still died. Or at least been confined to a nursing home. She would have been a vegetable.

No one was to blame—except maybe nature, Melody's DNA, or as Abigail couldn't help noting, God—but everyone seemed to want to hold somebody responsible. Hailey blamed Melody's doctor for not connecting the dots of Melody's chronic hypertension, her mild heart problems, and her family history—Melody's grandmother had died young of an aneurysm, too. Lou blamed Abigail for leaving and consequently sending Melody's blood pressure through the roof. Even Abigail needed someone to fault. She wavered between blaming herself and blaming Hailey. Wouldn't all those years of mothering Hailey be enough to destabilize anyone's health? There was more than enough guilt to go around.

The vigil for Melody Bennett was poorly attended, but though they would have never admitted it, the family actually wanted it that way. Their restrained mourning, the tears they shed over the now plastic-looking face of their petite wife and mother were solitary offerings meant to polish the smooth lines of her casket, not to impress the neighbors with the scope of their sorrow.

Mrs. Manning and Dr. Madsen came as well as several family friends and twenty or so members of St. Mary's who had known Melody through her occasional attendance at a Ladies Aid baby shower or the biannual quilting circle. All in all, fewer than fifty people walked heavy-footed through the doors of St. Mary's and peered over the edge of her candlelit casket. Most hardly remembered the young woman Lou had married or the energetic new mother who had ecstatically raised her first daughter for five years before everything was irreversibly altered.

Melody had been a lively young thing in her day—vivacious almost—yet also sweet and dazzlingly pretty. But after giving birth to Hailey, all that had slowly started to change. When her placenta ruptured after the long and agonizing labor that brought Hailey into the world, Melody had bled so hard and fast that the doctors didn't waste time doing a complete hysterectomy. The cause of the abruption was never really diagnosed (her high blood pressure even then?), but as soon as Melody had been given an extra unit of blood and was officially considered stable, it didn't really matter. She had only ever wanted two children anyway, and her wish had been granted. Though part of Melody had hoped for a son for Lou, it didn't take her long to realize that Hailey would do just fine.

Her recovery took longer than she anticipated, and Melody suffered from a mild case of post-partum depression that she tried to mask by claiming exhaustion. It worked, and no one pressed her, but in the subsequent weeks and months she began the gloomy process of fading away. Melody's skin and hair, her bright eyes and trim figure, even her lively personality, never quite recovered. By this time Lou had found a new love, his baby, and Melody's gradual decline was chalked up to age. She was, after all, the mother of two young girls. Didn't every woman undergo the transformation from vibrant young wife to rumpled, middle-aged mother?

At any rate, the woman the Bennetts buried was not the same one Lou had married, and no one was the wiser but the ageless husband and lover who lived only in midnight dreams. Since Lou never remembered his dreams, he was left with nothing more than a haunting love for Melody that aged subtly with the years instead of losing intensity. He mourned her greatly.

Everyone did.

Abigail stayed home for five weeks, and during that time she asked herself every single day if she would be able to get back on a plane for Florida when the new semester began. *Can I? Can't I? Will I? Won't I?* She went back and forth endlessly, pulled in every direction the compass pointed because she felt obligated to her family but also loyal to herself, duty-bound to stay but desperate to leave. And she missed her mom. More than anything, she missed her mom.

In the end, Abigail realized that she had made her decision the moment Hailey had announced on the phone, "Mom's dead." She was going back to Florida. What was there for her in Newcastle? A father who blamed her? A sister who drained her?

"You can't go," Lou told her when she mentioned that school started in less than a week.

"I have to. My professors gave me extensions for the fall semester and I've finished all my work. I'm not even behind."

"I don't care if you've done the work. You can't leave us like this." Lou's face was chiseled marble; he didn't even take his eyes off the TV when he spoke to her.

"I've already bought my ticket."

"With whose money?"

"Mine," Abigail said. "You know I got a huge out-of-state grant. You know I've been saving for college since I was thirteen."

Lou just grunted.

"I leave on Friday. Classes start Monday."

"I'm not taking you."

"Mrs. Manning already said she would. She's going to cook you supper once a week. She even told me she'd teach Hailey how. And I'll be back for spring break. You'll be fine."

"Your mother is dead," Lou said cruelly, finally

tearing his gaze from the flickering TV and glaring at Abigail. "How can you leave us?"

"I'm not leaving you. Hailey will be sixteen in a few months—she's practically a woman. You have each other. You're going to be fine, and I'm going to get my degree." Abigail almost said, "I'll move back when I'm done," but she couldn't bring herself to lie so blatantly to his face.

Lou's lips contorted for a moment. Abigail thought he almost looked like he was going to cry, but then he managed, "Hailey's sick, Abigail Rose. I can't take care of her on my own."

"She's not sick. Everything is under control. She's been fine, hasn't she?" All at once Abigail regretted her question. Living in Florida had kept her out of the loop where Hailey was concerned. Maybe she didn't want to know anymore. Maybe she didn't want to hear about the tantrums, the self-mutilation, the suicide attempts.

But Lou didn't go into specifics. "Something like this will send her over the edge," he stated bleakly.

"She's still seeing Dr. Madsen. He'll catch it if something is going to happen. He'll change her meds, do more counseling . . ."

Lou went perfectly still. His eyes glazed over and slid away from her. "I'm alone," he whispered.

Abigail felt her heart sink past her stomach, past even her legs, her feet, until it poured out between the soft piles of brown shag carpet on the floor. "You're not alone," she whispered back. She hardly dared do it, but she moved to the edge of the couch. She sat down. "You have us."

Her father acted as if he hadn't heard her. "I'm alone," he murmured again.

"No, Dad . . . ," Abigail started, but she knew it was futile. He was mourning—they all were—and he had to deal with the loss of Melody in his own way. She patted his hand, and when he didn't flinch, Abigail tentatively put her arms around his shoulders and squeezed. "Hailey's here. And I'm a phone call away."

For her part, Hailey barely reacted to Abigail's announcement. "I knew you'd go back," she said, but there wasn't an ounce of hostility in her voice. It was as if she were merely observing the weather. *I knew it would rain today.*

"You're going to be fine, right?" Abigail said more to herself than to Hailey.

"This is what people do when someone dies," Hailey confessed dully. "They go on. Persevere. Endure. I guess we're going on."

"I guess we are."

"I'll try my best." Hailey reached behind the pillow she was wrapped around and handed Abigail a small bundle. "Here. Take these. I think Mom would have wanted you to have them."

Abigail didn't know that she was reaching for her mother's rosary and prayer book until they were folded between her hands. "No," she said, trying to hand them back, "she would have wanted *you* to have them."

"I have my own."

"But you and Mom . . ." Abigail hesitated, working around a lump in her throat. How could she admit that this was something Hailey and Melody shared, something that she was not a part of? After Hailey's confirmation, the lines of her mother's spiritual devotion deepened, too. It was a place where they could meet each other, where they could find a square of common ground on which to stand. Abigail couldn't meet them there. Maybe she didn't want to.

"Believe me, Abby," Hailey said. "These are for you."

What could she do but run her fingers across the embossed cover and feel the weight of the beads in her palm? "Thank you," Abigail whispered, knowing she held a small treasure. She leaned down and wrapped her sister in a hug. "I love you," Abigail said because it was the only thing left to say. *I love you and I can't help fearing for you at least a little*. But she couldn't say the last part.

"I love you, too."

Lou and Hailey lasted six months in Newcastle without Melody. They waited until Hailey was done with school for the year; then they sold their citron home, liquidated Melody's modest life insurance policy, and rented a small U-Haul with a car dolly to transport the few things they had decided to keep.

By the middle of June, Lou and Hailey were the proud owners of a single-wide prefabricated home at the edge of Bayou Vista, an ancient but well-kept trailer park on the outskirts of Rosa Beach, Florida.

When they showed up at the door of the on-campus apartment Abigail had rented for the summer, she didn't know whether to laugh at the ridiculousness of it or cry, so she did both. She laughed for them. And when Lou and Hailey had left and she was alone—for the moment at least—Abigail cried for herself.

It took me two weeks to gather the courage to go back to Hailey's apartment. Exactly fourteen days and two hours passed between the moment I first discovered her slumped inside the chipped porcelain bathtub until I could force myself to return and begin the process of erasing the signs of her existence.

Though removing Hailey was the last thing I wanted, I couldn't help but see it that way: like a purging almost, a deletion of Hailey Anne Bennett in every form but memory or photograph. No longer would there be a lease agreement in her name, pinning her to this time and place, assuring me that she was here and more or less safe with, at the very least, a roof over her head. No longer would there be a maxed-out credit card bearing her signature, a subscription to Vogue that she would thumb through over a cup of weak coffee, or a valid driver's license with Hailey looking unduly charming instead of gray-skinned and horrible like everyone else's frightening ID photos.

And it was my job to expunge all these tokens, these little guarantees of life. I had to sort them and box them, sell them, give them away, or store them in some closet where they could sit in ambush, waiting to remind and devastate at just the wrong moment.

I put it off for two weeks, but I would have gladly postponed my return to Hailey's apartment for two years.

When I slid my key into her front door lock for one of the last times, I half expected the small rooms to have darkened, succumbed in some visible way to grief in Hailey's absence. But the apartment was exactly as I had left it—minus, of course, the men in uniform. I closed the door behind me with a careful click, then stepped out of my shoes and crossed the floor barefoot and silent, waiflike and solemn as if I were treading on holy ground. As if her spirit hovered over me, watching. The undeniable truth was, she was everywhere I turned. And in between the places filled by her, there was something entirely unexpected: remnants of him. Of Tyler Kamp.

Of course I knew the name. Though my contact with Hailey was sporadic at best, and I had never actually met the most recent love of her life, I knew who he was. I knew what he meant to my sister. Most significantly, I knew that Hailey had anticipated him to be the person who would finally come to her rescue.

What I didn't know was everything else about him. Where did he work? Where did he live? What was he like? What were his intentions with my sister? How could he be so in love with Hailey one minute and then gone the next?

I had scanned the crowd at Hailey's vigil and at

370

her funeral, and as far as I could tell, Tyler hadn't shown up. I felt like I would recognize him instantly—Hailey never dated anything less than perfection. Her boyfriends were all legendarily attractive, more often than not whispering to her in exotic accents and radiating an air of enticing mystery. One had been a model, one an aspiring actor. Once Hailey dated a man nearly twenty years her senior who owned a yacht and took her to the Miami Bay Regatta, where she christened his new boat with a bottle of two-hundred-dollar Veuve Clicquot.

Tyler, the latest in a long line of remarkable men, would have to be equally impressive.

But no such Apollo showed up to say his final good-byes to Hailey. In fact, none of them had come at all. Her funeral mass was much like my mother's: intimate, small, almost lonely.

As I sorted through Hailey's dresser drawers, extracting the leftovers that Tyler had forgotten when he cleaned out his things and left my sister, I raged at him in my mind. Had he lived with her? or only spent the occasional night? Had he made promises that broke her heart? Or did she misinterpret his intentions? The only crime I could convict him of with any certainty was abandonment, but that didn't stop me from vilifying him for a hundred different sins that I was sure he had committed.

Hating him was cathartic, but my fury reached a

new level when I slid the nightstand drawer open and found Hailey's dreams nestled inside. A glossy print magazine stared up at me, replete with the photo of a stunning bride swathed in white. Though the magazine was new, it had obviously been thumbed through dozens of times, and there were dog-eared corners throughout. With my heart in my throat, I sank to the bed and turned to the pages she had marked.

For the rest of the afternoon, I lived the wedding that I was sure my sister had imagined. Her dress was strapless but simple, elegant in the lay of the exquisite fabric instead of the flashy sparkle of faux gems and sequins. Her ring was a platinum band encircling a square-cut diamond. Her flowers were pink roses. And I would have stood beside her in a knee-length, chocolate-colored dress.

Near the back of the magazine I found a page bookmarked with a square of creamy linen cardstock, the logo of a local greenhouse embossed in the corner. The note was short and I read it in a glance, but I held it for many long minutes studying each word as if I could uncover a secret code in his profession. There was no cloak-and-dagger mystery, but his lie had proven deadly.

I ripped the card down the middle, splitting I love you and forever, and rending Tyler's name in two.

XIII

℞ AFTER SPENDING CANADA DAY with Eli and Tyler, Abigail found herself to be the honorary member of some slapdash sort of makeshift family. The two men were already family, but Eli intentionally pulled back to make room for her in a way that was both heartwarming and disconcerting. Tyler watched from the sidelines, apparently wary of the mixed messages Abigail continued to send him, but he didn't seem opposed to seeing more of her and watching where this all would go.

As for Abigail, for the first time in years, maybe decades, she felt like there was a space carved out just for her. There was an emptiness here that she alone could fill; she didn't have to move over to make room for Hailey, another coworker, or anyone else for that matter. Deep down, Abigail feared it was useless to form any sort of attachments, and she tried to distance herself from the indefinable role that Eli seemed ready for her to satisfy. But as much as she rebelled against the possibility of letting things get muddled, she found that her defenses were steadily weakening.

Revenge, she told herself, lying in the darkness of the trailer when the stars were burning holes in the midnight sky and she couldn't sleep. *Remember why I'm here: revenge.*

But that wasn't entirely true. Abigail had pre-meditated nothing when she stepped on a plane bound for the West Coast. True, she had imagined a handful of different scenarios, of confrontations and shouting matches, of accusations that would defer some of the guilt she felt to the shoulders of the man who should rightfully bear it. She wanted to make Tyler pay. But mostly she had gone because her life was in shambles, her mind was besieged, and she felt she couldn't go on without looking into the eyes of the man who gave Hailey enough of a reason to finally kill herself. Who was he? Was he the monster she expected?

Meeting Tyler and then facing the violence that lay dormant in her own broken heart was more than Abigail had bargained for. Was she really capable of killing this man? of paying the blood sacrifice that Hailey's life, Hailey's unforgivable sin, demanded? Now that she knew Tyler was everything she had steeled herself against yet nothing she had anticipated, was she capable of going through with the penance that she believed Hailey's death required?

The way Abigail saw it, Hailey's suicide note and her two terse sentences were indicative of the tragically codependent nature of her sister's entire life. Abigail could finish Hailey's sentences for her. *I don't blame you* for twenty-six years of failing me. *I don't blame Tyler* for failing me the rest of my life. And yet somebody had to pay for their failure. Somebody had to pay for what happened, didn't they?

Because living in the tension between what she wanted to do and couldn't, and what she shouldn't do but wanted to, was so difficult, Abigail gave in for a while. She suspended the materialization of her hazy intentions and let life sweep her along as if none of what brought her to British Columbia in the first place mattered. It went so against her organized, sensible nature that Abigail felt like an off-balance centrifuge—tipping, spinning, falling. It was a jarring but not altogether disagreeable feeling. She went with it.

A few weeks after a bridge had been crossed the night they talked over salmon and wine, Eli opened up his home to Abigail and offered her the use of his downstairs bathroom. It was across the house from the little mudroom commode that she had been utilizing at night, and it featured a roomy shower with fantastic water pressure and, somewhat surprisingly, a lovely marble-topped cabinet, where she could finally store her toiletries for good.

At first, Abigail felt a little strange sliding Eli's house key out from underneath the geranium pot where he placed it just for her use. It was even harder to make herself tiptoe down the narrow hallway past the black-and-white portraits of Eli's ancestors in discolored gilt-edged frames. Once in a while, Abigail would hear footsteps above her

375

and she'd freeze, terrified of getting caught, terrified that Tyler would descend the steps and find her there, crouching in the darkness like some criminal. But then, Eli had invited her in.

Abigail had used the extra bathroom in Eli's house for a while when it struck her that the service shed locker room had gone untended since the last time she set foot in it days before. Dismayed that she had overlooked one of her responsibilities when Eli was being so nice to her, Abigail snuck to the service shed one Sunday to scour the bathroom she had neglected.

Eli usually frowned at doing work of any kind at the winery on Sundays, but she reasoned that the situation warranted it. When Eli left for church early in the morning, Abigail stole through the vineyards dressed in the stained, grubby clothes she used for cleaning out barrels. She was equipped with armfuls of towels and rags from her own stash and ready to plunge headfirst into what she knew would be a disaster zone.

The bathroom turned out to be even worse than she had expected. The floor was blotted with dirty footprints, and the mirrors were splattered with gray water. Even the lockers bore marks from muddied hands. It was so filthy, Abigail kicked one of the open metal doors with an aggravated grunt. It made such a glorious slamming sound that she opened the door and did it again. *Slam! Take that,* she thought. *Slam! And that.* But the object of her frustrations was unclear even to Abigail.

With a sigh, she dropped the towels on the short bench and crossed the room to grab the bucket of cleaners from beneath the filthy sink. But Abigail could instantly feel that the bucket was too light, and when she lifted out the industrial-size all-purpose spray, she realized the bottle was nearly empty. So was the toilet bowl cleaner and the glass spray. She couldn't clean this sort of grime with plain old water.

Abigail sighed and put her hands on her hips to survey the compact room. She knew there was a metal utility cabinet in the entryway between the bathroom and the rest of the shed, but the door was padlocked, just like the door that led to where the equipment and tools were kept.

Normally, Abigail would be too decorous to do anything other than mention the shortage to Eli and then clean the bathroom at the next opportunity she got. But there was a certain ease in her growing familiarity with Eli, and Abigail was sure that she had learned some things about her employer. One such revelation was the knowledge that he didn't keep his keys on a key chain—he hid them.

Abigail went back to the sink and got down on her knees, feeling inside the gaping cupboard and around the edges. No key as far as she could tell. Next she stood on the bench and combed the dusty tops of the four side-by-side lockers. Nothing. Searching inside the lockers, behind the plastic-framed mirror, and along the top edge of the shower stall produced the same result.

Exhausting the hiding places in the bathroom, Abigail left the dingy room and went to stand in the center of the square entryway. It was nothing more than a truncated hall, really, a ten-by-ten enclosure with doors on three sides and a utility cabinet on the fourth. One door led outside, one door led to the bathroom, and one door led to the equipment shed proper and was heavily padlocked. The only place left to look was on or around the utility cabinet itself.

Abigail slid her hands all over the cabinet but found nothing. She was too short to see the top of the metal closet, but she was determined enough to find the key that she went back into the bathroom and dragged the little bench across the floor so she could stand on it. The bench helped, but Abigail still couldn't see if there was anything on the top of the cabinet. She stood on her tiptoes and reached as far as she could, displacing an inch of dust in the process. Abigail erupted in a succession of sneezes and was about to give up when she inadvertently knocked something to the floor. The tinny clink of metal on concrete told her she had found what she was looking for.

Thompson Hills was a ghost town on Sunday morning, and Abigail celebrated her find with an uncharacteristic whoop. She hopped to the ground and retrieved the key from underneath the bench. Dusting it off, Abigail tried it in the padlock and let out another triumphant cry when it clicked. She removed the rusted lock and hooked it on the belt loop of her jean shorts, then swung the double doors wide open.

A glance at the interior of the cabinet showed Abigail that extra cleaning supplies were not stored inside. In fact, the cabinet was mostly empty, save two pairs of crusted over old work boots on the bottom shelf and a limp tool belt sagging on a ledge near the middle. Straining to see the top shelves, Abigail noted that there was a cardboard box near the top. It was just tall enough to contain a few stacked bottles of cleaning solution, and since she had gone through so much trouble to open the metal chest in the first place, she positioned the bench so she could reach the box and see for herself.

Something inside the box thudded dully when she pulled it down. It didn't slosh or feel heavy enough to contain bottles of cleaner, but Abigail peeled back the cardboard tabs anyway and peered inside. There were a handful of dirty rags that she pawed out of the way, then a stack of old newspapers and outdated *National Geographic* magazines that she ignored. Sticking her hand deep into the box, Abigail patted the dark recesses until her fingers struck something cold and hard. Confused by the smooth feel of icy metal, she gripped the object and lifted it to the light.

The moment it was in her palm, Abigail knew what she was holding, but that didn't stop her from letting a choked gasp escape her lips when the handle of a graphite-colored handgun appeared above the edge of the box. Shock sent a series of stinging tremors from her scalp to her fingertips, and she instinctively tightened her grip.

Abigail was holding the barrel of the gun, a long, cool cylinder that was rounded on the bottom and squared on the top with a raised sight at the tip of each end. Biting her lip, she carefully aligned the weapon in her right hand, gripping the notched black handle so that the barrel lay flat in her left palm. She avoided the trigger so vigilantly, it might have been tipped with poison.

Etched into the side of the gun was the word *Glock*, and then, after a short space, 22. The *G* of *Glock* was elongated and misshapen; it encompassed the entire word, wrapping around it so the only truly legible letters were *lock*. Something about the brand, the distinctive logo, stirred a forgotten corner of Abigail's memory. She was an avid news buff and read every issue of *Newsweek* cover to cover. Surely there had been an article about Glock handguns. Were they used by law enforcement professionals?

Confused and slightly afraid, Abigail turned the weapon over and over. It was very cold and much,

much heavier than she had imagined a gun would be. She had never held a gun before, and it filled her with a sort of hostile dread—she hated the way it felt in her hands, the way it pressed her arms down and forced her to hold it up almost against her will. *Guns don't kill people,* she thought. *People kill people.* With the ominous weight of cold metal in her palms, Abigail had to agree. Lifting this weapon, peering down the line of sight, and pulling the trigger would have to be an act of intention.

With a very deliberate motion and a disproportionately unsteady hand, Abigail raised the gun and pointed it at the round, silver lock of the bathroom door. There was an obvious scored grip at the end of the barrel, and she grasped it in between her thumb and the knuckle of her forefinger and pulled. It stuck.

Abigail wasn't strong enough to chamber a round with the gun raised, so she lowered it and pushed down on the handle while she tried again. It took her three tries, but eventually there was the smooth clack-clack-clack of metal on metal, and Abigail saw the brassy flash of a bullet before the chamber snapped closed so hard she jumped. Then, filling her lungs with as much air as they would hold, she held the gun in her right hand and supported the bottom with her left. Abigail found the door lock, closed one eye, and aligned the sights.

When the barrel was perfectly in line with her target, Abigail put her finger on the trigger. *"Bang,"* she whispered.

That one little word sent shock waves down her taut spine. It startled Abigail so much, it sounded so definitive, so harsh, that she dropped the gun.

The clatter of the Glock hitting the floor made her scream. Abigail sprang away from the discarded weapon as if it were a cobra, coiled and ready to strike, instead of a neglected piece of man-made hardware. Her heart was thudding so hard it ached in her chest, and she pressed the heel of her hand to her breastbone in the hope of easing the pain.

With her hand in place over her heart, Abigail impulsively crossed herself. It was something she rarely did, something that signified a childhood that had been less than idyllic, that she tried to forget. But with the strange black gun at her feet, somehow it felt appropriate. Forehead, chest, shoulder, shoulder. Each touch deliberate, almost calculated.

"Elijah Dixon," Abigail said, "what in the world are you doing with a gun in your cabinet?"

Abigail had a vague awareness of the fact that guns were far more strictly regulated in Canada than they were in the U.S., and she was sure that Eli would be in serious trouble if anyone knew there was a Glock hidden in his equipment shed. Had he crossed the border with it? Why was it so recklessly abandoned in the bottom of a nonde-script cardboard box? Why was it loaded? Abigail knotted her fingers in her hair and held her head. *Was* it loaded? Had she seen a bullet? Or were her eyes playing tricks on her?

Regret expanded against Abigail's rib cage until she was sure that she could hear the crack of sepa-rating bones. She wished with all her being that she had never gone snooping for more cleaning supplies. She wished she could forget what she had uncovered.

She had to make it go away.

Abigail grabbed the gun with two fingers and thrust it back into the box. She arranged the maga-zines and newspapers over the top of it, then scat-tered the rags so they covered everything. As she wove the four cardboard tabs together, Abigail sti-fled a sickened shiver. She was putting a loaded gun in a flimsy box meant for nothing more threat-ening than a few bottles of cleaner. Thankfully, it looked like no one had touched it for years, and she wondered if there was a way she could return the thick layer of dust to the box. But no, that was impossible. She'd have to just put it back where she found it, lock the cabinet, and pray that no one noticed that the accumulation of dusty soot had been displaced.

Abigail arranged everything just the way it had been, including the padlock key at the far right corner of the cabinet top, and cautiously backed out of the equipment shed casting guilty glances over her shoulder. No one was around. No one had seen her. And yet she couldn't shake a feeling of culpability, as if she were the one who had put the gun there instead of merely being the person who found it.

But as she sprinted from the service shed, Abigail knew that her conscience was troubled for good reason. For even as she hated the feel of that gun, even as she lamented the fact that she had found it in the first place, some small part of her soul rang with the knowledge that if she hoped to make Tyler pay for what he had done, she now had a way to do it.

If there was a way to thrive with Lou and Hailey transplanted in Florida, Abigail never discovered it. When her father and sister made the transition to Rosa Beach, Abigail wanted nothing more than to ignore their presence. How could they do this to her? How could they invade her new life, wreck her chance at a fresh start?

But as much as she resented the intrusion, Abigail also understood that Lou's intention was never to ruin her life. He merely wanted to preserve his own.

Abigail had been in Florida for less than a year, and in the months of her absence Hailey had undergone yet another personality evolution. At sixteen years old, she was a force to be reckoned with for more reasons than simply her disarming good looks.

There had always been a bit of an edge to Hailey Bennett, but the almost-woman she had become in her adolescence had such a wild fierceness to her it was downright alarming. She seemed taut, ready to burst at any moment, to dissolve into tears or fly into a rage at the smallest hint of provocation. Abigail quickly realized that Hailey's growing instability was a secret that first Melody and then Lou had carefully guarded from her.

But no one could hide it anymore. Whether she liked it or not, Abigail was once again thrust into the multifaceted role of mother, caretaker, and disciplinarian, never mind sister and friend.

Although it wasn't like Hailey wanted her sister to step into that role. Hailey was reveling in the anonymity of being the new girl in a new town. Nobody knew her or her past. No one had heard alarming stories about that "pretty Bennett girl" or told their kids to stay away from that "strange child."

School wasn't in session, but that didn't mean that Hailey wasn't instantly popular—she trawled the mall and made friends by merit of her striking blue eyes and flippant ways. She was perfectly imperfect with her eccentric ideas and lightning flash of changing moods. Hailey was the definition of cool because she was the most beautifully astonishing person anyone could ever hope to meet.

Beautiful, astonishing, eccentric, striking . . . Hailey was many things. But just below the surface she was also unstable, and within the first month that Lou and Hailey lived in Florida, she proved the extent of her unpredictability.

Abigail had a work-study job in the library of South Seminole, and she was busy fixing the bindings on aging books one day when the phone at the front desk rang.

"Phone for you, Abigail," the head librarian called over the return counter. Her voice was soft and melodious, but there was a peculiar look on her face that said, "You shouldn't be receiving calls on the job."

"Thank you," Abigail said, ducking her head. She put down the book that she had been working on and tried to hurry over to the phone without disrupting the hushed air of the nearly empty library.

Taking the phone and turning her back on her boss with an apologetic smile, Abigail muttered into the mouthpiece, "Yes?"

"Abby, you gotta come and pick me up."

"Hailey?"

"Who'd you think it was? Seriously, Sis, sometimes you are so opaque."

"Dense, Hailey. Be normal—say *dense*."

"Impenetrable."

"Whatever. Where are you?"

"In the security office at the Sawgrass Sands Mall."

"What?"

"I got in a fight."

"What?" Abigail's voice hurdled over the acceptable threshold of noise.

"Shhh!"

Abigail swiveled to face her employer, her cheeks ashen. "Sorry," she mouthed. Then she turned away again and whispered into the phone, "Hailey Bennett, you did not get into a fight."

"Oh, but I did." Her voice dropped. "And I won. You should see the other girl."

"You got into a catfight?"

"That's not what we call it. We call it a—"

"Hailey."

"Whatever. Just come pick me up. They won't let me go until a parent or guardian comes to collect me."

Abigail wanted to say, "I'm neither of those things," but she strangled the phone instead. She was going to tell Hailey that she'd be there after work; cooling her heels in the mall security office for a couple of hours would do her sister a little good. But before Abigail could say another word, Hailey hung up on her.

Abigail stopped just short of slamming the receiver down and had a full-blown argument with herself over what to do. Should she call Lou? go down there herself? She didn't get off work for another two and a half hours. Could she let Hailey wither beneath the cold stares of angry security

387

guards for that long? Then again, Hailey hardly sounded like she was in wallflower mode. More likely than not she'd hold up just fine on her own.

But whether or not Hailey would be permanently damaged by a short stay in the custody of beefy mall guards, Abigail couldn't bring herself to abandon her sister. Melody hadn't even been gone a year—who knew what sort of emotional turmoil the already-scarred Hailey was enduring?

Though the head librarian was less than impressed that an employee was going to skip out of work early, Abigail didn't give her a choice. "Family crisis," she explained, not waiting for permission to leave.

The security office of Sawgrass Sands wasn't hard to find. Abigail parked near a Guess? outlet at the posh, pedestrian mall and followed the wrought-iron road signs to a narrow hallway between the Gap and Banana Republic. At the end of the brick walkway was a well-lit and modern-looking office. And there, behind the glass door marked Security, Abigail could just make out the kitten heel of one of Hailey's new black sandals. It was bobbing, bobbing, bobbing.

Taking a steadying breath, Abigail pushed open the door and intentionally turned away from her sister. On the opposite side of the room was a burly man in a white collared shirt behind a high counter. "Hi," she said evenly, extending her hand. "I'm Abigail Bennett. I'm here to pick up Hailey."

The guard gave her a bored look, completely ignored her outstretched hand, and turned back to the papers in front of him. "I need to speak with her parent or guardian."

"I'm her sister."

"Good for you."

Abigail sighed. "Our mother died last year and our father is . . . He's not equipped to deal with this sort of thing. I'm the closest thing Hailey's got to a functioning parent."

The guard squinted at Abigail for a moment, apparently trying to decide if her story was a farce intended to pull his heartstrings or something close to the truth.

"I'm a junior at South Seminole majoring in accounting," Abigail offered as if the reference to her education would impress him. "I'll take responsibility for whatever my sister has done."

"You don't look like your sister," the guard assessed coolly.

Abigail shot Hailey a glance, taking in her miniskirt and layered, skin-hugging tank tops. "Tell me about it," she muttered.

"You don't look old enough to be in college."

"Would you like to see my ID?" Abigail retorted.

The guard paused, deliberating, and then pushed himself off the stool he was sitting on and moved in front of the counter. "Fine. You can have her. You're lucky—the other girl's family doesn't want to press charges since you'd probably just sue back. But this young woman is effectively banned from Sawgrass Sands. I don't want to see her here again." He crossed his arms and glared at Hailey. "Got that, missy?"

"Missy?" Hailey questioned, her eyebrows arching dramatically.

Abigail all but jumped across the small room and grabbed her sister's arm. "Come on."

Hailey was standing now, towering over Abigail in her little heels. Abigail could feel the electricity in her sister's body, the way she leaned slightly toward the security guard as if she wanted to go after him, too. Why had he called her missy?

"Let's go." Abigail pushed Hailey in front of her and turned to the security guard to distract him from the antagonism in the younger girl's eyes. "I'm so sorry about what happened," Abigail said, even though what happened had absolutely nothing to do with her. "It won't happen again. I'll make sure of that."

Then they were out the door and Hailey's heels were a staccato of angry sound on the patterned red bricks. "Can you believe that?" she fumed.

"Now is not the time for you to get all indignant."

"But he—"

"But nothing. You got in a fight!" Abigail nearly shouted. "What were you thinking?"

Hailey didn't even bother to shrug.

"What happened?"

"Nothing."

Abigail glowered at her and suddenly caught sight of a rosy purple bruise that was beginning to form on the delicate line of Hailey's well-defined jaw. She reached out, unable to control the spontaneous, motherly gesture. "You're hurt."

Hailey swatted her hand away. "I'm fine."

"I should see the other girl, right?"

Hailey laughed.

"Is she okay?"

"The other girl?"

Abigail groaned in exasperation.

"She's fine," Hailey answered.

"What happened? If you don't tell me, I'll go back and ask that security guard."

"She called me crazy." Hailey laughed suddenly, twisting her face up and spinning her finger around her temple as if to underline the other girl's point.

Abigail stared at her, trying to penetrate the thick wall of sickness, the jumble of her confused mind. "You're not taking your pills, are you?"

"No," Hailey admitted freely.

"You haven't found a new psychologist, have you?"

"Dr. Madsen didn't really do anything anyway."

"Yes, he did. And you can't be off your meds. You need them." Abigail threw her shoulders back a little and tried to live up to the promise that she had made the security guard: *I'll take responsi-*

bility. "You have to take your medication. That's not a request."

Hailey's eyes flashed with a spark of ice blue fire for a split second. Then she smiled calmly and reached into her purse. Extracting a pack of Camel Lights, she tapped out a single cigarette, placed it between her full, pouty lips, and lit it with a hot pink lighter. She took a long drag, then gracefully pulled the cigarette from her mouth and winked at Abigail. "Make me."

જ *I knew it could be potentially ruinous to let myself be dragged down into the mire of questions that surrounded Hailey. And yet, sitting in the dusty, filtered light of her tomblike apartment with the magazine that boasted her dreams in my hands, I suddenly knew that I could not go on until I had at least spoken to her boyfriend. Former boyfriend? Where was he?*

Will you marry me? *The words swept across the bottom of the bridal magazine as if in imitation of the question Hailey had obviously longed to hear. Were they merely a wish? or an actuality? I suspected that Tyler had formally asked her no such thing—there was no ring for proof, no gleeful call to anyone she loved—but it was not impossible to imagine that they had talked about it. Didn't he know her well enough? Didn't he know enough about her to realize that toying with her emotions in any way was flirting with disaster?*

I surged off Hailey's bed and sought out the black purse that I had earlier avoided. Turning the bag upside down, I unearthed a small bottle of lotion, two tubes of lipstick in Red Rebellion and Soft Nude, a leather-bound calendar that proved to be all but empty, a crumpled napkin, a purse pack of tissues, Hailey's faux snakeskin wallet, and her cell phone. The charge on Hailey's phone was completely dead, but I would plug it in and check her missed calls and her address book later—I would find him, track him down, make him tell me why. But not just now.

For now, her wallet contained exactly what I was looking for. Folded between a coupon for a local spa and a coffee shop receipt, I found a photograph with rumpled edges. It was a snapshot that had been cut down so it could fit in the slender pocket reserved for business cards and notes. The background had been completely trimmed away, and the only thing that remained inside the frame of the white, curled border was my sister's lovely face and the profile of a slightly disheveled man.

Hailey was gorgeous as always, but my eyes were instantly drawn to the man. He had a surfer-boy look to him; his dark tan and sun-highlighted hair were accented by blue green eyes the color of the ocean where the sand dropped down and away, into the deep. There was a shock of maple gold hair that looked like it was about to fall over his eyes, but he wasn't paying attention to it—his gaze was fixed on Hailey. His lips were slightly parted, as if he was just about to say her name or maybe kiss her.

This was the man, I knew it, and all at once I wanted to reach through the photograph and grab him. I wanted to spin him around, wipe that little half smirk off his lips. I'd demand to know what happened.

"Tyler," I said thickly, "what have you done?"

XIV

❧ AFTER SHE FOUND the gun, Abigail paced like a caged animal for days. Never before had she felt so trapped at Thompson Hills. She felt chained, bound by her sham of a job and the false relationships that she had allowed herself to form. But that was only a part of it. The cause of her entrapment was ultimately Hailey, and Abigail was sick to death of trying to right impossible wrongs. She was sick of living like an imposter, sick of lying and scheming, of trying to feed a fading hate for Tyler even as she questioned her own ability to follow through with any vicious plan she managed to concoct.

Two months of her life had been spent in British Columbia, and in that time Abigail had accomplished nothing. Nothing. Eli had carved a somewhat-tender spot for himself in her heart, and she genuinely and rather curiously enjoyed her job and the small town of Revell, but who was she trying to fool? Herself? She couldn't stay here in this heartbreaking limbo. This couldn't go on. Abigail admonished herself for not having the courage to confront Tyler, to utter Hailey's name in his presence and hear what he had to say. And she resented the discovery of the mysterious gun, the way it mocked her with the means to do what she hardly even dared to think about.

Abigail's life was an awkward suspension, a careful balance between where she was and where she wanted to be. The truth was, she wasn't ready to go back to Florida, but it was becoming too painful to stay.

"What's up with you?" Paige asked one morning when Abigail slumped up the steps to Thompson Hills.

"Nothing," she grunted because that one word seemed to sum up her entire life.

"Liar," Paige accused. "You look like Eli chewed you up and spit you out."

Abigail threw her arms up. "What is it with everyone vilifying Eli? He's a decent guy, you know."

Paige narrowed her eyes as if considering whether or not Abigail was serious. Finally she said, "You're right. Eli's okay. It's just part of the culture around here. We pour wine, we smile nice, and we complain about Eli."

"Then the culture around here sucks."

"Maybe a little. Maybe we just need to be countercultural, eh?" Paige smiled and snapped her fingers. "I know what you need. You need to get away. Have you had a single day off all summer? Eli works you like he owns you." The smile fluttered on her pretty face. "No offense."

"None taken."

"Good." Paige threw a sly look over her shoulder and then unzipped her purse in one fluid movement. Snaking her hand inside, she groped around until she emerged victorious with a set of keys clutched in her fist. "You don't look well, Abigail. I think you are definitely coming down with something."

"I feel fine," Abigail protested.

"No, you don't. You feel awful." Paige thrust the keys at Abigail. "My car is the silver Honda. You'd better take it into town and get yourself something for that pounding headache."

"But I—"

Paige grabbed Abigail's wrist and turned her hand palm up. "And then I think you'd better put your feet up somewhere. A little R & R will do you a world of good. You'll be a different person tomorrow." She dropped the keys into Abigail's hand and forced her fingers to curl around them.

"Eli will—"

"Oh, for heaven's sake, get in that car before I smack you."

Abigail tried to scowl but couldn't stop herself from smiling instead. "Thank you."

"No thanks needed. I'll just add it to your tab. Covering for you with Eli breathing down my neck should be worth a small fortune at least." When Abigail raised a cautionary eyebrow, Paige amended herself. "Not that he's not a nice guy and all."

"You're such a nonconformist," Abigail teased.

Paige gave her a little shove. "Get out of here

before he sees you looking all healthy and put together. Disappear."

Disappear. The perky waitress couldn't have said anything more inviting. "I will." Abigail's words were as solemn as a promise.

Paige's car was immaculately clean and smelled of watermelon. Somehow it felt homey to Abigail; it reminded her of her own little Passat and the strawberry air freshener that her mechanic sprayed under the floor mats when she had it serviced. The scent, the feel of the car lanced Abigail with a sharp pang of homesickness that she quickly stifled under the thrill of skipping out of work.

Driving Paige's car was different from driving Eli's. She felt free to have a little fun with it, to drive it like it was her car and not a loaner. Best of all, the silver Honda had a standard transmission; the clutch was just a smidge stiff but the gears were fluid. As Abigail pulled out of the parking lot of Thompson Hills, she decided she might never come back. The thought excited her, but somewhere buried deep she had to acknowledge that she would actually miss Eli when the day to leave did finally come.

The light feeling carried Abigail for several kilometers as she drove back the way she had come to Revell—winding up the rocky cliffs and heading toward the crisscrossing web of mountains. When she had coasted into town all those weeks ago, it had been dark and Abigail had missed the charming fruit stands and profusion of cheerful signs. Billboards proclaiming fresh cherries, apricots, peaches, plums, pears, and apples dotted the countryside, competing for attention with bolder, brighter colors and asserting that they were all the consummate best.

Since it was the beginning of August, Abigail knew that peaches and apricots were just hitting the peak of their season. She drove past nearly a dozen fruit stands before she turned into a field driveway and headed back for the smallest, most nondescript of the bunch. The middle-aged caretaker helped her select three perfect peaches, which she carried over to a picnic table for breakfast à la carte.

There was a small hand pump near the picnic table with a green produce basket turned upside down beneath it. A wooden sign hung around the neck of the faucet, declaring, "If you just can't wait . . ."

Abigail put two of her peaches on the table, then primed the pump once or twice and washed the final piece of fruit beneath a spray of ice-cold water. She ran her fingers over the soft fuzz until the peach felt smooth; then she wiped it on her shirt and ate it like an apple.

Peach juice trickled down her chin and ran in rivulets along her hands and arms until it dripped off her elbows. For some reason, Abigail didn't mind the sticky sweetness. In this one moment, away from the winery and separated by thousands of miles from her father, her job, her obligations, she was more than content to play the part of a child. Abigail licked her syrupy fingers instead of scrubbing them under the pump.

Although she was happy for the break, when Abigail got back into the car, she realized that she had no idea what to do next. The beach seemed out of the question—she couldn't stomach the thought of lounging in the sand with nothing to distract her mind from all the things that troubled her. Shopping? No, the only shops in and around Revell were touristy T-shirt joints that sold flip-flops and cheap clothes with mass-produced witticisms like "My grandpa and grandma went to the Summerlands and all I got was this lousy T-shirt." A spontaneous grin twisted Abigail's lips at the thought of buying something like that for Lou. But no, she had no desire to shop. Or eat or sightsee or drive down long, lonely roads. What, then?

It was never Abigail's intention to pull into the parking lot of the Sunny Grove Inn and RV Park, but as she drove past the distinctive L-shaped building, she found the tug irrepressible. Suddenly she was stepping on the brakes, spinning the wheel, and coasting into the only territory other than Thompson Hills that she could consider truly familiar in Revell. She hoped Jane was around.

Abigail found the older woman sweeping a long-handled net over the surface of the outdoor pool. The accountant-cum-sommelier smiled unreservedly, happy to find things as she had left them, happy to have something even marginally recognizable that she could sink into for a while. She unlatched the heavy gate and stepped beneath the grapevine arbor, where she found the exact same chair that she had sat in at the beginning of the summer. Abigail sank into the plastic-banded lounger with a sigh.

"You're lucky," Jane said without turning around. "You've got the pool to yourself for a while. Seems like all those families with the little kids went down to the beach for the day."

"Perfect," Abigail exhaled. "I was hoping for some peace and quiet."

Abigail was sure that there was no way Jane could possibly recognize her voice, but the motel proprietor spun around instantly as if she did. "Abigail?"

"You remembered my name!"

"Of course I did! I've been waiting for you to stop by for weeks. What happened to getting ice cream together?"

"I'm sort of partial to wine now."

Jane laughed. "Well, how about lemonade instead? Could I talk you into a glass of lemonade? It's Country Time—you stir the powder into some water—but it tastes okay on ice."

"Sounds great."

Abandoning the net by the side of the pool, Jane crossed over to where Abigail was sitting. For a moment the two women struggled with the strange impulse to hug each other, but then Jane merely extended her arm and took Abigail's hand in both of her own.

"You smell like peaches," Jane commented with a wide smile. "It's nice to see you. I'm glad you came to say hi."

"Me too."

Jane hurried over to the motel office and came back a few minutes later carrying two mismatched glasses and a squat pitcher that tinkled merrily with ice cubes. She set them down on a table near Abigail and pulled up a chair beside her.

"The pool is usually packed by this time every day. If you would have stopped by yesterday, we wouldn't have been able to hear each other over the din."

"Has it been a good summer?" Abigail asked, gesturing toward the line of rooms. She didn't know what else to say. Only moments ago it had felt so right to stop at the Sunny Grove, but now that she was here, Abigail didn't know how to make conversation with this woman who was a virtual stranger. She smiled awkwardly, but Jane didn't seem to notice.

"Oh, it's always a good summer. People come; they go. . . . I clean the pool and take their money." Jane laughed at her own joke as she poured a glass of lemonade. "How about you? Has it been a good summer?"

Abigail cocked her head, considering. "I suppose so. It's beautiful here."

"Yes, it is," Jane agreed. "Where are you these days? Are you still in Revell?"

"I'm a bit embarrassed to tell you where I am," Abigail admitted. "I don't think you're a huge fan of my boss."

Jane took a sip of her lemonade, raising her eyebrows above the rim of the glass in obvious interest.

"I'm working at Thompson Hills," Abigail said in response to her unspoken query. She studied Jane's face for any sign of surprise, but the older woman didn't seem shocked at all. Nor did her eyes flash with any betraying emotion about Elijah Dixon. Abigail was confused. Hadn't Jane warned her about Eli?

"What makes you think I'm not a fan of Elijah?" Jane wondered.

"We talked about him. Remember? You said . . ."

"I said he was a miserable old bear. If you've been working with him all summer, you know full well that he's a bit of a bear. As for miserable, well, I think you may have misinterpreted my meaning."

Abigail was speechless. She had assumed that Jane meant Eli was miserly, unpleasant, and mean. Her conjecture was underscored by her coworkers, but Abigail had never really taken the time to wonder why Eli was the gruff perfectionist she had come to know and respect.

"I haven't seen him in well over a year," Jane admitted. "But the last time I spoke with Elijah, he was a very miserable old man." She looked pointedly at Abigail. "And by that I mean sad. Depressed."

"Why?" The question was out of Abigail's mouth before she could stop it. She didn't mean to pry, but it was hard not to wonder what sort of sadness shaped her boss.

"I don't think it's my place to tell Elijah's story," Jane said. "But he has much to regret, as I'm sure we all do."

The women were silent as they took turns staring into the foggy depths of their lemonade and looking off over the cool face of the sparkling blue water. Abigail could see white puffs of clouds reflected on the smooth surface of the pool. She looked up and saw the mirror image floating in the expanse of sky above her. For a moment she wondered which clouds were real and which were merely reflections—they were the same: white on blue and white on blue.

Jane eventually asked Abigail another question and they moved to less uncertain ground, chatting about safer things. They talked for almost an hour, and by the time Abigail's glass was nearly empty, she felt a sort of defiant calm settle over her as if she intended to wrench a little relaxation out of her day even if it meant she had to ignore the doubts that crowded her mind. Regret, misery, secrets . . . Abigail drowned such thoughts with one last gulp of sandy-textured lemonade.

As Abigail handed Jane her glass, a minivan pulled into the Sunny Grove parking lot.

"Good timing," Jane commented, indicating the well-traveled family that all but fell out of the still-moving van. "I needed something to get myself in gear. I could sit here and chitchat all day long."

The two women watched as a trio of kids spotted the pool and let out a series of excited cries. They raced over to the gate in direct disobedience to their father's command to "Stay here!"

"It's gonna get noisy," Abigail observed.

"Well," Jane said, getting to her feet and gathering the pitcher and glasses, "I'm glad you stopped by. It was so nice to see you."

"It was nice to see you, too."

"Will you come back again?"

"Yeah," Abigail said, wishing in spite of herself that this was a relationship she could continue to form.

"Lucky for you, if you ever want to see me again, you know exactly where I'll be." Jane grinned and started to walk away.

With a cheeky lilt in her voice, Abigail called after her, "Too bad I don't believe in luck."

Jane stopped. Turned around. "Neither do I." Her eyes glinted at Abigail, mirroring the clouds in the water, the sky. "Some people would just rather hear 'you're lucky' than 'you're blessed.' " She winked and gave Abigail a jaunty little bow. "But since you don't believe in luck either, I suppose I can call you what you are: blessed."

The word snagged on an exposed corner of Abigail's carefully veiled heart and floated there, a balloon anchored by the sharp edge of her skepticism. Blessed? Jane had no idea what she was talking about. How in the world could anyone consider Abigail Bennett's life blessed? Would Jane call her blessed if she knew that Abigail had held that gun and pointed it, practicing? wondering if she could pull the trigger when the barrel was aimed at something other than the lock on a bathroom door? And yet Abigail couldn't help wanting to cling to that small word, that token of something more. Against all odds, hope unfurled a tentative wing, stroked the sky.

As Abigail watched Jane walk away, she found it hard not to hope that her friend was right. Maybe the end of her story hadn't been written yet.

It was time to find out.

The rest of the day melted away, the minutes and hours of freedom rendered languorous and dreamlike by the draining sun. Abigail went back to the winery around midafternoon, when she knew it was busy and when she suspected that Eli had slipped into his dark, cool office for a short catnap with his head on the desk. She parked Paige's car close to the building, cracked the windows an inch for ventilation, and hid the keys under the mat. Paige would find them, and Abigail wasn't at all worried about theft in this harmless little town.

Back at the trailer with no one around, Abigail unearthed her neglected phone and plugged it into one of the outlets in Eli's downstairs bathroom. She let it charge for an hour or so while she cleaned up. Then she turned her cell phone on, ready to pay the exorbitant roaming fees.

Once every ten days or so, Abigail touched base with her other life. She phoned the Four Seasons Manor Home and made contact with Johnson, McNally & Bennett. Even though Abigail didn't believe them, the ladies at the Four Seasons told her, *Your father needs you.* And if she was talking to Marguerite, she always heard, *Your clients need you. We need you.* Both calls always ended the same: *When are you coming home?*

As far as she was concerned, they could not have possibly posed a more difficult question. There were so many variables, so many uncertainties. *I don't know,* she answered, her response as predictable as their query. But today, with Jane's unwitting encouragement, she felt ready to be more definitive. She felt capable of saying, *Soon.*

Finding the handgun in Eli's locked cabinet, then spending time in the soothing, normalizing presence of someone as down-to-earth as Jane had been a sort of wake-up call for Abigail. Her time at Thompson Hills and her distance from Hailey's suicide were granting her a perspective that she hadn't bargained for.

It was with a sense of urgency that Abigail waited for the evening to fade. She avoided Eli's house and made sure that she was out of sight when Eli and Tyler came home around dinnertime. But when the sun tucked itself below the edge of the horizon and a cooling, purple veil unfolded across the sky, Abigail took a few shuddering breaths, whispered something that may have been classified as a desperate prayer, and crossed the driveway to Eli's side door.

Something inside her recoiled at the thought of seeing Eli right now—she couldn't stand the idea of looking into his face, of disregarding his kindness toward her, his subtle influence, and boldly asking to see his nephew. She knocked twice and muttered almost inaudibly, "Let it be Tyler."

It was. Tyler opened the door with his lips forming a question, but instead of asking it, he swallowed and said, "I'll get Eli."

"No." Abigail stopped him. "Actually I was looking for you."

Tyler shrugged. "You found me."

"Yeah. Um . . ." Abigail berated herself for not planning this out better. What was she supposed to say? "I was just . . . I was wondering if you knew what tonight was."

The quizzical look Tyler shot her was far from encouraging.

"I mean, tonight isn't necessarily a *special* night, but it is a *moonless* night." *Stupid,* she thought. *I sound so stupid.* But she fumbled on. "It's the once-a-year, most perfect night for seeing the Perseids."

"You lost me at *tonight.*"

Abigail could hardly blame Tyler for being diffi-cult, but it took all her patience to forge ahead. "The Perseids are a meteor shower. They stretch along the orbit of the comet Swift-Tuttle, and they're very, uh, easy to see with the naked eye."

"Meteors?"

"I like that stuff." Abigail bobbed her head almost shyly and caught a ragged breath. She looked at Tyler through downturned lashes. "You know, meteors, stars, comets . . ."

"*Star Trek*?"

"No, not *Star Trek.*"

"*Star Wars*?"

"Is this a test?"

"Nah, I'm just giving you a hard time." Tyler put his hand on the doorframe and let a thin smile crack his chiseled face. "So the Perseids are hap-pening tonight?"

"Yes."

"And . . . ?"

"I was wondering if you'd like to watch with me." The words cartwheeled over each other in their rush to escape. *I did it!* Abigail thought. *Now all he has to do is say . . .*

"Sure. But I thought you were sick."

"I'm feeling better."

Tyler's eyes narrowed. "I thought you didn't like me."

"I'm making amends." Abigail took a tiny gulp.

"Okay . . ." Tyler drew out the syllables, stalling. "Where and when?"

"Somewhere high, away from light pollution. Anytime after eleven."

Tyler checked his watch. "I'll meet you in two hours, right here. We can walk the vineyards to the ridge at the border of Warkentin's orchards."

Abigail nodded. Tyler mimicked her assent, then closed the door slowly, as if he half expected her to say something more. She didn't.

The two hours passed quickly for Abigail, for what were mere minutes in light of all the weeks and months that she had waited to confront Tyler? A solitary journey to the service shed to retrieve the gun erased nearly an hour because although Abigail tried to convince herself that stealing the Glock from its hiding place was no big deal, she stood in front of the cabinet for many long minutes before she worked up the courage to reach for the key. By the time Abigail returned to the little trailer, there was nothing left for her to do but turn the weapon over and over in her hands, turn everything over and over in her mind.

Abigail was arranging the hood of a bulky sweat-shirt around her neck when Tyler emerged from Eli's darkened house. She felt like a gangland thug in the silly ensemble, but it was chilly, and the only other long-sleeved shirts she had were either dressy or in the wash. All the same, she hoped she didn't look like she was hiding something. Even though she was.

Tyler mumbled hello and Abigail responded similarly. They didn't wave or smile or greet each other with enthusiasm; they sized up the situation warily, hesitant to set the tone for what was ahead.

When Tyler took off on a path that led away from the winery, Abigail fell into step beside him. She tucked her hands in the large front pocket of her hoodie so she could mangle her fingers in secret. It was dark and her hands were hidden, but she was sure that she was white-knuckled around the chill of the weighted metal.

They walked in silence for several minutes, stepping on their own shadows cast by the dirty yellow rays of Eli's yard light. The dim, narrow ghosts that lay before them got smaller and smaller, fainter and fainter until they disappeared completely and the pair found themselves shrouded in the utter blackness of a stark, moonless night.

"Good thing I took this," Tyler said, pulling a flashlight from the cargo pocket of his frayed shorts.

He clicked it on and trained the beam on the

ground in front of him, but Abigail reached over to stop him. For a moment it seemed as if she was going to put her hand on his arm, but she couldn't do it. Instead she pointed up and instructed, "Turn it off."

Tyler complied without argument and raised his eyes heavenward, following the line of her finger.

The sky above them had the same luminous quality as the ebony marble-topped cabinet in Eli's bathroom. It shimmered. It pulsed and breathed and hummed like a lovely, living thing. The enormity of darkness was stunning, a sable pool of fine ink spilled across the heavens, but it was also staggeringly bright. It glittered with a million points of light, a million distant fireflies that flickered endlessly against the black.

As they watched, a handful of meteors trembled free from their jeweled settings and careened across the vastness, disappearing into the horizon or flickering out unnoticed in some far-flung universe. Just as one meteor faded into nothingness, another took its place and began the swift fall to oblivion. Abigail wondered, as she always did, if and where they landed, these little pieces of heaven. These so-called falling stars.

"Wow," Tyler breathed, and Abigail was surprised to hear real wonder in his voice.

"This is the peak," Abigail explained. "We should be able to see fifty to eighty meteors an hour tonight."

"I've never seen so many falling stars in my life."

"They're not stars," Abigail corrected Tyler before she could stop herself.

The air was thick and viscous, impenetrable, but Abigail could make out the contour of Tyler's face as he turned toward her. "Meteors," he amended. "So you're an astronomer in another life?"

"Among other things." Abigail paused, considering how much to disclose and how much to hold tight. "Actually my sister had a thing for the sky. Anything I know about stars, constellations, *meteors* . . . it all came from her." She waited for Tyler to say something in recognition, to tell her that he once dated a girl who loved stars, who was born beneath the standard of a well-known comet, but he didn't say anything.

Tyler switched on the flashlight again. "Let's find a place to sit."

Abigail fell in step behind him, single file, and tried to keep pace as his long legs swallowed up the path in front of them. Tyler was tense; she could sense it—she could trace the outline of his nervous energy as surely as she could feel the sharp rim of the gun's sight beneath her fingertip. But she didn't know what to say to him, and she didn't know how to put him at ease nor did she necessarily want to. So she walked in silence, listening to the thud and shuffle of their feet on the ground, and waited for Tyler to tell her that they had arrived.

The hike took about fifteen minutes, and as they emerged on the lip of a small cliff above the straight rows of gnarled cherry trees, Abigail turned a slow circle. As far as she could tell, there were no farms nearby, no homes lit up with the glow of a television or maybe a nightstand lamp. What would a gunshot sound like in this place? How far would it echo? Would anyone be close enough to hear and wonder, *What was that? A rancher shooting a coyote? A crow cannon going off accidentally?*

"I didn't think to bring a blanket," Tyler said.

Abigail spun to see him standing there, arms akimbo, the flashlight pointed at the ground uselessly. She flipped up her hood. "Me either, but this will work just fine."

Tyler may have smiled, maybe not, but he did switch off the flashlight and lower himself to the ground. Abigail moved beside him, close but not too close, and lay back stiffly, seemingly intent to watch the drama unfold in the sky above them. He stayed sitting, arms looped around his knees.

Instead of looking at the sky, Abigail studied Tyler's muscular back, the curve of his arms. There were questions she wanted to ask him, things she had to know, but there was no easy way to slip into the role of interrogator. So Abigail just lay there for a while, her heart thrumming a wild beat, and waited for Tyler to say something.

"How do you like working at Thompson Hills?"

414

he ventured after a while. He didn't turn around, but the question seemed friendly enough.

"It's nice," Abigail admitted. "It's . . . kind of homey and exotic all at once. I didn't know much about wine before I came. How about you? How is it working for your uncle?"

"Eli was my mom's only sibling. He's been like a dad to me." Tyler laughed a little, but it sounded forced. "So I guess it's been good and bad. Can you imagine working for your dad?"

"No. No, that wouldn't go well at all."

The conversation stalled again. To Abigail it felt like they were walking in thick mud, fighting for every little step, getting dragged down. Or maybe she was getting dragged down. Maybe this would be easy if her mind wasn't anchored with thoughts of Hailey. Maybe this would be easy if her hands weren't fingering the hard lines of what she hid in her sweatshirt pocket.

"What happened to your mom?" Abigail blurted without thinking.

Tyler's pause was heavy with uncertainty. "How do you know something happened to my mom?"

Abigail fumbled. Had she given too much away already? Did Tyler suspect that she knew more about him than he realized? "You said 'was.' You said, 'Eli *was* my mom's only sibling.' I just thought . . . I didn't mean to pry."

With a sigh, Tyler sank back onto the ground beside Abigail. He kept looking up, but Abigail could just make out the silhouette of his face in profile. It reminded her of the photo in Hailey's purse. She could almost picture the longing look in his eyes.

"I'm being oversensitive," Tyler said. "In answer to your question, my mom died in May after a long battle with cancer."

"I'm sorry for your loss." Abigail forced herself to form the words.

"That's why I came home. I lived in Florida for four years. But when Mom was near the end . . . it just felt right to come home."

Abigail tried to forget that she knew Tyler had lived in Florida. What was a logical question? What should she say next if she didn't know what she had already learned about Tyler?

But thankfully she didn't have to say anything. Tyler continued talking. "Thompson Hills was my mom's before my dad died. I grew up here. Family business."

Abigail guessed that there was a rich history, a long heritage that upheld the small estate. Under different circumstances, she'd love to know. But for now she could only focus on Tyler. "How old were you?"

"When?"

"When your father died."

"Six. I don't remember him much. But my mom remarried when I was ten, and Murray was a decent stepfather. He adopted me and everything."

"But he didn't want to stay at Thompson Hills?"

"Nah, Murray's a city man. We moved to Vancouver a week after their wedding."

"And Eli took over." Abigail filled in the blanks.

"No, actually. Eli was living in Washington State. He didn't move back until a few years later. Not until after the—" Tyler stopped and swiveled his head to seek Abigail out of the darkness. "You've got me telling stories that aren't mine to tell."

Abigail opened her mouth to speak twice before sound finally came out. "I didn't mean to pry."

"You said that already, and don't worry, I don't think you're prying. I'm going overboard. I've been blamed for that before." Tyler blew a puff of air from between his pursed lips as if this frustrated him. "But if you want to know about Eli, you're going to have to ask him yourself."

"Okay," Abigail said. She decided to try another tactic. "What brought you to Florida?"

"I wanted to get as far away from my family as I could possibly get."

A wry smile flitted across Abigail's face. Apparently she had more in common with Tyler Kamp than just a relationship with Hailey. "Pretty bad?"

"No, my mom was great. And Murray was fine, I guess. In retrospect. But I was messed up. Hurt. You know."

Abigail could feel him withdraw even as he

clipped out those few short words. Too personal. They were getting too personal. Though her head was splitting with the effort of trying to hold everything together, Abigail managed to spit out another question. "How can a Canadian just pick up and move to Florida?"

"How can an American just pick up and move to BC?"

"Touché."

"Actually, I'm a dual citizen. Our family has always lived with one foot in each country."

Abigail closed her eyes and watched the stars burn like cold pricks of light against the backs of her eyelids. "Did you like Florida?"

"It was hot."

"It's hot here."

"A different sort of hot."

They melted into silence again. Abigail's fingers clenched and unclenched. Her heart stopped and stuttered and raced.

Suddenly Tyler moved beside her, propped himself up on his elbow, and leaned over her.

Abigail was too startled to move, so she cowered against the hard earth, searching the darkness for his eyes, trying to understand what he was doing and why. *Now.* Could she do it now? Should she? Did she want to? Would it solve anything? What would she feel? relief? a sense of completion? the slam of a door forever closing? *Yes,* she decided, *it would be a release* . . . even if it was only temporary.

Abigail skimmed her finger over the trigger, felt the firmness of it, the way it resisted her gentle pressure. She couldn't pull it by accident. It couldn't be an accident.

Tyler interrupted her deluge of thoughts before she could do anything. "What are we doing here?" he asked, his voice edged with something tough, unflinching.

"I don't know what—"

"Abigail, seriously. You've avoided me all summer. You look at me as if you can hardly stand the sight of me. . . . What are we doing here? Why did you all of a sudden invite me to watch the stars with you?"

"Meteors." The word slipped out in a whisper before Abigail could stop it.

Tyler laughed. *Meteors.*

"Why did you come?" Abigail asked, her voice barely loud enough to hear.

She held her breath, convinced that Tyler hadn't heard her. But then he said, "Because I wanted to."

Tyler sat up and extended a hand to help Abigail up, too. When she didn't reach for it, he snagged her under the elbows and pulled her into a sitting position. "Listen, maybe I'm feeling brave because it's so pitch-dark out here that I can't see your face. And maybe you'll hate me forever after tonight, but I'm going to talk for a few minutes and you're here without a flashlight, so I guess you're stuck listening."

Abigail was rendered speechless. This had been her idea. She was supposed to be gathering the information she needed. She was supposed to be in control. How had he hijacked everything? Abigail's knees felt hot where they touched his legs, and the horizon dipped so low behind the hill where they were sitting, it seemed a few stars were sprinkled like sparks in Tyler's hair. She could feel everything about him radiating heat. He was a flame to her, burning.

"I came tonight," Tyler began, "because I happen to like you. Interpret that however you want to. I don't care. But I've liked you since the first time you came to Thompson Hills—and not when Eli hired you, when I waited on your table."

"You recognized me?" Abigail choked.

"I'm not a romantic sort of guy, so don't think I went home and pined over you. You're really not even my type."

Understatement, Abigail thought in spite of herself, her mind flashing over a fading memory of Hailey.

"But there's just . . . well, there's something about you."

For the first time all night, Abigail abandoned the gun and put her hands to her face so she could rub her tired eyes. She was sick of straining to see him in the darkness. She was sick of trying to make sense of this.

"I'm *not* trying to ask you out—we've been

through that," Tyler clarified. "But I can't help feeling that we have this . . . connection."

Yeah, we killed Hailey. You and me. We have a connection.

Tyler laughed again, his voice ringing out in the stillness with such intensity that Abigail wanted to cover her ears. "Why am I telling you this?" He put his elbows on his knees and rested his head on his forearms. He exhaled loudly and it ended in a quiet shout of angst. "Look, my mom died a few months ago, and before that I extracted myself from the most dysfunctional, codependent mess of a relationship you could ever imagine. I guess I'm still dealing. And now I'm babbling nonsense to you. A virtual stranger. A woman who doesn't even like me."

Dysfunctional, codependent . . . "That bad?" Abigail breathed shallowly, aware of how close they were to brushing up against the edges of *her*. Of saying her name.

"You tell me: how much do you dislike me?"

"That's not what I meant." Abigail struggled to rewind the conversation in her mind. "I mean, your 'mess of a relationship.' It was . . . awful?"

"Worse. But I don't want to talk about it. Let's go back," Tyler said, pushing himself to his feet. "The stars are nice. The meteors are nice. But I'd like to go back."

Even in the dimness Abigail could see him offer his hand. The gun was heavy against her stomach, but she ignored it and reached for his fingers. She had never touched him, not in all the weeks she had been at Thompson Hills. She couldn't bring herself to do it. Now, she had to know if his fingers smoldered, if there was something elemental and inescapable in his touch. She wanted to know if he would burn her.

Tyler's hands didn't burn. They didn't fill her with loathing or rage. Instead, they were large and strong and they covered her own small hands as if she were a child. He pulled her to her feet carefully, aware of the unfamiliar footing and the blackness all around them. Though he could have let go the second she was on her feet, he held her for just a moment, making sure she was steady, that she wouldn't stumble or fall.

When Abigail was upright, she stood there, feeling the warmth of his breath on her hair and taking in the proximity of him: the spread of his shoulders above her, the slight scent of soap.

He was a man. He was just a man. Not a monster or a murderer or even as cold and heartless as she had once imagined him to be. Abigail could almost picture him at six, losing his father, or at ten, finding himself thrown into a new family. He was a twentysomething leaving home and a wiser man coming back. He was the man in Hailey's photograph, loving her maybe, leaving her for sure, but probably never intending for things to end the way they did.

For a second it seemed that Tyler leaned toward her. Abigail held her ground, felt him enter the close circle of air pressing against her, and held her breath. But then he backed away and turned around. He clicked on the flashlight almost sheepishly, as if the brightness would make his shadowed confessions appear as silly as he seemed to fear they were. It didn't. Abigail didn't feel like anything about the night had been silly at all.

Tyler didn't say another word and neither did Abigail. He just struck off in the direction of home and she followed him, feeling a sort of hollowness carve her from the inside out.

Abigail wondered if Tyler even knew that Hailey was dead.

"I feel hollow when I'm on my meds," Hailey tried to explain. "Empty, cavernous, vacuous. Otiose, even. Do you know what *otiose* means?"

"I'm not in the mood to play spelling bee with you." Abigail threw the car into park in front of Lou and Hailey's quaint trailer.

"I'm not spelling anything. I'm expanding your vocabulary. *Otiose* means useless or futile, lacking value, use, or substance."

"Fine. I know what *otiose* means."

"You're not listening." Hailey twisted around in her seat and grasped Abigail's hands, made her sister look at her. "I don't feel like myself when I'm on medication. I feel . . . sterile. Like I'm living in vain—like I'm not really living at all."

Abigail closed her eyes. Her head was so heavy, so weary from always being the strong one, from bailing her sister out of problem after problem. Hailey was before her, gripping her wrists and showing way too much skin in a miniskirt that had crept up and up as they drove home from Sawgrass Sands, and Abigail simply couldn't bring herself to look at her anymore. She let her aching head fall until her forehead rested on Hailey's shoulder.

"Hey," Hailey said softly. "I'm trying to be transparent here." She jiggled her arm.

"Don't," Abigail whispered. "Just don't."

"Don't wiggle my shoulder?"

"Don't do this."

"What's *this*?"

"Go off your meds, get into fights, do crazy things, smoke . . ." Reminded by her final plea, Abigail sat up with a sigh and reached for Hailey's purse. She yanked it open and took out the pack of Camel Lights. Hailey didn't even try to stop her. "Don't smoke these."

"Okay."

"And please don't go off your medication."

Hailey took her purse back hesitantly and pressed it against her stomach. She wrapped her arms around it as if it gave her strength somehow, as if it could offer more protection than the cheap piece of fabric that passed for her tank top. "I'm sorry. I have to do this."

"Please no." Abigail's voice hardly rose above a whimper.

"You'll see. I'll be good. I'll be better than ever. I'll be myself."

Abigail had to remind herself that beneath the tough girl exterior, beneath the instability and sometimes even ruthless nature of Hailey's personality, she was still a fragile little girl.

"You *are* yourself," Abigail told her. "You know we love you, Dad and me."

"I know. But *I have to do this*." Hailey punctuated each word by softly hitting her purse with a closed fist. "I mean it. You can't stop me." Then she opened the car door and eased out gradually, inch by inch as if she fully expected her big sister to try to do exactly that: to stop her.

Abigail didn't. She didn't even bother to watch Hailey go. Instead, she slammed the car in reverse and left a skid mark on the cracked concrete of the short driveway.

For over a year, Hailey was more or less okay off her medication. She did all right in school, and Abigail never had to deal with another aggravated mall security guard—or any security guard for that matter.

But there were small things that hinted at the inner turmoil Hailey lived with every day. She didn't sleep much and she didn't eat much. Hailey got so thin her figure rivaled the gaunt, skeletal

425

frame of a runway model. And she jittered a lot. Sometimes her hands trembled when she reached for something, and whenever she was sitting, some part of her had to be moving, moving, moving. She crossed her legs and swung her foot. She drummed her fingers. She tapped her thighs like they were djembe drums.

"You need lessons," Abigail teased her once.

Hailey just gave her a thin smile, a bland look of disinterest, as if she hadn't even heard her. Then she stopped drumming and a moment later began to tap her toe. She was a bright spark of constant, directionless energy.

Abigail seized the occasional opportunity to suggest that Hailey should go back on her medication. Or see a new doctor to determine if there were other courses of treatment. But Hailey demurred, and Lou didn't back Abigail up in her infrequent but heartfelt pleas.

I can't do it for her, Abigail told herself over and over again. *I can't make things right for her. I can't fix her problems. I can't do the work that only Hailey Anne Bennett can do.* But even though she knew those things, accepting her helpless role didn't lessen the burden of guilt that had secured itself around Abigail's shoulders like a shroud. When she was feeling sad and weak, the voice in her head whispered, *If only I could love her more. If only I could say the right things. If only I keep trying . . . If only, if only, if only.*

But all of Abigail's *if only*s crumbled to dust the day Lou called her shortly after Hailey's eighteenth birthday.

"I need you!" he croaked, his voice shattering.

They were words Abigail had never expected to hear from her father, words that left her feeling a strange mix of powerful and powerless. *"I need you."* Why her? Why now? What could he possibly *need*?

And then, all at once, she knew.

In the span of a moment Abigail grieved, wondered how Hailey had finally done it, and endured a momentary vision of Hailey's funeral. She could almost hear the deep, resonant song of the tenor bells.

The world flickered, like a candle sputtering out, and Abigail felt her insides writhe with the tingle of all her fears. This was it. This was the event that would be the axis of her life—everything that had been and everything that was yet to come would forever hinge on this event. Hailey was gone.

Abigail drove as fast as she could to the trailer that Lou and Hailey shared. Some isolated part of her mind wondered at her ability to handle a car, stop at the stop signs, observe traffic patterns, and stay between the dotted line and the curb. But then again, maybe she only convinced herself that she was doing okay. Maybe she only arrived at the trailer in one piece by the grace of God.

When she pulled up, Lou threw the door open

and stood in the rotting frame, waving his cane at her like the frantic encouragement could make her move faster. "I went to sit by the lake today, and when I got home, she was gone!"

"Dad," Abigail said firmly, cutting through the wheeze and grind of his rattling sobs. She felt frighteningly calm, detached. "Have you called 911?"

Lou stepped back to let Abigail in. He slumped onto the chintz couch and covered his face with his hands, leaving Abigail to shut the door on the blistering Florida heat and take charge. She stopped just inside the musty-smelling home, wondering where Hailey was. Her bedroom? The bathroom? The thought made Abigail's heart heave and pitch.

She shook her head to clear it and forced herself to focus on Lou. "Did you call 911?" she asked again.

"I did! Of course I did. What do you think I am?"

"What did they say? Is somebody coming?"

"They can't really *do* anything. . . ."

Abigail could tell that Lou was on the very edge of reason. Dropping to her haunches on the matted carpet, she placed her hands firmly on his knees. She squeezed, hoping her touch would ground him in reality.

Lou let his hands drop from his head, and Abigail moved her face toward his, filling the line of his vision with herself so he had no choice but to look at her or close his eyes.

"What do you mean they can't do anything? That's their job. Did you call 911? Are you sure?" Abigail cast around for the phone, reasoning somehow that if it was still in its cradle, Lou was probably only imagining the call that he had intended to make.

"I talked to a dispatcher and then to an officer," he whimpered.

The concrete answer snapped Abigail's attention back to her father. "Tell me what they said."

"They filed a missing persons report, but they don't suspect—" his voice cracked—"foul play."

"Missing persons?" Abigail repeated, trying to make sense of those words. "Missing?"

"That's what I told you! She's gone!" He pointed to the narrow hallway that led to the two small bedrooms and equally tiny bathroom.

Abigail pushed herself up, accepting the fact that her father was in no shape to walk her through what had happened. She had to make the discovery herself. Sucking in her breath and holding it fast, Abigail left Lou in the living room and headed to Hailey's bedroom.

There was her bed, her desk, the posters on her wall of movie stars and rock bands. There was no Hailey. Abigail realized that the bed looked empty to her. She had expected her sister to be on the bed. She had expected her to be *gone*.

But it didn't take Abigail long to learn that *gone* didn't mean dead; it meant missing. Disappeared.

Vanished. But not without a trace. Hailey had packed a suitcase, taking most of her clothes, all her toiletries, and the stuffed polar bear she kept on her bed and claimed she didn't sleep with anymore. She took those things and she *left*.

Hailey left.

Abigail seethed with the audacity of it. After eighteen years of giving and giving, eighteen years of worry, sweat, and tears, Hailey repaid her selfless gift with abandonment. Abigail had never asked for anything in return. Never. But she expected better than this. She deserved it.

Abigail cursed and yelled and spit. She kicked Hailey's bedroom wall and slammed the door. She hoped that she never saw Hailey again. And for the first time in her life, she actually meant it.

I went back to work almost immediately, even though everyone tried to talk me out of it. Of course, I didn't work on the days leading up to Hailey's funeral, and I didn't work on the day that I went to clean out her apartment, but other than those brief disruptions in my hectic schedule, life went on as normal. I'm a professional, I reminded myself. And then I donned an indomitable smile and acted the part.

But after I initiated the process of clearing out my sister's apartment, something began to nag at the frayed edges of my consciousness. I had tucked the photo of Hailey and Tyler into my purse as a sort of talisman, and though I knew it was crazy, I found myself searching for his face wherever I went. He was on the street, in the grocery store, driving the car beside me. . . . He was everywhere. And nowhere, because each time I turned around, I had to admit that it wasn't him. It was never him. But for some reason I couldn't stop. I couldn't shake the suspicion that he held the key to why Hailey finally gave up. I was convinced he had the answers I was so desperately searching for.

There were other things, too—little things that made me wonder if I was dealing with my sister's death in a normal, healthy way. Sometimes, in the middle of the day as I was speaking to a client or even doing something as mundane as standing by the watercooler, from somewhere deep inside, I'd feel a warning chill. A single violent pulse of adrenaline would bubble at the core of my abdomen and seep like poison through my body. My fingers, my toes, even my lips would begin to tingle, and then my heart would gallop away from a suitable rhythm, threatening to rise out of my throat and leave my body.

It was an attack of some sort, I knew that much. An anxiety attack? Maybe. But it didn't really feel like nerves to me. More often than not it simply stung like a cruel reminder: Hailey was dead and I was alive. I breathed, my heart continued to beat, and though I hated the brutal ache that each attack thrust on me, I had to acknowledge and appreciate the fact that at the very least I was still able to feel something—even if it was the feverish chill of panic.

I was afraid that other people noticed my rest-lessness, too.

"How are you doing?" Colton asked one afternoon, poking his head in my office.

"Doing good," I chirped, looking up just long enough to prove it with a smile. "Busy though."

He must have taken my response as an invitation because he stepped into my office, pulling the door behind him. "Do you mind if I shut this?"

"Not at all."

The door clicked softly.

432

Colton hesitated just over the threshold, his hand still on the oiled bronze knob. I kept my eyes on the papers in front of me, but I could sense his unease and wasn't surprised when he crossed the plush carpet one careful step at a time. It seemed he was fortifying himself to bring up whatever he had come to talk about, and since I didn't want to hear it, I wasn't about to make things easy for him. I didn't say a word.

"You know," he eventually began, his voice artificially bright, "we really don't mind—in fact, we totally understand—if you'd like to take some time off."

"No thank you," I protested. "I want to work. I'm fine."

He sighed. "Abigail, we'd like you to take some time off."

"Hey," I joked, "I thought I was a partner in this firm. I thought I was capable of making my own decisions."

"You are; of course you are. But it must be so hard . . ."

I looked up to see Colton perched on the end of one of the wingback chairs facing my desk. His hands were clasped between his knees, and he was leaning forward with such an earnest expression that I couldn't stop myself from softening a little. He cared. He was only trying to help.

"It's hard," I admitted. "But I want to do this. I want to be here. It helps me feel normal."

Colton's eyes changed suddenly, and he looked down at his hands to hide his expression. He had never been very good at being subtle. "Abigail . . ." He drew my name out with unhurried deliberation, stalling on the syllables, working up to what he had come to say. "You just don't seem okay to us."

"What do you mean?"

"I've seen you sometimes," Colton confessed, "pale as a ghost and shaking. You breathe like you've run a marathon. And sometimes you just space out."

"Space out?"

"Like you're not even here."

"I know what space out means," I said, bristling. "I'm just surprised that you think I do it. Haven't I been a good employee? Haven't I done everything you've ever asked of me and more?"

"Yes. Oh, heavens yes." A delicate drop of spittle formed on Colton's lips as he rushed to reassure me. "It's just that you recently lived through one of the most difficult tragedies that anyone could ever face, and it's got to affect you."

"I'm dealing."

"I know." Now that a crack had formed in the dam of Colton's pent-up thoughts, he let his concerns freefall, tumbling out in an uncensored rush. "But Hailey was your only sister and I know you were like a mother to her. And you found her, Abigail; you found her. I can't even imagine what you must be going through. Anyone in your situa-

tion would be so confused and hurt. . . . You must be dealing with so many emotions right now: anger and grief and uncertainty . . . guilt . . . "

"Guilt?" The word startled me so much I had to say it again. "Guilt?"

Colton looked horrified. "Not that you're to blame. I don't mean that it's your fault."

"It's not," I whispered. But my partner had touched a raw nerve, an almost-primal fear that I had tried not to acknowledge in the days after Hailey's suicide. I had often blamed myself before for Hailey's shortcomings. I had wondered if there was some way that I could have done more to prevent her from making such life-altering mistakes. Love wins, *someone once told me. So maybe I didn't love her enough. Maybe I could never quite be all she needed. I was willing to accept my part in some of her suffering. But this was too big. I couldn't shoulder this burden.*

Right there, sitting across from Colton in the soothing, air-conditioned comfort of my beautiful office, I felt one of those attacks shudder to life at the center of my being. I shivered, and then a wave of unnamable emotions blindsided me. The furious pulse of it was so relentless I had to breathe in desperate little gasps.

Colton stood and reached across the desk for me. His hands found mine and held them tight. "I'm sorry."

"It's not my fault," I forced out. I was panting,

helpless to prevent the attack and mortified that it was happening in front of Colton. But as each inhalation and exhalation shortened into one tiny burst of pain after another, I realized that someone was to blame. If it wasn't me, who was it?

I closed my eyes, I breathed, and suddenly I knew that my entire being was pulsing with the only alternative: Ty-ler. Ty-ler. Ty-ler. *"It's not my fault," I wheezed. "It's Tyler's."*

In that moment, as I gave breath to the words, my muttered accusation became my truth.

XV

CR AFTER TYLER DISAPPEARED behind the shadowed door of Eli's log cabin, Abigail paced the driveway. She walked as far as she dared into the darkness, letting the crunch of the gravel beneath her feet guide her path and keep her from getting lost in the black night. But when the outline of the house and trailer became dull and indistinct, just one more variation on the subtle shades of ebony, she turned back.

Abigail knew she should take refuge in the trailer so she could try to work through her infuriatingly uneventful encounter with Tyler. But she couldn't stop walking. She paced to the edge of oblivion feeling severed from the world around her, then turned and marched straight back to the reassuring comfort of her little trailer home. Back and forth, back and forth, Abigail wandered in circles until exhaustion overtook her and she finally mounted the rusty metal steps to the door of the ancient Navigator.

When she woke the following morning, her legs ached with the need to keep moving. *Keep moving.*

Abigail showered in double time and then took off across the vineyards in the hopes of arriving at Thompson Hills before Eli. But she had no such luck. Before Abigail had made it halfway to the creamy yellow buildings, she heard footsteps approaching from behind.

"You over it?" Eli called, jogging lightly to catch up to her.

She turned for just a second, framed in moving reel between the arching rows of grapevines. But she didn't slow down.

"Excuse me?" Abigail threw the query over her shoulder, knowing full well what Eli was referring to. She didn't want to spend time with Eli, and she didn't feel like being conversational. Most of all, she didn't want to complicate what had happened—and what *hadn't* happened—with her growing fondness for Tyler's uncle.

"Have you *healed*, girl? Are you feeling better?"

"I'm fine," Abigail reiterated when she felt the older man step beside her and match her hurried pace.

"Could've fooled me."

Normally Abigail would mutter something cheeky back, and the two of them would banter. Sometimes Eli's sharpness stung, but Abigail had become accustomed to it and was able to ignore the rough quality of his interactions—she had even learned to anticipate it. But instead of engaging his obvious barb, she lengthened her stride.

"Where you off to in such a hurry?"

"I wanted to get to the winery early," Abigail all but sang. "You know, start making up for yesterday." Her voice was so synthetically cheerful that it dripped with sarcasm. She felt Eli stiffen beside her. And although she tried to harden her heart and be indifferent to the fact that she had stung him, Abigail was instantly seized with regret. She hadn't meant to be so harsh. Eli had done nothing to deserve such treatment. None of her problems were his fault.

Abigail stopped, kicking up a small cloud of dust with her sudden change in momentum. She rubbed her cheeks with her palms and sighed.

Eli stopped, too, a few paces beyond Abigail. Then he turned to survey her with an analytical look, a disapproving tightness in his lips that told Abigail he was not at all impressed with her attitude.

"Sorry I'm being so . . . ." Abigail searched for the right word, but the only terms that seemed fitting were definitely not appropriate to say. So she met his eyes with an apology in her gaze. "I just had a really, really rough night." She hadn't planned on admitting that last part, and the second the hurried words were out of her mouth, she questioned them. Why was she letting Eli in?

But he just clicked his tongue in reprimand and shook his head. "You were with Tyler. What did you expect?" Then he turned on his heel and walked off toward the winery.

Abigail stood there speechless, surprised that Eli knew whom she was with, but also taken aback, as always, that he could be so flippant about his nephew. A faint smile passed her lips in spite of the heavy tug of her heart. She called after him, "For someone who loves Tyler as much as you claim to, you sure don't think much of him, do you?"

"Oh, I think the world of that boy. He's smart and he's handsome. Got a way with people, too. But he carries old baggage around like he's some kind of masochistic luggage handler, and he messes up relationships by encouraging obsession. Doesn't understand healthy boundaries, that boy." Eli paused to let Abigail catch up. He tilted his head as if considering something for the first time. "You know, I think that might explain why he's so drawn to you. You're probably the furthest thing from clingy he's ever met."

Abigail was so stunned by Eli's unsolicited analysis of Tyler and his motivations she couldn't speak.

"You're probably the first girl that he couldn't make obsess over him." Eli laughed.

Swallowing hard, Abigail muttered, "You've given this a lot of thought."

"I think about my nephew all the time. I *pray* for him all the time."

Hearing Eli mention prayer made Abigail even more uncomfortable than she already was. She squirmed thinking of him offering prayers for Tyler—it was an intimate admission, something that made her feel the way she often had as a child:

on the outside looking in. Eli spoke of prayer, and all Abigail could think about was the gun she had crammed into the cupboard of the unused trailer bathroom. It made her feel dirty.

"Well, enough about Tyler," Abigail said, brushing her hands together as if ridding them of dust. "I guess we'd better get to work."

Eli ignored her obvious attempt to change the conversation. He had settled into a subject, and it was hard to sway him when he had things he wanted to say. "I think I've told Tyler dozens of times about the life of a vine, the art of winemaking, and do you think he's listened to me even once? I don't think so." He wagged his finger at Abigail. "If you ask me, anyone who works in a vineyard or a winery should know what the process takes."

Abigail tried not to look blank, but confusion must have stolen across her face because Eli suddenly lit up.

"We've talked about everything from politics to religion, haven't we? But I don't think I've ever told you about *wine*."

No, Abigail thought, *you haven't. But right now, I just don't care to hear it.* She didn't want to be preached to, educated, or forcefully illuminated in any way. She didn't want to have to nod and smile, act like she was paying attention. She didn't want to hear about wine. What she wanted was to be left alone. And although it almost contradicted her earlier apology, she steeled her resolve and said firmly, "Maybe some other time."

The gleam in Eli's eyes faded at her words. He gave her one last penetrating look, then veered away abruptly. He didn't even try to protest.

Abigail walked several paces behind him all the way to the winery.

Abigail had expected the day to be difficult, but it turned out to be mundane. The winery was busy, and she volunteered for tour guide duty rather than taking her place behind the high counter with Paige and Natalie. Abigail wanted to be alone, and though leading tours arguably required more inter-action with people, her words could be more or less rote, memorized from the regular sessions with Eli and then regurgitated nearly verbatim. No one on the tours ever asked her about herself. She was able to go on autopilot.

Even after the winery closed, Abigail's mood didn't improve much. Hoping to avoid her coworkers, she slipped out the back door in the cellar beneath the tasting room when everyone else was gathering their things and spending a few min-utes chatting in the empty parking lot. She didn't feel like struggling through another variation on the theme of the conversation that she had endured with Eli hours earlier. It was getting harder and harder for Abigail to fit comfortably in the life she had created for herself, and she didn't want to be reminded of the way things were spinning out of control.

Abigail gulped down a solitary supper of a peanut butter sandwich folded unceremoniously in half and one of the leftover peaches from the roadside stand. Then she gave in to the compulsion of her legs and went for a run. Usually she would never dream of running after she had just eaten, but Abigail set an easy pace for herself, loping past the winery and along the road that led to Mack's. She left Thompson Hills behind, barely breaking a jog and aiming for the water.

It was nearing dark when Abigail finally trotted back through the picturesque grounds of the winery. She had stayed away as long as she could, anxious to preserve her self-inflicted solitude and even more eager to dodge an awkward meeting with either Tyler or Eli. But now that dusk was rolling in, she risked the possibility of not being able to find her way home in the dark. Abigail had no choice but to return.

As she neared the front doors of the main building at Thompson Hills, she noticed that one of the wide double doors was ajar. At first Abigail thought her eyes were playing tricks on her, that the advancing twilight was merely casting shadows on the rich and varied hues of the polished wood grain. But she slowed anyway, relaxing her light jog to a quick walk that became an unhurried stroll. She was sure that it was an optical illusion, but it was impossible to ignore the mirage of the open door now that she had seen it.

By the time Abigail was close enough to distinguish between shadows and reality, she knew her eyes hadn't deceived her. The west door of the winery was indeed open a few inches, and from deep inside the building, Abigail thought she could just make out the lilt and roll of a sound that was definitely not organic to the surrounding flora and fauna. Was that a voice? Was someone inside the winery?

Abigail trotted up the steps, repressing a surge of sudden possessiveness. Why would someone be in the winery at this time of night? She was sure that whoever had opened the door and crept inside had nothing but ill intentions. Without pausing to think, she placed her palm on the thick, hand-crafted door and eased it open just enough to slip into the dim interior.

It was cool inside and very quiet; the noisy hum of life outside was almost immediately hushed behind the barrier of the heavy door. Abigail walked in a few paces and paused, wondering if she had jumped to conclusions, if her momentary visions of teenage vandals or youthful hoodlums looking for a buzz had been rash and unfounded. Maybe someone had simply left the door open. But hadn't she heard a voice?

Abigail held her breath, listening, and after nearly a minute had passed, she convinced herself that the open door had been nothing more than an oversight. The winery was still and serene. It emanated a sort of drowsy aura as it lay blanketed in long shadows that were quickly obscuring every familiar landmark in the spectacular entryway. The effect was calming, and because Abigail felt safe and alone, she closed her eyes and soaked in the peace of the place. Unbidden, a word rose from her subconscious and lingered, defining the feeling of the quiet building for Abigail: *sanctuary*.

But somehow the tranquility, the sense of refuge, rankled her. *I shouldn't be here,* she thought. *I have no right to be here*. All at once she turned to leave, ignoring the sweet atmosphere of the unexpected safe haven. The gentle spell was completely broken when Abigail realized that she would have to seek out Eli and tell him that the front doors of the main building were unlocked.

Abigail hurried back the way she had come. And then a few notes rang out in the expanse of air around her. It was just a few notes, a handful of lush and husky tones that echoed and rose and fell, but they halted the motion of Abigail's hand as she reached for the door. She was transfixed, her arm outstretched, and someone was singing behind her.

Although she knew she should leave right then, Abigail couldn't bring herself to walk out of the building. As if in a trance, she put her back to the open air of the unfolding night and took a few hesitant steps deeper into the entrance, toward the slight sound.

But whoever was singing had stopped, and the vast hall was getting darker by the second. She faltered, confused and disoriented. Had she only imagined the music?

Maybe she had. Maybe she was losing her mind. But she didn't care. Without making a sound, Abigail crossed to the stacked rock wall, arms spread out in front of her so she wouldn't crash into it in the darkness. When she reached the stones, they were unexpectedly warm and jagged beneath her fingers. She clung to them like a rock climber and moved deftly along the face of the artesian wall, feeling her way to where it ended and she knew the tasting room spread open before her. Within seconds, her hands found empty space; she peered around the edge.

There, in the center of the massive room, was a small table. It was covered with a linen tablecloth and glowing softly as if enchanted beneath the light of a single tapered candle. Eli was seated at the table alone, his hands folded in front of him and his head bowed almost deferentially over an uncorked bottle of red wine. There was also something dark and squat on the table, but Abigail couldn't quite make out what it was.

Abigail tilted her head at the sight of Eli sitting there in repose and was surprised to discern the tender slant of his shoulders. As she watched, he pressed his lips together and began again to hum the lingering strains of the song that she now knew had never been given voice—the indefinite sound that she had heard earlier was Eli breathing out one resonant note after another, picking his way as if he couldn't quite remember the tune.

Something about the unexpectedness of it all—the candles, the wine, the strangely lovely music—was breathtakingly beautiful. It seemed sacred somehow, almost holy. After a few more notes Abigail thought she could make out the melody of the song. But then he stopped again and the moment evaporated.

Though Abigail could have remained against the wall for hours watching the mysterious drama before her unfold, something inside her cringed at her own intrusion into Eli's private moment. She had stumbled upon something intensely intimate; whatever Eli was doing, it was not intended for an audience. Abigail allowed herself one last look before she tore herself away with a sigh.

The soft exhalation was entirely unintentional and much louder than Abigail imagined a sigh could ever be. Her gaze sprang to Eli in fright, and in that same moment she saw him look up. She yanked herself behind the wall and cowered there, panting.

"Who's there?" Eli barked.

Abigail pressed her hands to her heart in an effort to silence its furious thump. Maybe if she was still enough, he'd assume that the drafty building was playing games with him. Some of the waiters had caught a bird in the expansive rafters a few weeks before. Maybe Eli would chalk up whatever he had heard and seen to nature or to the predictable moans and grumblings of a large and aging building.

But Eli wasn't stupid. "Who's there?" he called again. This time his voice was commanding, powerful.

What choice did Abigail have? She had no intention of sprinting out of the building, tripping over her own feet in the darkness, and taking off across the fields. She had been caught spying, and while she could explain away her presence by expressing concern over the open door, she couldn't justify invading a secret moment that Eli may never forgive her for uncovering. Hiding would only make everything worse.

It was with a sense of resignation that Abigail stepped away from the wall and presented herself at the north entrance to the tasting room. She waited for his harsh reprimand.

"Abigail?"

She realized that he probably couldn't tell who was standing in the shadows. The faint light of the candle didn't reach her downcast eyes. "Yes, Eli, it's me."

"What are you doing here? Is something wrong? Are you okay?"

"I'm fine," Abigail assured him, answering his questions in reverse order. "And nothing's wrong. But I was out for a jog and I noticed that the front door was open. . . . I was afraid someone had broken in."

"I left the front door open?" Eli seemed puzzled by this revelation and sat still for a long moment, considering the woman before him through squinted eyes. Abigail couldn't tell if he was glaring at her or merely trying to make out her features across the dim room. But then he smiled and pushed back from the table. He grabbed a second chair and placed it across from where he had been sitting.

"Why don't you join me?" he invited, indicating her spot by tapping his palms lightly against the curved wood of the chair's high back.

Abigail was stunned. Join him? Surely Eli didn't mean it. Maybe this was a test of some sort, and she was going to be lectured for making the wrong choice. But even at such a distance, Abigail could tell that something like concern was mingling in Eli's eyes. It reminded her of the first time they met, on the beach when Nan had knocked her down. Eli had given her the same indiscernible look then—it was a baffling mixture of worry, compassion, and . . . hope?

"No." Abigail hooked a thumb over her shoulder. "I should get back."

"To the trailer? Nonsense. Sitting there alone is

unhealthy." Eli tipped the chair up an inch or two and let the back legs fall to the floor with a convincing thud. "Come. Sit."

Abigail didn't want to move, but she found herself drawn to him. Her steps were tentative because she felt like she was nearing a table that had been laid for her. Yet there was no way Eli could have known she was coming. Abigail looked at the open seat, and although she acknowledged with a secret rush of affection that it had been placed there especially for her, she lowered herself into the chair almost awkwardly.

Eli smiled at her and nodded once.

They sat in silence, Eli studying Abigail and Abigail taking in the table before her. The bottle of wine at the center of the table glittered like melted rubies in the faint candlelight. There were two wineglasses beside it, each refracting the single flame into tiny rainbows that winked at her with a certain impossibly magical quality. Why two? But Abigail didn't have time to contemplate the second glass because beneath the subtle scent of the wine, an earthy aroma of fresh bread stung the back of her tongue and made her mouth water. The brown object she had glimpsed from the door was a dark, crusty round loaf of bread dimpled with grains and seeds.

"What are you doing?" she breathed.

"I'm celebrating communion."

Everything clicked into place. Abigail's eyes

shot to Eli's face. "You can't do that. Only a priest can perform the sacrament of communion."

"Report me," he challenged, his eyes flashing. "I'm a broken man. My church only administers communion a few times a year. A *year*. I need the body and blood a little more than that. What are you going to do about it?"

"But—"

"I love the Lord. I am a son of God, and his supper is a family meal. I don't think he'd deny me his gift."

"It's just . . ."

"What?"

"Sacrilegious."

"I find it wholly reverent."

They frowned at each other, and Abigail almost made up an excuse so she could flee his questionable nighttime ritual.

But then Eli grinned and shook his head at her. "You Catholics."

"Lapsed Catholic," Abigail reminded him, unable to stop herself from smiling back.

"Whatever. I do this for those times in between, those long stretches of waiting when I start to forget about the miracle. The mystery. The power of God for those who believe." The corner of Eli's mouth was still upturned mischievously, but his voice was tinged with awe. "It's a mighty thing, girl."

Abigail didn't know what to say, but the room

was cool, the candlelight was soft, and she found that she didn't want to leave anymore. Let him talk about miracles and mysteries. She knew they were fairy tales. Let him have his communion. She knew that no matter how you spun it, wine was wine and bread was bread.

Eli eyed her suspiciously. "I see how it is. You think I'm nuts."

"No, I—"

"A while back you told me about purgatory," he broke in, "about contrition for our sins and the resulting consequences. Ultimately, I think, we were talking about judgment."

What did he want her to say? Abigail tilted her head in a halfhearted nod.

"Just being sorry doesn't fix it. But I also don't believe it rests on our shoulders," Eli explained. "I believe the cross was enough: it's not about judgment; it's about forgiveness."

Not for me, Abigail thought. *Not for the things I've done. Or* haven't *done. Not even for Hailey.* "What do you need forgiveness for?" she teased, trying to lighten the mood.

Eli wouldn't be baited. He gave her a long, hard look, and Abigail knew that he was going to say something she would regret hearing. She raised her hand as if the physical act could stop him, but it was too late. Without a word of warning, without anything to prepare her for what she was about to hear, Eli said, "I killed a man."

Abigail's heart stopped beating.

"It happened thirteen years, four months, and eleven days ago."

Stuttering back to life with a few ragged beats, Abigail's heart pounded so fiercely she was afraid she would not be able to hear Eli speak when he opened his mouth again. She decided to cut him off instead of learning what had happened. She didn't want to know. "You don't," Abigail croaked, cleared her throat, and tried again. "You don't have to tell me anything."

"It's no secret. Besides, sometimes I feel like I *should* tell my story. I feel like I should tonight."

"Really, I—"

"I wasn't incarcerated or anything. I'm not some psycho murderer." Eli's attempts to reassure her only made her more edgy, but Eli didn't seem to notice. "It's all pretty straightforward actually."

"Eli—"

"I'd been a cop in Spokane for twelve years," he said, cutting her off. "One night my partner and I pulled over an SUV for reckless driving. The vehicle stopped for us, but before we could get out of our squad car, the driver of the SUV hopped out and started coming at us. I shouted at him to stop, but he didn't. He just . . . he just came."

The silence in the room was absolute.

"I didn't understand," Eli continued, and Abigail could tell he was lost in a memory that had cost him much. "I didn't understand, and I had never . . . Nothing like that had ever . . ."

"Eli, no," Abigail whispered. "Just . . . no. You don't have to say any more."

"We screamed at him, both of us, but he kept coming." Eli ran his fingers through his short hair in one quick, frustrated motion. "When the driver reached for something in his back pocket, I shot him."

"No."

"It was ruled self-defense. I wasn't culpable for anything."

"He was reaching for a gun?" Abigail exhaled.

"He was reaching for his wallet."

Abigail moaned.

"I could have stayed on the force, but I couldn't handle it, you know? They prep you for that sort of thing at police academy, but I don't think anyone could ever be truly ready for . . . *that*."

"I'm so sorry."

"Me too."

Eli didn't say anything more for a while, and neither did Abigail. They watched the flame on the candle dance and sway, each dealing with their own demons, their own fears and sorrows.

Finally Eli rubbed his face with his hands and took a few uneven breaths. "He was just a college kid. A total punk who thought his quick temper gave him the right to rule. . . . They told me he was a physical science major."

Eli's expression glazed over, and Abigail could just imagine the invented life that Eli had constructed for his young victim. She had done it a thousand times with Hailey. What would her sister look like in five years? ten? Would she have married someday? filled Abigail's life with sweet nieces and nephews? Abigail wanted to tell Eli that she understood, but she couldn't get the words out.

"I quit the force and moved back here to rot my life away in the place where I was born. End of story."

Abigail studied him for a moment. "No. Not really."

"You're right, Abby. That wasn't the end of my story."

"Abigail," she whispered.

"I think Abby suits you. May I call you Abby?"

Abigail shook her head.

Eli shrugged. "Okay."

"How could you . . . go on?" she asked, surprising herself with the question but incapable of stopping herself from asking it.

"I tried to tell you about it this morning, but you weren't in a chatty mood."

It was Abigail's turn to shrug.

Eli grinned. "I learned about wine."

"What in the world is that supposed to mean?"

"When I took these vineyards over, I hardly knew a thing about growing grapevines. The first year, I was so miserable and so absorbed in my own grief that I just let them do their thing—I figured a plant knew how to grow on its own."

"Pretty common assumption," Abigail mumbled.

"Turns out, a grapevine needs someone to tend it if it's going to produce any fruit." He leaned forward in his chair, warming to his story now that the painful part of the telling was over. "Vineyards take a lot of hands-on work, a lot of time and patience and effort."

"Don't all crops?"

"To a certain extent, but grapevines are different. Basically, every spring Josh and I have to practically kill each vine. We leave the cordon—that's the main vine—but we cut off nearly all the canes and burn them."

"Canes?"

"All the other vines. Or most of them at least." Eli narrowed his eyes at her. "You give tours, girl. Don't you know anything?"

"I've listened to every word you ever said," Abigail said, straight-faced.

Eli released a short burst of a laugh. "Sure you have."

"I just call them vines."

"Whatever. But you're going to learn something now." Eli pointed at Abigail with his index and middle finger, then brought the fingers to his own eyes. "Listen and learn. Where was I?"

"Canes."

"Oh yeah. You wouldn't believe how many

canes we hack off. Then we get rid of the new growth and even remove many of the leaves to allow the sunshine in. It's almost . . . violent."

"Why do you do it?"

"Because that's how you get a grapevine to produce fruit."

Abigail considered the man before her, watching the light in his face as it seemed to illuminate the table instead of the other way around.

"Vineyards need a lot of care. They're very susceptible to disease, they need just the right amount of water and sunlight, and if you want fruit, you have to work at it. But they are also very resilient—if a vine has a good root system, it's almost impossible to kill it."

"It's lovely to know all that, but what does it have to do with what you went through?"

"Because Christ is the vine and we are the branches. You've heard the metaphor. You were a church girl once."

"It's just a metaphor."

"Not to me." Eli lifted the bottle of wine and tipped it in his hands so that it looked as if he intended to pour it over the table. When the scarlet liquid had slid to the very end of the long-necked bottle, Eli tilted it upright again. "Why do you think Jesus used wine to symbolize his blood?"

Abigail didn't know what to say, but she raised her shoulder slightly, an indication for Eli to keep talking.

457

"I think the Lord used wine for dozens of reasons, but one of the most convincing for me is the fact that crafting a glass of fine wine is nothing less than a very intentional, almost sacrificial, act of love. The labor, the heart and soul that goes into first producing a fine grape, is only reflected in the further arts of harvesting and destemming, crushing, primary fermentation, cold and heat stabilization, secondary fermentation, aging . . . And then we test and blend, preserve, filter, and bottle. After that comes *more* aging."

Though Abigail wondered if she was supposed to be responding to any of Eli's passionate musings, he didn't really give her a chance. But she didn't mind him rambling. Because she cared for him, she gave him the benefit of the doubt. She listened.

"It's the process of a lifetime, really. A few years to prepare the ground, several more for the vines to produce fruit . . . but a real fruitful vine needs *years* to mature. Then it's another year or two before the wine is ready for bottling. After that, reds need a good decade before they begin to taste like all they're capable of. If you want a really amazing wine, wait a quarter century or more."

Eli paused just long enough to regard the bottle in his hands. "This beautiful Bordeaux has been in my cellar for nearly eleven years. It's a mix of cabernet sauvignon, merlot, and Shiraz, though I bought the Shiraz grapes from a fellow vintner since we don't grow them at Thompson Hills." He lifted a bushy eyebrow at Abigail and gave her a conspiratorial smile. "I was experimenting."

"Is it any good?"

Eli grunted. "What do you think? It's excellent. It's beautiful and complex and rich. It's gone through a deepening, a process of hard trial, difficult growth, and a long journey in the same direction. That's the Christian life: a long journey in the same direction. It's about perseverance. Obedience. And a whole lot of grace. The hand of the master winemaker, forever pruning, producing fruit, and then making something profound and lovely out of our meager harvest."

Abigail was quiet. Her eyes were on Eli, but when he fell silent, she found she couldn't look at him anymore. "I can't say I've ever thought of it that way," she finally said.

"Neither did I until I took over this place. Then all of a sudden, here I was, pruned all but naked and stuck at a crossroads: produce fruit or be cut from the vine."

Part of Abigail wanted very much to believe all that Eli was saying, all that he was implying with his stories. There was something powerful about his metaphors, those full and living symbols. But they were nothing more than sentimental tales, emotional restructurings that helped him understand everything that had happened to him and why it had happened. Did he really believe all that?

Hailey had believed. Or at least, there were definite points throughout her short life when she tried. But wasn't that the crux of it all? that Hailey had wanted to believe but that she was prevented from any kind of peace by the illness she had been born with? Could the master gardener grow a vine so sick and frail that he was compelled to sever the work of his own hands?

Eli broke into her reverie with a few gentle words. "I'm getting way off track, talking about the life of a vine. We were supposed to talk about these things this morning."

Abigail wrinkled her forehead in confusion. "Did you plan this?" she asked, her voice laced with skepticism.

"No, but I hoped for it. I've been leaving that door open for months. I figured one of these days you'd walk through it." Eli indicated the second wineglass. "It's yours."

"But I can't . . . I can't have communion with you," Abigail protested. "I haven't been to confession. I'm *Catholic*."

"Lapsed," Eli reminded.

"No. I won't do it. I'm not . . . I'm not ready—"

"For what?" Eli interrupted. "I told you before, the Lord's Supper is a family affair. We're all invited to be part of the family; we're all invited to the table." He lowered his gaze. "And I've been watching you since that day on the beach. You're about as lost and lonely as they come. You could use a good, old-fashioned family meal."

"But I—"

"Remember what I said? I need it. I think you do, too."

Abigail's chest collapsed against the knowledge of what he wanted from her—what he wanted to give her. She didn't feel ready; she didn't feel deserving. But wasn't that the point? that she was undeserving? Abigail had sat in a church pew for almost twenty years, and she had absorbed enough to know that there was nothing she could do now or ever to earn what had been sacrificed in her name. Suddenly the song that Eli had been humming emerged bright and obvious from the shadows of her memory: "Amazing Grace."

"We are called out of death, Abigail Bennett. We are reconciled. And this—" Eli took the bread in his calloused hands and tore it so that two jagged pieces rested in each outstretched palm—"is the body of our Lord Jesus Christ. Who on the night he was betrayed took bread, and when he had given thanks, he broke it and said, 'This is my body, broken for you. Do this in remembrance of me.'"

Eli offered the bread to Abigail, held it for her in an offering so sweet and so heartbreaking that she had no choice but to take it. It was heavy and fragrant in her hands. It was dark and exquisite. It was holy. The little sound that slipped from her lips was neither a gasp nor a sob but a fragment chiseled from the shattered heart that she tried so hard to contain.

"The body of Christ, Abigail, given for you."

She pulled off a piece, and though her throat was suddenly and inexplicably strangled with tears, she placed it in her mouth like an obedient child and felt the perfect subtlety of it. It was slightly warm. It filled her mouth. It overwhelmed her with a sense of vulnerability.

Eli took the wine and raised a glass. "In the same way, he took the cup, and when he had given thanks, he poured it and said, 'This is my blood, poured out for you, for the complete forgiveness of all your sins. Do this in remembrance of me.'"

Abigail accepted the glass and brought it to her face. She drank deeply of the scent, letting the complexity of it overcome her until her senses were filled with the extravagance of the earth and minerals, the extraordinary fruit.

"The blood of Christ, Abigail, given for you."

The wine exploded in her mouth, the shock of it almost painful after the simple delicacy of the bread. She let it wash over her tongue before she swallowed it, before she took it into herself and felt the warmth of it inside her. It burned a little going down; it left a hot trail from the tip of her tongue to her center.

Abigail didn't know if she deserved it, if she had the right to sit at this table to eat and drink, to partake of something that she felt she had no part in. But for this one moment in time, with the candle glowing and the bread and wine before her, inside of her, it didn't matter. She was drowning, but she didn't struggle for air; she opened her mouth and took it in. It washed over her, in her. Abigail felt it fold against every hidden place, every secreted thought and hope. It felt absolute, unconditional.

It felt like home.

Hailey didn't come home the following day or the next. She didn't come home the day after that.

Lou nearly lost his mind with fear and grief, but Abigail was convinced that Hailey was fine. Or maybe not *fine* but certainly not dead or in danger. Abigail was sure that her sister had left of her own volition, that her abandonment was nothing more than a cruel and narcissistic act designed to allow Hailey to fulfill her own selfish and self-destructive desires. The level-headed accountant could almost picture the gorgeous men, the wild parties. It made her sick.

And though they were motivated by two very different emotions, both Lou and Abigail were desperate to find Hailey. They called her high school and talked with the guidance counselor. They got the names of a few people whom the teachers considered to be Hailey's friends and tried to solicit their help, but no one seemed to know where she had disappeared to or why. Lou and Abigail even prowled her regular haunts in the hope of catching a glimpse, of hearing a telling snatch of conversation, *anything*. But their hands were tied.

Even the police couldn't do much. After Hailey had been gone for forty-eight hours, an officer came to Lou's trailer to check things out. Since Hailey was eighteen, he explained that she was no longer a minor and was legally allowed to take off on her own. But all the same, he poked around in Hailey's room and asked Lou a dozen questions, all the while writing something on a small notepad. A half hour later, he told the distraught father that he would keep his eyes and ears open. He promised to call if anything came up.

Five nights after Hailey disappeared from her father's trailer, Abigail's phone rang in the middle of the night. She had been sound asleep, and when the little device on her nightstand began to sing, Abigail almost screamed in shock. But some small part of her was tense and ready, waiting for the call that would interrupt her life with news of Hailey.

Tossing the thin sheet off, Abigail sat up straight in bed and turned to place her feet flat on the floor. She needed the stability, the grounding presence of the solid floor beneath her. Flexing her toes against the cold laminate, Abigail took a deep breath and reached for the humming device.

It was a number she didn't recognize. Abigail clicked on the phone. "Hello?" Her voice was hesitant, tinged with fear.

"Abby?"

"*Hailey?* Where are you?" Abigail demanded, her words splintered with concern even though she had promised herself that if her sister called, she would be as cold and resolute as steel.

On the other end of the line, Hailey began to sob. "I . . . I don't know."

"What do you mean you don't know? Are you drunk? high?"

Hailey didn't answer. "Please come and get me. I want to come home."

"You have to tell me where you are."

"It's a big stucco house with a circle driveway and a fountain in the middle."

"You just described thousands of houses in Rosa Beach. I need an address."

There was a shuffling sound on the line, followed by a few hard sniffs and then the thud of muffled footsteps.

"You still there?" Abigail asked.

"I'm going outside," came the faint reply. Did it sound slurred? Was Hailey slurring her words?

After several seconds of silence, punctuated only by indiscernible sounds that made Abigail's heart thump painfully, Hailey said, "The house number is 1562."

"It's a start, but I need a street name." Abigail reached for a pen and a scrap of paper in the drawer of her nightstand. Finding it, she squinted at the paper and scrawled 1562.

Hailey was silent for a while. "I'm two houses from the corner," she finally said. "Want me to walk to the intersection and read the sign?"

"Are you in a good neighborhood?"

"What?"

"Are you safe? Is it a safe neighborhood?"

"It looks fancy," Hailey replied.

"Go ahead then; walk to the corner."

More shuffling, more time. Eventually Hailey told her: "I'm at the corner of Riviera and Middleton."

"Is there a bush nearby? a place you can hide?"

"Yes." Hailey sniffled.

"I want you to stay there. Don't go back to the house, okay?"

"But—"

"Just listen to me. Stay there. I'll find you."

Abigail terminated the call before Hailey could protest. Then she tossed on a pair of running shorts and a sweatshirt and raced for her computer. A quick Internet search informed her that the intersection of Riviera and Middleton was less than six miles from her apartment. Since it was the middle of the night, she could be there in ten minutes, tops. As she grabbed her car keys, Abigail couldn't help but wonder if Hailey had been there the whole time. Only ten minutes away from her building yet her sister might as well have been halfway across the world.

It was with a thrill of anticipation that Abigail acknowledged she wouldn't have to fly halfway across the world to fit her fingers around Hailey's scrawny neck.

But when Abigail pulled up to the four-way stop at Riviera and Middleton, daydreams of strangling her sister had taken a backseat to her fear of finding the girl at all. Would she be here? Or had she gone back to the strange house undoubtedly filled with strange people? What sort of a state would she be in? What had she done in her absence?

No cars or pedestrians were around at 2 a.m., and Abigail put her car in park at the stop sign and got out. "Hailey?" she called softly, scanning the darkness for signs of life. "Hailey, it's me."

For a moment, all was still. Then, amidst a whisper of rustling leaves, the unkempt girl emerged from behind a swath of ornamental grasses flanking a short, white bench. She stood there for the span of a few heartbeats, deliberating, until reason apparently won out and she came forward one cautious step at a time. It was as if she was afraid to approach Abigail with too much enthusiasm, too much transparent relief. But Abigail could read her face even at such a distance, and it was suffused with blatant gratitude.

As Hailey closed the space between them, Abigail boiled in a melting pot of emotions. Anger and resentment bubbled prominently, but underneath her fury, Abigail couldn't help but pity the forlorn young woman approaching her. Hailey cut such a pathetic silhouette in the darkness, so frail and wretched and sorry that Abigail felt the stirrings of compassion for her. She knew better than anyone that her sister was incapable of making sane and logical decisions; she could hardly be held responsible for herself. And no matter what she had done, the sad fact remained that whatever had made her run away was also the thing that made her life miserable.

"Hey," Abigail said when Hailey was only a few paces away.

Hailey stopped for a minute, staring at her with eyes made cloudy by tears. Then she jogged forward in a few stumbling steps and threw herself against Abigail.

The two girls all but crashed against the car, Abigail pinned beneath the slight weight of her sister as Hailey clung to her.

"I'm so sorry," Hailey wept. "I'm so sorry I ran away. I'm so sorry I did this to you and Dad."

The hands that had wanted to strangle Hailey clenched and unclenched. Abigail faltered, torn and confused because a part of her wanted to push her sister off and shout at her for being so self-centered and egotistical. But relief was mingling with the heat of anger in her blood, and Abigail reluctantly wrapped her arms around Hailey. She smoothed her hair away from her face just like their mother once did and lifted the long, golden strands off her sweaty neck. She soothed her, and though it was more or less mechanic, her hands were tender.

"Let's go home," Abigail whispered.

There was no question as to what Abigail meant by home. Neither girl wanted to face Lou in the middle of the night—not after he was rendered unconscious by his prescription sleep aid—so Abigail drove back to her apartment, the swanky flat that she had bought when Johnson & McNally hired her a year before.

The drive back to Abigail's place was silent and so was the quick trip up the stairs.

But when both women were inside the apartment, Abigail slid the dead bolt home and turned on her sister. "Where have you been?"

Hailey closed her eyes. "I know. I should have never—"

"I didn't ask for an apology. I asked for an explanation."

"It's complicated. I—"

"Hailey."

She pressed her fingers to her temples and massaged the gentle curve of skin. "You wouldn't understand."

"No, I probably won't. But you're going to tell me anyway. You owe me that at least."

Hailey's eyes snapped open and she fixed Abigail with a cold stare. "I don't owe you anything."

"We're family," Abigail countered, her gaze equally as chilly. "I've spent the last eighteen years of my life trying to be a good sister to you."

For a moment, the two women played tug-of-war with their eyes. Each was determined, each unwilling to give in because each was sure she was right.

Then Hailey sighed and moved around the kitchen island to sink onto a stool. "I know. And you *are* a good sister. But you don't understand, and sometimes I feel like you've never even tried to."

"What do you mean I haven't tried to?"

"You haven't tried to understand me."

"I know what you were saying. I just don't know what you *meant*. I fully understand that you have an illness," Abigail explained, hardening her hands and gesturing calmly, logically, as if the stiff planes of her fingers could prove her knowledge of the situation before her. "I know your diagnosis. I'm well aware of the medications you're supposed to be on. . . . I've even been to therapy with you. Multiple times!"

"That's not what I'm talking about."

"Then help me understand, because I have no idea what you're talking about!" Abigail didn't mean to shout, but Hailey crouched as if she expected her sister to slap her. Abigail withered a little, then came across the kitchen to bend over the island, her forearms on the faux marble surface and her face level with Hailey's. "What do you mean?" she tried, softer this time. "Why don't I understand you?"

"It's just . . . you have no idea how hard this is."

"I know it's—"

"You have no idea how trapped I am," Hailey interrupted. "What it feels like to live inside this mind, knowing that I should feel one way or another but I just *can't*. I can't. There are times when everything in my life tells me that I should be happy, elated even, with the way things are going, with the way my life is turning out . . . but I can't. There's a disconnect somewhere that won't let me feel what I know a normal person would feel. *Should* feel."

"Then take your meds," Abigail tried to reason.

Hailey's eyes went dull. Blank. "You don't get it."

"No. No, I'm trying."

"Forget it."

Abigail was at a loss for words. She didn't know how to bridge the distance between them, how to be strong and gentle, authoritative and encouraging. So she left the murky waters that they had somehow entered and set herself on higher ground, reverting to the question that still had not been answered. "Why did you leave?"

"Escape," Hailey said simply. "I needed to escape."

There was nothing more to say. How could Abigail counter that? *Read a book. A nice beach read with a happy ending. Escape into that. Or watch some mindless TV. Go for a run, take a long bath, go to church. . . .* "Have you found a church in Rosa Beach?"

Hailey's lips curved slightly, a token smile that was bittersweet and short-lived. "I've been going to Christ the King for nearly two years. I've invited you to go with me at least a dozen times."

Abigail shrugged off the guilt trip that Hailey was obviously trying to burden her with. She hadn't brought up the topic of church to censure herself. "What about that? Have you prayed about your illness? Have you . . . have you asked for healing?"

"Every single day," Hailey said, her voice thick with emotion, "for the last thirteen years, I'd guess."

"So where's your answer?" Abigail was surprised at the ferocity behind her words, the wrath.

"I've gotten it," Hailey assured her. "His answer is no."

Abigail settled Hailey on the couch with an afghan that Melody had made when her eldest graduated from eighth grade. At first, Abigail tried to convince her sister to take her bed, but Hailey flat-out refused, insisting that the couch was more than fine. Abigail suspected the small act of sacrifice was a sort of penance, one tiny way of making up for the agony that she had caused by disappearing.

And though her heart twisted at the sight of Hailey curled in a fetal position on the narrow couch, Abigail couldn't help feeling that maybe a little atonement was a good thing for her. After all, she had abandoned her family and done heaven only knows what while she was gone. When Abigail bent to give her sister a one-armed hug before making her way to her own bedroom, she was sure that she caught the sickly sweet scent of something illicit. Alcohol? Drugs? Either way, it didn't matter. Abigail didn't want to know.

In the silence of her bedroom, minutes ticked by and then one hour and two, but no matter which way she flipped, Abigail could not find the elusive spot that promised sleep. She tossed and turned, wondering and worrying about the troubled woman on her couch and trying to decide if she should go back out there and try to build a bridge between them.

But she didn't have to. Hailey came to her.

When the shadow first appeared in her doorway, Abigail caught her breath, wondering if Hailey had decided to leave again. Or maybe she was ill. Maybe she needed something. Was she sleep-walking?

Abigail decided not to say anything. She stayed perfectly still, her eyes fine slits that betrayed nothing of her wakefulness in the dim room.

Hailey tiptoed slowly across the plush carpet, as if she was afraid of startling her sister. At the edge of the bed, she paused, seeming to search in the darkness for any clue that would alert her to Abigail's state.

After a moment, she must have decided that her sister was asleep, because she carefully lifted the corner of the sheet and lowered herself inch by inch until she was lying on the edge of the bed. She balanced there for a second, her feet still on the floor. Then she lifted her legs, too, and lay stretched out beside the prone shape of the woman who was her substitute mother, her sister, her role model, her friend. She took a shuddering breath.

For once Abigail didn't feel the least bit conflicted or confused. She reached out a strong arm and circled it around her sister's waist. She pulled her close.

Hailey didn't seem startled. She put her hand on top of Abigail's and whispered, "Someday I'll be well. I'll find some incredible guy who will understand, who will be able to *really* know me. . . . You know, keep me sane. We'll have a kid or two. It'll be great. You'll see."

"I'm sure I will," Abigail whispered back. "You'll make an amazing wife. A great mother."

They were words, nothing but words. Neither woman believed them for a second. But it was comforting to say them out loud, to claim them.

Abigail and Hailey were quiet, lying there together in a communion that couldn't be duplicated in a hundred years of trying. They breathed.

They listened to the sound of stillness in the quiet haven of the room.

And then Abigail asked, "Do you still go to church? I mean, have you gone recently?"

Hailey squeezed her sister's hand, answered as if she knew the question was coming. "Yes."

"Why do you go?"

"Because I love the sights and sounds. The candles, the icons, the incense . . . And I have an affinity with the Virgin Mary. Can you imagine what it must have been like to be her? I'm sure everyone thought she was crazy, too."

Though it seemed insensitive somehow, Abigail couldn't help but grin.

"And there's something about Jesus . . ." Hailey said it so softly that Abigail almost missed the words. "He knows what it means to suffer. He *knows*. And I can't help but trust him. He says, 'Come to Me, all who are weary and heavy-laden, and I will give you rest.'" She paused so long that Abigail was sure she couldn't continue. But then, into the darkness Hailey breathed a desire so weighted with longing it seemed directed heavenward. "I want to rest."

Something in Abigail's chest collapsed. *I can give you rest,* she thought. *I try.* But she wasn't what Hailey was looking for and she knew it. "Why do you believe him?" she asked, jealous of her sister's blind faith, maybe even jealous of the object of Hailey's faith, and yet pricked with a spreading ache she hadn't planned on and felt powerless to control. It tingled through her veins. It made her numb.

"I believe because I have to trust that who I am, what I'm living through isn't an accident. I have to trust that I am loved unconditionally. That there is a plan for my life. Otherwise . . ."

The caution hung in the air.

It jarred Abigail to the bone. She felt a tremor from her head to her toes, and she tightened her grip on Hailey. Though she wanted to say something, nothing felt right. Her quick answers rang trite in her mind, and she couldn't bring herself to utter something that was only patent fluff. Abigail wanted to affirm her sister's conviction, but she couldn't quite get past her anger at the same God who had made Hailey the way she was. And she had no idea what to do with the person of Jesus, this suffering savior. This God and man who understood, who offered rest.

The tears that were suddenly hot and insistent in the corners of her eyes were unexpected. Abigail tried to swallow but couldn't. She tried to clear her throat, but eighteen years of emotion clogged the narrow space. What else could she do? Abigail raised herself on her elbow and kissed her sister's perfect cheek in benediction. In love.

Hailey left again a few months later. And came home. Then disappeared shortly after that. By the time she was twenty, she no longer lived under Lou's roof for more than the occasional couch crash that happened only because she was between boyfriends or currently out of favor with her friends. She worked a succession of different jobs that ranged from secretarial to questionable—Abigail once caught her in a Hooters T-shirt. And Hailey learned that the men who bought her drinks when she was eighteen would buy her a dress when she was twenty. Or let her borrow their car or bankroll a few months' rent. She stayed in sporadic contact with Abigail, but their communication was usually borne out of Hailey's need for quick cash and only necessary when she was in one of her infrequent and short-lived slumps.

It was a five-year spiral that cycled from hope to despair, from celestial highs to ruinous lows. Sometimes things were more or less good, and Abigail heard of or even met her sister's ever-changing lovers. Sometimes things were horrible, and neither Lou nor Abigail heard from Hailey for months. Those were long weeks filled with fear and a horrifying sense of premature loss. Once Abigail went so far as to jot down notes for Hailey's funeral.

But all that changed around Christmastime when Hailey was twenty-five. She started calling Abigail daily; she even dropped by Johnson, McNally & Bennett, where she charmed Abigail's coworkers to the point of infatuation. She stopped dabbling in whatever depressants and stimulants she normally used to dampen the dry heat of her own tumultuous emotions. And though it shocked Abigail, Hailey made an appointment with a psychologist and actually showed up at the scheduled time.

When Hailey breezed into the the Four Seasons Manor Home for Christmas dinner, Abigail knew that something significant had shifted. The young woman smiled, captivated the nurses, and hugged her father. Then she pulled Abigail aside and whispered with a twinkle in her eye, "Remember what I told you? all those years ago? about the incredible guy and the kids? the life I was created for?"

"Yes," Abigail said slowly, searching her sister's eyes for the fever of intoxication, the betraying twitch that would tell her Hailey was not in her right mind. It wasn't there.

"I found him," she cried. "I found him and he's perfect and everything is going to change."

Abigail felt a cold sweat prickle between her shoulder blades; her palms went clammy. She held her breath.

Hailey didn't seem to notice. Instead, she laughed. "His name is Tyler."

℘ *For those first few agonizing weeks after Hailey died, I visited Lou every day. I went when I knew he'd be confined to bed, finished with his daily regimen of three square meals, rec time in his wheelchair, and an early evening dose of Jeopardy! By the time I slipped through his door, he was always reclining in bed, the blankets tucked neatly beneath his limp arms, and his head centered on the hard pillow as if he had measured it to make sure each ear was perfectly equidistant from the squared edges. He didn't turn when I came in, but his gaze flicked in the direction of the door, and I knew that he expected me.*

We never did much. We just sat there in each other's presence and fixed our eyes, unseeing, on the glinting light of the television suspended from the corner near the ceiling. Every once in a while I felt brave enough to attempt a conversation of sorts, but Lou grunted away my feeble efforts and I stopped trying. Strange as it sounds, I think I just wanted to be near him, even though it seemed he didn't want to be near me.

But one day I walked into Lou's room at the Four Seasons, and he responded very differently to me than all those times before.

I had been cleaning at Hailey's apartment, boxing and sorting the last of her things, and I worked up a decent sweat running up and down the stairs from her rooms to my car. As I prepared to descend the steps one last time, I glanced in the box I was holding and noticed one of Hailey's silk scarves poking out from between the folded flaps. I yanked the lemony cream swath of fabric out of the box and hastily folded it into a misshapen triangle. Then I swept the damp tendrils of hair from my face and neck and wrapped the makeshift bandana around my head, tying it at the nape of my neck as if I were some sweet housewife from the 1950s instead of an unattached career woman in the throes of watching her life disintegrate.

When I arrived at the Four Seasons an hour later to check in on Lou, it hadn't crossed my mind to remove the lovely scarf.

The look on his face when I walked through the door should have been enough to alert me that something was not as it should be. Though his eyes were fixed on the TV, when I rapped on the doorframe, he gave me his usual courtesy of a passing glance. But this time, as Lou began to look away, he spun back toward me with more than just his eyes—his whole body shifted to take me in as I stood outlined in the frame of the doorway.

"What?" I asked, doing a self-conscious once-over to make sure that everything was in place. Was I dirty? Had I lost a button?

But Lou wasn't staring at me in disdain; he was

drinking me in with thirsty, longing eyefuls. "I love it when you wear your hair back," he told me, his voice low with a mixture of transparent pain and thinly veiled hope.

Mystified, I lifted a hand to my hair and felt it. The scarf. Realization hit me at the same time as panic—Lou thought I was Hailey. The milky yellow bandana hid my dark hair and fell like a long ponytail across one shoulder. Standing in the half-light between the bright hallway and his dim room, I must have appeared like an unexpected angel. Lou was certainly looking at me as if I was one.

I didn't know what to do. Lou didn't have Alzheimer's, but he was on the brink of eighty-three and he had lived a long and strenuous life. His mind was clear for the most part, but this wasn't the first time he had become confused. Sometimes he called me by the name of the nurse on duty or complained that Melody had forgotten again that he hated margarine: "Is it too much to ask for a little real butter?" Whenever he mixed something up, I would just give him a bland nod and ignore it.

This, however, was way beyond my experience. What was I supposed to do? Whip off the scarf and tell him that I was Abigail, not Hailey? Or should I go along with it? pretend to be my sister so that he could have a brief moment of peace? Maybe I could just tell him I loved him and disap-

pear. Maybe he'd think I was an apparition, a dream.

"Come here," Lou said before I had a chance to formulate a plan. He held out his hand to me.

I stepped forward because his face was flushed with happiness. The dark line of his usually furrowed brow was smooth and relaxed. And his lips were parted in a smile that made him look young again, like the father of my youth. How could I not go to him?

When Lou caught my hand, he pulled me toward him as if he was reeling me in. He looked up at me, taking in my features with hopeful eyes, his eyebrows knitting when he saw the dark shimmer of my brown eyes, then absorbing the golden sweep of fabric that was not hair . . . and I watched as he relived her death by degrees.

"Abby?" he whispered, anguished.

"Yeah, Dad. It's me." Though I expected him to turn away, I put my free hand over his and held it tight. "I'm sorry."

But my father didn't turn from me this time. He knew she was gone, knew it was me, but instead of putting my sister between us, Lou tugged me down. We were nose to nose for the briefest of seconds, and in his eyes I could see the recognition that we shared this grief. We bore it silently and alone, but we bore the same sorrow.

Then Lou crushed me against his chest, wrapping his arms around me and sobbing until I had no choice but to let my tears join his. We stayed like that for a long while, holding each other and mourning for her.

When he was finally able to talk, Lou murmured against the scarf that still covered my hair, "Why?"

"I don't know," I whispered back.

"I just want to know why."

Sitting up reluctantly, I passed the back of my hand across my cheeks, beneath my nose. I sniffed. "She was sick."

"My little girl didn't do this on her own," Lou insisted, hitting the blankets with his fist. "Someone did this to her. Someone made her believe that she couldn't go on. If I were a younger man . . ."

The threat hung in the air between us, for I knew that my father would move heaven and earth to avenge his daughter's death, even if there was nothing to avenge. Even if she had just succumbed to her illness like we always feared she would.

But I knew there was more to it than that. There had to be. And because he had held me, because he realized that I was Abigail and he had still chosen to fold me in his arms, I knew what I had to do.

I picked up his hand and kissed it, sealing a promise that he didn't even know I had made.

XVI

ભ THOUGH ELI WANTED to accompany Abigail back to the trailer, she insisted on walking alone. Her unexpected nighttime encounter had been far more powerful and perplexing than she ever imagined an experience could be. She felt shell-shocked, dizzy, and spent, and she needed time to process what had happened.

"Take the flashlight at least," Eli told her. He handed her a heavy silver Maglite that could have easily passed for a billy club. Winking at her, he said, "Don't worry. You'll only need it for the light."

"What about you? How will you get back?"

Eli swept his palm across the flame of the candle, nearly snuffing it out. "I'll light my path the old-fashioned way."

"Just don't start a fire."

"Don't you worry about that. I'll be fine."

Abigail left him to clean up the remnants of their symbolic meal and made her way back to the dark entrance. At the wall she paused, tempted to take one last look over her shoulder at the table, the bread, and the wine. She wanted to preserve the memory in her mind, tuck it into some exclusive vault where she could easily retrieve it later for careful examination. But she didn't, because in some incomprehensible way, she hoped for more.

This is the first, she thought, *but maybe it doesn't have to be the last.*

The world outside the winery was still; there wasn't even a breath of breeze in the leaves of the vines that spread around Abigail. But above her, the heavens were a dynamic, living thing. Though the meteor shower had slowed, there was still an unnatural profusion of diamond light that fell around her in intermittent bursts. Abigail breathed deeply, taking it in, and couldn't suppress the feeling that the evening was a gift, a reprieve from everything that had brought her to Revell in the first place. She lingered on the way between the buildings of Thompson Hills and her little home.

By the time Abigail arrived at the trailer, she was nearly vibrating in anticipation. It occurred to her as she walked that the Bible she had taken from the hotel in Everett was still tucked in her attaché. She felt a delicious ripple of interest; it startled her, but it wasn't unwelcome because for the first time since she had stolen the book, she was actually curious to hold it and flip through the pages.

The attaché was hidden behind the driver's seat of the antiquated motor home, slid in the small space between the seat back and the bench of the kitchenette booth. Abigail yanked it out and scooted onto the bench. She clicked off the flash-light and turned on the lamp that sat on the counter. True to his word, the first day that Abigail spent in the Navigator, Tyler ran an extension cord from the outlet beside Eli's cement patio and snaked it through a small tear in the kitchen window screen. He even duct taped the opening so that no bugs could sneak through the hole.

When a warm circle of light bathed the inside of the trailer in a soft, yellow glow, Abigail couldn't help but think about Tyler. She sat immobile for a while and probed the thought with careful fingers. She outlined her emotions in tentative, cautious strokes. The acute and wrenching ache that she usually felt when she took the time to truly focus on Tyler was gone, and in its place was an emptiness that made her wonder if she could understand the phantom pain of an amputee. What had been so agonizing was now only the bitter memory of something terrible but absent. Was she capable of letting go? Was one sacred encounter enough to change everything?

It was complicated, and Abigail wasn't sure she was ready to answer those questions. So she put them aside and focused on the bag in front of her. Unzipping the long pocket, she reached blindly for the hard edges of the Gideons' inadvertent gift. Instead of finding the book, her hand swept across the flat line of a forgotten manila envelope. She tensed, remembering.

It shouldn't have been a big deal, even when Abigail pulled it out of her Florida mailbox over two months ago. After all, she knew what the autopsy report would say. Though it was very obvious to her how Hailey had died, an autopsy was standard procedure when the cause of death was even marginally unclear. All the same, Abigail had no desire to read the report and come face-to-face with those cold, hard facts. It made everything so final.

But now, with the taste of the bread and wine still lingering on her tongue, Abigail felt capable of looking inside. She took the envelope and laid it on the table in front of her. "Give me strength," she whispered, prayerlike.

Sliding her finger under a corner of the thick paper, Abigail broke the gummy seal and pulled out the packet that was waiting inside. The front page bore the official seal of the Office of the Medical Examiner of Bluegrass County, Florida. As she removed the thick paper clip holding the document together, she glanced over the first few lines. She noted the Jonathan P. Berkowitz Forensic Center logo and Hailey's full name and case number as well as official dates, signatures, and the embossed stamp of a notary public.

She sighed heavily. So far, so good. She could do this.

The second page had only a few lines, but they were hard ones to read. Hailey's name and case number appeared again, followed by two short, boldfaced paragraphs: Cause of Death and Manner of Death. Abigail was able to read *overdose*, *self-inflicted*, and *suicide* before she had to rip her eyes from the page. She removed the sheet from the pile and placed it facedown with unsteady hands.

There were at least half a dozen more pages to flip through and a glance told Abigail that these were chock-full of typed information. She had made it this far; maybe two pages were enough for tonight. Maybe the power of what she had experienced was enough to get her through those pages and nothing more. Two pages today, two more tomorrow, and so on until the entire file had been examined. Then she could burn the whole document. Abigail longed to let the flame from Eli's candle lick the edges of these hateful papers. But they were lying in front of her right now, and she couldn't ignore them any more than she could forget that Hailey had died.

With trembling fingers, Abigail flipped through the pages. Though she tried not to read anything too closely, she noticed the headings: *History*, *Autopsy*, *Evidence of Medical Intervention*. On the next page there were *Clothing*, *External Appearance*, and *Internal Examination*. Then *Heart*, *Kidneys*, and *Gastrointestinal Tract*. *Neck Organs*, *Head*, *Histology*, *Toxicology* . . . The titles went on and on, cataloging every little thing about Hailey Anne Bennett in death.

Single words like *temporal*, *parietal*, and *occip-ital* swam off the page and made an indelible mark on Abigail's consciousness, and the numbers followed by ounces and pounds stood out simply because they were different. Everything had been measured and weighed, recorded as carefully as the length, weight, and head circumference of a newborn baby. Hailey was reduced to several pages filled with numbers and notations, most of which meant nothing to Abigail.

Though she could sweep over most of the categories, for some reason her eyes alighted on a short paragraph beginning with reproductive systems. Did they leave no stone unturned? Abigail was about to flip to the final page when a phrase from the unanticipated section jumped off the paper and strangled her: *gravid uterus at 8–10 weeks gestation.* Gestation? She tore through the rest of the paragraph and found, *fetal length, .90 inches* and *fetal weight, .075 ounces.*

Fetus? Hailey was . . . *pregnant?* Abigail thrust herself away from the table, stumbling over her own two feet in her rush to get away from the devastating pages. "No," she said, the pebbly scratch of her voice startling her. *"No."*

But she knew what she had read. A horrified glimpse reconfirmed it. Those words, printed in unmistakable black and white, didn't lie.

Abigail began to hyperventilate. Air, she needed more air. But the more she breathed, the more she felt like she was going to explode. Her chest burst beneath the terrible weight of knowing that it was not just Hailey's death that she mourned; it was also the death of a child. Her nephew. Maybe her niece.

Pressing her palms to her mouth, Abigail struggled to contain what was threatening to spill from her. A scream? A sob? She was sure there was more at stake than a cry of anguish that would stop at the four walls of the trailer. Her very soul writhed in agony. It seemed capable of crawling up from the pit of her being to slip away into the night, a dark and wounded specter.

Hailey had been pregnant. With Tyler's baby?

Tyler's baby.

The realization roused Abigail from whatever attack had momentarily claimed her. Without pausing to consider what she was doing, she staggered lead footed to the bathroom and bent to throw open the tiny cabinet door. The Glock was there, loaded and ready. It felt good in her hand.

Abigail yanked open the trailer door and lurched with unsteady, halting motions across the driveway. Somewhere in the recesses of her mind, she was coherent enough to note that Eli couldn't possibly be back from the winery yet. That meant the soft light of the television emanating from between the slats of the venetian blinds had to be for Tyler. She could picture him half-asleep and prostrate on the couch.

Slipping her shaking fingers around the handle of the side door, Abigail held her breath and turned the knob. The door popped open with a muted click. Tyler hadn't bothered to lock it.

Nan came trotting across the carpet, his tongue lolling in welcome. Abigail hesitated long enough to give the dog a distracted scratch; then she grabbed a scruff of fur at Nan's collar and pulled him out of the house. She stepped inside and had the forethought to lock the door behind her.

"Eli?" Tyler called.

She emerged slowly from the shadows of the mudroom into the darkened kitchen. Since the main living space was an open great room, Abigail could peer past the stylish island and see Tyler sprawled on the couch in front of *SportsCenter*. The TV was the only source of light in the house.

"Abigail," Tyler said, pulling himself to a sitting position. "What are you doing here? Is everything okay?"

Her aching mind registered that he was wearing a white T-shirt and jeans, the same outfit Hailey had donned to climb in a bathtub and bring her own life to a close.

"Did you know she was pregnant?" Abigail whispered, pressing herself against the island, hiding the gun beneath the line of smooth countertop.

"Excuse me?" Tyler cocked his head at her, his eyes filled with confusion.

"She was pregnant," Abigail yelled this time. "Did you know that?"

"What in the world are you talking about?" Tyler stood, the look on his face betraying the fact that he felt something menacing in the room. He took a few tentative steps toward her. "Are you okay? You seem—"

"Stop," Abigail muttered, the pitch of her voice enough to render the man across from her statuesque. "I asked you a question."

"I have no idea what you're talking about," Tyler said, holding his hands up in entreaty. "Is this some movie I was supposed to watch?"

Abigail wiped her forehead with the back of her free wrist and took a shuddering breath. She couldn't control the tremors stealing through her entire body, and she watched Tyler note her involuntary movement with alarm.

"You're not okay," he insisted, answering his own question. "Did something happen? Do you need a doctor?"

"No!" Abigail didn't mean to shout, but it did make Tyler take a step back. "My name is Abigail Bennett," she said, a little softer but no less forcefully. She clipped each syllable, all but spitting out the final *T*. "*Bennett.* Does that name mean anything to you?"

Tyler didn't skip a beat. "I dated a girl with the same last name, but that was months ago." Then a sudden wash of understanding spilled over his features. "Wait, Hailey had a sister. Her name was . . ."

"Abby?"

"Are you telling me you're Hailey's sister? I would have never guessed." Tyler grinned through his bewilderment, apparently trying to lighten whatever hung dark and heavy in the air. "Small world. But how did you know I dated Hailey? And what are you doing *here*? I thought . . ." Abigail was still looking at him with apparent malice, so he swallowed the last of his musings. In a different tone he said, "How is Hailey? I haven't seen her since March."

Abigail shook her head as if to clear it. He didn't know? How could he not know? "Hailey's dead," she said, her gaze boring into him with caustic precision. "And so is her baby. *Your* baby."

She may as well have taken the gun and leveled it at Tyler's head. He hardened into something implacable, his face chiseled into a mask of unrealistic calm. Abigail could see that he didn't believe her, that none of this made sense to him. But she was deadly serious, and the gravity of her words, the rigidity of her posture as she stood before him didn't take long to prove convincing. *Hailey's dead*. The words settled over him, a mantle so burdensome he bowed beneath the load and was forced to put his hands on the arm of the couch for support. *Your baby . . .*

"What?" he gasped.

"Hailey killed herself on March 14. Her birthday,"

Abigail added almost to herself. "She took her baby with her."

Tyler's eyes were wide and unblinking, but Abigail could tell he wasn't looking at her. He wasn't even aware of where he was. It was obvious that his mind's eye had rewound the clock five months to the last time he had seen Hailey alive. "But I saw her. She was . . . she was upset . . . but . . ."

"What did you say to her?" Abigail demanded, choking on the intensity of her longing to know. "What happened between you two?"

"We broke up," Tyler confessed. All at once tears dripped from his eyes. Abigail was convinced that the wetness startled him by the way he hurriedly brought his hands to his face and tried to erase the evidence with his palms.

"When?"

"I don't know. . . . A few days before I left for Vancouver." Tyler's words trickled over each other, an avalanche of explanation. "It was, uh . . . My plane left on the twelfth, and it happened before . . . just before I left. But I didn't know that. . . . I didn't *know*."

Two days. She had lasted two days without him. "Why?" Abigail pleaded. "Why did you break up with her?"

"Because we were a mess," Tyler said. "Because she pulled me down."

Abigail growled. If she had even a drop of sympathy for him, it evaporated with that one statement. "So you knocked her up and left her?" She was so furious she jerked away from the island and started toward Tyler.

"What?" he sputtered again.

"You heard me! My sister was pregnant with your baby!"

Tyler went down on his knees, a supplicant before Abigail's livid, approaching form. "She told me she was pregnant, but I thought it was just a ploy to get me to stay. I didn't think . . . I didn't know it was for real."

"It was!" Abigail screamed, throwing her arms in the air, lashing out at nothing and everything. She didn't point the gun at him, but it loomed ominous in her hand. It was a hostile, animate thing. It hovered like a bird of prey; it reigned over them as fateful as a rumbling, oppressive cloud.

When Tyler caught sight of it, he went so pale Abigail feared he might pass out. "Wh-what are you doing, Abigail?" The words wavered in the stillness before flickering out.

"I'm atoning. You killed my sister."

Tyler shook his head, slowly at first, but faster and faster as he realized the implications. "She killed herself."

"Because of you."

"No."

"You left her pregnant and alone. You knew she was sick."

"I knew she saw a psychologist. I knew she took pills." Tyler's head still jerked from side to side. "I didn't know she was suicidal."

Abigail's head hurt. Her heart hurt. And she became conscious that her right arm hurt, too. Looking up, she realized that the gun was still clutched in her hand, raised over her head as a talisman, a warning. It was heavy and angular. It was hard to hold. She lowered it slowly, holding it out. Pointing it at Tyler. "She wasn't well. There is no way you could not have known."

"Don't be stupid," he pleaded. "I loved her; I did. If I had known . . . Don't. Just don't. This won't solve anything. It won't fix anything." He focused behind her, but Abigail was too intent on the barrel of the gun to turn around.

Her finger was on the trigger and her mind was spinning with the unyielding burden of everything she knew. She saw Hailey in the bathtub, gray and lifeless. She saw the light go out of her father's eyes when she told him about his baby girl. She saw the long, dark road to Revell and the troubling sparkle of the mirror where she peered into her own soul. There were the unexplored emotions of the moonless night she spent with Tyler. And rising slower still, but surfacing all the same, were memories of Hailey, sparks from her childhood like the final shimmer of fading fireworks against a cloudy sky.

Suffusing every thought, bathing her memories

in a stain of unexpected crimson, was the wine she shared with Eli, the invitation she had accepted.

But Abigail didn't know what to do with all that. She didn't know how to reconcile what had happened, the lives that had been lost, with a sacrifice she couldn't claim to understand.

"You don't get it," she said, though she didn't know if she was talking to herself or to Tyler.

When he made a little noise in the back of his throat, Abigail tore her eyes away from the gun and glanced at the man on the floor in front of her. He was looking past her, and in a flash of instinct Abigail knew that someone was behind her. She jumped away and spun around in time to see Eli lunge for her and stumble into empty space.

The older man straightened up slowly, putting his hands in front of him as if to show her that he had nothing to hide. There was a key in his hand, and he laid it on the counter in one unhurried, deliberate movement. "Hey." His voice was so calm, his movements so reassuring that for a moment everything seemed perfectly normal and sane.

Abigail just stared at him. But then Tyler called out his uncle's name, and Abigail remembered the gun in her hand. She aimed it into the room at no one in particular because she couldn't bring herself to point it at Eli.

"I heard everything. I was coming up from the fields and I saw you come out of your trailer with

498

the gun in your hand." Eli's eyes softened. "I'm sorry for your loss."

Though Abigail hadn't shed a single tear since reading the sickening autopsy report, with Eli before her looking so composed and comforting, she felt something inside her break. In an instant her cheeks were streaked. "She was pregnant."

"I know."

"I should have been there for her. I should have known."

"It wasn't your fault."

"It was *Tyler's* fault."

"No, Abigail. It wasn't anybody's fault. She had an illness, a disease." Eli took a step toward her. "What did she suffer from?"

The question startled Abigail, but she answered because she didn't know what else to do. "Hailey was severely bipolar. But there were other things, too. ADHD, maybe even borderline personality disorder . . ."

Eli nodded as if he understood. "She was pursued. Can you imagine what it must feel like to be so relentlessly pursued?"

"Eli . . . ," Abigail whispered, warning him.

"Can you imagine how hard that must have been for her?" he repeated, moving a little closer. "Your sister was overcome."

"What does that mean?" Abigail cried, sniffling.

"She was hunted. Like cancer taking a victim, her illness took her."

"Where?" Abigail demanded. "Where does my sister get to go?"

Understanding widened Eli's eyes. "You think she's in hell, don't you? Or in between, stuck in some nebulous purgatory."

"I don't know," Abigail confessed, using the hand that wasn't holding the gun to run shaky fingers through her tangled hair. She caught a handful of it at the back of her head and moaned.

"Maybe God wants to be merciful."

"But that doesn't change anything."

"What do you mean?"

"That communion you orchestrated, all that stuff about forgiveness and grace . . . Hailey still killed herself. And I . . ." She was at a loss for words. She waved the gun as if it explained everything.

"You what? You don't think the sacrifice of the cross is enough to cover you? He paid it all, Abigail; all you have to do is accept the gift."

She pressed her eyes shut for a second but whisked them open when she heard Eli's socks swish across the carpet. He was a few feet away from her.

"I know what you're doing," he told her. "I've worked by your side for months now, and I can put the pieces together. You think this is your penance, don't you? You think it's your job to somehow make this all right."

"I'm her sister," Abigail said. "I was practically her mother. I *have* to."

"That's not true. You don't have to do anything. We talked about wine, remember?" Eli searched her face. "What if your life is an offering poured out in a single glass? What if surrender is exactly what God is asking from you? What if surrender is *all* he is asking from you? A moment of forgiveness. An act of grace."

"But I promised . . ."

"What did you promise? Who did you promise?"

Abigail could hardly form the words. "My father," she mouthed. When nothing came out, she said it again, the tiny breath of sound barely loud enough to hear: "My father."

Something in Eli's face shifted. "Your father wants you to kill Tyler?"

Just hearing him say it made Abigail shake her head with unexpected vehemence. "No, no, he never said that. He doesn't . . ."

"Of course he doesn't."

"Then what am I supposed to do?" she shouted.

"There's nothing you *can* do other than love her, grieve for her, and let her go."

Abigail watched him until her eyes were so filled with tears that Eli's face was completely obscured.

"Maybe this time it's not about judgment," he said. "Maybe it's about grace."

She didn't like hearing her words turned around on her, but Abigail couldn't stop herself from grasping at Eli's proclamation as if it could be true.

For a moment she faltered, hoping. But that was too easy. It had to be. "What if you're wrong?"

"What if I'm not? What if God—?"

"It's his fault. He made her that way," she accused, venom spiking each syllable as it fell from her lips.

"And he loves her. Surrender Hailey," Eli pleaded. "Just let go."

"No."

"Give me the gun." He took another step closer.

"I can't."

"Yes, you can."

She aimed it at him.

"You don't want to use it anyway."

The tip of the barrel dipped the tiniest bit, and in less than a second Eli was gripping her wrist, pointing the gun at the floor.

Abigail's hand shook so badly that Eli had to come beside her and pry the weapon from her fingers, one stiff knuckle at a time. Then the Glock was in his hand, and he removed the chambered bullet, ejected the magazine, and stuffed the useless husk of gun in the belt of his khaki pants.

When the weapon was safely dismantled, Eli put one firm arm around Abigail's shoulders and was ready and waiting to sweep the other beneath her knees when she sagged against him. He picked her up.

XVII

 I WOULD BE LYING if I said that it was a relief to find myself back in Rosa Beach.

Honestly I don't remember much about the trip home other than snatches of almost-robotic awareness: I recall packing my bags with apathy, pulling out my credit card to pay for the extraordinarily expensive and poorly routed plane ticket home, and turning rather rudely from one of the suited flight attendants when she asked me if I preferred water or orange juice.

Other than that, the fourteen-hour trip from Kelowna to Vancouver, Vancouver to Seattle, Seattle to Denver, Denver to Chicago, and Chicago to the Fort Myers airport was a mind-numbing blur.

When I got off the plane, the first thing that hit me was the temperature. Surviving a mid-August heat wave in southern Florida is akin to persevering for weeks in a pressure cooker. I should have known that. I should have been ready. But although I had lived in Rosa Beach for twelve years, I wasn't prepared for the physical impact of stepping out the door of the ice-cold Boeing 747.

With my skin prickling in the intolerable heat, I took the shuttle to my car in a long-term parking lot a few miles from the airport. Clicking off the locks, I melted onto the soft gray leather seats, vanishing back into my real life. Trying it on for size. I couldn't tell if it fit or not. I was too tired, too used up, so I turned the ignition in my poor, neglected Passat, and headed south, slanting my car toward the ocean and home.

Home? Was my chic apartment home? Was Florida? Startled by my own train of thought, I had to dig even deeper. Had Minnesota felt like home to me? I contemplated my childhood, those years under the same roof as Lou and Melody, as Hailey. No, Newcastle didn't feel much like home either.

I decided right then and there that if home is where the heart is, my heart has been homeless for a very long time.

After Eli disarmed me the night I pulled a gun on his nephew, we spent some time talking about home. I thought that after what I did to Tyler, my relationship with Eli would be over, the beautiful evening we spent in the winery sharing a supper I never dreamed I'd be a part of again would be a meaningless blip on the shaky radar of my messed-up life. But Eli didn't turn on me. He lifted me up, carried me to his couch, and when I had wept long enough to render myself dry for the rest of my life, he talked to me.

"I'm so . . . I'm so *sorry*," I whispered once my tears were gone and there was nothing left for me to do but face the man before me.

Eli was standing, obviously uncomfortable with my emotional display but unable to bring himself to abandon me in such a terrible state. When I spoke, he started to lower himself to his haunches, but he stalled halfway down and groaned. "These old knees can't handle that." He pulled the coffee table a little closer and sat on it.

"I'm sorry," I whispered again.

"I know." Eli sighed heavily. "That definitely wasn't the smartest thing you've ever done." He pulled the gun from his waistband with a flourish. "Thanks for finding this for me. I've been looking for it for years."

Confusion must have creased my face because he rushed to explain. "When I quit the force and moved back here, the only thing I took with me was the car that I was driving and my backup piece tucked in a cardboard box in the trunk." The corner of Eli's lip pulled up in a sardonic grin. "Border patrol never thought to ask."

I watched him, waiting for him to continue. Why keep his backup? Before I could open my mouth to ask, it clicked. He kept the gun *just in case* . . . Just in case he found that he couldn't live with himself and decided to take the coward's way out. Just in case he decided to end things like Hailey had. I felt a rush of fury blaze bright and hot in my eyes and knew that Eli had seen it when he raised his hands in defense.

"It's not like that," he said, acquitting himself before I had a chance to accuse. "Not anymore. At one time I believed the only way to end the suffering was to *end* it. I know it sounds cliché, but I believe that God works in mysterious ways."

I glared at him, but his gaze was guileless.

He considered the gun for a moment. "And I can't help also believing there's a purpose in everything."

"In aiming a gun at someone? trying to gather the courage to pull the trigger?"

"Even that." Eli laid the Glock on the coffee table beside him and leaned close to me. "But I don't think you would have done it."

I brushed my hands across my cheeks and took a long, steadying breath. Sitting up, I pulled my legs beneath me and sat cross-legged in front of Eli. "I don't know what I'm capable of anymore."

"Great things, Abigail Bennett. You're capable of great things."

"So was Hailey."

Eli clasped his hands in front of him and gazed at the carpet. "She was a beautiful girl. I saw her once in a tiny photo on Tyler's phone before he deleted it."

At the mention of Tyler, I looked around the room. I don't know if I expected him to be hovering in some corner, waiting to abuse me for what I tried to do, or if I imagined he'd be penitent, filled with sorrow at the loss of someone who could have been everything to him. "Where is he?"

"He left."

There were so many questions tied into that one small statement, I didn't know where to begin.

"Tyler can't handle something like this," Eli said, rescuing me from the pain of trying to articulate all I felt. "Not now."

"But . . ." What had I expected? Did I really imagine he'd stick around to talk this through?

"He's growing, but he's got a long way to go."

"I—"

"You know, I should have seen it coming." Eli put a hand to his forehead and rubbed the weathered skin of his temples. "Do you know why we keep rosebushes at the end of every row of vines?"

The sudden shift in conversation unnerved me, and I shook my head as if to clear it.

Eli interpreted my gesture as an invitation to continue. "Grapevines are delicate plants, but roses are even more fragile. If we see fungus, insect damage, mildew—you name it—on one of the rosebushes, we know that our vines could be in serious trouble. And then we can take the appropriate steps to prevent anything really horrible from happening." He sighed. "I saw so many signs. . . . I should have been paying attention."

"Don't be ridiculous," I muttered, shifting as if to get up. "Where is he? I need to . . . I just—"

"Someday," Eli interrupted me again, but this time his tone was commanding. "There will be time to put this all to rights someday. But not now. Not today."

That wasn't quite enough for me, but I could tell it was all I was going to get out of Eli. I sank back and picked at the seam of my running shorts. "What happened between them? Did he ever tell you?"

"He's kind of a private man," Eli said. "But I know that he carries a lot of deep hurts. Tyler never got over his father's death, even though he was young when it happened. And he never quite accepted Murray as his dad. Nice enough guy but not much interested in being a father."

I bit my lip, stared at my fingers as they curled and uncurled in my lap. "He just . . . he seems so arrogant, so in charge."

"Isn't that often the case when people are trying to cover up for their own self-perceived inadequacies?"

I didn't respond.

"When Tyler's mom was about to die," Eli continued, "I think it made him reexamine everything. He told me that he came home because he wanted to start over."

"He said Hailey pulled him down."

"Doesn't misery love company? Doesn't brokenness beget more brokenness? I can only imagine how two hurting people like them could wallow together in some sad pit of their own making."

"She wasn't miserable," I told him. "She thought he was her redemption."

Though he had been tender with me from the

508

moment he walked in the door, Eli fixed me with a hard look. "She was wrong."

"Hailey was lost," I replied. "She spent twenty-six years trying to stifle herself, trying to control what was uncontrollable. For some reason, she believed that Tyler could fix what was broken in her."

"He couldn't."

"It doesn't matter. She pinned everything on him." I scowled at him, daring him to contradict me. "It's not fair."

"No, it's not."

"When he broke up with her, I'm sure she panicked. Pregnant and alone? Hailey couldn't take care of herself. How could she take care of a baby?"

"One final rejection," Eli said, filling in the blanks. Then he added carefully, "And you . . . you—"

"I found her," I breathed, stopping him with a sigh so low he clamped his mouth shut. "I found her in her apartment when she missed our lunch date. I was supposed to be taking her out for her birthday." I paused, remembering the excited phone call, the happy tremor in her voice when she contacted me of her own volition. "We had set it up a week earlier. She told me that she had big news to tell me. *Big* news—something that would change everything."

Though Eli wasn't the sentimental sort, I could

see this last bit of information strummed a raw nerve. "The baby?"

"I don't know, but I found a bridal magazine in her apartment. I think she thought Tyler was going to marry her."

"He was going to be the father of her child," Eli murmured. Then he heaved a long, anguished sigh. "Oh, that poor girl."

His reaction stirred me; it made me want to talk. All at once I wanted to remember her, honor her, to take the time to consider all the small things about my sister that made her who she was.

"Hailey was brilliant," I asserted. "She loved words, and she had an amazing memory. There was always something going on inside of her that I couldn't begin to follow or understand."

When Eli looked up to meet my gaze, I went on. "Of course she was beautiful, but she was much more, too. She was strong and smart and capable and persuasive. . . . You know, she was born when Halley's Comet was visible from earth. My mom told her the story all the time when she was little; it was almost a fairy tale at our house."

Eli exhaled in something that could have been considered a restrained chuckle.

"Of course, Hailey grew up loving the sky. When she was in fifth grade and her teacher read *The Adventures of Tom Sawyer*, she learned that Mark Twain had been born when Halley's Comet was visible, and he died seventy-five years later when

510

it passed the earth again." I shrugged as if it made perfect sense. "She always said she wanted to die the same way—beneath the banner of the comet."

"Her birthday was a close second," Eli commented.

A chill splintered icy fingers through me. "I suppose."

"I think it was Mark Twain who called life 'the heaviest curse devisable by divine ingenuity.'"

"They were soul mates," I said dryly.

We were silent for a while then, and for the first time since Hailey died, I let the full force of it wash over me. I knew how she did it and why, but I would never understand the reasoning that brought her to that place. I would never grasp the pain that she must have endured to find herself curled up in a bathtub, the razor in her hands. And nothing—*nothing*—could ever erase what she had done, the gap that she had left in my life. Not Tyler's life. Not even my own.

"I miss her so much," I whimpered, my voice collapsing on the words. But even though I could barely speak, I was suddenly bursting with things I wanted to say. "And I'm so *angry* at her. She had no *right*. She caused so much *pain*. She almost made me . . . I almost . . ."

"You can't almost do anything," Eli said, his tone matter-of-fact. "You either do something or you don't. And you didn't."

"I wanted to."

"No, you didn't. You felt compelled to. You didn't understand that her debt wasn't yours to pay."

I didn't know what else to say. My tears were gone and so was my voice, but in the stillness I was gripped by the desire to inhale, to breathe in as much air as I could hold, to let it fill my lungs and expand my chest, because I *could*. Because when I opened my mouth, I found that I could breathe past the ache. And when I was finally full, something small and fledgling fought to put down tenuous roots. I felt like I had been bled dry, but in the wake of all that loss I could accept the possibility that maybe Eli was right. About many things. Maybe about everything.

After a long while, I tentatively reached for his hand. When Eli saw me move, he grabbed my hand and crushed it in both of his own.

"I have to go," I told him.

"Now?"

"Yes."

"Florida?"

"Yes."

"I'll take you to the airport tomorrow."

"Thank you." My eyes were on my legs, but I could feel Eli looking at me. I lifted my head.

"If you need somewhere . . ." He fumbled for a moment and I snuck a peek at him, but the second my eyes met his, he glanced away. "I think that the *where* matters," he said, his voice thick.

I couldn't help but smile a little, thinking of his *terroir*, his wine.

"You have a home here," he said. And though he got up the very next minute and walked away, I believed that he meant every word.

But I couldn't stay in Revell. Not after what had happened. Not after what I had done. Nothing made sense for me but to go back to the place I had called home for over a decade. It was the logical, most Abigail-like thing I could possibly do.

The day after I arrived in Rosa Beach, I tried more or less to pick up my life where I had left off. When I showed up at Johnson, McNally & Bennett, everyone acted as if I were a conquering hero, returning from some noble quest. It killed me, knowing that they had no idea where I had been or why. How would they react if they knew?

But I wasn't about to tell my coworkers a thing, so I accepted their hugs and pats on the back and ducked out as quickly as I could. Even though it was the last thing on earth I wanted to do, at eight o'clock sharp the following morning, I was poised and ready, sitting behind my desk. After all, resuming my life as normal was the reason I had returned.

I don't know what I anticipated, but I didn't think that everything would feel so strange. That first day back at work was an enormous battle for me, a frustrating duel between the part of me that wanted to pretend everything could go back to the way it had been and the rest of my soul that knew such hopes were sheer foolishness.

Those long, agonizing hours at the job I had once loved ended with me all but running out of the office at exactly 5 p.m. I felt claustrophobic, held captive by my custom Herman Miller chair, and laden with old responsibilities and expectations that only seemed to loom larger after a few months' hiatus from the real world.

"It's great to have you back," Colton told me as I slipped out of the office. He was leaning against the front desk and laughing about something with Marguerite. But he turned his head to watch me go, and though an easy smile still rested on his face, something in his eyes seemed uncertain.

I'm not crazy, I wanted to tell him. *But you don't know me.* I felt like no one knew me. Not really.

"Thanks," I said for his benefit. "It's great to be back."

"Just don't take off on us again, okay? I don't think your clients liked me very well."

"I don't think they *trusted* you," Marguerite corrected him, winking at me as if we shared an inside joke.

I didn't get it.

Sadly, catching up with my father wasn't any simpler.

Since I wasn't ready to face him right away, I didn't stop by the Four Seasons until I had been in

Florida for a few days. But when I eventually gathered the courage to see him, I was surprised to find that Lou had changed much in my absence.

The nurses told me that it could be a matter of days or weeks. Maybe months but not likely. Lou's body was shutting down slowly, system by system. Though the doctors couldn't pinpoint exactly what was causing his gradual decline, the nurses assured me that my father was dying of a broken heart.

"Failure to thrive," one called it. "He's not interested in food or drink. Actually he's not interested in living anymore."

"He's lived a long life," another told me. She laid her hand on my arm and offered me a sad, sympathetic smile.

"I know," I said, not sure I could tell her that I was actually happy for him.

The nurse was right; Lou wasn't interested in living anymore. But how could I blame him? What's wrong with submitting to the gentle embrace of death when it reaches to enfold you after you've struggled through eighty-three years of life on this planet? I didn't begrudge my father's longing one bit.

Instead of trying to talk him into fighting, I showed up every day at his bedside and loved him the best way I knew how: I was there for him.

One night as I walked into Lou's bedroom, I found him sound asleep. I could tell instantly that nothing would rouse him, not my footsteps on the hard floor nor even the subtle movement of my hand covering his. He was succumbing more and more often to sleep of this sort, this steadfast and seemingly bottomless rest. It was the kind of slumber that I knew he might never wake from. Though my heart wrenched to see him lying there as vulnerable as a child, I was also somewhat relieved to find him sleeping.

Creeping quietly across the floor even though my silence was unnecessary, I slid into the chair beside my father and took his wrinkled hands in mine. Then I prayed over him, reciting the Lord's Prayer as best I remembered it, and kissed the jumble of fingers in my hands. When I had said *amen*, so shall it be, over his motionless form, I reached into my purse and extracted a little box. It was a smudged Altoids tin that even after all these years still carried with it the faint scent of cinnamon.

The metal case opened like a book, and inside I had fitted two photographs—one of me and one of Hailey. It was actually one photo, the print from her nightstand, but I didn't feel bad cutting it apart. We were still together, face-to-face in the ancient tin turned picture frame. But for some reason, we made more sense to me this way.

I left the small metal box in Lou's hands, knowing that he'd feel it when he woke up. He'd see us there, and he'd know that I loved him, that I understood. Or, at least, that I forgave him.

Walking away from my father that night, I knew that I could forgive Hailey, too. Eli was right: my sister was pursued. Who was I to judge whether or not she was weak, whether or not she should have fought off her attacker longer than she already had?

I *wish* that she had continued to fight—there are still many nights when I wake in the midst of darkness because my heart is cleft with a sense of deep loss. And sometimes I ache with a feeling of uncontainable regret—there is so much that she will miss, so much that we could have shared . . . *if*. There is always an *if*. But I think I can let her go now. I think I can accept that it wasn't me. It wasn't Tyler.

Hailey's death, like her life, is an unfathomable mix of brokenness. And, I think, grace.

Maybe, just maybe, if I in my weakness and failings can forgive Hailey, the God who gave so freely of his own is able to forgive her, too.

Lately I've been thinking a lot about snow. It's October, two and a half months since I left Revell, and for some reason I can't stand the fact that it's still hot. The heat, the incessant humidity plagues me, and I find myself longing for the autumns of my youth. I remember the rains that crusted into ice, and later, the snow that gentled the world. That covered a multitude of sins. A part of me wants very much to buy a plane ticket and make my way back to Newcastle, Minnesota.

But there's nothing there for me anymore. And in a matter of days, weeks, there won't be anything for me here either.

I can't help wondering, does it snow in the Summerlands?

I did an Internet image search, typing in just a few keywords: *snow in the Summerlands*. It seemed like such a strange thing to write, such an obvious incongruity, but sure enough, seconds later my computer screen was filled with images in gray and white. There were long rows of dormant vines, slick with ice and blanketed in a thick, wooly covering of pure, silvery snow. It was a delicious, unexpected irony for me. Snow in the Summerlands . . .

Kind of like water into wine. Life through death. Freedom from sacrifice.

I'm ready to go back. I want to see Thompson Hills swathed in white, a sleeping bride. Waiting. I want to taste the harvest of wine from the banquet of my summer. Most of all, I want to see Eli again. I need to know if he meant what he said—that I have a home. Maybe I'll let him call me Abby.

here is the deepest secret
nobody knows
(here is the root of
the root and the bud
of the bud
and the sky of the sky
of a tree called life;
which grows
higher than soul can
hope or mind can hide)
and this is the wonder
that's keeping
the stars apart

i carry your heart
(i carry it in my heart)

†

E. E. CUMMINGS
"I CARRY YOUR HEART WITH ME"

ACKNOWLEDGMENTS

ભ A BOOK IS NEVER a solo effort, and *The Moment Between* is no exception. I am indebted to my family, friends, acquaintances, and even complete strangers for your many contributions to this book and unyielding enthusiasm while I wrote it. Your generosity, thoughtfulness, encouragement, and sage advice continue to surprise and delight me.

Special thanks to Mom and Dad Baart as well as the entire Baart clan (Dan and Danielle Kampen and Adam and Jenine Baart) for introducing me to British Columbia's unparalleled wine country, the Okanagan Valley. I have many fond memories of summer vacations on the lake, and I will never forget my first experience at a bona fide winery. It was love at first sip.

Early inspirations for this story owe their existence to many special people in my life, including Jamin and Kate Ver Velde, *nouveaux* wine connoisseurs and intrepid taste testers in our unofficial wine club. Also, my deepest gratitude to Mark and Miriam Buss for showing me the beauty and complexity of the relationship between winemaking and God.

Thank you to Roxy Harlow for teaching me much about life, love, and what it means to be a friend. Please be patient with me; I'm still learning.

New friends Francine Rivers and Lisa McKay proved invaluable as they helped me negotiate the sometimes-baffling publishing world. Thank you, Francine, for taking the time to advise and counsel me. You are as gracious, approachable, and kind as you are talented. And thank you, Lisa, for sharing the experience. I wish we could curl up with a cup of coffee and talk at least once a week. When's the next conference?

I'm grateful to early readers Arlana Huyser, Kate Ver Velde, Tiffany Postma, and Susan Stanley for reading first-draft copies and giving honest feedback. Also to Dad, Mom, Amber, and Aaron for oohing and aahing in all the right places.

Expert advice on guns and everything gun-related came from Mike Halma. Though I couldn't help but be intimidated by your uniform, I'm forever grateful that you were willing to let me hold, aim, and inspect your firearm. It wasn't loaded, right? And thank you to Ronda Wells, MD, for answering all my gruesome autopsy questions. Other professional counsel came in the form of winery tours, most notably at Mission Hill and Tinhorn Creek in the Okanagan. The cellars alone at Mission Hill were worth the cost of the tour.

Writing a book with an agent was a new experience for me this time around, and now I find myself wondering how I managed before. Danielle Egan-Miller, Joanna MacKenzie, and Lauren Olson were worth their weight in gold. Thank you for your dedication to this book and your commitment to excellence. I hope I've done you proud.

To Karen Watson, Stephanie Broene, Lorie Popp, Babette Rea, Vicky Lynch, and Jessie McGrath, as well as the rest of the amazing team at Tyndale House: thanks. I am so grateful that you have given me the chance to do what I've always wanted to do. The way you make it all come together is pure magic.

My deepest appreciation to Todd Diakow for walking with me every step of the way. As always, this book has your fingerprints all over it.

Love and thanks to my family and friends . . . Mom and Dad, Andrew and Amber, Nick and Lisa, my Bible study girls, all the amazing men and women in our small group (past and present), as well as the new people I've met along the way and everyone else I've forgotten to mention. I love you all dearly, and I am blessed beyond measure to have you in my life.

Finally I am nothing without my boys. Aaron, Isaac, and Judah, you are my everything. I love you and I love what we have.

Lord, make my life an offering.

ABOUT THE AUTHOR

ℭℜ NICOLE BAART WAS born and raised in a small town in Iowa.

She is the mother of two young sons and the wife of a pastor. After the adoption of their infant son, Nicole discovered a deep passion for global issues and is a founding member of One Body, One Hope, a nonprofit organization that works with a church and orphanage in Liberia. Visit www.one-bodyonehope.org for more information.

The Moment Between is Nicole's third book.

She and her family live in Iowa.

DISCUSSION QUESTIONS

1. "Abigail Bennett was the definition of unexpected." Explain. Do you agree or disagree with this statement? Why? How does Abigail change throughout the book? What is the impetus for that change?

2. Hailey's mental illness affects everyone around her. What sort of emotions does Hailey evoke in you? Do you like her or dislike her? Do you have compassion for her or does she frustrate you? Explain.

3. How is Abigail shaped by her youth? What role does Lou play in her life? What role does Melody play in her life? What about Hailey?

4. Abigail calls herself a "lapsed Catholic." Why do you think she has allowed her faith to lapse? Hailey, on the other hand, seems to cling to her faith. Why is her belief system so important to her?

5. Why is Abigail so driven to atone for her sister's death? Do you understand her motivations? Why or why not? Why does she blame Tyler? Do you agree with her assessment of Tyler's guilt?

6. Though she doesn't claim to be a Christian, until she finds herself obsessed with Tyler, Abigail lives an exemplary, by-the-book life. Hailey, on the other hand, is a Christian, but there seems to be a disconnect between Hailey's faith and her lifestyle choices. What does this seem to say about faith and actions? Do you agree or disagree? Why?

7. What does Eli mean when he asks Abigail, "What if your life is an offering poured out in a single glass?" Do you agree or disagree with his assessment of Abigail's role in Hailey's death?

8. In the final chapter, Abigail says, "If home is where the heart is, my heart has been home-less for a very long time." And earlier in the book we learn that "her heart existed in many more places than simply the cage behind her arching rib bones." What does she mean by that? Was there ever a time in your life when you could relate to these statements?

9. The symbol of communion is used repeatedly throughout the book in both obvious and subtle ways. Locate several references to the sacrament of communion. What purpose does this symbol serve?

10. Throughout history and even today there are many religious groups that consider suicide to be an unpardonable sin. In fact, some churches won't even allow victims of suicide to be buried in the same cemetery as people who die of natural causes. Do you agree or disagree with this conviction? Why or why not?

11. Near the end of the book, Abigail narrates, "Hailey's death, like her life, is an unfathomable mix of brokenness. And, I think, grace." What does she mean by this? Do you agree that Hailey's life is a mix of brokenness and grace? Use specific examples from the book.

12. In the final paragraphs of the book, Abigail talks about the irony of snow in the Summerlands. What other ironies can you pick out as you look back over the book? What metaphors stand out to you? What symbols do you find meaningful?

Center Point Publishing

600 Brooks Road • PO Box 1
Thorndike ME 04986-0001 USA

(207) 568-3717

US & Canada:
1 800 929-9108
www.centerpointlargeprint.com